THE BEST OF BOVA

VOLUME II

BAEN BOOKS
by Ben Bova

✳ ✳ ✳

Mars, Inc.
Laugh Lines
The Watchmen
The Exiles Trilogy
The Best of Bova: Volume I
The Best of Bova: Volume II

With Les Johnson
Rescue Mode

THE BEST OF
BOVA
VOLUME II

BEN BOVA

BEST OF BEN BOVA: VOLUME TWO

This is a work of fiction. All the characters and events portrayed in this book are fictional, and any resemblance to real people or incidents is purely coincidental.

Introduction © 2016 by Ben Bova; "The Angel's Gift" first published in The First Omni Book of Science Fiction © January 1984; "Isolation Area" first published in The Magazine of Fantasy & Science Fiction © October 1984; "The Lieutenant and the Folksinger" first published in Maxwell's Demons © September 1978; "The Next Logical Step" first published in Analog Science Fiction and Fact © May 1962; "Sword Play" first published in Escape Plus © December 1984; "The Shining Ones" first published in Notes to a Science Fiction Writer © September 1975; "The Sightseers" first published in Future City © July 1973; "The Supersonic Zeppelin" first published in Analog Science Fiction and Fact © January 2005; "The Secret Life of Henry K." first published in Maxwell's Demons © September 1978; "Jovian Dreams" first published in Thrilling Wonder Stories–Summer 2007 © July 2007; "Brillo" first published in Analog Science Fiction/Science Fact © August 1970; "Answer, Please Answer" first published in Amazing Stories © October 1962; "The Man Who Saw "Gunga Din" Thirty Times" first published in Showcase © June 1973; "Out of Time" first published in Omni © November 1984; "Béisbol" first published in Analog Science Fiction/Science Fact © November 1985; "Re-entry Shock" first published in The Magazine of Fantasy & Science Fiction © January 1993; "The System" first published in Analog Science Fiction -> Science Fact © January 1968; "Battle Station" first published in Battle Station © October 1987; "Primary" first published in Isaac Asimov's Science Fiction Magazine © February 1985; "Those Who Can" first published in Maxwell's Demons © September 1978; "The Mask of the Rad Death" first published in Challenges © July 1993; "Thy Kingdom Come" first published in Science Fiction Age © March 1993; "Love Calls" first published in The Best of Omni Science Fiction No. 4 © 1982; "In Trust" first published in Tombs © June 1995; "Appointment in Sinai" first published in Analog Science Fiction and Fact © June 1996

A Baen Books Original

Baen Publishing Enterprises
P.O. Box 1403
Riverdale, NY 10471
www.baen.com

ISBN: 978-1-4767-8159-4

Cover art by Adam Burn

First Baen printing July 2016

Distributed by Simon & Schuster
1230 Avenue of the Americas
New York, NY 10020

Library of Congress Cataloging-in-Publication Data

Names: Bova, Ben, 1932- author.
Title: The best of Bova / by Ben Bova.
Description: Riverdale, NY : Baen Books, [2016] | "A Baen Books
  original"--Title page verso.
Identifiers: LCCN 2015049941 | ISBN 9781476781211 (paperback)
Subjects: | BISAC: FICTION / Science Fiction / High Tech. | FICTION / Science
  Fiction / General. | FICTION / Short Stories (single author).
Classification: LCC PS3552.O84 A6 2016 | DDC 813/.54--dc23 LC record available at
http://lccn.loc.gov/2015049941

Printed in the United States of America

10 9 8 7 6 5 4 3 2 1

To Toni and Tony and the radiant,
resplendent, romantic Rashida.

And to Lloyd McDaniel,
without whose unstinting help this book
would never have seen the light of day.

CONTENTS

INTRODUCTION ✳ 1

THE ANGEL'S GIFT ✳ 3

ISOLATION AREA ✳ 11

THE LIEUTENANT AND THE FOLKSINGER ✳ 37

THE NEXT LOGICAL STEP ✳ 51

SWORD PLAY ✳ 59

THE SHINING ONES ✳ 69

THE SIGHTSEERS ✳ 95

THE SUPERSONIC ZEPPELIN ✳ 99

THE SECRET LIFE OF HENRY K. ✳ 127

JOVIAN DREAMS ✳ 141

BRILLO ✳ 145

ANSWER, PLEASE ANSWER ✳ 181

THE MAN WHO SAW "GUNGA DIN" THIRTY TIMES ✳ 199

OUT OF TIME ✳ 205

BÉISBOL ✳ 219

RE-ENTRY SHOCK ✳ 229

THE SYSTEM ✳ 241

BATTLE STATION ✳ 243

PRIMARY ✳ 289

THOSE WHO CAN ✳ 297

THE MASK OF THE RAD DEATH ✳ 311

THY KINGDOM COME ✳ 319

LOVE CALLS ✳ 361

IN TRUST ✳ 373

APPOINTMENT IN SINAI ✳ 393

The reasonable man adapts himself to the world; the unreasonable one persists in trying to adapt the world to himself. Therefore all progress depends on the unreasonable man.

—George Bernard Shaw

THE BEST OF BOVA

BOVA

VOLUME II

INTRODUCTION

Here it is, a lifetime's work in three volumes containing eighty stories published over fifty-four years, from 1960 to 2014. They range from the Baghdad of *The Thousand Nights and a Night* to the eventual end of the entire universe, from the green hills of Earth to the fiery surface of a dying star, from corporate board rooms to a baseball field in heaven. With plenty of stops in between.

Re-reading these stories—some of them for the first time in decades—I am struck with a bitter-sweet sadness, recalling friends who have died along the way, passions and problems that drove the invention of the various tales. It's as if I'm a ghost visiting departed scenes, people whom I have loved, all gone now.

Yet they live on, in these stories, and perhaps that is the real reason why human beings create works of fiction: they are monuments to days gone by, memories of men and women who have been dear to us—or visions of what tomorrow may bring.

Every human society has had its storytellers. There is a fundamental need in the human psyche to produce tales that try to show who we truly are, and why we do the things we do.

Most of the stories in this collection are science fiction: that is, the stories involve some aspect of future science or technology that is so basic to the tale that if that element were removed, the story would collapse.

To me, science fiction is the literature of our modern society.

Humankind depends on science and technology for its survival, and has been doing so since our earliest ancestors faced saber-toothed cats. We do not grow fangs or wings, we create tools. Tool-making—technology—is the way we deal with the often-hostile world in which we live.

Over the past few centuries, scientific studies of our world have led to vastly improved technologies, better tools with which to make ourselves healthier, richer and more free. Science fiction is the literature that speaks to this.

Every organism on Earth is struggling to stay alive, to have offspring, to enlarge its ecological niche as widely as possible. We humans have succeeded so well at that quest that there are more than seven billion of us on this planet, and we are driving many, many of our fellow creatures into extinction.

The stories in this collection examine various aspects of humankind's current and future predicaments. Some of the tales are somewhat dated: written half a century ago, they deal with problems that we have already solved, or bypassed. Many of the stories tell of the human race's drive to expand its habitat—its ecological niche—beyond the limits of planet Earth. Many deal with our interactions with our machines, which are becoming more intelligent with every generation.

The people in these stories include heroes and heels, lovers and loners, visionaries and the smugly blind.

I hope you enjoy their struggles.

—**Ben Bova**
Naples, Florida
November 2014

THE ANGEL'S GIFT

Everybody from Goethe to the high school kid next door has written a story about a deal with the devil: you know, a tale in which a man sells his soul in exchange for worldy wealth and power. Sometimes the story ends happily, as in Stephen Vincent Benét's "The Devil and Daniel Webster." More often it's a tragedy, such as "Faust."

Here's a story about a man making a deal with an angel. He has to give up all his worldly wealth and power in order to save his soul. I believe that this story explains the seemingly inexplicable fall of a former President of the United States.

Sort of.

HE STOOD AT HIS BEDROOM WINDOW, gazing happily out at the well-kept grounds and manicured park beyond them. The evening was warm and lovely. Dinner with the guests from overseas had been perfect; the deal was going smoothly, and he would get all the credit for it. As well as the benefits.

He was at the top of the world now, master of it all, king of the hill. The old dark days of fear and failure were behind him now. Everything was going his way at last. He loved it.

His wife swept into the bedroom, just slightly tipsy from the champagne. Beaming at him, she said, "You were magnificent this evening, darling."

He turned from the window, surprised beyond words. Praise from her was so rare that he treasured it, savored it like expensive wine, just as he had always felt a special glow within his breast on those extraordinary occasions when his mother had vouchsafed him a kind word.

"Uh . . . thank you," he said.

"Magnificent darling," she repeated. "I am so proud of you!"

His face went red with embarrassed happiness.

"And these people *are* so much nicer than those Latin types," she added.

"You . . . you know, you were . . . you *are* . . . the most beautiful woman in this city," he stammered. He meant it. In her gown of gold lamé and with her hair coiffed that way, she looked positively regal. His heart filled with joy.

She kissed him lightly on the cheek, whispering into his ear, "I shall be waiting for you in my boudoir, my prince."

The breath gushed out of him. She pirouetted daintily, then waltzed to the door that connected to her own bedroom. Opening the door, she turned back toward him and blew him a kiss.

As she closed the door behind her, he took a deep, sighing, shuddering breath. Brimming with excited expectation, he went directly to his closet, unbuttoning his tuxedo jacket as he strode purposefully across the thickly carpeted floor.

He yanked open the closet door. A man was standing there, directly under the light set into the ceiling.

Smiling, the man made a slight bow. "Please do not be alarmed, sir. And don't bother to call your security guards. They won't hear you."

Still fumbling with his jacket buttons, he stumbled back from the closet door, a thousand wild thoughts racing through his mind. An assassin. A kidnapper. A newspaper columnist!

The stranger stepped as far as the closet door. "May I enter your room, sir? Am I to take your silence for assent? In that case, thank you very much."

The stranger was tall but quite slender. He was perfectly tailored in a sky-blue Brooks Brothers three-piece suit. He had the youthful, innocent, golden-curled look of a European terrorist. His smile revealed perfect, dazzling teeth. Yet his eyes seemed infinitely sad, as though filled with knowledge of all human failings. Those icy blue eyes pierced right through the man in the tuxedo.

"Wh . . . what do you want? Who are you?"

"I'm terribly sorry to intrude this way. I realize it must be a considerable shock to you. But you're always so busy. It's difficult to fit an appointment into your schedule."

His voice was a sweet, mild tenor, but the accent was strange. East coast, surely. Harvard, no doubt.

"How did you get in here? My security . . ."

The stranger gave a slightly guilty grin and hiked one thumb ceilingward. "You might say I came in through the roof."

"The roof? Impossible!"

"Not for me. You see, I am an angel."

"An . . . angel?"

With a self-assured nod, the stranger replied, "Yes. One of the Heavenly Host. Your very own guardian angel, to he precise."

"I don't believe you."

"You don't believe in angels?" The stranger cocked a golden eyebrow at him. "Come now. I can see into your soul. You do believe."

"My church doesn't go in for that sort of thing," he said, trying to pull himself together.

"No matter. You do believe. And you do well to believe, because it is all true. Angels, devils, the entire system. It is as real and true as this fine house you live in." The angel heaved a small sigh. "You know, back in medieval times people had a much firmer grasp on the realities of life. Today . . ." He shook his head.

Eyes narrowing craftily, the man asked, "If you're an angel, where are your wings? Your halo? You don't look anything like a real angel."

"Oh." The angel seemed genuinely alarmed. "Does that bother you? I thought it would be easier on your nervous system to see me in a form that you're accustomed to dealing with every day. But if you want . . ."

The room was flooded with a blinding golden light. Heavenly voices sang. The stranger stood before the man robed in radiance, huge white wings outspread, filling the room.

The man sank to his knees and buried his face in his hands. "Have mercy on me! Have mercy on me!"

He felt strong yet gentle hands pull him tenderly to his feet. The angel was back in his Brooks Brothers suit. The searing light and ethereal chorus were gone.

"It is not in my power to show you either mercy or justice," he said, his sweetly youthful face utterly grave. "Only the Creator can dispense such things."

"But why . . . how . . ." He babbled.

Calming him, the angel explained, "My duty as your guardian angel is to protect your soul from damnation. But you must cooperate, you know. I cannot *force* you to be saved."

"My soul is in danger?"

"In danger?" The angel rolled his eyes heavenward. "You've just about handed it over to the enemy, gift-wrapped. Most of the millionaires you dined with tonight have a better chance to attain salvation than you have, at the moment. And you know how difficult it is for a rich man."

The man tottered to the wingback chair next to his king-sized bed and sank into it. He pulled the handkerchief from his breast pocket and mopped his sweaty face.

The angel knelt beside him and looked up into his face pleadingly. "I don't want to frighten you into a premature heart seizure, but your soul really is in great peril."

"But I haven't done anything wrong! I'm not a crook. I haven't killed anyone or stolen anything. I've been faithful to my wife."

The angel gave him a skeptical smile.

"Well . . ." He wiped perspiration from his upper lip. "Nothing serious. I've always honored my mother and father."

Gently, the angel asked, "You've never told a lie?"

"Uh, well . . . nothing big enough to . . ."

"You've never cheated anyone?"

"Um."

"What about that actor's wife in California? And the money you accepted to swing certain deals. And all the promises you've broken?"

"You mean things like that—they count?"

"Everything counts," the angel said firmly. "Don't you realize that the enemy has your soul almost in his very hands?"

"No. I never thought—"

"All those deals you've made. All the corners you've cut." The angel suddenly shot him a piercing glance. "You haven't signed any documents in blood, have you?"

"No!" His heart twitched. "Certainly not!"

"Well, that's something, at least."

"I'll behave," he promised. "I'll he good. I'll be a model of virtue."

"Not enough," the angel said, shaking his golden locks. "Not nearly enough. Things have gone much too far."

His eyes widened with fear. He wanted to argue, to refute, to debate the point with his guardian angel, but the words simply would not force their way through his constricted throat.

"No, it is not enough merely to promise to reform," the angel repeated. "Much stronger action is needed."

"Such as . . . what?"

The angel got to his feet, paced across the room a few steps, then turned back to face him. His youthful visage brightened. "Why not? If *they* can make a deal for a soul, why can't we?"

"What do you mean?"

"Hush!" The angel seemed to be listening to another voice, one that the man could not hear. Finally the angel nodded and smiled. "Yes. I see. Thank you."

"What?"

Turning back to the man, the angel said, "I've just been empowered to make you an offer for your soul. If you accept the terms, your salvation is assured."

The man instantly grew wary. "Oh no you don't. I've heard about deals for souls. Some of my best friends—"

"But this is a deal to *save* your soul!"

"How do I know that?" the man demanded. "How do I know you're really what you say you are? The devil has power to assume pleasing shapes, doesn't he?"

The angel smiled joyfully. "Good for you! You remember some of your childhood teachings."

"Don't try to put me off. I've negotiated a few tricky deals in my day. How do I know you're really are an angel, and you want to save my soul?"

"By their fruits ye shall know them," the angel replied.

"What are you talking about?"

Still smiling, the angel replied, "When the devil makes a deal for a soul, what does he promise? Temporal gifts, such as power, wealth, respect, women, fame."

"I have all that," the man said. "I'm on top of the world, everyone knows that."

"Indeed."

"And I didn't sign any deals with the devil to get there, either," he added smugly.

"None that you know of," the angel warned. "A man in your position delegates many decisions to his staff, does he not?"

The man's face went gray. "Oh my God, you don't think . . ."

With a shrug, the angel said, "It doesn't matter. The deal that I offer guarantees your soul's salvation, if you meet the terms."

"How? What do I have to do?"

"You have power, wealth, respect, women, fame." The angel ticked each point off on his slender, graceful fingers.

"Yes, yes, I know."

"You must give them up."

The man lurched forward in the wingchair. "Huh?"

"Give them up."

"I can't!"

"You must, if you are to attain the Kingdom of Heaven."

"But you don't understand! I just can't drop everything! The world doesn't work that way. I can't just . . . walk away from all this."

"That's the deal," the angel said. "Give it up. All of it. Or spend eternity in hell."

"But you can't expect me to—" He gaped. The angel was no longer in the room with him. For several minutes he stared into empty air. Then, knees shaking, he arose and walked to the closet. It too was empty of strange personages.

He looked down at his hands. They were trembling.

"I must he going crazy," he muttered to himself. "Too much strain. Too much tension." But even as he said it, he made his way to the telephone on the bedside table. He hesitated a moment, then grabbed up the phone and punched a number he had memorized months earlier.

"Hello. Chuck? Yes, this is me. Yes, yes, everything went fine tonight. Up to a point."

He listened to his underling babbling flattery into the phone, wondering how many times he had given his power of attorney to this weakling and to equally venal deputies.

"Listen, Chuck," he said at last. "I have a job for you. And it's got to be done right, understand? Okay, here's the deal—" He winced inwardly at the word. But, taking a deep manly breath, he plunged ahead.

"You know the Democrats are setting up their campaign quarters in that new apartment building—what's it called, Watergate? Yeah. Okay. Now I think it would serve our purposes very well if we bugged the place before the campaign really starts to warm up . . ."

There were tears in his eyes as he spoke. But from far, far away, he could hear a heavenly chorus singing.

ISOLATION AREA

Here's Sam Gunn again, the leather-lunged, sawed-off, skirt-chasing entrepreneur who bends the rules into pretzels in his quest to strike it rich.

"Isolation Area" deals with the period of Sam's life when he takes that first scary step toward becoming the solar system's premier big-time space entrepreneur. In a subtler way it is also the story of the friendship between two men, and of the new freedoms that we will find as we begin to live and work—and love—in space.

* 🌐 *

THEY FACED EACH OTHER SUSPICIOUSLY, floating weightlessly in emptiness.

The black man was tall, long-limbed, loose, gangling; on Earth he might have made a pro basketball player. His utilitarian coveralls were standard issue, frayed at the cuffs and so worn that whatever color they had been originally had long since faded into a dull gray. They were clean and pressed to a razor sharpness, though. The insignia patch on his left shoulder said *Administration*. A strictly nonregulation belt of royal blue, studded with rough lumps of meteoric gold and clamped by a heavy gold buckle, cinched his narrow waist and made him look even taller and leaner.

He eyed the reporter warily. She was young, and the slightly greenish cast to her pretty features told him that she had never been in orbit before. Her pale blond hair was shoulder length, he judged, but she had followed the instructions given to groundlings and tied it up in a zero-gee snood. Her coveralls were spanking new white. She filled them nicely enough, although she had more of a figure than he cared for.

Frederick Mohammed Malone was skeptical to the point of being hostile toward this female interloper. The reporter could see the resentment smoldering in the black man's eyes. Malone's face was narrow, almost gaunt, with a trim little Vandyke jutting out from his chin. His forehead was high, receding; his hair cropped close to the skull. She guessed Malone's age at somewhere in the early forties, although she knew that living in zero gravity could make a person look much younger than his or her calendar age.

She tried to restart their stalled conversation. "I understand that you and Sam Gunn were, uh, friends."

"Why're you doing a story on Sam?" Malone asked, his voice low and loaded with distrust.

The two of them were in Malone's "office": actually an observation blister in the central hub of space station *Alpha*. Oldest and still biggest of the Earth-orbiting stations, *Alpha* was built on the old wheels-within-wheels scheme. The outermost rim, where most of the staff lived and worked, spun at a rate that gave it almost a full Earth gravity. Two thirds of the way toward the hub there was a wheel that spun at the Moon's one-sixth gee. The hub itself, of course, was for all practical purposes at zero gee, weightless.

Malone's aerie consisted of one wall, on which were located a semicircular sort of desk and communications center, a bank of viewing screens that were all blankly gray at the moment, and an airtight hatch that led to the spokes that radiated out to the various wheels. The rest of the chamber was a transparent plastic bubble, from which Malone could watch the station's loading dock—and the overwhelming majesty of the huge, curved, incredibly blue and white-flecked Earth as it slid past endlessly, massive, brilliant, ever-changing, ever-beautiful.

To the reporter, though, it seemed as if they were hanging in empty space itself, unprotected by anything at all, and falling, falling, falling toward the ponderous world of their birth. The background rumble of the bearings that bore the massive station's rotation while the hub remained static sounded to her like the insistent bass growl of a giant grinding wheel that was pressing the breath out of her.

She swallowed bile, felt it burn in her throat, and tried to concentrate on the job at hand.

She said to Malone, "I've been assigned to do a biography of Mr. Gunn for the Solar Network."

Despite himself, Malone suddenly grinned. "First time I ever heard him called *Mr.* Gunn."

"Oh?" The reporter's microchip recorder, clipped to her belt, was already on, of course. "What did the people here call him?"

That lean, angular face took on an almost thoughtful look. "Oh . . . Sam, mostly. 'That tricky bastard,' a good many times." Malone actually laughed. "Plenty times I heard him called a womanizing sonofabitch."

"What did you call him?"

The suspicion came back into Malone's eyes. "He was my friend. I called him Sam."

Silence stretched between them, hanging as weightlessly as their bodies. The reporter turned her head slightly and found herself staring at the vast bulk of Earth. Her mind screamed as if she were falling down an elevator shaft. Her stomach churned queasily. She could not tear her eyes away from the world drifting past, so far below them, so compellingly near. She felt herself being drawn toward it, dropping through the emptiness, spinning down the deep swirling vortex . . .

Malone's long-fingered hand squeezed her shoulder hard enough to hurt. She snapped her attention to his dark, unsmiling face as he grasped her other shoulder and held her firmly in his strong hands.

"You were drifting," he said, almost in a whisper.

"Was I . . . ?"

"It's all right," he said. "Gets everybody at first. Don't be scared. You're perfectly safe."

His powerful hands steadied her. She fought down the panic surging inside.

"If you got to upchuck, go ahead and do it. Nothing to be ashamed of." His grin returned. "Only, use the bags they gave you, please."

He looked almost handsome when he smiled, she thought. After another moment, he released her. She took a deep breath and dabbed at the beads of perspiration on her forehead. The retch bags that the technicians had attached to her belt were a symbol to her now. I won't need them, she insisted to herself. I'm not going to let this get me.

"Feel better?" he asked. There was real concern in his eyes.

"I think I'll be all right. Thanks."

"*De nada*," he said. "I appreciate your coming out here to the hub for the interview."

His attitude had changed, she saw. The sullenness had thawed. He had insisted on conducting the interview in the station's zero-gravity area. He had allowed no alternative. But she was grateful that the shell of distrust seemed to have cracked.

It took several moments before she could say, "I'm not here to do a hatchet job on Mr. Gunn."

Malone made a small shrug. "Doesn't make much difference, one way or t'other. He's dead; nothing you say can hurt him now."

"But we know so little about him. I suppose he's the most famous enigma in the solar system."

The black man made no response.

"The key question, I guess . . . the thing our viewers will be most curious about, is why Sam Gunn exiled himself up here. Why did he turn his back on Earth?"

Malone snorted with disdain. "He didn't! Those motherfuckers turned their backs on him."

"What do you mean?"

"It's a long story," Malone said.

"That's all right. I've got as much time as it takes." Even as she said it, the reporter wished that Malone would volunteer to return back to the outer wheel, where gravity was normal. But she dared not ask the man to leave his office. Once a subject starts talking, never interrupt! That was the cardinal rule of a successful interview. Besides, she was determined not to let weightlessness get the better of her.

"Would you believe," Malone was saying, "that it all started with a cold?"

"A cold?"

"Sam came down with a cold in the head. That's how the whole thing began."

"Tell me about it."

* * *

Sam was a feisty little bastard—Malone reminisced—full of piss and vinegar. If there were ten different ways in the regulations to do a job, he'd find an eleventh, maybe a twelfth or a fourteenth, just because he couldn't abide being bound by the regs. A free spirit, I guess you'd call him.

He'd had his troubles with the brass in Houston *and* Washington. Why he ever became an astronaut in the first place is beyond me. Maybe he thought he'd be like a pioneer out on the frontier, on his own, way out in space. How he made it through training and into flight operations is something I'll never figure out. I just don't feature Sam sitting still long enough to get through kindergarten, let alone flight school and astronaut training.

Anyway, when I first met him, he was finished as an astronaut. He had put in seven years, which he said was a biblical amount of time, and he wanted out. And the agency was glad to get rid of him, believe me. But he had this cold in the head, and they couldn't let him go back Earthside until it cleared up.

"Eight billion people down there with colds, the flu, bad sinuses, and postnasal drips, and the assholes in Houston won't let me go back until this goddamned sniffle clears up."

Those were the first words Sam ever said to me. He had been assigned to my special isolation ward, where I had reigned alone for nearly four years. *Alpha* was under construction then. We were in the old Mac-Dac Shack, a glorified tin can that passed for a space station back in those primitive days. It didn't spin, it just hung there; everything inside was weightless.

My isolation ward was a cramped compartment with four zero-gee bunks jammed into it, together with lockers to stow personal gear. Nobody but me had ever been in it until that morning. Sam shuffled over to the bed next to mine, towing his travel bag like a kid with a sinking balloon.

"Just don't sneeze in my direction, Sniffles," I growled at him.

That stopped Sam for about half a second. He gave me that lopsided grin of his—his face sort of looked like a scuffed-up soccer ball, kind of round, scruffy. Little wart of a nose in the middle of it. Longest hair I ever saw on a man who works in space; hair length was one of the multitudinous points of contention between Sam and the agency. His eyes sparkled. Kind of an odd color, not quite blue, not really green. Sort of in between.

"Malone, huh?" He read the name tag clipped over my bunk.

"Frederick Mohammed Malone."

"Jesus Christ, they put me next to an Arab!"

But he stuck out his hand. Sam was really a little guy; his hand was almost like a baby's. After a moment's hesitation I swallowed it in mine.

"Sam," he told me, knowing I could see his last name on the name tag pinned to his coveralls.

"I'm not even a Muslim," I said. "My father was, though. First one in Arkansas."

"Good for him." Sam disengaged his cleated shoes from the grillwork floor and floated up onto the cot. His travel bag hung alongside. He ignored it and sniffed at the air. "Goddamned hospitals all smell like somebody's dying. What're you in for? Hangnail or something?"

"Something," I said. "Acquired immune deficiency syndrome."

His eyes went round. "AIDS?"

"It's not contagious. Not unless we make love."

"I'm straight."

"I'm not."

"Terrific. Just what I need, a gay black Arab with AIDS." But he was grinning at me.

I had seen plenty of guys back away from me once they knew I had AIDS. Some of them had a hang-up about gays. Others were scared out of their wits that they would catch AIDS from me, or from the medical personnel or equipment. I had more than one reason to know how a leper felt, back in those days.

Sam's grin faded into a frown. "How the hell did the medics put me in here if you've got AIDS? Won't you catch my cold? Isn't that dangerous for you?"

"I'm a guinea pig."

"You don't look Italian."

"Look," I said, "if you're gonna stay in here, keep off the ethnic jokes, okay?"

He shrugged.

"The medics think they've got my case arrested. New treatment that the genetic researchers have come up with."

"I get it. If you don't catch my cold, you're cured."

"They never use words like 'cured.' But that's the general idea."

"So I'm a guinea pig, too."

"No, you are a part of the apparatus for this experiment. A source of infection. A bag of viruses. A host of bacteria. Germ city."

Sam hooked his feet into his bunk's webbing and gave me a dark look. "And this is the guy who doesn't like ethnic jokes."

The Mac-Dac Shack was one of the first space stations the agency had put up. It wasn't fancy, but for years it had served as a sort of research laboratory, mainly for medical work. Naturally, with a lot of M.D.s in it, the Shack sort of turned into a floating hospital in orbit. With all the construction work going on in those days, there was a steady stream of injured workmen and technicians.

Then some bright bureaucrat got the idea of using the Shack as an isolation ward, where the medics could do research on things like AIDS, Legionnaires' disease, the New Delhi virus, and various paralytic afflictions that required either isolation or zero gravity or both. The construction-crew infirmary was moved over to the yet-unfinished *Alpha*, while the Shack was turned into a pure research facility with various isolation wards for guinea pigs like me.

Sam stayed in my ward for three, four days: I forget the exact time. He was like an energetic little bee, buzzing all over the place, hardly ever still for a minute. In zero gee, of course, he could literally climb the curved walls of the ward and hover up on the ceiling. He terrified the head nurse in short order by hanging near the ceiling or hiding behind one of the bunks and then launching himself at her like a missile when she showed up with the morning's assortment of needles.

Never once did Sam show the slightest qualm at having his blood sampled alongside mine. I've seen guys get violent from their fear that they'd get a needle contaminated by me, and catch what I had. But Sam never even blinked. Me, I never liked needles. Couldn't abide them. Couldn't look when the nurse stuck me; couldn't even look when she stuck somebody else.

"All the nurses are women," Sam noticed by the end of his first day.

"All six of them," I affirmed.

"The doctors are all males?"

"Eight men, four women."

"That leaves two extra women for us."

"For you. I'm on the other side."

"How come all women nurses?" he wondered.

"I think it's because of me. They don't want to throw temptation in my path."

He started to frown at me but it turned into that lopsided grin. "They didn't think about *my* path."

He caused absolute havoc among the nurses. With the single-mindedness determination of a sperm cell seeking blindly for an ovum, Sam pursued them all: the fat little redhead, the cadaverous ash-blonde, the really good-looking one, the kid who still had acne—all of them, even the head nurse, who threatened to inject him with enough estrogen to grow boobs on him if he didn't leave her and her crew alone.

Nothing deflected Sam. He would be gone for long hours from the ward, and when he'd come back, he would be grinning from ear to ear. As politely as I could, I'd ask him if he had been successful.

"It matters not if you win or lose," he would say. "It's how you play the game . . . as long as you get laid."

When he finally left the isolation ward, it seemed as if we had been friends for years. And it was damned quiet in there without him. I was alone again. I missed him. I realized how many years it had been since I'd had a friend.

I sank into a real depression of self-pity and despair. I had caught Sam's cold, sure enough. I was hacking and sneezing all day and night.

One good thing about zero gravity is that you can't have a postnasal drip. One bad thing is that all the fluids accumulate in your sinuses and give you a headache of monumental proportions. The head nurse seemed to take special pleasure in inflicting upon me the indignity of forcing tubes up my nose to drain the sinuses.

The medics were overjoyed. Their guinea pig was doing something interesting. Would I react to the cold like any normal person, and get over it after a few days? Or would the infection spread and worsen, turn into pneumonia or maybe kill me? I could see them writing their learned papers in their heads every time they examined me, four times a day.

I was really unfit company for anyone, including myself. I went on for months that way, just wallowing in my own misery. Other patients came and went: an African kid with a new strain of polio; an asthmatic who had developed a violent allergy to dust; a couple of burn victims from the *Alpha* construction crew. I stayed while they were treated and sent home. Then, without any warning, Sam showed up again.

"Hello, Omar, how's the tent-making business?" My middle name had become Omar as far as he was concerned.

I gaped at him. He was wearing the powder-blue coveralls and shoulder insignia of Global Technologies, Inc., which in those days was just starting to grow into the interplanetary conglomerate it has become.

"What the hell you doing back here?" My voice was a full octave higher than normal, I was so surprised. And glad.

"I work here."

"Say what?"

He ambled over to me in the zero-gee strides we all learn to make: maintain just enough contact with the grillwork on the floor to keep from floating off toward the ceiling. As Sam approached my bunk, the head nurse pushed through the ward's swinging doors with a trayful of the morning's indignities for me.

"Global Technologies just won the contract for running this tin can. The medical staff still belongs to the government, but everybody else will be replaced by Global employees. I'll be in charge of the whole place."

Behind him, the head nurse's eyes goggled, her mouth sagged open, and the tray slid from her hand. It just hung there, revolving slowly, as she turned a full one-eighty and flew out of the ward without a sound.

"You're in charge of this place?" I laughed. "No shit?"

"Only after meals," Sam said. "I've got a five-year contract."

We got to be *really* friends then. Not lovers. Sam was the most heterosexual man I have ever seen. One of the shrinks aboard the station said he had a Casanova complex: he had to take a shot at any and every female creature he saw. I don't know how good his batting average was, but he surely kept busy—and happy.

"The thrill is in the chase, Omar, not the capture," he said to me many times. Then he would always add, "As long as you get laid."

But Sam could be a true friend, caring, understanding, bringing out the best in a man. Or a woman, for that matter. I saw him help many of the station's female employees, nurses, technicians, scientists, completely aside from his amorous pursuits. He knew when to put his

Casanova complex in the backseat. He was a helluva good administrator, and a leader. Everybody liked him. Even the head nurse grew to grant him a grudging respect, although she certainly didn't want anybody to know it, especially Sam.

Of course, knowing Sam, you might expect that he would have trouble with the chain of command. He had gotten himself out of the space agency, and it was hard to tell who was happier about it, him or the agency. You could hear sighs of relief from Houston and Washington all the way up where we were, the agency was so glad to be rid of the pestering little squirt who never followed regulations.

It didn't take long for Sam to find out that Global Technologies, Inc., had its own bureaucracy, its own set of regulations, and its own frustrations.

"You'd think a multibillion-dollar company would want to make all the profits it can," Sam grumbled to me about six months after he had returned to the Shack. "Half the facilities on *Alpha* are empty, right? They overbuilt, right? I show them how to turn *Alpha* into a tourist resort and they reject the goddamned idea. 'We're not in the tourism business,' they say. Goddamned assholes."

I found it hard to believe that Global Tech didn't understand what a bonanza they could reap from space tourism. But they just failed to see it. Sam spent weeks muttering about faceless bureaucrats who sat on their brains, and how much money a zero-gravity honeymoon hotel could make. It didn't do him a bit of good. At least, that's what I thought at the time.

The big crisis was mostly my fault. Looking back on it, if I could have figured out a different way to handle things, I would have. But you know how it is when your emotions are all churned up; you don't see any alternatives. Truthfully, I still don't see how I could have done anything else except what I did.

They told me I was cured.

Yeah, I know I said they never used words like that; but they changed their tune. After more than five years in the isolation ward of the station, the medics asked me to join them in the conference room. I expected another one of their dreary meetings; they made me attend them at least once a month, said it was important for me to "maintain a positive interaction with the research staff." So I dragged myself down to the conference room.

They were all grinning at me, around the table. Buckets of champagne stood at either end, with more bottles stashed where the slide projector usually hung.

I was cured. The genetic manipulations had finally worked. My body's immune system was back to normal. My case would be in the medical journals; future generations would bless my memory (but not my name, they would protect my anonymity). I could go back home, back to Earth.

Only, I didn't want to go.

"You don't want to go?" Sam's pudgy little face was screwed up into an incredulous expression that mixed in equal amounts of surprise, disapproval, and curiosity.

"Back to Earth? No, I don't want to go," I said. "I want to stay here. Or maybe go live on *Alpha* or one of the new stations they're building."

"But why?" Sam asked.

We were in his office, a tiny little cubbyhole that had originally been a storage locker for fresh food. I mean, space in the Shack was *tight.* I thought I could still smell onions or something faintly pungent. Sam had walled the chamber with a blue-colored spongy plastic, so naturally it came to be known as the Blue Grotto. There were no chairs in the Grotto, we just hung in midair. You could nudge your back against the slightly rough wall surfacing and that would hold you in place well enough. There wasn't much room to drift around in. Two people were all the chamber could hold comfortably. Sam's computer terminal was built into the wall; there was no furniture in the Grotto, no room for any.

"I got nothing to go back there for," I answered, "and a lot of crap waiting for me that I would just as soon avoid."

"But it's *Earth,*" he said. "The world . . ."

So I told him about it. The whole story, end to end. I had been a soldier, back in that nasty little bitch of a war in Mexico. Nothing glamorous, not even patriotism. I had joined the army because it was the only way for a kid from my part of Little Rock to get a college education. They paid for my education, and right after they pinned a lieutenant's gold bars on my shoulders they stuck me inside a heavy tank. Well, you know how well the tanks did in those hills. Nothing to shoot at but cactus, and we were great big noisy targets for those smart little missiles they brought in from Czechoslovakia or wherever.

They knocked out my tank. I was the only one of the crew to survive, and I wound up in an army hospital where they tried to put my spine back together again. That's where I contracted AIDS, from one of the male nurses who wanted to prove to me that I hadn't lost my virility. He was a very sweet kid, very caring. But I never saw him again once they decided to ship me to the isolation ward up in orbit.

Now it was five years later. I was cured of AIDS, a sort of anonymous hero, but everything else was still the same. Earth would still be the same, except that every friend I ever knew was five years' distance from me. My parents had killed themselves in an automobile wreck while I was in college. I had no sisters or brothers. I had no job prospects: soldiers coming back home five years after the war aren't greeted with parades and confetti, and all the computer stuff I had learned in college was obsolete by now. Not even the army used that kind of equipment anymore.

And Earth was dirty, crowded, noisy, dangerous—it was also *heavy*, a full one gee. I tried a couple of days in the one-gee wheel over at *Alpha* and knew that I could never live in Earth's full gravity again. Not voluntarily.

Sam listened to all this in complete silence, the longest I had ever known him to go without opening his mouth. He was totally serious, not even the hint of a smile. I could see that he understood.

"Down there I'd be just another nobody, an ex-soldier with no place to go. I can't handle the gravity, no matter what the physical therapists think they can do for me. I want to stay here, Sam. I want to make something of myself and I can do it here, not back there. The best I can be back there is another veteran on a disability pension. What kind of a job could I get? I can *be* somebody up here, I know I can."

He put his hand on my shoulder. "You're sure? You're absolutely certain this is what you want?"

I nodded. "I can't go back, Sam." I pleaded. "I just can't."

The faintest hint of a grin twitched at the corners of his mouth. "Okay, pal. How'd you like to go into the hotel business with me?"

You see, Sam had already been working for some time on his own ideas about space tourism. If Global Tech wouldn't go for a hotel facility over on *Alpha*, complete with zero-gee honeymoon suites, then Sam figured he could get somebody else interested in the idea. The people who like to bad-mouth Sam say that he hired me to cover his ass so he could spend his time working on his tourist hotel idea while he was still collecting a salary from Global. That isn't the way it happened at all; it was really the other way around.

Sam hired me as a consultant and paid me out of his own pocket. To this day I don't know where he got the money. I suspect it was from some of the financial people he was always talking to, but you never knew, with Sam. He had an inexhaustible fund of rabbits up his sleeves. Whenever I asked him about it, he just grinned at me and told me not to ask questions. I was never an employee of Global Technologies. And Sam worked full-time for them, eight hours a day, six days a week, and then some. They got his salary's worth out of him. More. But that didn't mean he couldn't spend nights, Sundays, and the odd holiday here and there wooing financiers and lawyers who might come up with the risk capital he needed for his hotel.

Sure, sometimes he did his own thing during Global's regular office hours. But he worked plenty of overtime hours for Global, too. They got their money's worth out of Sam.

Of course, once I was no longer a patient whose bills were paid by the government, Global sent word up from corporate headquarters that I was to be shipped back Earthside as soon as possible. Sam interpreted that to mean when he was good and ready. Weeks stretched into months. Sam fought a valiant delaying action, matching every query of theirs with a detailed memorandum and references to obscure government health and safety regulations. It would take Global's lawyers a month to figure out what the hell Sam was talking about, and then frame an answer.

In the meantime, he moved me from the old isolation ward into a private room—a coffin-sized cubbyhole—and insisted that I start paying for my rent and food. Since Sam was paying me a monthly consultant's stipend, he was collecting my rent and food money out of the money he was giving me as his consultant. It was all done with the Shack's computer system, no cash ever changed hands. I had the feeling that there were some mighty weird subroutines running around inside that computer, all of them programmed by Sam.

While all this was going on, the Shack was visited by a rather notorious U.S. Senator, one of the most powerful men in the government. He was a wizened, shriveled old man who had been in the Senate almost half a century. I thought little of it; we were getting a constant trickle of VIPs in those days. The bigwigs usually went to *Alpha,* so much so that we began calling it the Big Wheel's Big Wheel. Most of them avoided the Shack; I guess they were scared of getting contaminated from our isolation ward patients. But a few of the VIPs made their way to the Shack now and then.

Sam took personal charge of the Senator and his entourage, and showed him more attention and courtesy than I had ever seen him lavish upon a visitor before. Or since, for that matter. Sam, kowtowing to an authority figure? It astounded me at the time, but I laughed it off and forgot all about it soon enough.

Then, some six months after the Senator's visit, when it looked as if Sam had run out of time and excuses to keep me in the Shack and I would have to pack my meager bag and head down the gravity well to spend the rest of my miserable days in some overcrowded ghetto city, Sam came prancing weightlessly into my microminiaturized living quarters, waving a flimsy sheet of paper.

"What's that?" I knew it was a straight line, but he wasn't going to tell me unless I asked.

"A new law." He was smirking, canary feathers all over his chin.

"First time I ever seen you happy about some new regulation."

"Not a regulation," he corrected me. "A *law.* A federal law, duly passed by the U.S. Congress and just signed today by the President."

I wanted to play it cool, but he had me too curious. "What's it say? Why's it so important?"

"It says," he made a flourish that sent him drifting slowly toward the ceiling as he read, "No person residing aboard a space facility owned by the United States or by a corporation or other legal entity licensed by the United States may be compelled to leave said facility without due process of law."

My reply was something profound, like, "Huh?"

His scrungy little face beaming, Sam said, "It means that Global can't force you back Earthside! As long as you can pay the rent, Omar, they can't evict you."

"You joking?" I couldn't believe it.

"No joke. I helped write this masterpiece, kiddo," he told me. "Remember when old Senator Winnebago was up here last year?"

The Senator was from Wisconsin, but his name was not Winnebago. He had been a powerful enemy of the space program—

until his doctors told him that degenerative arthritis was going to make him a pain-racked cripple unless he could live in a low-gee environment. All of a sudden he became a big space freak. His visit to the Shack had proved what his doctors had told him: in zero gee the pains that hobbled him disappeared and he felt twenty years younger. That's when Sam convinced him to sponsor the "pay your own way" law, which provided that neither the government nor a private company operating a space facility could force a resident out as long as he or she was able to pay the going rate for accommodations.

"Hell, they've got laws that protect tenants from eviction in New York and every other city," Sam said. "Why not here?"

I was damned glad of it. Overjoyed, in fact. It meant that I could stay, that I wouldn't be forced to go back Earthside and drag myself around at my full weight. What I didn't realize at the time, of course, was that Sam would eventually have to use that law for himself. Obviously, *he* had seen ahead far enough to know that he would need such protection, sooner or later. Did he get the law written for his own selfish purposes? Sure he did. But it served *my* purpose, too, and Sam knew that when he was bending the Senator's tin ear. That was good enough for me. Still is.

For the better part of another year I served as Sam's legman—a job I found interesting and amusingly ironic. I shuttled back and forth from the Shack to *Alpha*, generally to meet big-shot business persons visiting the Big Wheel. When Sam was officially on duty for Global, which was most of the time, he'd send me over to *Alpha* to meet the visitors, settle them down, and talk to them about the money that a tourist facility would make. I would just try to keep them happy until Sam could shake loose and come over to meet them himself. Then he would weave a golden web of words, describing how fantastic an orbital tourist facility would be, bobbing weightlessly around the room in his enthusiasm, pulling numbers out of the air to show how indecently huge would be the profit that investors would make.

"And the biggest investors will get their own suites, all for themselves," Sam promised, "complete with every luxury—and every service that the staff can provide."

He would wink hard enough to dislocate an eyelid at that point, to make certain the prospective investor knew what he meant.

I met some pretty interesting people that way: Texas millionaires,

Wall Street financiers, Hollywood sharks, a couple of bullnecked types I thought might be Mafia but turned out to be in the book and magazine distribution business, even a few very nice young ladies who were looking for "good causes" in which to invest. Sam did not spare them his "every service that the staff can provide" line, together with the wink. They giggled and blushed.

"It's gonna happen!" Sam kept saying. Each time we met a prospective backer his enthusiasm rose to a new pitch. No matter how many times the prospect eventually turned sour, no matter how often we were disappointed, Sam never lost his faith in the idea or in the inevitability of its fruition.

"It's gonna happen, Omar. We're going to create the first tourist hotel in space. And you're going to have a share of it, pal. Mark my words."

When we finally got a tentative approval from a consortium of Greek and Italian shipping people, Sam nearly rocked the old Shack out of orbit. He whooped and hollered and zoomed around the place like a crazy billiard ball. He threw a monumental party for everybody in the Shack, doctors, nurses, patients, technicians, administrative staff, security guards, visitors, and even the one consultant who lived there: me. Where he got the caviar and fresh Brie and other stuff, I still don't know. But it was a party none of us will ever forget. It started Saturday at five p.m., the close of the official workweek. It ended, officially, Monday at eight a.m. There are those who believe, though, that it's still going on over there at the Shack.

Several couples sort of disappeared during the party. The Shack isn't so big that people can get lost in it, but they just seemed to vanish. Most of them showed up, looking tired and sheepish, by Monday morning. Three of those couples eventually got married. One pair of them was stopped by a security guard when they tried to go out an air lock while stark naked.

Sam himself engaged in a bit of EVA with one of the nurses, a tiny little elf of fragile beauty and uncommon bravery. She snuggled into a pressure suit with Sam, and the two of them made several orbits around the Shack, outside, propelled by nothing more than their own frenetic pulsations and Newton's Third Law of Motion.

Two days after the party, however, the Beryllium Blonde showed up.

Her real name was Jennifer Marlow, and she was as splendidly beautiful as a woman can be. A figure right out of a high school boy's wettest dreams. A perfect face, with eyes of china blue and thickly glorious hair like a crown of shining gold. She staggered every male who saw her, she stunned even me, and she sent Sam into a complete tailspin.

To top things off, she was Global Technology's ace troubleshooter. Her official title was Administrative Assistant (Special Projects) to the President. The word we got from Earthside was that she had a mind like a steel trap, and a vagina much the same.

The official reason for her visit was to discuss Sam's letter of resignation with him.

"You stay right beside me," Sam insisted as we drifted down the Shack's central corridor, toward the old conference room. "I won't be able to control myself if I'm in there alone with her."

His face was as white as the Moon's. He looked like a man in shock.

"Will you be able to control yourself *with* me in there?" I wondered.

"If I can't, rap me on the head. Knock me out. Give me a Vulcan nerve pinch. Anything! Just don't let me go zonkers over her."

I smiled.

"I'm not kidding, Omar!" Sam insisted. "Why do you think they sent her up here, instead of some flunky? They know I'm susceptible. God knows how many scalps she's got nailed to her teepee."

I grabbed his shoulder and dug my cleats into the corridor's floor grid. We skidded to a stop.

"Look," I said, "maybe you want to avoid meeting with her altogether. I can represent you. I'm not . . . uh, susceptible."

His eyes went so wide I could see white all around the pupils. "Are you nuts? Miss a chance to be in the same room with her? I want to be protected, Omar, but not that much!"

What could I do with him? He was torn in half. He knew the Beryllium Blonde was here to talk him out of resigning, but he couldn't resist the opportunity of letting her try her wiles on him any more than Odysseus could resist listening to the Sirens.

Like a couple of schoolboys dragging ourselves down to the principal's office, we made our way slowly along the corridor and pushed through the door to the conference room. She was already seated at the head of the table, wearing a Chinese-red jumpsuit that fit her like skin. I gulped down a lump in my throat at the sight of her. She smiled a dazzling smile and Sam gave a little moan and rose right off the floor.

He would have launched himself at her like a missile if I hadn't grabbed his belt and yanked him down into the nearest chair. Wishing there were safety harnesses on the seats, I sat down next to Sam, keeping the full length of the polished imitation-wood table between us and the Blonde.

"I think you know why I'm here," she said. Her voice was music.

Sam nodded dumbly, his jaw hanging open. I thought I saw a bit of saliva bubbling at the corner of his mouth.

"Why do you want to leave us, Sam? Don't you *like* us anymore?"

It took three tries before Sam could make his voice work. "It's . . . not that. I . . . I . . . I want to go into business for myself."

"But your employment contract has almost two full years more to run."

"I can't wait two years," he said in a tiny voice. "This opportunity won't keep."

"Sam, you're a very valued employee of Global Technologies, Incorporated. We want you to stay with us. *I* want you to stay with us."

"I . . . can't."

"But you signed a contract with us, Sam. You gave us your word."

I stuck in my dime's worth. "The contract doesn't prohibit Sam from quitting. He can leave whenever he wants to."

"But he'll lose all his pension benefits and health-care provisions."

"He knows that."

She turned those heartbreakingly blue eyes on Sam again. "It will be a big disappointment to us if you leave, Sam. It will be a *personal* disappointment to me."

To his credit, Sam found the strength within himself to hold his ground. "I'm awfully sorry . . . but I've worked very hard to create this opportunity and I can't let it slip past me now."

She nodded once, as if she understood. Then she asked, "This opportunity you're speaking about: does it have anything to do with the prospect of opening a tourist hotel on space station *Alpha?*"

"That's right. Not just a hotel, a complete tourist facility. Sports complex, entertainment center, zero-gravity honeymoon suites."

He stopped abruptly and his face turned red. Sam *blushed!* He actually blushed.

Miss Beryllium smiled her dazzling smile at him. "But Sam, that idea is the proprietary property of Global Technologies. Global owns the idea, not you."

For a moment the little conference room was absolutely silent. I could hear nothing except the faint background hum of the air-circulation fans. Sam seemed to have stopped breathing.

Then he squawked, *"What?"*

With a sad little shake of her gorgeous head, the Blonde replied, "Sam, you developed that idea while an employee of Global Technologies. We own it."

"But you turned it down!"

"That makes no difference, Sam. Read your employment contract. It's ours."

"But I made all the contacts. I raised the funding. I worked everything out—on my own time, goddammit! *On my own time!*"

She shook her head again. "No, Sam. You did it while you were a Global employee. It's not your possession. It belongs to us."

Sam leaped from his chair and bounded to the ceiling. This time he was ready to make war, not love. "You can't do this to me!"

The Blonde looked completely unruffled by his display. She sat there patiently, a slightly disappointed little frown on her face, while I calmed Sam down and got him back into his chair.

"Sam, dear, I know how you must feel," she said. "I don't want us to be enemies. We'd be happy to have you take part in the tourist hotel program—as a Global employee. There could even be a raise in it for you."

"It's mine, dammit!" Sam screeched. "You can't steal it from me! It's mine!"

She shrugged. "Well, I expect our lawyers will have to settle it with your lawyers. In the meantime, I suppose there's nothing for us to do but accept your resignation. With reluctance. With my personal and very sad reluctance."

That much I saw and heard with my own eyes and ears. I had to drag Sam out of the conference room and take him back to his own quarters. She had him whipsawed, telling him that he couldn't claim possession of his own idea, and at the same time practically begging him to stay on with Global and run the tourist project for them.

What happened next depends on whom you ask. There are as many different versions of the story as there are people who tell it. As near as I can piece it all together, though, it went this way:

The Beryllium Blonde had figured that Sam's financial partners would go along with Global Technologies once they realized that Global had muscled Sam out of the tourist business. But she probably wasn't as sure of everything as she tried to make Sam think. After all, those backers had made their deal with the little guy; maybe they wouldn't want to do business with a big multinational corporation. Worse still, she didn't know exactly what kind of deal Sam had cut with his backers; if Sam had a legally binding contract with them that named him as their partner, they might scrap the whole project when they learned that Global had cut Sam out.

So she showed up at Sam's door that night. He told me that she was still wearing the same jumpsuit, with nothing underneath it except her own luscious body. She brought a bottle of incredibly rare and expensive wine with her. "To show there's no hard feelings."

The Blonde's game was to keep Sam with Global and get him to go through with the tourist hotel idea. Apparently, once Global's management got word that Sam had actually closed a deal for building a tourist facility on *Alpha*, they figured they might as well go into the tourist business for themselves. *Alpha* was still underutilized; a tourist facility suddenly made sense to those jerkoffs.

So instead of shuttling back to Phoenix, as we had thought she would, the Blonde knocked on Sam's door that night. The next morning I saw him floating along the Shack's central corridor. He looked kind of dazed.

"She's staying here for a few days," Sam mumbled. It was like he was talking to himself instead of to me. But there was a happy little grin on his face.

Everybody in the Shack started to make bets on how long Sam could hold out. The best odds had him capitulating in three nights. Jokes about Delilah and haircuts became uproariously funny to everybody—except me. My future was tied up with Sam's; if the tourist hotel project collapsed, it wouldn't be long before I was shipped back Earthside, I knew.

After three days there were dark circles under Sam's eyes. He looked weary. The grin was gone.

After a week had gone by, I found Sam snoring in the Blue Grotto. As gently as I could I woke him.

"You getting any food into you?" I asked.

He blinked, gummy-eyed. "Chicken soup. I been taking chicken soup. Had some yesterday . . . I think it was yesterday . . ."

By the tenth day, more money had changed hands among the bettors than on Wall Street. Sam looked like a case of battle fatigue. His cheeks were hollow, his eyes haunted.

"She's a devil, Omar," he whispered hoarsely. "A devil."

"Then get rid of her, man!" I urged.

He smiled wanly. "And quit show business?"

Two weeks to the day after she arrived, the Blonde packed up and left. Her eyes were blazing anger. I saw her off at the docking port. She looked just as perfectly radiant as she had the day she first arrived at the Shack. But what she was radiating now was rage. *Hell hath no fury* . . . I thought. But I was happy to see her go.

Sam slept for two days straight. When he managed to get up and around again, he was only a shell of his old self. He had lost ten pounds. His eyes were sunken into his skull. His hands shook. His chin was stubbled. He looked as if he had been through hell and back. But his crooked little grin had returned.

"What happened?" I asked him.

"She gave up."

"You mean she's going to let you go?"

He gave a deep, soulful, utterly weary sigh. "I guess she figured she couldn't change my mind and she couldn't kill me—at least not with the method she was using." His grin stretched a little wider.

"We all thought she had you wrapped around her . . . eh, her little finger," I said.

"So did she."

"You outsmarted her!"

"I outlasted her," Sam said, his voice low and suddenly sorrowful. "You know, at one point there, she almost had me convinced that she had fallen in love with me."

"In love with you?"

He shook his head slowly, like a man who had crawled across miles of burning sand toward an oasis that turned out to be a mirage.

I said, "You had me worried, man."

"Why?" His eyes were really bleary.

"Well . . . she's a powerful hunk of woman. Like you said, they sent her up because you're susceptible."

"Yeah. But once she tried to steal my idea from me, I stopped being susceptible anymore. I kept telling myself, 'She's not a gorgeous hot-blooded sexpot of a woman, she's a company stooge, a bureaucrat with boobs, an android they sent here to nail you.'"

"And it worked," I said.

"By a millimeter. Less. She damned near beat me. She damned near did. She should have never mentioned marriage. That woke me up."

What had happened, while Sam was fighting the Battle of the Bunk, was that when Sam's partners realized that Global was interested in the tourist facility, they become absolutely convinced that they had a gold mine and backed Sam to the hilt. *Their* lawyers challenged Global's lawyers, and once the paper-shufflers in Phoenix saw that, they realized that Miss Beryllium's mission at the Shack was doomed to fail. The Blonde left in a huff when Phoenix ordered her to return. Apparently, either she was enjoying her work or she thought that she had Sam weakening.

"Now lemme get another week's worth of sleep, will you?" Sam asked me. "And, oh, yeah, find me about a ton of vitamin E."

So Sam became the manager and part-owner of the human race's first extraterrestrial tourist facility. I was his partner and, the way he worked things out, a major shareholder in the project. Global got some rent money out of it. Actually, so many people enjoyed their vacations aboard the Big Wheel so much that a market eventually opened up for low-gravity retirement homes. Sam beat Global on that, too. But that's another story.

Malone was hanging weightlessly near the curving transparent dome of his chamber, staring out at the distant Moon and the cold, unblinking stars.

The reporter had almost forgotten her fear of weightlessness. The black man's story seemed finished; she blinked and adjusted her attention to here and now. Drifting slightly closer to him, she turned the recorder off with an audible click, then thought better of it and clicked it on again.

"So that's how this facility came into being," she said.

Malone nodded, turning in midair to face her. "Yep. Sam got it built, got it started, and then lost interest in it. He had other things on his mind. He went into the advertising business, you know."

"Oh, yes, everybody knows about that," she replied. "But what happened to the woman, the Beryllium Blonde? And why didn't Sam ever return to Earth again?"

"Two parts of the same answer," Malone said. "Miss Beryllium thought she was playing Sam for a fish, using his Casanova complex to literally screw him out of the hotel deal. Once she realized that *he* was playing *her*, fighting a delaying action until his partners got their lawyers into action, she got damned mad. Powerfully mad. By the time it finally became clear back at Phoenix that Sam was going to beat them, she took her revenge on Sam."

"What do you mean?"

"Sam wasn't the only one who could riffle through old safety regulations and use them for his own benefit. She found a few early NASA regs, then got some bureaucrats in Washington—from the Office of Safety and Health, I think—to rewrite them so that anybody who'd been living in zero gee for a year or more had to undergo six months' worth of retraining and exercise before he could return to Earth."

"Six months? That's ridiculous!"

"Is it?" Malone smiled without humor. "That regulation is still on the books, lady. Nobody pays any attention to it anymore, but it's still there."

"She did that to spite Sam?"

"And she made sure Global put all its weight behind enforcing it. Made people think twice before signing an employment contract for working up here. Stuck Sam, but good. He wasn't going to spend any six months retraining! He just never bothered going back to Earth again."

"Did he want to go back?"

"Sure he did. He wasn't like me. He *liked* it back there. There were billions of women on Earth! He wanted to return, but he just couldn't take six months out of his life for it."

"That must have hurt him."

"Yeah, I guess. Hard to tell with Sam. He didn't like to bleed where people could watch."

"And you never went back to Earth," the reporter said.

"No," Malone said. "Thanks to Sam, I stayed up here. He made me manager of the hotel, and once Sam bought the rest of this Big Wheel from Global, I became the manager of the entire *Alpha* station."

"And you've never had the slightest yearning to see Earth again?"

Malone gazed at her solemnly for long moments before answering. "Sure I get the itch. But when I do, I go down to the one-gee section of the Wheel here. I sit in a wheelchair and try to get around with these crippled legs of mine. The itch goes away then."

"But they have prosthetic legs that you can't tell from the real thing," she said. "Lots of paraplegics—"

"Maybe *you* can't tell them from the real thing, but I guarantee you that any paraplegic who uses those things can tell." Malone shook his head. "No, once you've spent some time up here in zero gee, you realize that you don't need legs to get around. You can live a good and useful life here, instead of being a cripple hack down there."

"I see," the reporter said.

"Yeah. Sure you do."

An uncomfortable silence stretched between them. She turned off the recorder on her belt, for good this time. Finally Malone softened. "Hey, I'm sorry. I shouldn't be nasty with you. It's just that . . . thinking about Sam again. He was a great guy, you know. And now he's dead and everybody thinks he was just a trouble-making bastard."

"I don't, not anymore," she said. "A womanizing sonofabitch, like you said. A male chauvinist of the first order. But after listening to you tell it, even at that he doesn't sound so terrible."

The black man smiled at her. "Look at the time! No wonder I'm hungry! Can I take you down to the dining room for some supper?"

"The dining room in the full-gravity area?"

"Yes, of course."

"Won't you be uncomfortable there? Isn't there a dining area in the low-gravity section?"

"Sure, but won't you be uncomfortable there?"

She laughed. "I think I can handle it."

"Really?"

"Certainly. And maybe you can tell me how Sam got himself into the advertising business."

"All right. I'll do that."

As she turned, she caught sight of the immense beauty of Earth sliding past the observation dome; the Indian Ocean a breathtaking swirl of deep blues and greens, the subcontinent of India decked with purest white clouds.

But she looked at Malone, then asked in a whisper, "Don't you miss being home, being on Earth? Don't you feel isolated here, away from—"

His booming laughter shocked her. "Isolated? Up here?" Malone pitched himself forward into a weightless somersault, then pirouetted in midair. He pointed toward the ponderous bulk of the planet and said, "*They're* the ones who're isolated. Up here, I'm free!"

He offered her his arm and they floated together toward the gleaming metal hatch, their feet a good eight inches above the chamber's floor.

THE LIEUTENANT AND
THE FOLKSINGER

Here is Chet Kinsman again. This is the last short story I wrote about him. Paradoxically enough, it depicts a key event at the very beginning of his adult life, when he was (is?) eighteen years old.

FROM THE REAR SEAT OF THE T-38 JET, San Francisco Bay was a sun-glittering mirror set among the brown California hills. Fog was still swirling around the stately towers of the Golden Gate Bridge, but the rest of the Bay was clear and brilliant, the late morning sky brazen, the city on the hills far enough below them so that it looked shining white and clean.

"Like it?" asked the pilot.

Chet Kinsman heard his voice as a disembodied crackle in his helmet earphones over the shrill whine of the turbojet engines.

"Love it!" he answered to the bulbous white helmet in the seat in front of him.

The cockpit was narrow and cramped; Kinsman could barely move in his seat without bumping his own helmet into the plexiglass canopy that covered them both. The straps of his safety harness cut into his shoulders. He had tugged the harness on too tightly. But he felt no discomfort.

This is flying! he said to himself. *Five hundred knots at the touch of a throttle.*

"How high can we go?" he asked into his helmet microphone.

A pause. Then, "Oh, she'll do fifty thousand feet easy enough."

Kinsman grinned. "A lot better than hang gliders."

"I like hang gliding," the pilot said.

"Yeah, but it doesn't compare to this. This is *power,* man."

"Right enough."

It had been a disappointing week. Kinsman had flown to California on impulse. Life at the Air Force Academy was rigid, cold, and a first-year man was expected to obey everyone's orders rather than make friends. So when the first week-long break in the semester came, he dashed to La Jolla with his roommate.

While his fellow cadet was engulfed by his family, Kinsman wandered alone through the beautiful but friendless La Jolla area. His own family was a continent away and would have no part of a son of theirs stooping to the military life, no matter what his reason. Finally Kinsman rented a car and drove north along the spectacular coast highway, up into the Bay area. Alone.

Then on Friday night, at a topless bar in North Beach, where he had to wear his uniform to avoid the hassle of I.D. checks, he bumped into a Navy flier in the midst of the naked dancers and their bouncing, jiggling breasts.

Now he was flying. And happy.

Suddenly the plane's nose dropped, and Kinsman's stomach disappeared somewhere over his right shoulder. The pilot rolled the plane, wingtips making full circles in the empty air, as they dived toward the water—which now looked hard as steel. Kinsman swallowed hard and felt his pulse racing in every part of his body.

"Try a low-level run. Get a real sensation of speed," the pilot said.

Kinsman nodded, then realized he couldn't be seen. "Okay. Great."

In less than a minute they were skimming across the water, engines howling, going so fast that Kinsman could not see individual waves on the choppy Bay, only a blur of blue-gray whizzing just below them. The roar of the engines filled his helmet and the whole plane was shaking, bucking, as if eager to get back up into the thinner air where it was designed to fly.

He thought he saw the International Airport along the blur of hills and buildings off to his left. He knew the Bay Bridge was somewhere up ahead.

"Whoops! Freighter!"

The control stick between Kinsman's knees yanked back toward his crotch. The plane stood on her tail, afterburners screaming, and a microsecond's flicker of a ship's masts zipped past the corner of his eye. He felt the weight of death pressing on his chest, flattening him into the contoured seat, turning it into an invalid's couch. He couldn't lift his arms from his lap or even cry out. It was enough to try to breathe.

They leveled off at last, and Kinsman sucked in a great sighing gulp of oxygen.

"Damned sun glare does that sometimes," the pilot was saying, sounding half-annoyed and half-apologetic. "Damned water looks clear, but there's a whole friggin' fleet hidden by the glare off the water. That's why I'd rather fly under a high overcast—over water, anyway."

"That was a helluva ride," Kinsman said at last.

The pilot chuckled. "I'll bet there's some damned pissed sailors down there. Probably on the horn now, trying to get our tail number."

They headed back to Moffett Field. The pilot let Kinsman take the controls for a few minutes, directing him toward the Navy base where the airfield and the NASA research station were.

"You got a nice steady touch, kid. Make a good pilot."

"Thanks. I used to fly my father's plane. Even the business jet, once."

"Got your license?"

"Not yet. I figure I'll qualify at the Academy."

The pilot said nothing.

"I'm going in for astronaut training as soon as I qualify," Kinsman went on.

"Astronaut, huh? Well, I'd rather fly a plane. Damned astronauts are like robots. Everything's done by remote control for those rocket jockeys."

"Not everything," Kinsman said.

He could sense the pilot shaking his head in disagreement. "Hell, I'll bet they have machines to do their screwing for them."

They called it a coffee shop, but the bar served mainly liquor. *Irish coffee is what they mean,* Kinsman told himself as he hunched over a cold beer and listened to the girl with the guitar singing.

> "Jack of diamonds, queen of spades,
> Fingers tremble and the memory fades,
> And it's a foolish man who tries to bluff the dealer."

Through the coffee shop's big front window, Kinsman could see the evening shadows settling over the Berkeley streets. Students, loungers, street people eased along the sidewalks, most of them looking shabby in denims and faded Army fatigues. Kinsman felt out of place in his sky-blue uniform; he had worn it to the Navy base to help get past the security guards for his meeting with the pilot.

But now as he sat in the coffee shop and watched the night come across the clapboard buildings, and the lights on the Bay Bridge form a twinkling arch that led back to San Francisco, he was just as alone as he had been at the Academy, or back home, or all week long here in California, except for that one hour's flight in the jet.

> "You can't win,
> And you can't break even,
> You can't get out of the game . . ."

She has a lovely voice, all right, he realized. *Like a silver bell. Like water in the desert.*

It was a haunting voice. And her face, framed by long midnight-black hair, had a fine-boned dark-eyed ascetic look to go with it. She sat on a high stool, under a lone spotlight, blue-jeaned legs crossed and guitar resting on one knee.

As Kinsman was trying to work up the nerve to introduce himself to her and tell her how much he enjoyed her singing, a dozen kids his own age shambled into the place. The singer, just finished her song, smiled and called to them. They bustled around her.

Kinsman turned his attention to his beer. By the time he had finished it, the students had pushed several tables together and were noisily ordering everything from Sacred Cows to Diet 7-Up. The singer had disappeared. It was full night outside now.

"You alone?"

He looked up, startled, and it was her. The singer.

"Uh . . . yeah." Clumsily he pushed the chair back and got to his feet.

"Why don't you come over and join us?" She gestured toward the crowd of students.

"Sure. Great. Love to."

She was tall enough to be almost eye level with Kinsman, and as slim and supple as a young willow. She wore a black long-sleeved turtleneck pullover atop the faded denims.

"Hey, everybody, this is . . ." She turned to him with an expectant little smile. All the others stopped their conversation and looked up at him.

"Kinsman," he said. "Chet Kinsman."

Two chairs appeared out of the crowd, and Kinsman sat down between the singer and a chubby blonde girl who was intently rolling a joint for herself.

Kinsman felt out of place. They were all staring at him, except for the rapt blonde, without saying a word. *Wrong uniform,* he told himself. He might as well have been wearing a Chicago policeman's riot suit.

"My name's Diane," the singer said to him, as the bar's only waitress placed a fresh beer in front of him.

"That's Shin, John, Carl, Eddie, Delores . . ." She made a circuit of the table and Kinsman forgot the names as soon as he heard them. Except for Diane's.

They were still eying him suspiciously.

"You with the National Guard?"

"No," Kinsman said. "Air Force Academy."

"Going to be a flyboy?"

"A flying pig!" said the blonde on his left.

Kinsman stared at her. "I'm going in for astronaut training."

"An orbiting pig," she muttered.

"That's a stupid thing to say."

"She's upset," Diane told him. "We're all on edge after what happened at Kent State today."

"Kent State?"

"You haven't heard?" It was an accusation.

"No. I was flying this afternoon and—"

"They gunned down a dozen students."

"The National Fuckin' Guard."

"Killed them!"

"Where?"

"At Kent State. In Ohio."

"The students were demonstrating against the Cambodian invasion and the National Guard marched onto the campus and shot them down."

"Christ, don't they let you see the newspapers?"

"Or TV, even?"

Kinsman shook his head weakly. It was like they were blaming him for it.

"We'll show them, those friggin' bastards!" said an intense, waspish little guy sitting a few chairs down from Kinsman. *Eddie?* he tried to remember. The guy was frail-looking, but his face was set in a smoldering angry mold, tight-lipped. The thick glasses he wore made his eyes look huge and fierce.

"Right on," said the group's one black member. "We gonna tear the campus apart."

"How's that going to help things in Cambodia?" Kinsman heard his own voice asking. "Or in Kent State?"

"How's it gonna *help?*" They looked aghast at his blasphemy.

"Yeah," Kinsman answered, wanting to bounce some of their hostility back at them. "You guys tear up the campus. Big deal, what do you accomplish? Maybe the National Guard shoots you. You think Nixon or anybody else in Washington will give a damn? They'll just call you a bunch of Commies and tell everyone we've got to fight harder over in 'Nam because the whole country's full of subversives."

"That doesn't make any sense," Eddie said.

"Neither does ripping up the campus."

"But you don't understand," Diane said. "We've got to do *something.* We can't let them kill students and draft us into a war we never declared. We've got to show them that we'll fight against them!"

"I'd go after my Congressmen and Senators and tell them to get us out of Vietnam."

They laughed at him. All but Eddie, who looked angrier still.

"You don't understand anything about how the political process works, do you?" Eddie accused.

Now I've got you! "*Well,*" Kinsman answered, "an uncle of mine is a U.S. Senator. My grandfather was Governor of the Commonwealth of Pennsylvania. And a cousin is in the House of Representatives. I've been involved in political campaigns since I was old enough to hold a poster."

Silence. As if a leper had entered their midst.

"Jesus Christ," said one of the kids at last. "He's with the Establishment."

"Your kind of politics," Diane said to him, "doesn't work for us. The Establishment won't listen to us."

"We've got to fight for our rights."

"Demonstrate."

"Fight fire with fire!"

"Action!"

"Bullshit," Kinsman snapped. "All you're going to do is give the cops an excuse to bash your heads in—or worse."

The night, and the argument, wore on. They swore at each other, drank, smoked, talked until they started to get hoarse. Diane had to get up and sing for the other customers every hour, but each time she finished she came back and sat beside Kinsman.

And still the battle raged. The bar finally closed and Kinsman found that his legs had turned rubbery. But he went with them along the dark Berkeley streets to someone's one-room pad, four flights up the back stairs of a dark old house, yammering all the way, arguing with them all, one against ten. And Diane was beside him.

They started drifting away from the apartment. Kinsman found himself sitting on the bare wooden floor, halfway between the stained kitchen sink and the new-looking waterbed, telling them: "Look, I don't like it any more than you do. But violence is their game. You can't win that way. Blow up the whole damned campus, and they'll blow up the whole damned city to get even with you."

One of the students, a burly shouldered kid with a big beefy face and tiny squinting eyes, was sitting on the floor in front of Kinsman.

"You know your trouble flyboy? You're chicken." Kinsman shrugged at him and looked around the floor for the can of beer he had been working on.

"You hear me? You're all talk. But you're scared to fight for your rights."

Kinsman looked up and saw that Diane, the blonde girl, and two of the guys were the only ones left in the room.

"I'll fight for my rights," Kinsman said, very carefully because his tongue wasn't always obeying his thoughts. "And I'll fight for your rights, too. But not in any stupid-ass way."

"You callin' me stupid?" The guy got to his feet. *A weight lifter,* Kinsman told himself. *And he's going to show off his muscles on me.*

"I don't know you well enough to call you anything," he said.

"Well I'm callin' you chicken. A gutless motherfuckin' coward."

Slowly Kinsman got to his feet. It helped to have the wall behind him to lean against.

"I take that, sir, to be a challenge to my honor," he said, letting himself sound drunk. It took very little effort.

"Goddam' right it's a challenge. You must be some goddam' pig— secret police or something."

"That's why I'm wearing this inconspicuous uniform."

"To throw us off guard."

"Don't be silly."

"I'm gonna break your head, wise-ass."

Kinsman raised one finger. "Now hold on. You challenged me. I get the choice of weapons. That's the way it works in the good ol' *code duello.*"

"Choice of weapons?" The guy looked confused.

"You challenged me to a duel, didn't you? You have impeached my honor. I have the right to choose the weapons."

The guy made a fist the size of a football. "This is all the weapon I need."

"But that's not the weapon I choose," Kinsman countered. "I believe that I'll choose sabers. I won a few medals back East with my saber fencing. Now where can we find a pair of sabers at this hour of the morning . . ."

The guy grabbed Kinsman's shirt. "I'm gonna knock that fuckin' grin off your face."

"You probably will. But not before I kick your kneecaps off. You'll never see the inside of a gym again, muscleman."

"That's enough, both of you," Diane snapped.

She stepped between the two of them, forcing the big student to let go of Kinsman.

"You'd better get back to your place, Ray," she said, her voice iron hard. "You're not going to break up my pad and get me thrown out on the street."

Ray pointed a thick, blunt finger at Kinsman. "He's a narc. Or something. Don't trust him."

"Go home, Ray. It's late."

"I'll get you, blue-suit," Ray said.

"I'll get you." Kinsman said, "When you find the sabers, let me know."

"Shut up!" Diane hissed at him. But she was grinning. She half pushed the lumbering Ray out of the door.

The others left right after him, and suddenly Kinsman was alone with Diane.

"I guess I ought to get back to my hotel," Kinsman said, his insides shaking now that the danger had passed.

"Where's that?"

"The Stanhope . . . in the city."

"God, you *are* Establishment!"

"Born with a silver spoon in my ear. To the manner born. Rich or poor, it pays to have money. Let 'em eat cake. Or was it coke?"

"You're drunk!"

"How can you tell?"

"Well, for one thing, your feet are standing in one place, but the rest of you is swaying like a tree in the breeze."

"I am drunk with your beauty . . . and a ton and a half of beer."

Diane laughed. "I can believe the second one."

Looking around for a phone, Kinsman asked, "How do you get a cab around here?"

"You won't. Not at this hour. No trains, either."

"I'm stuck here?"

She nodded.

"A fate worse than death." Kinsman saw that the room's furnishings consisted of a bookshelf crammed with sheet music, the waterbed, a Formica-topped table and two battered wooden chairs that didn't match, the waterbed, a pile of books in one corner of the floor, a few pillows strewn around here and there, and the waterbed.

"You can share the bed with me," Diane said.

He felt his face turning red. "Are your intentions honorable?"

She grinned at him. "The condition you're in, we'll both be safe enough."

"Don't be too sure."

But he fell asleep as soon as he sank into the soft warmth of the bed.

It was sometime during the misty, dreaming light of earliest dawn that he half awoke and felt her body cupped next to his. Still half in sleep, they moved together, slowly, gently, unhurried, alone in a pearly gray fog, feeling without thinking, caressing, making love.

Kinsman lay on his back, smiling dazedly at the cracked ceiling.

"Was that your first time?" Diane asked. Her head was resting on his chest.

He suddenly felt embarrassed. "Well, uh, yeah . . . it was."

She stroked the flat of his abdomen.

Awkwardly, he said, "I guess I was pretty clumsy, wasn't I?"

"Oh no. You were fine."

"You don't have to humor me."

"I'm not. It was marvelous. Terrific."

It wasn't your first time, he knew. But he said nothing.

"Go to sleep," Diane said. "Get some rest and we can do it again."

It was almost noon by the time Kinsman had showered in the cracked tub and gotten back into his wrinkled uniform. He was looking into the still-steamy bathroom mirror, wondering what to do about his stubby chin, when Diane called through the half-open door: "Tea or coffee?"

"Coffee."

Kinsman came out of the tiny bathroom and saw that she had set up toast and a jar of Smuckers grape jelly on the table by the window. A teakettle was on the two-burner stove, with a pair of chipped mugs and a jar of instant coffee alongside.

They sat facing each other, washing down the crunchy toast with the hot, strong coffee. Diane watched the people moving along the street below them. Kinsman stared at the clean sky.

"How long can you stay?" she asked.

"I've got a date with this guy to go flying this afternoon. Then I leave tonight."

"Oh."

"Got to report back to the Academy tomorrow morning."

"You have to."

He nodded. "Wish I didn't."

She gave him a *so do I* look. "But you're free this afternoon?"

"I'm supposed to meet this Navy guy; he's going to take me up with him."

"Come down to the campus with me instead," Diane said, brightening. "The demonstration will be starting around two and you can help us."

"Me?"

"Sure! You're not going to let them get away with it, are you? They'll be sending *you* to Cambodia or someplace to get killed."

"Yeah, maybe, but—"

She reached across the table and took his free hand in both of hers. "Chet . . . please. Not for me. Do it for yourself. I don't want to think of you being sent out there to fight a war we shouldn't be fighting. Don't let them turn you into a robot."

"But I'm going into astronaut training."

"You don't believe they'll give you what you want, do you? They'll use you for cannon fodder, just like all the others."

"You don't understand."

"No, you don't understand!" she said earnestly. Kinsman saw the intensity in her eyes, the devotion. *Is she really worried that much about me?*

"We've got to stop them, Chet. We've got to use every ounce of courage we can muster to stop this war and stop the killing."

"Tearing up the campus isn't going to do it."

"I know that. This is going to be a peaceful demonstration. It's the pigs that start the violence."

He shook his head.

"Come and see, if you don't believe me! Come with me."

"In my uniform? Your friends would trash me."

"No they won't. It'd make a terrific impact for somebody in uniform to show up with us. We've been trying to get some of the Vietnam veterans to show themselves in uniform."

"I can't," Kinsman said. "I've got a date with a guy to go flying this afternoon."

"That's more important than freedom? More important than justice?"

He had no answer.

"Chet . . . please. For me. If you don't want to do it for yourself, or for the people, then do it for me. Please."

He looked away from her and glanced around the shabby, unkempt room. At the stained, cracked sink. The faded wooden floor. The unframed posters scotch-taped to the walls. The waterbed, with its soiled sheet trailing onto the floor.

He thought of the Academy. The cold gray mountains and ranks of uniforms marching mechanically across the frozen parade ground. The starkly functional classrooms, the remorsely efficient architecture devoid of all individual expression.

And then he turned back, looked past the woman across the table from him, and saw the sky once again.

"I can't go with you," he said quietly, finally. "Somebody's got to make sure you don't get bombed while you're out there demonstrating for your rights."

For a moment Diane said nothing. Then, "You're trying to make a joke out of something that's deadly serious."

"I'm being serious," he said. "You'll have plenty of demonstrators out there. Somebody's got to protect and defend you while you're exercising your freedoms."

"It's our own government we need protection from!"

"You've got it. You just have to exercise it a little better. I'd rather be flying. There aren't so many of us up there."

Diane shook her head. "You're hopeless."

He shrugged.

"I was going to offer to let you stay here . . . if you wanted to quit the Air Force."

"Resign?"

"If you needed a place to hide . . . or you just wanted to stay here, with me."

He started to answer, but his mouth was dry. He swallowed, then in a voice that almost cracked, "I can't. I . . . I'm sorry, Diane, but I just can't." He pushed his chair back and got to his feet.

At the door, he turned back toward her. She was at the table still. "Sorry I disappointed you. And, well, thanks . . . for everything."

She got up, walked swiftly across the tiny room to him, and kissed him lightly on the lips.

"It was my pleasure, General."

"Lieutenant," he quickly corrected. "I'll be a lieutenant when I graduate."

"You'll be a general someday."

"I don't think so."

"You could have been a hero today," she said.

"I'm not very heroic."

"Yes you are." She was smiling at him now. "You just don't know it yet."

That afternoon, forty thousand feet over the Sacramento Valley, feeling clean and free and swift, Kinsman wondered briefly if he had made the right choice.

"Sir?" he asked into his helmet microphone. "Do you really think astronaut training turns men into robots?"

The man's chuckle told him the answer. "Son, any kind of training is aimed at turning you into a robot. Just don't let 'em get away with it. The main thing is to get up and fly. Up here they can't really touch us. Up here we're free."

"They're pretty strict over at the Academy," Kinsman said. "They like things done their way."

"Tell me about it. I'm an Annapolis man, myself. You can still hold onto your own soul, boy. You have to do things their way on the outside, but you be your own man inside. Isn't easy, but it can be done."

Nodding to himself, Kinsman looked up and through the plane's clear plastic canopy. He caught sight of a pale ghost of the Moon, riding high in the afternoon sky.

I can do it, he said to himself. *I can do it.*

THE NEXT LOGICAL STEP

Since the 1950s computer experts have been producing ever-more sophisticated models of the world's economic, ecological and geopolitical systems to help Washington's decision-makers to forecast what the world will be like over the next few decades. Of course, there are many problems with such computer world models. "The Next Logical Step," which was written more than fifty years ago, examines one such problem—and its solution.

※ 🌀 ※

"I DON'T REALLY SEE where this problem has anything to do with me," the CIA man said. "And, frankly, there are a lot of more important things I could be doing."

Ford, the physicist, glanced at General LeRoy. The general had that quizzical expression on his face, the look that meant he was about to do something decisive.

"Would you like to see the problem firsthand?" the general asked, innocently.

The CIA man took a quick look at his wrist watch. "Okay, if it doesn't take too long. It's late enough already."

"It won't take very long, will it, Ford?" the general said, getting out of his chair.

"Not very long," Ford agreed. "Only a lifetime."

The CIA man grunted as they went to the doorway and left the general's office. Going down the dark, deserted hallway, their footsteps echoed hollowly.

"I can't overemphasize the seriousness of the problem," General LeRoy said to the CIA man. "Eight ranking members of the General Staff have either resigned their commissions or gone straight to the violent ward after just one session with the computer."

The CIA man scowled. "Is this area secure?"

General LeRoy's face turned red. "This entire building is as Secure as any edifice in the Free World, mister. And it's empty. We're the only living people inside here at this hour. I'm not taking any chances."

"Just want to be sure."

"Perhaps if I explain the computer a little more," Ford said, changing the subject, "you'll know what to expect."

"Good idea," said the man from CIA.

"We told you that this is the most modern, most complex and delicate computer in the world . . . nothing like it has ever been attempted before—anywhere."

"I know that *they* don't have anything like it," the CIA man agreed.

"And you also know, I suppose, that it was built to simulate actual war situations. We fight wars in this computer . . . wars with missiles and bombs and gas. Real wars, complete down to the tiniest detail. The computer tells us what will actually happen to every missile, every city, every man . . . who dies, how many planes are lost, how many trucks will fail to start on a cold morning, whether a battle is won or lost—"

General LeRoy interrupted. "The computer runs these analyses for both sides, so we can see what's happening to them, too."

The CIA man gestured impatiently "Wargames simulations aren't new. You've been doing them for years."

"Yes, but this machine is different," Ford pointed out. "It not only gives a much more detailed war game. It's the next logical step in the development of machine-simulated war games." He hesitated dramatically.

"Well, what is it?"

Ford said, "We've added a variation of the electroencephalograph."

The CIA man stopped walking. "The electro-what?"

"Electroencephalograph. You know, a recording device that reads the electrical patterns of your brain. Like the electrocardiograph."

"Oh."

"But you see, we've given the EEG a reverse twist. Instead of using a machine that makes a recording of the brain's electrical wave output, we've developed a device that will take the computer's readout tapes and turn them into electrical patterns that are put *into* your brain!"

"I don't get it."

General LeRoy took over. "You sit at the machine's control console. A helmet is placed over your head. You set the machine in operation. You *see* the results."

"Yes," Ford went on. "Instead of reading rows of figures from the computer's printer . . . you actually see the war being fought. Complete visual and auditory hallucinations. You can watch the progress of the battles, and as you change strategy and tactics you can see the results before your eyes."

"The idea, originally, was to make it easier for the General Staff to visualize strategic situations," General LeRoy said.

"But everyone who's used the machine has either resigned his commission or gone insane," Ford added.

The CIA man cocked an eye at LeRoy. "You've used the computer."

"Correct."

"And you have neither resigned nor cracked up."

General LeRoy nodded. "I called you in."

Before the CIA man could comment, Ford said, "The computer's right inside this doorway. Let's get this over with while the building is still empty."

They stepped in. The physicist and the general showed the CIA man through the room-filling rows of massive consoles.

"It's all transistorized and sub-miniaturized, of course," Ford explained. "That's the only way we could build so much detail into the machine and still have it small enough to fit inside a single building."

"A single building?"

"Oh yes: this is only the control section. Most of this building is taken up by the circuits, the memory banks and the rest of it."

"Hmmmn."

They showed him finally to a small desk, studded with control buttons and dials. The single spotlight above the desk lit it brilliantly, in harsh contrast to the semidarkness of the rest of the room.

"Since you've never run the computer before," Ford said, "General LeRoy will do the controlling. You just sit and watch what happens."

The general sat in one of the well-padded chairs and donned a grotesque headgear that was connected to the desk by a half-dozen wires. The CIA man took his chair, slowly. When they put one of the bulky helmets on him, he looked up at them, squinting a little in the bright light. "This . . . this isn't going to . . . well, do me any damage, is it?"

"My goodness no," Ford said. "You mean mentally? No, of course not. You're not on the General Staff, so it shouldn't . . . it won't . . . affect you the way it did the others. Their reaction had nothing to do with the computer *per se*."

"Several civilians have used the computer with no ill effects," General LeRoy said. "Ford has used it many times."

The CIA man nodded, and they closed the transparent visor over his face. He sat there and watched General LeRoy press a series of buttons, then turn a dial.

"Can you hear me?" The general's voice came muffled through the helmet.

"Yes," he said.

"All right. Here we go. You're familiar with Situation One-Two-One? That's what we're going to be seeing."

Situation One-Two-One was a standard war game. The CIA man was well-acquainted with it. He watched the general flip a switch, then sit back and fold his arms over his chest. A row of lights on the desk console began blinking on and off, one, two, three . . . down to the end of the row, then back to the beginning again, on and off, on and off.

And then, somehow, he could see it!

He was poised, incredibly, somewhere in space, and he could see it all in a funny, blurry, double-sighted, dreamlike way. He seemed to be seeing several pictures and hearing many voices, all at once. It was all mixed up, and yet it made a weird kind of sense.

For a panicked instant he wanted to rip the helmet off his head. *It's only an illusion*, he told himself, forcing calm on his unwilling nerves. *Only an illusion.*

But it seemed strangely real.

He was watching the Gulf of Mexico. He could see Florida off to his right, and the arching coast of the southeastern United States. He could even make out the Rio Grande River.

Situation One-Two-One started, he remembered, with the discovery of missile-bearing enemy submarines in the Gulf. Even as he watched the whole area—as though perched on a satellite—he could see, underwater and close-up, the menacing shadowy figure of a submarine gliding through the crystal-blue sea.

He saw, too, a patrol plane as it spotted the submarine and sent an urgent radio warning.

The underwater picture dissolved in a bewildering burst of bubbles. A missile had been launched. Within seconds, another burst—this time a nuclear depth charge—utterly destroyed the submarine.

It was confusing. He was everyplace at once. The details were overpowering, but the total picture was agonizingly clear.

Six submarines fired missiles from the Gulf of Mexico. Four were immediately sunk, but too late. New Orleans, St. Louis and three Air Force bases were obliterated by hydrogen-fusion warheads.

The CIA man was familiar with the opening stages of the war. The first missile fired at the United States was the signal for whole fleets of American missiles and bombers to launch themselves at the enemy. It was confusing to see all the world at once; at times he could not tell if the fireball and mushroom cloud was over Chicago or Shanghai, New York or Novosibirsk, Baltimore or Budapest.

It did not make much difference, really. They all got it in the first few hours of the war; as did London and Moscow, Washington and Peking, Detroit and Delhi, and many, many more.

The defensive systems on all sides seemed to operate well, except that there were never enough antimissiles. Defensive systems were expensive compared to attack rockets. It was cheaper to build a deterrent than to defend against it.

The missiles flashed up from submarines and railway cars, from underground silos and stratospheric jets; secret ones fired off automatically when a certain airbase command post ceased beaming out a restraining radio signal. The defensive systems were simply overloaded. And when the bombs ran out, the missiles carried dust and germs and gas. On and on. For six days and six fire-lit nights. Launch, boost, coast, reenter, death.

And now it was over, the CIA man thought. The missiles were all gone. The airplanes were exhausted. The nations that had built the weapons no longer existed. By all the rules he knew of, the war should have been ended.

Yet the fighting did not end. The machine knew better. There were still many ways to kill an enemy. Time-tested ways. There were armies fighting in four continents, armies that had marched overland, or splashed ashore from the sea, or dropped out of the skies.

Incredibly, the war went on. When the tanks ran out of gas, and the flamethrowers became useless, and even the prosaic artillery pieces had no more rounds to fire, there were still simple guns and even simpler bayonets and swords.

The proud armies, the descendants of the Alexanders and Caesars and Temujins and Wellingtons and Grants and Rommels, relived their evolution in reverse.

The war went on. Slowly, inevitably, the armies split apart into smaller and smaller units, until the tortured countryside that so recently had felt the impact of nuclear war once again knew the tread of bands of armed marauders. The tiny savage groups, stranded in alien lands, far from the homes and families that they knew to be destroyed, carried on a mockery of war, lived off the land, fought their own countrymen if the occasion suited, and revived the ancient terror of hand-wielded, personal, one-head-at-a-time killing.

The CIA man watched the world disintegrate. Death was an individual business now, and none the better for no longer being mass-produced. In agonized fascination he saw the myriad ways in which a man might die. Murder was only one of them. Radiation, disease, toxic gases that lingered and drifted on the once-innocent winds, and—finally—the most efficient destroyer of them all: starvation.

Nine billion people (give or take a meaningless hundred million) lived on the planet Earth when the war began. Now, with the tenuous thread of civilization burned away, most of those who were not killed by the fighting itself succumbed, inexorably, to starvation or disease.

Not everyone died, of course. Life went on. Some were lucky.

A long darkness settled on the world. Life went on for a few, a pitiful few, a bitter, hateful, suspicious, savage few. Cities became pestholes. Books became fuel. Knowledge died. Civilization was completely gone from the planet Earth.

The helmet was lifted slowly off his head. The CIA man found that he was too weak to raise his arms and help. He was shivering and damp with perspiration.

"Now you see," Ford said quietly, "why the military men cracked up when they used the computer."

General LeRoy, even, was pale. "How can a man with any conscience at all direct a military operation when he knows that *that* will be the consequence?"

The CIA man struck up a cigarette and pulled hard on it. He exhaled sharply. "Are all the war games . . . like that? Every plan?"

"Some are worse," Ford said. "We picked an average one for you. Even some of the 'brushfire' games get out of hand and end up like that."

"So . . . what do you intend to do? Why did you call me in? What can *I* do?"

"You're with CIA," the general said. "Don't you handle espionage?"

"Yes, but what's that got to do with it?"

The general looked at him. "It seems to me that the next logical step is to make damned certain that *They* get the plans to this computer . . . and fast!"

SWORD PLAY

This story is not science fiction. It is not fantasy. It is autobiography. This event actually happened while I was a member of the fencing club of the Arch Street YMCA in Philadelphia. I include this tale here because so many science-fiction readers are enamored of sword-wielding superheroes that I thought it would be fun to show what fencing is really like.

* 🌀 *

"What're you grinnin' at?" Jimmy Matthews shrugged without answering. But he kept on grinning.

"C'mon, Jimmy . . . what's going on inside your pointy head?" Paul asked.

"Nothing," said Jimmy, still showing a lot of teeth.

The boys were standing on the corner in front of Weston High, waiting for the bus that would take them into the city. It was a chilly late autumn afternoon. School was over for the day. Windswept clouds covered the sun and brittle leaves rustled along lawns and pavements.

Paul poked a toe into the equipment bag at his feet. It rattled like a plumber's tool kit.

"You're still grinning," he said.

Jimmy shrugged and dug his hands deeper into his windbreaker pockets. He was tall for a sophomore, with the lanky yet muscular body of a good swimmer. A big mop of dark-brown hair flopped over his eyes.

"Come on," Paul nearly begged. "What's so funny?" Paul was shorter and stockier, with sandy hair and pale blue eyes. He was the kid who got to where he wanted to go by working stubbornly until he made it. He and Jimmy studied together a lot, after school. Paul got As and Bs. Jimmy, just as bright, barely squeaked through with Cs and Ds.

"Nothing's funny," Jimmy said, as if he didn't really mean it. "What makes you think something's got to be funny? Can't a guy just stand on a street corner and smile?"

"Something's buzzing in your BB brain."

Jimmy rubbed the side of his nose. "Well . . ."

"Yeah? What?"

"I was thinking how hard it's going to be not to laugh when I see you in that fancy outfit."

"My fencing uniform?"

"Yeah. With the knee pants."

Paul frowned. "You won't laugh so hard when you try it yourself. It's a tough sport."

"Sure," Jimmy chuckled. "In those pretty outfits. With the neat little knee pants."

Paul kicked harder at the equipment bag. "You're always making fun of everything. Always goofing off."

"You sound like Old Lady McNiff," Jimmy complained. His voice went into a trembling falsetto: "James, you have a million-dollar brain, but you're only using ten cents worth of it."

Both boys broke up laughing.

"Hey, here comes the bus," Jimmy said. Paul became serious again. "You won't goof up the fencing class, will you? No clowning around?"

"I'll try not to laugh."

"I'll bet you'll like it, if you just pay attention and don't try any horseplay."

The bus pulled up with a hiss of air brakes. Paul hefted his equipment bag and slung it over his shoulder. Jimmy carried only a sweatshirt and shorts, in a paper bag. As Paul scampered up the bus steps, Jimmy booted him in the rear. Lightly. With a big grin.

The Y was an old, brick building, in the middle of the downtown area. It wasn't a good neighborhood to be in, especially after dark.

The gym was big, but old. High ceiling with dim lights that were covered by wire screening. Bare wooden floors. Basketball hoops without netting and backboards that looked as if they'd crumble if just one more ball banged into them. It smelled of a century of sweat, and Jimmy wrinkled his nose as he and Paul walked through it, heading for the locker room.

But his grin returned as Paul dressed in the white knee pants and high-necked white jacket of his fencing outfit. Jimmy himself simply took off his shirt and pulled a sweatshirt over his head. His jeans and sneakers completed his outfit. "You look just *swell*," he said as they walked out of the locker room.

Paul was about to reply when he spotted the fencing instructor talking to a few other kids at the far end of the gym. He also wore a jacket and knee pants, but they were gray with wear and age, and looked very different from Paul's spanking-white three-week-old uniform.

"Come on," Paul said. "I'll introduce you."

Mr. Martinez was small and wiry. A friendly smile was the main feature of his tan face.

"Welcome to the fencing club, Jim. I hope you learn to enjoy fencing." He took Jimmy's hand in a strong grip.

"Uh, thanks . . . I hope so."

"We'll be starting in a few minutes, just as soon as the others show up. Paul, why don't you show Jim a few limbering-up exercises until we're ready for the starting lineup."

Jimmy snickered as Paul demonstrated the deep hip bends and arm-stretching exercises.

"You look like you're gonna dance a ballet, not try to stick some clown with a sword."

Frowning, Paul said, "You try it and see if it's so easy."

But Jimmy was watching the other kids. Some wore sweatshirts with their school initials. Most of them were from the downtown schools. Three were girls.

Jimmy stood off to one side as Mr. Martinez lined everybody up and put them through a set of opening exercises. He demonstrated how to lunge with a foil: an explosion of purposeful motion, like a snake striking, so fast that Jimmy couldn't follow it.

After about ten sweat-popping minutes, Mr. Martinez let the class drop to the floor and relax. He walked up to Jimmy, a chest protector and mask in one hand.

"See if these fit you. You've got to have the right protection when you fence. There's no real danger in this sport if you're properly equipped—unless you break a blade and fall against your opponent with the broken end. But that almost never happens, unless the fencers aren't working correctly and they get too close to each other."

Jimmy strapped on the chest protector, wormed the fencing mask over his head, and Mr. Martinez started to show him how to lunge. But Jimmy kept getting it all mixed up. He couldn't seem to get his arms and legs working together right.

Finally Mr. Martinez whipped off his mask. His face was very grave. "Why did you come here this afternoon?" he asked.

Jimmy was surprised by the question. "Huh? Well, I guess I wanted to see what fencing is like."

"And what do you think of it?"

"It's all right, I guess."

Mr. Martinez said, "You'll never enjoy fencing or anything else if you don't apply yourself. You've got the size and reflexes to be an outstanding fencer, but you're just not interested, are you? Why not?"

Staring down at his sneakers, Jimmy said, "Well, it's kind of silly. Not like football or basketball. All you try to do is touch each other with these dumb fake swords."

"You think football is tougher? Or basketball?"

"Yeah."

"All right. Try this little exercise, then. Maybe it'll show you there's more to fencing than dancing around."

Mr. Martinez called one of the girls. "Donna, will you show Jimmy here the glove exercise?"

Donna worked the fencing glove off her right hand and held it against the wall a little higher than her shoulder. "You take the on-guard position. When I drop the glove, you lunge and pin it against the wall with the point of your foil before it hits the floor."

"Is that all? That's easy!"

She grinned at him. "Try it."

Jimmy squatted into the on-guard position and held his foil the way Mr. Martinez had shown him. Trying hard to remember how to make a good lunge, he noticed that Donna was smirking, as if she knew something he didn't. She dropped the glove.

Jimmy lunged smartly. And missed. The glove slithered down the wall and hit the floor.

"Let's try that again," he said.

They did. And again. And again. Each time Jimmy's lunge was too slow to catch the glove against the wall. Once he lost his balance and fell on the seat of his pants.

He mopped sweat from his eyes.

"There's gotta be a trick to it."

"No," Donna said. "You've just got to be fast."

"Let's see you do it, then." Jimmy held the glove and Donna speared it. She missed a couple of times, but she hit it more often than she missed. He could feel his face getting red.

"If you can do it, I can do it!"

They reversed positions again, and still Jimmy missed the glove as Donna let it fall. His face twisted into a tight frown of concentration. *On guard, watch her hand, lunge!* And again he missed.

"Can I tell you something that Mr. Martinez told me last week?" she asked.

"Sure, go ahead."

"He said I should try to think that the point of my blade is alive, and that it's *pulling* me to the target. Stop thinking about making a lunge; don't worry about your arms and feet at all. Just let the point *pull* you to the target."

Shrugging, Jimmy said, "Okay." But it didn't make much sense.

She held the glove up against the wall again. Jimmy stared at it and pointed the tip of his foil at it. She dropped it and the blade leaped at it.

"You did it!"

He had caught the glove by a corner of its cuff; a fraction of an inch more and he would have missed it again.

"Let's try a couple more," Jimmy said.

He still missed more than he caught, but he hit the glove squarely twice.

"That's terrific," Donna said, looking really pleased. "I didn't hit the glove at all the first day I tried."

Jimmy's legs were trembling with exertion. "It's not as easy," he puffed, "as it looks."

Paul came up with a mask under his arm. "You want to try a little fencing?"

Jimmy thought about asking him to wait until he had caught his breath. But he saw the crooked grin on Paul's face, and answered, "Sure!"

"Okay, put on your mask," Paul said. "You're gonna need it!" He cut a "Z" through the air with his blade.

"We'll fence along this line," Paul said, pointing to a barely visible, red line along the worn floorboards. "Don't get too close. That's the way you break blades, and then you have to pay for a new one. Just try a couple of lunges at me . . . try to hit my body. Arms and legs and head are foul territory."

Paul stood fairly straight and held his blade down, to give Jimmy a clear shot. Jimmy lunged and hit him squarely on the chest.

"Not bad!"

They tried a half-dozen lunges. Then Paul showed Jimmy the two simplest parries—the way you blocked your opponent's blade with your own blade, to make him miss the target.

Jimmy lunged and Paul parried. Then Paul lunged and Jimmy parried, but too late. Paul's point hit Jimmy on the shoulder. They lunged and parried, and soon they were moving back and forward. *Hey, just like the movies!* Jimmy suddenly realized he was really fencing. And it was fun.

"Gotcha!"

"Naw, you missed."

They went at it again, more furiously than ever. Mr. Martinez shouted, "Hey, you boys . . ."

But Jimmy couldn't hear him. He and Paul were locked in mortal combat: *Zorro and his enemy.*

"You're too close! Stop!" Mr. Martinez raced toward them.

Jimmy hacked at Paul's blade and then lunged. He saw his foil hit his friend's chest, bend almost double, then snap in half. Horrified, he felt himself falling off-balance against Paul, the broken end of his foil still in his outstretched hand. Like watching a slow-motion film, he saw the jagged end of the blade enter Paul's body just under the right armpit.

The two boys collided and went down in a tangled heap. Paul was clutching at his right side, and Jimmy could see his grimace of pain even through the fencing mask.

Mr. Martinez yanked Paul's mask off, and he and Jimmy gently unbuttoned the high-necked fencing jacket and eased it off Paul's shoulders. Everyone else was standing around them in a tight, silent knot.

"Doesn't look very bad," Mr. Martinez said, examining the gash under Paul's arm. It was bleeding slightly. "Donna, go over to my fencing bag and get the first aid kit."

"I," Paul's voice was shaky. "I taste blood in my mouth."

"Oh no," Donna gasped.

"Punctured lung," somebody whispered. Mr. Martinez' jaw muscles tensed. "Help me lift him . . . gently," he said to Jimmy. "We've got to rush him to the hospital."

Dazed, scared, wordless, Jimmy took one of Paul's shoulders. Mr. Martinez took the other and a couple of other boys lifted Paul's legs. As gently as they could they hurried him out of the gym and down the musty-smelling hallway. The whole class followed.

They went through the Y lobby, where they startled a couple of old men playing chess, and out into the street. It was getting dark. A chilly wind was blowing. Jimmy felt nothing; he was numb.

They carried Paul down the shabby street, past a restaurant with grease-streaked windows, an empty store, an abandoned church, a group of tired people waiting for a bus. One of the kids sprinted out into the street ahead of them and held up his arms to stop the traffic. Jimmy barely noticed the cars and buses and trucks growling in the city's end-of-the-day traffic snarl.

A tough-looking gang of kids and young men stood on the street corner and watched them as they hurried past. Jimmy saw that the next building was the hospital; gray cement walls and a faded old sign lit by a single bare bulb: OUTPATIENT CLINIC—CASHIER—EMERGENCY.

They hustled Paul right past the startled receptionist, through a half-filled waiting room, and through a double swinging door into the emergency treatment area. There was an empty white-sheeted table on their right, and they laid Paul down.

A frowning nurse bustled up to them, but before she could say anything, Mr. Martinez puffed, "Punctured lung accident."

Her mouth clicked shut. She said, "I'll get an intern. You go to the waiting room, all of you."

They clumped into the waiting room, suddenly filling it to overflowing. Donna took Jimmy by the arm and sat him in one of the creaking plastic chairs, next to a fat woman who scowled at the gang of silent, scared kids. Mr. Martinez went over to the receptionist, who pulled out a long, blue-paper form and started asking him questions.

Suddenly Jimmy wanted to cry. He held back the tears, just barely. But he sank his head into his hands.

"My best buddy," he heard himself say, his voice sounding all choked up. "I stabbed him."

"It wasn't your fault," Donna said gently.

"Maybe he'll die . . ."

"You didn't do it on purpose. It was an accident."

Jimmy straightened up and looked at her. She reached out and put a hand on his shoulder. "It wasn't your fault," she repeated.

"Yes, it was," Jimmy knew. "I was goofing off. Just like I always do. If I hadn't been such a jerk . . ."

A doctor pushed through the double doors. He looked very serious, almost angry. Mr. Martinez went over from the receptionist's desk to the white-jacketed intern.

"You brought in the boy with the laceration under his arm?" the doctor asked.

"Yes," Mr. Martinez said. "His lung . . ."

The doctor shook his head. "He tasted blood in his mouth?"

"Yes."

"That's because he bit his tongue. There's nothing wrong with his lung."

Mr. Martinez' jaw dropped open. Then he smiled. Jimmy felt himself take a deep, relieved breath.

"He's just got a scratch," the doctor said. "He'll be out in a minute."

Jimmy wanted to laugh, to jump to his feet and shout. But he felt too weak to move.

In a few minutes Paul came back out into the waiting room, grinning sheepishly. There was a bandage under his right arm. They all clustered around him.

"Where's my jacket?" he asked.

Jimmy started to make a teasing answer, then realized that this was no time for being funny. "We must've left it back in the gym."

"We'll have to walk back to the Y dressed like this?" Donna looked aghast.

Jimmy realized that they were an odd-looking crew: wearing knee-length fencing pants, or shorts, or sweatshirts, or chest protectors.

Mr. Martinez grinned. "I guess we'll have to walk the two blocks dressed this way, all right. We'd better stick close together."

"Maybe we should've brought our foils," one of the kids said. They all laughed and started for the door of the waiting room.

"All for one, and one for all," somebody shouted.

Mr. Martinez pulled up beside Jimmy. "Do you still think fencing is for sissies?"

Jimmy could feel his face go red. "Naw, I guess not. It's a tough game. I'll have to work real hard at it."

"You're coming back next week?" Paul asked.

Jimmy nodded, and inside his head he realized that something good had come out of all this. "Yep. I'll be back. And no more goofing off. I want to see if I can really become a good fencer."

"Good!" said Mr. Martinez. "We have our first competition against another team at the end of the month. I want to be able to depend on both you boys for our team."

"You can," they said together, then laughed at how much alike they sounded.

THE SHINING ONES

If you have read my book of advice to writers, Notes To a Science Fiction Writer, *then you have seen a structural analysis of this story,* "The Shining Ones." *Rather than repeat that analysis here, let me tell you how censorship affects the publishing business.*

"The Shining Ones" was originally written at the request of a publishing house which wanted to start a series of short novels for "reluctant readers": that is, people of young adult age who had not learned to read much beyond the grammar-school level. The basic ideas in the plot, and the characterizations of the main personages in the story, were carefully reviewed and approved by the book company's editor. When I delivered the manuscript, the editor reported, at first, that she liked it very much. But she had to get approval from a board of "experts" that the publisher had hired: a group of teachers and psychologists whose main function, as I understood it, was to decide if the story would be readable by its intended audience.

The "experts" approved the story, but with a catch. They felt that the hero's fatal disease was too depressing, and that aspect of the story should be dropped. When I was informed of this by the editor I pointed out that Charles Dickens' "A Christmas Carol" would hardly be the memorable story it is if Tiny Tim had suffered merely from acne, instead of a crippling, life-threatening disease. No use. The "experts" were adamant. Although I was not allowed to meet them or argue my case with them, their decision was final: change the story or have it rejected.

I withdrew the story and published it elsewhere. As far as I know, no one has ever suffered mental or emotional disability because of this story. Particularly if they read to the end of it!

I

JOHNNY DONATO lay flat on his belly in the scraggly grass and watched the strangers' ship carefully.

It was resting on the floor of the desert, shining and shimmering in the bright New Mexico sunlight. The ship was huge and round like a golden ball, like the sun itself. It touched the ground as lightly as a helium-filled balloon. In fact, Johnny wasn't sure that it really did touch the ground at all.

He squinted his eyes, but he still couldn't tell if the ship was really in contact with the sandy desert flatland. It cast no shadow, and it seemed to glow from some energies hidden inside itself. Again, it reminded Johnny of the sun.

But these people didn't come from anywhere near our sun, Johnny knew. *They come from a world of a different star.*

He pictured in his mind how small and dim the stars look at night. Then he glanced at the powerful glare of the sun. *How far away the stars must be!* And these strangers have traveled all that distance to come here. To Earth. To New Mexico. To this spot in the desert.

Johnny knew he should feel excited. Or maybe scared.

But all he felt right now was curious. And hot. The sun was beating down on the rocky ledge where he lay watching, baking his bare arms and legs. He was used to the desert sun. It never bothered him.

But today something was burning inside Johnny. At first he thought it might be the sickness. Sometimes it made him feel hot and weak. But no, that wasn't it. He had the sickness, there was nothing anyone could do about that. But it didn't make him feel this way.

This thing inside him was something he had never felt before. Maybe it was the same kind of thing that made his father yell in fury, ever since he had been laid off from his job. Anger was part of it, and maybe shame, too. But there was something else, something Johnny couldn't put a name to.

So he lay there flat on his belly, wondering about himself and the strange ship from the stars. He waited patiently, like his Apache friends would, while the sun climbed higher in the bright blue sky and the day grew hotter and hotter.

The ship had landed three days earlier. *Landed* was really the wrong word. It had touched down as gently as a cloud drifts against the tops of the mountains. Sergeant Warner had seen it. He just happened to be driving down the main highway in his State Police cruiser when the ship appeared. He nearly drove into the roadside culvert, staring at the ship instead of watching his driving.

Before the sun went down that day, hundreds of Army trucks and tanks had poured down the highway, swirling up clouds of dust that could be seen even from Johnny's house in Albuquerque, miles away. They surrounded the strange ship and let no one come near it.

Johnny could see them now, a ring of steel and guns. Soldiers paced slowly between the tanks, with automatic rifles slung over their shoulders. Pretending that he was an Apache warrior, Johnny thought about how foolish the Army was to make the young soldiers walk around in the heat instead of allowing them to sit in the shade. He knew that the soldiers were sweating and grumbling and cursing the heat. As if that would make it cooler. They even wore their steel helmets; a good way to fry their brains.

Each day since the ship had landed, exactly when the sun was highest in the sky, three strangers would step out of the ship. At least, that's what the people were saying back in town. The newspapers carried no word of the strangers, except front-page complaints that the Army wouldn't let news reporters or television camera crews anywhere near the star ship.

The three strangers came out of their ship each day, for a few minutes. Johnny wanted to talk to them. Maybe—just maybe—they could cure his sickness. All the doctors he had ever seen just shook their heads and said that nothing could be done. Johnny would never live to be a full-grown man. But these strangers, if they really came from another world, a distant star, they might know how to cure a disease that no doctor on Earth could cure.

Johnny could feel his heart racing as he thought about it. He forced himself to stay calm. *Before you can get cured,* he told himself, *you've got to talk to the strangers. And before you can do that, you've got to sneak past all those soldiers.*

A smear of dust on the highway caught his eye. It was a State Police car, heading toward the Army camp. Sergeant Warner, most likely. Johnny figured that his mother had realized by now he had run away, and had called the police to find him. So he had another problem: avoid getting found by the police.

He turned back to look at the ship again. Suddenly his breath caught in his throat. The three strangers were standing in front of the ship. Without opening a hatch, without any motion at all. They were just *there,* as suddenly as the blink of an eye.

They were tall and slim and graceful, dressed in simple-looking coveralls that seemed to glow, just like their ship.

And they cast no shadows!

2

THE STRANGERS stood there for several minutes. A half-dozen people went out toward them, two in Army uniforms, the others in civilian clothes. After a few minutes the strangers disappeared. Just like that. Gone. The six men seemed just as stunned as Johnny felt. They milled around for a few moments, as if trying to figure out where the strangers had gone to. Then they slowly walked back toward the trucks and tanks and other soldiers.

Johnny pushed himself back down from the edge of the hill he was on. He sat up, safely out of view of the soldiers and police, and checked his supplies. A canteen full of water, a leather sack that held two quickly made sandwiches and a couple of oranges. He felt inside the sack to see if there was anything else. Nothing except the wadded-up remains of the plastic wrap that had been around the other two sandwiches he had eaten earlier. The only other thing he had brought with him was a blanket to keep himself warm during the chill desert night.

There wasn't much shade, and the sun was getting really fierce.

Johnny got to his feet and walked slowly to a clump of bushes that surrounded a stunted dead tree. He sat down and leaned his back against the shady side of the tree trunk.

For a moment he thought about his parents.

His mother was probably worried sick by now. Johnny often got up early and left the house before she was awake, but he always made sure to be back by lunchtime.

His father would be angry. But he was always angry nowadays—most of the time it was about losing his job. But Johnny knew that what was really bugging his father was Johnny's own sickness.

Johnny remembered Dr. Pemberton's round red face, which was normally so cheerful. But Dr. Pemberton shook his head grimly when he told Johnny's father:

"It's foolish for you to spend what little money you have, John. It's incurable. You could send the boy to one of the research centers, and they'll try out some of the new treatments on him. But it won't help him. There is no cure."

Johnny hadn't been supposed to hear that. The door between the examination room where he was sitting and Dr. Pemberton's office had been open only a crack. It was enough for his keen ears, though.

Johnny's father sounded stunned. "But . . . he looks fine. And he says he feels okay."

"I know." Dr. Pemberton's voice sounded as heavy as his roundly overweight body. "The brutal truth, however, is that he has less than a year to live. The disease is very advanced. Luckily, for most of the time he'll feel fine. But towards the end . . ."

"Those research centers," Johnny's father said, his voice starting to crack. "The scientists are always coming up with new vaccines . . ."

Johnny had never heard his father sound like that: like a little boy who had been caught stealing or something, and was begging for a chance to escape getting punished.

"You can send him to a research center," Dr. Pemberton said, slowly. "They'll use him to learn more about the disease. But there's no cure in sight, John. Not this year. Or next. And that's all the time he has."

And then Johnny heard something he had never heard before in his whole life: his father was crying.

They didn't tell him.

He rode back home with his father, and the next morning his

mother looked as if she had been crying all night. But they never said a word to him about it. And he never told them that he knew.

Maybe it would have been different if he had a brother or sister to talk to. And he couldn't tell the kids at school, or his friends around the neighborhood. What do you say? "Hey there, Nicko, I'm going to die around Christmas sometime."

No. Johnny kept silent, like the Apache he often dreamed he was. He played less and less with his friends, spent more and more of his time alone.

And then the ship came.

It had to *mean* something. A ship from another star doesn't just plop down practically in your back yard by accident.

Why did the strangers come to Earth?

No one knew. And Johnny didn't really care. All he wanted was a chance to talk to them, to get them to cure him. Maybe—who knew?—maybe they were here to find him and cure him!

He dozed off, sitting there against the tree. The heat was sizzling, there was no breeze at all, and nothing for Johnny to do until darkness. With his mind buzzing and jumbling a million thoughts together, his eyes drooped shut and he fell asleep.

"Johnny Donato."

The voice was like a crack of thunder. Johnny snapped awake, so surprised that he didn't even think of being scared.

"Johnny Donato! This is Sergeant Warner. We know you're around here, so come out from wherever you're hiding."

Johnny flopped over on his stomach and peered around. He was pretty well hidden by the bushes that surrounded the tree. Looking carefully in all directions, he couldn't see Sergeant Warner or anyone else.

"Johnny Donato!" the voice repeated. "This is Sergeant Warner."

Only now the voice seemed to be coming from farther away. Johnny realized that the State Police sergeant was speaking into an electric bullhorn.

Very slowly, Johnny crawled on his belly up to the top of the little hill. He made certain to stay low and keep in the scraggly grass.

Off to his right a few hundred yards was Sergeant Warner, slowly walking across the hot sandy ground. His hat was pushed back on his head, pools of sweat stained his shirt. He held the bullhorn up to his mouth, so that Johnny couldn't really see his face at all. The sergeant's mirror- shiny sunglasses hid the top half of his face.

Moving still farther away, the sergeant yelled into his bullhorn, "Now listen, Johnny. Your mother's scared half out of her mind. And your father doesn't even know you've run away—he's still downtown, hasn't come home yet. You come out now, you hear? It's hot out here, and I'm getting mighty unhappy about you."

Johnny almost laughed out loud. *What are you going to do, kill me?*

"Dammit, Johnny, I know you're around here. Now, do I have to call in other cars and the helicopter, just to find one stubborn boy?"

Helicopters! Johnny frowned. He had no doubts that he could hide from a dozen police cars and the men in them. But helicopters were something else.

He crawled back to the bushes and the dead tree and started scooping up loose sand with his bare hands. Pretty soon he was puffing and sweaty. But finally he had a shallow trench that was long enough to lie in.

He got into the trench and pulled his food pouch and canteen in with him. Then he spread the blanket over himself. By sitting up and leaning forward, he could reach a few small stones. He put them on the lower corners of the blanket to anchor them down. Then he lay down and pulled the blanket over himself.

The blanket was brown, and probably wouldn't be spotted from a helicopter. Lying there under it, staring at the fuzzy brightness two inches over his nose, Johnny told himself he was an Apache hiding out from the Army.

It was almost true.

It got very hot in Johnny's hideout. Time seemed to drag endlessly. The air became stifling; Johnny could hardly breathe. Once he thought he heard the drone of a helicopter, but it was far off in the distance. Maybe it was just his imagination.

He drifted off to sleep again.

Voices woke him up once more. More than one voice this time, and he didn't recognize who was talking. But they were very close by— they weren't using a bullhorn or calling out to him.

"Are you really sure he's out here?"

"Where else would a runaway kid go? His mother says he hasn't talked about anything but that weirdo ship for the past three days."

"Well, it's a big desert. We're never going to find him standing around here jabbering."

"I got an idea." The voices started to get fainter, as if the men were walking away.

"Yeah? What is it?"

Johnny stayed very still and strained his ears to hear them.

"Those Army guys got all sorts of fancy electronic stuff. Why don't we use them instead of walking around here frying our brains?"

"They had some of that stuff on the helicopter, didn't they?"

The voices were getting fainter and fainter.

"Yeah—but instead of trying to find a needle in a haystack, we ought to play it smart."

"What do you mean?"

Johnny wanted to sit up, to hear them better. But he didn't dare move.

"Why not set up the Army's fancy stuff and point it at the ship? That's where the kid wants to go. Instead of searching the whole damned desert for him . . ."

"I get it!" the other voice said. "Make the ship the bait in a mousetrap."

"Right. That's the way to get him."

They both laughed.

And Johnny, lying quite still in his hideaway, began to know how a starving mouse must feel.

3

AFTER A LONG, hot, sweaty time Johnny couldn't hear any more voices or helicopter engines. And as he stared tiredly at the blanket over him, it seemed that the daylight was growing dimmer.

Must be close to sundown, he thought.

Despite his worked-up nerves, he fell asleep again. By the time he woke up, it was dark.

He sat up and let the blanket fall off to one side of his dugout shelter. Already it was getting cold.

But Johnny smiled.

If they're going to have all their sensors looking in toward the ship, he told himself, *that means nobody's out here. It ought to be easy to get into the Army camp and hide there. Maybe I can find someplace warm. And food!*

But another part of his mind asked, *And what then? How are you going to get from there to the ship and the strangers?*

"I'll cross that bridge when I come to it," Johnny whispered to himself.

Clutching the blanket around his shoulders, for warmth in the chilly desert night wind, Johnny crept up to the top of the hill once more.

The Army tanks and trucks were still out there. A few tents had been set up, and there were lights strung out everywhere. It almost looked like a shopping center decorated for the Christmas season, there were so many lights and people milling around.

But the lights were glaring white, not the many colors of the holidays. And the people were soldiers. And the decorations were guns, cannon, radar antennas, lasers—all pointed inward at the strangers' ship.

The ship itself was what made everything look like Christmas, Johnny decided. It stood in the middle of everything, glowing and golden like a cheerful tree ornament.

Johnny stared at it for a long time. Then he found his gaze floating upward, to the stars. In the clear cold night of the desert, the stars gleamed and winked like thousands of jewels: red, blue, white. The hazy swarm of the Milky Way swung across the sky. Johnny knew there were billions of stars in the heavens, hundreds of billions, so many stars that they were uncountable.

"That ship came from one of them," he whispered to himself. "Which one?"

The wind moaned and sent a shiver of cold through him, despite his blanket.

Slowly, quietly, carefully, he got up and started walking down the hill toward the Army camp. He stayed in the shadows, away from the lights, and circled around the trucks and tanks. He was looking for an opening, a dark place where there was no one sitting around or standing guard, a place where he could slip in and maybe hide inside one of the trucks.

I wonder what the inside of a tank is like? he asked himself. Then he shook his head, as if to drive away such childish thoughts. He was an Apache warrior, he told himself, sneaking up on the Army camp.

He got close enough to hear soldiers talking and laughing among themselves. But still he stayed out in the darkness. He ignored the wind and cold, just pulled the blanket more tightly over his thin shoulders as he circled the camp. Off beyond the trucks, he could catch the warm yellow glow of the strangers' ship. It looked inviting and friendly.

And then there was an opening! A slice of shadow that cut between pools of light. Johnny froze in his tracks and examined the spot carefully, squatting down on his heels to make himself as small and undetectable as possible.

There were four tents set up in a row, with their backs facing Johnny. On one side of them was a group of parked trucks and jeeps. Metal poles with lights on them brightened that area. On the other side of the tents were some big trailer vans, with all sorts of antennas poking out of their roofs. That area was well-lit too.

But the narrow lanes between the tents were dark with shadow. And Johnny could see no one around them. There were no lights showing from inside the tents, either.

Johnny hesitated only a moment or two. Then he quickly stepped up to the rear of one of the tents, poked his head around its corner and found no one in sight. So he ducked into the lane between the tents.

Flattening himself against the tent's vinyl wall, Johnny listened for sounds of danger. Nothing except the distant rush of the wind and the pounding of his own heart. It was dark where he was standing. The area seemed to be deserted.

He stayed there for what seemed like hours. His mind was saying that this was a safe place to hide. But his stomach was telling him that there might be some food inside the tents.

Yeah, and there might be some people inside there, too, Johnny thought.

His stomach won the argument.

Johnny crept around toward the front of the tent. This area was still pretty well lit from the lamps over by the trucks and vans. Peeking around the tent's corner, Johnny could see plenty of soldiers sitting in front of the parking areas, on the ground alongside their vehicles, eating food that steamed and somehow looked delicious, even from this distance. Johnny sniffed at the night air and thought he caught a trace of something filled with meat and bubbling juices.

Licking his lips, he slipped around the front of the tent and ducked inside.

It was dark, but enough light filtered through from the outside for Johnny to see that the tent was really a workroom of some sort. Two long tables ran the length of the tent. There were papers stacked at one end of one table, with a metal weight holding them in place. All sorts of instruments and gadgets were sitting on the tables: microscopes, cameras, something that looked sort of like a computer, other things that Johnny couldn't figure out at all.

None of it was food.

Frowning, Johnny went back to the tent's entrance. His stomach was growling now, complaining about being empty too long.

He pushed the tent flap back half an inch and peered outside. A group of men were walking in his direction. Four of them. One wore a soldier's uniform and had a big pistol strapped to his hip. The others wore ordinary clothes: slacks, windbreaker jackets. One of them was smoking a pipe—or rather, he was waving it in his hand as he talked, swinging the pipe back and forth and pointing its stem at the glowing ship, then back at the other three men.

Johnny knew that if he stepped outside the tent now they would see him as clearly as anything.

Then he realized that the situation was even worse. They were heading straight for this tent!

There wasn't any time to be scared. Johnny let the tent flap drop back into place and dived under one of the tables. No place else to hide.

He crawled into the farthest corner of the tent, under the table, and huddled there with his knees pulled up tight against his nose and the blanket wrapped around him.

Sure enough, the voices marched straight up to the tent and the lights flicked on.

"You'd better get some sleep, Ed. No sense staying up all night again."

"Yeah, I will. Just want to go over the tapes from this afternoon one more time."

"Might as well go to sleep, for all the good *that's* going to do you."

"I know. See you tomorrow."

"G'night."

From underneath the table, Johnny saw a pair of desert-booted feet walk into the tent. The man, whoever it was, wore striped slacks. He wasn't a soldier, or a policeman, and that let Johnny breathe a little easier.

He won't notice me under here, Johnny thought. *I'll just wait until he leaves and—*"You can come out of there now," the man's voice said. Johnny froze. He didn't even breathe.

The man squatted down and grinned at Johnny. "Come on, kid. I'm not going to hurt you. I ran away from home a few times myself."

Feeling helpless, Johnny crawled out from under the table. He stood up slowly, feeling stiff and achy all of a sudden.

The man looked him over. 'When's the last time you ate?"

"Around noontime."

Johnny watched the man's face. He had stopped grinning, and there were tight lines around his mouth and eyes that came from worry. Or maybe anger. He wasn't as big as Johnny's father, but he was solidly built. His hair was dark and long, almost down to his shoulders. His eyes were deep brown, almost black, and burning with some inner fire.

"You must be hungry."

Johnny nodded.

"If I go out to the cook van and get you some food, will you still be here when I come back?"

The thought of food reminded Johnny how hungry he really was. His stomach felt hollow.

"How do I know you won't bring back the State Troopers?" he asked.

The man shrugged. "How do I know you'll stay here and wait for me to come back?"

Johnny said nothing.

"Look kid," the man said, more gently, "I'm not going to hurt you. Sooner or later you're going to have to go home, but if you want to eat and maybe talk, then we can do that. I won't tell anybody you're here."

Johnny wanted to believe him. The man wasn't smiling; he seemed very serious about the whole thing.

"You've got to start trusting somebody, sooner or later," he said.

"Yeah." Johnny's voice didn't sound very sure about it, even to himself.

"My name's Gene Beldone." He put his hand out.

Johnny reached for it. "I'm Johnny Donato," he said. Gene's grip was strong.

"Okay Johnny," Gene smiled wide. "You wait here and I'll get you some food."

Gene came back in five minutes with an Army type of plastic tray heaped with hot, steaming food, and a mug of cold milk to wash it down. There were no chairs in the tent, but Gene pushed aside some of the instruments and helped Johnny to clamber up on the table.

For several minutes Johnny concentrated on eating. Gene went to the other table and fiddled around with what looked like a tape recorder.

"Did you really run away from home?" Johnny asked at last.

Gene looked up from his work. "Sure did. More than once. I know how it feels."

"Yeah."

"But . . ." Gene walked over to stand beside Johnny. "You know you'll have to go back home again, don't you?"

"I guess so."

"Your parents are probably worried. I thought I heard one of the State Troopers say that you were ill?"

Johnny nodded.

"Want to talk about it?"

Johnny turned his attention back to the tray of food. "No."

Gene gave a little one-shouldered shrug. "Okay. As long as you don't need any medicine right away, or anything like that."

Looking up again, Johnny asked, "Are you a scientist?"

"Sort of. I'm a linguist."

"Huh?"

"I study languages. The Army came and got me out of the university so I could help them understand the language the aliens speak."

"Aliens?"

"The men from the ship."

"Oh. Aliens—that's what you call them?"

"Right."

"Can you understand what they're saying?"

Gene grinned again, but this time it wasn't a happy expression. "Can't understand anything," he said.

"Nothing?" Johnny felt suddenly alarmed. "Why not?"

"Because the aliens haven't said anything to us."

"Huh?"

With a shake of his head, Gene said, "They just come out every day at high noon, stand there for a few minutes while we talk at them, and then pop back into their ship. I don't think they're listening to us at all. In fact, I don't think they're even *looking* at us. It's like they don't even know we're here!"

4

GENE LET JOHNNY LISTEN to the tapes of their attempts to talk to the aliens.

With the big padded stereo earphones clamped to his head, Johnny could hear the Army officers speaking, and another man that Gene said was a scientist from Washington. He could hear the wind, and a soft whistling sound, like the steady note of a telephone that's been left off the hook for too long. But no sounds at all from the aliens. No words of any kind, in any language.

Gene helped take the earphones off Johnny's head.

"They haven't said anything at all?"

"Nothing," Gene answered, clicking off the tape recorder. "The only sound to come from them is that sort of whistling thing—and that's coming from the ship. Some of the Army engineers think it's a power generator of some sort."

"Then we can't talk with them." Johnny suddenly felt very tired and defeated,

"We can talk *to* them," Gene said, "but I'm not even certain that they hear us. It's . . . it's pretty weird. They seem to look right through us—as if we're pictures hanging on a wall."

"Or rocks or grass or something."

"Right!" Gene looked impressed. "Like we're a part of the scenery, nothing special, nothing you'd want to talk to."

Something in Johnny was churning, trying to break loose. He felt tears forming in his eyes. "Then how can I tell them . . ."

"Tell them what?" Gene asked.

Johnny fought down his feelings. "Nothing," he said. "It's nothing."

Gene came over and put a hand on Johnny's shoulder. "So you're going to tough it out, huh?"

"What do you mean?"

Smiling, Gene answered, "Listen kid. Nobody runs away from home and sneaks into an Army camp just for fun. At first I thought you were just curious about the aliens. But now . . . looks to me as if you've got something pretty big on your mind."

Johnny didn't reply, but—strangely—he felt safe with this man. He wasn't afraid of him anymore.

"So stay quiet," Gene went on. "It's *your* problem, whatever it is, and you've got a right to tell me to keep my nose out of it."

"You're going to tell the State Troopers I'm here?"

Instead of answering, Gene leaned against the table's edge and said, "Listen. When I was about your age I ran away from home for the first time. That was in Cleveland. It was winter and there was a lot of snow. Damned cold, too. Now, you'd think that whatever made me leave home and freeze my backside in the snow for two days and nights— you'd think it was something pretty important, wouldn't you?"

"Wasn't it?"

Gene laughed out loud. "I don't know! I can't for the life of me remember what it was! It was awfully important to me then, of course. But now it's nothing, nowhere."

Johnny wanted to laugh with him, but he couldn't. "My problem's different."

"Yeah, I guess so," Gene said. But he was still smiling.

"I'm going to be dead before the year's over," Johnny said.

Gene's smile vanished. "What?"

Johnny told him the whole story. Gene asked several questions, looked doubtful for a while, but at last simply stood there looking very grave.

"That *is* tough," he said, at last.

"So I thought *maybe* the strangers—the aliens, that is—might do something, maybe cure it." Johnny's voice trailed off.

"I see," Gene said. And there was real pain in his voice. "And we can't even get them to notice us, let alone talk with us."

"I guess it's hopeless then."

Gene suddenly straightened up. "No. Why should we give up? There must be something we can do!"

"Like what?" Johnny asked.

Gene rubbed a hand across his chin. It was dark with stubbly beard. "Well . . . maybe they *do* understand us and just don't care. Maybe they're just here sightseeing, or doing some scientific exploring. Maybe they think of us like we think of animals in a zoo, or cows in a field—"

"But we're not animals!" Johnny said.

"Yeah? Imagine how we must seem to them." Gene began to pace down the length of the table. "They've travelled across lightyears— billions on billions of miles—to get here. Their ship, their brains, their minds must be thousands of years ahead of our own. We're probably no more interesting to them than apes in a zoo."

"Then why . . ."

"Wait a minute," Gene said. "Maybe they're not interested in us— but so far they've only seen adults, men, soldiers mostly. Suppose we show them a child, *you,* and make it clear to them that you're going to die."

"How are you going to get that across to them?"

"I don't know," Gene admitted. "Maybe they don't even understand what death is. Maybe they're so far ahead of us that they live for thousands of years—or they might even be immortal!"

Then he turned to look back at Johnny. "But I've had the feeling ever since the first time we tried to talk to them that they understand every word we say. They just don't *care.*"

"And you think they'll care about me?"

"It's worth a try. Nothing else we've done has worked. Maybe this will."

5

GENE TOOK JOHNNY to a tent that had cots and warm Army blankets.

"You get some sleep; you must be tired," he said. "I'll let the State Police know you're okay."

Johnny could feel himself falling asleep, even though he was only standing next to one of the cots.

"Do you want to talk to your parents? We can set up a phone link . . ."

"Later," Johnny said. "As long as they know I'm okay—I don't want to hassle with them until after we've talked to the aliens."

Gene nodded and left the tent. Johnny sat on the cot, kicked off his boots, and was asleep by the time he had stretched out and pulled the blanket up to his chin.

Gene brought him breakfast on a tray the next morning. But as soon as Johnny had finished eating and pulled his boots back on, Gene led him out to one of the big vans.

"General Hackett isn't too sure he likes our idea," Gene said as they walked up to the tan-colored van. It was like a civilian camper, only much bigger. Two soldiers stood guard by its main door, with rifles slung over their shoulders. It was already hot and bright on the desert, even though the sun had hardly climbed above the distant mountains.

The alien star ship still hung in the middle of the camp circle, glowing warmly and barely touching the ground. For a wild instant, Johnny thought of it as a bright beach ball being balanced on a seal's nose.

Inside, the van's air conditioning was turned up so high that it made Johnny shiver.

But General Hackett was sweating. He sat squeezed behind a table, a heavy, fat-cheeked man with a black little cigar stuck in the corner of his mouth. It was not lit, but Johnny could smell its sour odor. Sitting around the little table in the van's main compartment were Sergeant Warner of the State Police, several civilians, and two other Army officers, both colonels.

There were two open chairs. Johnny and Gene slid into them.

"I don't like it," General Hackett said, shaking his head. "The whole world's going nuts over these weirdos, every blasted newspaper and TV man in the country's trying to break into this camp, and we've got to take a little kid out there to do our job for us? I don't like it."

Sergeant Warner looked as if he wanted to say something, but he satisfied himself with a stern glare in Johnny's direction.

Gene said, "We've got nothing to lose. All our efforts of the past three days have amounted to zero results. Maybe the sight of a youngster will stir them."

One of the civilians shook his head. A colonel banged his fist on the table and said, "By god, a couple rounds of artillery will stir them! Put a few shots close to 'em—make 'em know we mean business!"

"And run the risk of having them destroy everything in sight?" asked one of the civilians, his voice sharp as the whine of an angry hornet.

"This isn't some idiot movie," the colonel snapped.

"Precisely," said the civilian. "If we anger them, there's no telling how much damage they could do. Do you have any idea of how much energy they must be able to control in that ship?"

"One little ship? Three people?"

"That one little ship," the scientist answered, "has crossed distances billions of times greater than our biggest rockets. And there might be more than one ship, as well."

"NORAD hasn't picked up any other ships in orbit around Earth," the other colonel said.

"None of our radars have detected *this* ship," the scientist said, pointing in the general direction of the glowing star ship. "The radars just don't get any signal from it at all!"

General Hackett took the cigar from his mouth. "All right, all right. There's no sense firing at them unless we get some clear indication that they're dangerous."

He turned to Gene. "You really think the kid will get them interested enough to talk to us?"

Gene shrugged. "It's worth a try."

"You don't think it will be dangerous?" the general asked. "Bringing him right up close to them like that?"

"If they want to be dangerous," Gene said, "I'll bet they can hurt anyone they want to, anywhere on Earth."

There was a long silence.

Finally General Hackett said, "Okay—let the kid talk to them."

Sergeant Warner insisted that Johnny's parents had to agree to the idea, and Johnny wound up spending most of the morning talking on the phone in the sergeant's State Police cruiser. Gene talked to them too, and explained what they planned to do.

It took a long time to calm his parents down. His mother cried and said she was so worried. His father tried to sound angry about Johnny's running away. But he really sounded relieved that his son was all right. After hours of talking, they finally agreed to let Johnny face the aliens.

But when Johnny at last handed the phone back to Sergeant Warner, he felt lower than a scorpion.

"I really scared them," he told Gene as they walked back to the tents.

"Guess you did."

"But they wouldn't have let me go if I'd stayed home and asked them. They would've said no."

Gene shrugged.

Then Johnny noticed that his shadow had shrunk to practically nothing. He turned and squinted up at the sky. The sun was almost at zenith. It was almost high noon.

"Less than two minutes to noon," Gene said, looking at his wristwatch. "Let's get moving. I want to be out there where they can see you when they appear."

They turned and started walking out toward the aliens' ship. Past the trucks and jeeps and vans that were parked in neat rows. Past the tanks, huge and heavy, with the snouts of their long cannon pointed straight at the ship. Past the ranks of soldiers who were standing in neat files, guns cleaned and ready for action.

General Hackett and other people from the morning conference were sitting in an open-topped car. A corporal was at the wheel, staring straight at the ship.

Johnny and Gene walked out alone, past everyone and everything, out into the wide cleared space at the center of the camp.

With every step he took, Johnny felt more alone. It was as if he were an astronaut out on EVA—floating away from his ship, out of contact, no way to get back. Even though it was hot, bright daylight, he could *feel* the stars looking down at him—one tiny, lonely, scared boy facing the unknown.

Gene grinned at him as they neared the ship. "I've done this four times now, and it gets spookier every time. My knees are shaking."

Johnny admitted, "Me too."

And then they were there! The three strangers, the aliens, standing about ten yards in front of Johnny and Gene.

It was spooky.

The aliens simply stood there, looking relaxed and pleasant. But they seemed to be looking right *through* Johnny and Gene. As if they weren't there at all.

Johnny studied the three of them very carefully. They looked completely human. Tall and handsome as movie stars, with broad shoulders and strong, square-jawed faces. The three of them looked enough alike to be brothers. They wore simple, silvery coveralls that shimmered in the sunlight.

They looked at each other as if they were going to speak. But they said nothing. The only sound Johnny could hear was that high-pitched kind of whistling noise that he had heard on tape the night before. Even the wind seemed to have died down, this close to the alien ship.

Johnny glanced up at Gene, and out of the corner of his eye, the three aliens seemed to shimmer and waver, as if he were seeing them through a wavy heat haze.

A chill raced along Johnny's spine.

When he looked straight at the aliens, they seemed real and solid, just like ordinary humans except for their glittery uniforms.

But when he turned his head and saw them only out of the corner of his eye, the aliens shimmered and sizzled.

Suddenly Johnny remembered a day in school when they showed movies. His seat had been up close to the screen, and off to one side. He couldn't make out what the picture on the screen was, but he could watch the light shimmering and glittering on the screen.

They're not real!

Johnny suddenly understood that what they were all seeing was a picture, an image of some sort. Not real people at all.

And that, his mind was racing, *means that the aliens really don't look like us at all!*

6

"THIS IS ONE OF OUR CHILDREN," Gene was saying to the aliens. "He is not fully grown, as you can see. He has a disease that will . . .

Johnny stopped listening to Gene. He stared at the aliens. They seemed so real when you looked straight at them. Turning his head toward Gene once more, he again saw the aliens sparkled and shimmered. Like a movie picture.

Without thinking about it any further, Johnny suddenly sprang toward the aliens. Two running steps covered the distance, and he threw himself right *off* his feet at the three glittering strangers.

He sailed straight *through* them, and landed sprawled on his hands and knees on the other side of them.

"Johnny!"

Turning to sit on the dusty ground. Johnny saw that the aliens—or really, the images of them—were still standing there as if nothing had happened. Gene's face was shocked, mouth open, eyes wide.

Then the images of the aliens winked out. They just disappeared.

Johnny got to his feet.

"What did you do?" Gene asked, hurrying over to grab Johnny by the arm as he got to his feet.

"They're not real!" Johnny shouted with excitement. "They're just pictures . . . they don't really look like us. They're still inside the ship."

"Wait, slow down," Gene said. "The aliens we've been seeing are images? Holograms, maybe. Yeah, that could explain . . ."

Looking past Gene's shoulder, Johnny could see a dozen soldiers hustling toward them. General Hackett was standing in his car and waving his arms madly.

Everything was happening so fast! But there was one thing that Johnny was sure of. The aliens—the *real* aliens, not the pretty pictures they were showing the Earthmen—the real aliens were still inside of their ship. They had never come out.

Then another thought struck Johnny. What if the ship itself was a picture, too? How could he *ever* talk to the star-visitors, get them to listen to him, help him?

Johnny had to know. Once General Hackett's soldiers got to him, he would never get another chance to speak with the aliens.

With a grit of his teeth, Johnny pulled his arm away from Gene, spun around and raced toward the alien star ship.

"Hey!" Gene yelled. "Johnny! No!"

The globe of the ship gleamed warmly in the sun. It almost seemed to pulsate, to throb like a living, beating heart. A heart made of gold, not flesh and muscle.

Johnny ran straight to the ship and, with his arms stretched out in front of him, he jumped at it. His eyes squeezed shut at the moment before he would hit the ship's shining hull.

Everything went black.

Johnny felt nothing. His feet left the ground, but there was no shock of hitting solid metal, no sense of jumping or falling or even floating. Nothing at all.

He tried to open his eyes, and found that he couldn't. He couldn't move his arms or legs. He couldn't even feel his heart beating.

I'm dead!

7

SLOWLY A GOLDEN LIGHT filtered into Johnny's awareness. It was like lying out in the desert sun with your eyes closed; the light glowed behind his closed eyelids.

He opened his eyes and found that he was indeed lying down, but not outdoors. Everything around him was golden and shining.

Johnny's head was spinning. He was inside the alien ship, he knew that. But it was unlike any spacecraft he had seen or heard of. He could see no walls, no equipment, no instruments; only a golden glow, like being inside a star—or maybe inside a cloud of shining gold.

Even the thing he was lying on, Johnny couldn't really make out what it was. It felt soft and warm to his touch, but it wasn't a bed or cot. He found that if he pressed his hands down hard enough, they would go *into* the golden glowing material a little way. Almost like pressing your fingers down into sand, except that this stuff was warm and soft.

He sat up. All that he could see was the misty glow, all around him.

"Hey, where are you?" Johnny called out. His voice sounded trembly, even though he was trying hard to stay calm. "I know you're in here someplace!"

Two shining spheres appeared before him. They were so bright that it hurt Johnny's eyes to look straight at them. They were like two tiny suns, about the size of basketballs, hovering in mid air, shining brilliantly but giving off no heat at all.

"We are here."

It was a sound Johnny could hear. Somewhere in the back of his mind, despite his fears, he was a little disappointed. He had been half-expecting to "hear" a telepathic voice in his mind.

"Where are you?"

"You are looking at us." The voice was flat and unemotional. "We are the two shining globes that you see."

"You?" Johnny squinted at the shining ones. "You're the aliens?"

"This is our ship."

Johnny's heart started beating faster as he realized what was going on. He was inside the ship. And *talking* to the aliens!

"Why wouldn't you talk with the other men?" he asked.

"Why should we? We are not here to speak with them."

"What *are* you here for?"

The voice—Johnny couldn't tell which of the shining ones it came from—hesitated for only a moment. Then it answered, "Our purpose is something you could not understand. You are not mentally equipped to grasp such concepts."

A picture flashed into Johnny's mind of a chimpanzee trying to figure out how a computer works. *Did they plant that in my head?* he wondered.

After a moment, Johnny said, "I came here to ask for your help . . ."

"We are not here to help you," said the voice.

And a second voice added, "Indeed, it would be very dangerous for us to interfere with the environment of your world. Dangerous to you and your kind."

"But you don't understand! I don't want you to change anything, just—"

The shining one on the left seemed to bob up and down a little. "We do understand. We looked into your mind while you were unconscious. You want us to prolong your life span."

"Yes!"

The other one said, "We cannot interfere with the normal life processes of your world. That would change the entire course of your history."

"History?" Johnny felt puzzled. "What do you mean?"

The first sphere drifted a bit closer to Johnny, forcing him to shade his eyes with his hand. "You and your people have assumed that we are visitors from another star. in a sense, we are. But we are also travelers in time. We have come from millions of years in your future."

"Future?" Johnny felt weak. "Millions of years?"

"And apparently we have missed our target time by at least a hundred thousand of your years."

"Missed?" Johnny echoed.

"Yes," said the first shining one. "We stopped here—at this time and place—to get our bearings. We were about to leave when you threw yourself into the ship's defensive screen."

The second shining one added, "Your action was entirely foolish. The screen would have killed you instantly. We never expected any of you to attack us in such an irrational manner."

"I wasn't attacking you," Johnny said. "I just wanted to talk with you."

"So we learned, once we brought you into our ship and revived you. Still, it was a foolish thing to do."

"And now," the second shining sphere said, "your fellow men have begun to attack us. They assume that you have been killed, and they have fired their weapons at us."

"Oh no . . ."

"Have no fear, little one." The first sphere seemed almost amused. "Their primitive shells and rockets fall to the ground without exploding. We are completely safe."

"But they might try an atomic bomb," Johnny said.

"If they do, it will not explode. We are not here to hurt anyone, nor to allow anyone to hurt us."

A new thought struck Johnny. "You said your screen would have killed me. And then you said you brought me inside the ship and revived me. Was . . . was I dead?"

"Your heart had stopped beating," said the first alien. "We also found a few other flaws in your body chemistry, which we corrected. But we took no steps to prolong your life span. You will live some eighty to one hundred years, just as the history of your times has shown us."

Eighty to one hundred years! Johnny was thunderstruck. *The "other flaws in body chemistry" that they fixed—they cured me!*

Johnny was staggered by the news, feeling as if he wanted to laugh and cry at the same time, when the first of the shining ones said:

"We must leave now, and hopefully find the proper time and place that we are seeking. We will place you safely among your friends."

"No! Wait! Take me with you! I want to go too!" Johnny surprised himself by shouting it, but he realized as he heard his own words that he really meant it. A trip through thousands of years of time, to who-knows-where!

"That is impossible, little one. Your time and place are here. Your own history shows that quite clearly."

"But you can't just leave me here, after you've shown me so much! How can I be satisfied with just one world and time when *everything's* open to you to travel to! I don't want to be stuck here-and-now. I want to be like you!"

"You will be, little one. You will be. Once we were like you. In time your race will evolve into our type of creature—able to roam through the universe of space and time, able to live directly from the energy of the stars."

"But that'll take millions of years."

"Yes. But your first steps into space have already begun. Before your life ends, you will have visited a few of the stars nearest to your own world. And, in the fullness of time, your race will evolve into ours."

"Maybe so," Johnny said, feeling downcast.

The shining one somehow seemed to smile. "No, little one. There is no element of chance. Remember, we come from your future. *It has already happened.*"

Johnny blinked. "Already happened . . . you—you're really from Earth! Aren't you? You're from the Earth of a million years from now! Is that it?"

"Good-bye grandsire," said the shining ones together.

And Johnny found himself sitting on the desert floor in the hot afternoon sunlight, a few yards in front of General Hackett's command car.

"It's the kid! He's alive!"

Getting slowly to his feet as a hundred soldiers raced toward him, Johnny looked back toward the star ship—the *time* ship.

It winked out. Disappeared. Without a sound or a stirring of the desert dust. One instant it was there, the next it was gone.

8

IT WAS A WEEK LATER that it really sank home in Johnny's mind.

It had been a wild week. Army officers quizzing him, medical doctors trying to find some trace of the disease, news reporters and

TV interviewers asking him a million questions, his mother and father both crying that he was all right and safe and *cured*—a wild week.

Johnny's school friends hung around the house and watched from outside while the Army and newspeople swarmed in and out. He waved to them, and they waved back, smiling, friendly. They understood. The whole story was splashed all over the papers and TV, even the part about the disease. The kids understood why Johnny had been so much of a loner the past few months.

The President telephoned and invited Johnny and his parents to Washington. Dr. Gene Beldone went along too, in a private Air Force twin-engine jet.

As Johnny watched the New Mexico desert give way to the rugged peaks of the Rockies, something that the shining ones had said finally hit home to him:

You will live some eighty to one hundred years, just as the history of your times has shown us.

"How would they know about me from the history of these times?" Johnny whispered to himself as he stared out the thick window of the plane. "That must mean that my name will be famous enough to get into the history books, or tapes, or whatever they'll be using."

Thinking about that for a long time, as the plane crossed the Rockies and flew arrow-straight over the green farmlands of the Midwest, Johnny remembered the other thing that the shining ones had told him:

Before your life ends, you will have visited a few of the stars nearest to your own world.

"When they said *you*," Johnny whispered again, "I thought they meant us, the human race. But—maybe they really meant *me!* Me! I'm going to be an interstellar astronaut!"

For the first time, Johnny realized that the excitement in his life hadn't ended. It was just beginning.

THE SIGHTSEERS

Some stories are little more than gags, but despite the brevity of this one, there's a bit more to it than the punch line at the end. (No fair peeking!)

Incidentally, this shortly led to my writing a short novel called City Of Darkness, *which takes up where this tale ends.*

* 🌀 *

MY HEART ALMOST WENT into fibrillation when I saw the brown cloud on the horizon that marked New York City. Dad smiled his wiser-than-thou smile as I pressed my nose against the plane's window in an effort to see more. By the time we got out of the stack over LaGuardia Airport and actually landed, my neck hurt.

The city's fantastic! People were crowding all over, selling things, buying, hurrying across the streets, gawking. And the noise, the smells, all those old gasoline-burning taxis rattling around and blasting horns. Not like Sylvan Dell, Michigan!

"It's vacation time," Dad told me as we shouldered our way through the crowds along Broadway. "It's always crowded during vacation time."

And the girls! They looked back at you, right straight at you, and smiled. They knew what it was all about, and they liked it! You could tell, just the way they looked back at you. I guess they really weren't any prettier than the girls back home, but they dressed . . . wow!

"Dad, what's a bedicab?"

He thought it over for a minute as one of them, long and low, with the back windows curtained, edged through traffic right in front of the curb where we were standing.

"You can probably figure it out for yourself," he said uncomfortably. "They're not very sanitary."

Okay, I'm just a kid from the north woods. It took me a couple of minutes. In fact, it wasn't until we crossed the street in front of one— stopped for a red light—and I saw the girl's picture set up on the windshield that I realized what it was all about. Sure enough, there was a meter beside the driver.

But that's just one of the things about the city. There were old movie houses where we saw real murder films. Blood and beatings and low-cut blondes. I think Dad watched me more than the screen. He claims he thinks I'm old enough to be treated like a man, but he acts awfully scared about it.

We had dinner in some really crummy place, down in a cellar under an old hotel. With live people taking our orders and bringing the food!

"It's sanitary," Dad said, laughing when I hesitated about digging into it. "It's all been inspected and approved. They didn't put their feet in it."

Well, it didn't hurt me. It was pretty good, I guess . . . too spicy, though.

We stayed three days altogether. I managed to meet a couple of girls from Maryland at the hotel where we stayed. They were okay, properly dressed and giggly and always whispering to each other. The New York girls were just out of my league, I guess. Dad was pretty careful about keeping me away from them . . . or them away from me. He made sure I was in the hotel room every night, right after dinner. There were plenty of really horrible old movies to watch on the closed-circuit TV. I stayed up past midnight each night. Once I was just drifting off to sleep when Dad came in and flopped on his bed with all his clothes on. By the time I woke up in the morning, though, he was in his pajamas and sound asleep.

Finally we had to go. We rented a sanitary car and decontaminated ourselves on the way out to the airport. I didn't like the lung-cleansing machine. You had to work a tube down one of your nostrils.

"It's just as important as brushing your teeth," Dad said firmly.

If I didn't do it for myself, he was going to do it for me.

"You wouldn't want to bring billions of bacteria and viruses back home, would you?" he asked.

Our plane took off an hour and a half late. The holiday traffic was heavy.

"Dad, is New York open every year . . . just like it is now?"

He nodded. "Yes, all during the vacation months. A lot of the public health doctors think it's very risky to keep a city open for more than two weeks out of the year, but the tourist industry has fought to keep New York going all summer. They shut it down right after Labor Day."

As the plane circled the brown cloud that humped over the city, I made up my mind that I'd come back again next summer. Alone, maybe. That'd be great!

My last glimpse of the city was the big sign painted across what used to be The Bronx:

NEW YORK IS A SUMMER FESTIVAL OF FUN!

THE SUPERSONIC
ZEPPELIN

This story actually did begin in a laboratory cafeteria, with a pair of friendly aerodynamicists pulling my leg about building a biplane that could reach supersonic speed without creating a sonic boom. The aerodynamics is all perfectly valid, and by the time lunch was over they had almost convinced themselves that a supersonic zeppelin could actually be built. They never carried the idea any further, but if they had . . . Well, read on.

* 🪐 *

LET'S SEE NOW. How did it all begin?

A bunch of the boys were whooping it up in the Malamute Saloon—no, that's not right; actually it started in the cafeteria of the Anson Aerospace plant in Phoenix.

Okay, then, how about:

There are strange things done in the midnight sun by the men who moil for gold—well, yeah, but it was only a little after noon when Bob Wisdom plopped his loaded lunch tray on our table and sat down like a man disgusted with the universe. And anyway, engineers don't moil for gold; they're on salary.

I didn't like the way they all looked down on me, but I certainly didn't let it show. It wasn't just that I was the newbie among them: I wasn't even an engineer, just a recently graduated MBA assigned to work with the Advanced Planning Team, aptly acronymed APT. As far as they were concerned I was either a useless appendage forced on them, or a snoop from management sent to provide info on which of them should get laid off.

Actually, my assignment was to get these geniuses to come up with a project that we could sell to somebody, anybody. Otherwise, we'd all be hit by the iron ball when the next wave of layoffs started, just before Christmas.

Six shopping weeks left, I knew.

"What's with you Bob?" Ray Kurtz asked. "You look like you spent the morning sniffing around a manure pile."

Bob Wisdom was tall and lanky, with a round face that was normally cheerful, even in the face of Anson Aerospace's coming wave of cutbacks and layoffs. Today he looked dark and pouchy-eyed.

"Last night I watched a TV documentary about the old SST."

"The *Concorde*?" asked Kurtz. He wore a full bushy beard that made him look more like a dog-sled driver than a metallurgical engineer.

"Yeah. They just towed the last one out to the Smithsonian on a barge. A beautiful hunk of flying machine like that riding to its final resting place on a converted garbage scow."

That's engineers for you. Our careers were hanging by a hair and he's upset over a piece of machinery.

"Beautiful, maybe," said Tommy Rohr. "But it was never a practical commercial airliner. It could never fly efficiently enough to be economically viable."

For an engineer, Rohr was unnervingly accurate in his economic analyses. He'd gotten out of the dot-com boom before it burst. Of the five of us at the lunch table, Tommy was the only one who wasn't worried about losing his job—he had a much more immediate worry: his new trophy wife and her credit cards.

"It's just a damned shame," Wisdom grumbled. "The end of an era."

Kurtz, our bushy-bearded metallurgist, shook his graying head. "The eco-nuts wouldn't let it fly supersonic over populated areas. That ruined its chances of being practical."

"The trouble is," Wisdom muttered as he unwrapped a soggy

sandwich, "you can build a supersonic aircraft that doesn't produce a sonic boom."

"No sonic boom?" I asked. Like I said, I was the newcomer to the APT group.

Bob Wisdom smiled like a sphinx.

"What's the catch?" asked Richard Grand in his slightly Anglified accent. He'd been born in the Bronx, but he'd won a Rhodes scholarship and came back trying to talk like Sir Stafford Cripps.

The cafeteria was only half-filled, but there was still a fair amount of clattering and yammering going on all around us. Outside the picture window I could see it was raining cats and elephants, a real monsoon downpour. Something to do with global warming, I'd been told.

"Catch?" Bob echoed, trying to look hurt. "Why should there be a catch?"

"Because if someone could build a supersonic aircraft that didn't shatter one's eardrums with its sonic boom, old boy, obviously someone could have done it long before this."

"We could do it," Bob said pleasantly. Then he bit it into his sandwich.

"Why aren't we, then?" Kurtz asked, his brows knitting.

Bob shrugged elaborately as he chewed on his ham and five-grain bread.

Rohr waggled a finger at him. "What do you know that we don't? Or is this a gag?"

Bob swallowed and replied, "It's just simple aerodynamics."

"What's the go of it?" Grand asked. He got that phrase from reading a biography of James Clerk Maxwell.

"Well," Bob said, putting down the limp remains of the sandwich, "there's a type of wing that a German aerodynamicist named Adolph Busemann invented back in the nineteen-twenties. It's a sort of biplane configuration, actually. The shock waves that cause a sonic boom are cancelled out between the two wings."

"No sonic boom?"

"No sonic boom. Instead of flat wings, like normal, you need to wrap the wings around the fuselage, make a ringwing."

"What's a ringwing?" innocent li'l me asked.

Bob pulled a felt-tip pen from his shirt pocket and began sketching on his paper placemat.

"Here's the fuselage of the plane." He drew a narrow cigar shape. "Now we wrap the wing around it, like a sleeve. See?" He drew what looked to me like a tube wrapped around the cigar. "Actually it's two wings, one inside the other, and all the shock waves that cause the sonic boom get cancelled out. No sonic boom."

The rest of us looked at Bob, then down at the sketch, then up at Bob again. Rohr looked wary, like he was waiting for the punch line. Kurtz looked like a puzzled Karl Marx.

"I don't know that much about aerodynamics," Rohr said slowly, "but this is a Busemann biplane you're talking about, isn't it?"

"That's right."

"Uh-huh. And isn't it true that a Busemann biplane's wings produce no lift?"

"That's right," Bob admitted, breaking into a grin.

"No lift?" Kurtz snapped.

"Zero lift."

"Then how the hell do you get it off the ground?"

"It won't fly, Orville," Bob Wisdom said, his grin widening. "That's why nobody's built one."

The rest of us groaned while Bob laughed at us. An engineer's joke, in the face of impending doom. We'd been had.

Until, that is, I blurted out, "So why don't you fill it with helium?"

The guys spent the next few days laughing at me and the idea of a supersonic zeppelin. I have to admit, at that stage of the game I thought it was kind of silly, too. But yet . . .

Richard Grand could be pompous, but he wasn't stupid. Before the week was out he just happened to pass by my phonebooth-sized cubicle and dropped in for a little chat, like the lord of the manor being gracious to a stable hand.

"That was rather clever of you, that supersonic zeppelin quip," he said as he ensconced himself in a teeny wheeled chair he had to roll in from the empty cubicle next door.

"Thanks," I noncommittalled, wondering why a senior engineer would give a compliment to a junior MBA.

"It might even be feasible," Grand mused. "Technically, that is."

I could see in his eyes the specter of Christmas-yet-to-come and the layoffs that were coming with it. If a senior guy like Grand was worried, I thought, I ought to be scared purple. Could I use the SSZ idea to move up Anson Aerospace's hierarchical ladder? The guys at the bottom were the first ones scheduled for layoffs, I knew. I badly needed some altitude, and even though it sounded kind of wild, the supersonic zeppelin was the only foothold I had to get up off the floor.

"Still," Grand went on, "it isn't likely that management would go for the concept. Pity, isn't it?"

I nodded agreement while my mind raced. If I could get management to take the SSZ seriously, I might save my job. Maybe even get a promotion. But I needed an engineer to propose the concept to management. Those suits upstairs wouldn't listen to a newly minted MBA; most of them were former engineers themselves who'd climbed a notch or two up the organization.

Grand sat there in that squeaky little chair and philosophized about the plight of the aerospace industry in general and the bleak prospects for Anson Aerospace in particular.

"Not the best of times to approach management with a bold, innovative concept," he concluded.

Omigod, I thought. He's talked himself out of it! He was starting to get up and leave my cubicle.

"You know," I said, literally grabbing his sleeve, "Winston Churchill backed a lot of bold, innovative ideas, didn't he? Like, he pushed the development of tanks in World War I, even though he was in the navy, not the army."

Grand gave me a strange look.

"And radar, in World War II," I added.

"And the atomic bomb," Grand replied. "Very few people realize it was Sir Winston who started the atomic bomb work, long before the Yanks got into it."

The Yanks? I thought. This from a Jewish engineer from the Bronx High School for Science.

I sighed longingly. "If Churchill were here today, I bet he'd push the SSZ for all it's worth. He had the courage of his convictions, Churchill did."

Grand nodded, but said nothing and left me at my desk. The next morning, though, he came to my cubicle and told me to follow him.

Glad to get away from my claustrophobic work station, I headed after him, asking, "Where are we going?"

"Upstairs."

Management territory!

"What for?"

"To broach the concept of the supersonic zeppelin," said Grand, sticking out his lower lip in imitation of Churchillian pugnaciousness.

"The SSZ? For real?"

"Listen, my boy, and learn. The way this industry works is this: you grab onto an idea and ride it for all it's worth. I've decided to hitch my wagon to the supersonic zeppelin, and you should too."

I should too? Hell, I thought of it first!

John Driver had a whole office to himself and a luscious, sweet-tempered executive assistant of Greek-Italian ancestry, with almond-shaped dark eyes and lustrous hair even darker. Her name was Lisa, and half the male employees of Anson Aerospace fantasized about her, including me.

Driver's desk was big enough to land a helicopter on, and he kept it immaculately clean, mainly because he seldom did anything except sit behind it and try to look important. Driver was head of several engineering sections, including APT. Like so many others in Anson, he had been promoted to his level of incompetency: a perfect example of the Peter Principle. Under his less-than-brilliant leadership APT had managed to avoid developing anything more advanced than a short-range drone aircraft that ran on ethanol. It didn't fly very well, but the ground crew used the corn-based fuel to make booze that would peel the paint off a wall just by breathing at it from fifteen feet away.

I let Grand do the talking, of course. And, equally of course, he made Driver think the SSZ was his idea instead of mine.

"A supersonic zeppelin?" Driver snapped, once Grand had outlined the idea to him. "Ridiculous!"

Unperturbed by our boss' hostility to new ideas, Grand said smoothly, "Don't be too hasty to dismiss the concept. It may have considerable merit. At the very least I believe we could talk NASA or the Transportation Department into giving us some money to study the concept."

At the word "money" Driver's frown eased a little. Driver was lean-faced, with hard features and a gaze that he liked to think was piercing. He now subjected Grand to his piercingest stare.

"You have to spend money to make money in this business," he said, in his best *Forbes* magazine acumen.

"I understand that," Grand replied stiffly. "But we are quite willing to put some of our own time into this—until we can obtain government funding."

"Your own time?" Driver queried.

We? I asked myself. And immediately answered myself, Damned right. This is *my* idea and I'm going to follow it to the top. Or bust.

"I really believe we may be onto something that can save this company," Grand was purring.

Driver drummed his manicured fingers on his vast desk. "All right, if you feel so strongly about it. Do it on your own time and come back to me when you've got something worth showing. Don't say a word to anyone else, understand? Just me."

"Right, Chief." I learned later that whenever Grand wanted to flatter Driver he called him Chief.

"Our own time" was aerospace industry jargon for bootlegging hours from legitimate projects. Engineers have to charge every hour they work against an ongoing contract, or else their time is paid by the company's overhead account. Anson's management—and the accounting department—was very definitely against spending any money out of the company's overhead account. So I became a master bootlegger, finding charge numbers for my APT engineers. They accepted my bootlegging without a word of thanks, and complained when I couldn't find a valid charge number and they actually had to work on their own time, after regular hours.

For the next six weeks Wisdom, Rohr, Kurtz and even I worked every night on the supersonic zeppelin. The engineers were doing calculations and making simulator runs in their computers. I was drawing up a business plan, as close to a work of fiction as anything on the Best Sellers list. My social life went to zero, which was—I have to admit—not all that much of a drop. Except for Driver's luscious executive assistant, Lisa, that is, who worked some nights to help us. I wished I had the time to ask her to dinner.

Grand worked away every night, too. On a glossy set of illustrations to use as a presentation.

* * *

We made our presentation to Driver. The guys' calculations, my business plan, and Grand's images. He didn't seem impressed, and I left the meeting feeling pretty gunky. Over the six weeks I'd come to like the idea of a supersonic zeppelin, an SSZ. I really believed it was my ticket to advancement. Besides, now I had no excuse to see Lisa, up in Driver's office.

On the plus side, though, none of the APT team was laid off. We went through the motions of the Christmas office party with the rest of the undead. Talk about a survivor's reality show!

I was moping in my cubicle the morning after Christmas when my phone beeped and Driver's face came up on my screen.

"Drop your socks and pack a bag. You're going with me to Washington to sell the SSZ concept."

"Yessir!" I said automatically. "Er . . . when?"

"Tomorrow, bright and early."

I raced to Grand's cubicle, but he already knew about it.

"So we're both going," I said, feeling pretty excited.

"No, only you and Driver," he said.

"But why aren't you—"

Grand gave me a knowing smile. "Driver wants all the credit for himself if the idea sells."

That nettled me, but I knew better than to argue about it. Instead, I asked, "And if it doesn't sell?"

"You get the blame for a stupid idea. You're low enough on the totem pole to be offered up as a sacrificial victim."

I nodded. I didn't like it, but I had to admit it was a good lesson in management. I tucked it away in my mind for future reference.

I'd never been to Washington before. It was chilly, gray and clammy; no comparison to sunny Phoenix. The traffic made me dizzy, but Driver thought it was pretty light. "Half the town's on holiday vacations," he told me as we rode a seedy, beat-up taxicab to the magnificent glass and stainless steel high-rise office building that housed the Transportation Department.

As we climbed out of the smelly taxi I noticed the plaque on the wall by the revolving glass doors. It puzzled me.

"Transportation and Urban Renewal Department?" I asked. "Since when . . ."

"Last year's reorganization," Driver said, heading for the revolving door. "They put the two agencies together. Next year they'll pull them apart, when they reinvent the government again."

"Welcome to TURD headquarters," said Tracy Keene, once we got inside the building's lobby.

Keene was Anson Aerospace's crackerjack Washington representative, a large round man who conveyed the impression that he knew things no one else knew. Keene's job was to find new customers for Anson from among the tangle of government agencies, placate old customers when Anson inevitably alienated them, and guide visitors from home base through the Washington maze. The job involved grotesque amounts of wining and dining. I had been told that Keene had once been as wiry and agile as a Venezuelan shortstop. Now he looked to me like he was on his way to becoming a Sumo wrestler. And what he was gaining in girth he was losing in hair.

"Let's go," Keene said, gesturing toward the security checkpoint that blocked the lobby. "We don't want to be late."

Two hours later Keene was snoring softly in a straightbacked metal chair while Driver was showing the last of his Powerpoint images to Roger K. Memo, Assistant Under Director for Transportation Research of TURD.

Memo and his chief scientist, Dr. Alonzo X. Pencilbeam, were sitting on one side of a small conference table, Driver and I on the other. Keene was at the end, dozing restfully. The only light in the room came from the little projector, which threw a blank glare onto the wan yellow wall that served as a screen now that the last image had been shown.

Driver clicked the projector off. The light went out and the fan's whirring noise abruptly stopped. Keene jerked awake and instantly reached around and flicked the wall switch that turned on the overhead lights. I had to admire the man's reflexes.

Although the magnificent TURD building was sparkling new, Memo's spacious office somehow looked seedy. There wasn't enough furniture for the size of it: only a government-issue steel desk with a swivel chair, a half-empty bookcase, and this slightly wobbly little conference table with six chairs that didn't match. The walls and floors were bare and there was a distinct echo when anyone spoke or even walked across the room. The only window had vertical slats instead of a curtain, and it looked out on a parking building. The only decoration on the walls was Memo's doctoral degree, purchased from some obscure "distance learning" school in Mississippi.

Driver fixed Memo with his steely gaze across the conference table. "Well, what do you think of it?" he asked subtly.

Memo pursed his lips. He was jowly fat, completely bald, wore glasses and a rumpled gray suit.

"I don't know," he said firmly. "It sounds . . . unusual . . ."

Dr. Pencilbeam was sitting back in his chair and smiling benignly. His PhD had been earned in the 1970s, when newly graduated physicists were driving taxicabs on what they glumly called "Nixon fellowships." He was very thin, fragile looking, with the long skinny limbs of a praying mantis.

Pencilbeam dug into his jacket pocket and pulled out an electronic game. *Reformed smoker*, I thought. *He needs something to do with his hands.*

"It certainly looks interesting," he said in a scratchy voice while his game softly beeped and booped. "I imagine it's technically achievable . . . and lots of fun."

Memo snorted. "We're not here to have fun."

Keene leaned across the table and fixed Memo with his best *here's something from behind the scenes* expression. "Do you realize how the White House would react to a sensible program for a supersonic transport? With the *Concorde* gone, you could put this country into the forefront of air transportation again."

"Hmm," said Memo. "But . . ."

"Think of the jobs this program can create. The President is desperate to improve the employment figures."

"I suppose so . . ."

"National prestige," Keene intoned knowingly. "Aerospace employment . . . balance of payments . . . gold outflow . . . the President would be terrifically impressed with you."

"Hmm," Memo repeated. "I see . . ."

I could see where the real action was, so I wangled myself an assignment to the company's Washington office as Keene's special assistant for the SSZ proposal. That's when I started learning what money and clout—and the power of influence—are all about.

As the months rolled along, we gave lots of briefings and attended lots of cocktail parties. I knew we were on the right track when no less than Roger K. Memo invited me to accompany him to one of the swankiest parties of the season. Apparently he thought that since I was from Anson's home office in Phoenix, I must be an engineer and not just another salesman.

The party was in full swing by the time Keene and I arrived. It was nearly impossible to hear your own voice in the swirling babble of chatter and clinking glassware. In the middle of the sumptuous living room the Vice President was demonstrating his golf swing. Several Cabinet wives were chatting in the dining room. Out in the foyer, three Senators were comparing fact-finding tours they were arranging for themselves to the Riviera, Bermuda, and American Samoa, respectively.

Memo never drank anything stronger than ginger ale, and I followed his example. We stood in the doorway between the foyer and the living room, hearing snatches of conversation among the three junketing Senators. When the trio broke up, Memo intercepted Senator Goodyear (R., Ohio) as he headed toward the bar.

"Hello, Senator!" Memo shouted heartily. It was the only way to be heard over the party noise.

"Ah . . . hello." Senator Goodyear obviously thought that he was supposed to know Memo, and just as obviously couldn't recall his name, rank, or influence rating.

Goodyear was more than six feet tall, and towered over Memo's paunchy figure. Together they shouldered their way through the crowd around the bar, with me trailing them like a rowboat being towed behind a yacht. Goodyear ordered bourbon on the rocks, and therefore so did Memo. But he merely held onto his glass while the Senator immediately began to gulp at his drink.

A statuesque blonde in a spectacular gown sauntered past us. The Senator's eyes tracked her like a battleship's range finder following a moving target.

"I hear you're going to Samoa," Memo shouted as they edged away from the bar, following the blonde.

"Eh . . . yes," the Senator answered cautiously, in a tone he usually reserved for news reporters.

"Beautiful part of the world," Memo shouted.

The blonde slipped an arm around the waist of one of the young, long-haired men and they disappeared into another room. Goodyear turned his attention back to his drink.

"I said," Memo repeated, standing on tiptoes, "that Samoa is a beautiful place."

Nodding, Goodyear replied, "I'm going to investigate ecological conditions there . . . my committee is considering legislation on ecology, you know."

"Of course. Of course. You've got to see things firsthand if you're going to enact meaningful legislation."

Slightly less guardedly, Goodyear said, "Exactly."

"It's a long way off, though," Memo said.

"Twelve hours from LAX."

"I hope you won't be stuck in economy class. They really squeeze the seats in there."

"No, no," said the Senator. "First class all the way."

At the taxpayers' expense, I thought.

"Still," Memo sympathized, "it must take considerable dedication to undergo such a long trip."

"Well, you know, when you're in public service you can't think of your own comforts."

"Yes, of course. Too bad the SST isn't flying anymore. It could have cut your travel time in half. That would give you more time to stay in Samoa . . . investigating conditions there."

The hearing room in the Capitol was jammed with reporters and camera crews. Senator Goodyear sat in the center of the long front table, as befitted the committee chairman. I was in the last row of spectators, as befitted the newly promoted junior Washington representative of Anson Aerospace Corp. I was following the industry's routine procedure and riding the SSZ program up the corporate ladder.

All through the hot summer morning the committee had listened to witnesses: my former boss John Driver, Roger K. Memo, Alonzo Pencilbeam and many others. The concept of the supersonic zeppelin unfolded before the news media and started to take on definite solidity in the rococo-trimmed hearing chamber.

Senator Goodyear sat there solemnly all morning, listening to the carefully rehearsed testimony and sneaking peeks at the greenery outside the big sunny window. Whenever he remembered the TV cameras he sat up straighter and tried to look lean and tough. I'd been told he had a drawer full of old Clint Eastwood flicks in his Ohio home.

Now it was his turn to summarize what the witnesses had told the committee. He looked straight into the bank of cameras, trying to come on strong and determined, like a high plains drifter.

"Gentlemen," he began, immediately antagonizing the women in the room, "I believe that what we have heard here today can mark the beginning of a new program that will revitalize the American aerospace industry and put our great nation back in the forefront of international commerce—"

One of the younger Senators at the far end of the table, a woman, interrupted:

"Excuse me, Mr. Chairman, but my earlier question about pollution was never addressed. Won't the SSZ use the same kind of jet engines that the *Concorde* used? And won't they cause just as much pollution?"

Goodyear glowered at the junior member's impudence, but controlled his temper well enough to say only, "Em . . . Dr. Pencilbeam, would you care to comment on that question?"

Half-dozing at one of the front benches, Pencilbeam looked startled at the mention of his name. Then he got to his feet like a carpenter's ruler unfolding, went to the witness table, sat down and hunched his bony frame around the microphone there.

"The pollution from the *Concorde* was so minimal that it had no measurable effect on the stratosphere. The early claims that a fleet of SSTs would create a permanent cloud deck over the northern hemisphere and completely destroy the ozone layer were never substantiated."

"But there were only a half-dozen *Concordes* flying," said the junior Senator. "If we build a whole fleet of SSZs—"

Before she could go any further Goodyear fairly shouted into his microphone, "Rest assured that we are well aware of the possible pollution problem." He popped his Ps like artillery bursts. "More importantly, the American aerospace industry is suffering, employment is in the doldrums, and our economy is slumping. The SSZ will provide jobs and boost the economy. Our engineers will, I assure you, find ways to deal with any and every pollution problem that may be associated with the SSZ."

I had figured that somebody, sooner or later, would raise the question of pollution. The engineers back in Phoenix wanted to look into the possibilities of using hydrogen fuel for the SSZ's jet engines, but I figured that just the mention of hydrogen would make people think of the old *Hindenburg*, and that would scuttle the program right there and then. So we went with ordinary turbojet engines that burned ordinary jet fuel.

But I went a step further. In my capacity as a junior (and rising) executive, I used expense-account money to plant a snoop in the organization of the nation's leading ecology freak, Mark Sequoia. It turned out that, unknown to Sequoia, Anson Aerospace was actually his biggest financial contributor. Politics make strange bedfellows, doesn't it?

You see, Sequoia had fallen on relatively hard times. Once a flaming crusader for ecological salvation and environmental protection, Sequoia had made the mistake of letting the Commonwealth of Pennsylvania hire him as the state's Director of Environmental Protection. He had spent nearly five years earnestly trying to clean up Pennsylvania, a job that had driven four generations of the original Penn family into early Quaker graves. The deeper Sequoia buried himself in the solid waste politics of Pittsburgh, Philadelphia, Chester, Erie and other hopelessly corrupted cities, the fewer dedicated followers and news media headlines he attracted. After a very credible Mafia threat on his life, he quite sensibly resigned his post and returned to private life, scarred but wiser. And alive.

When the word about the SSZ program reached him, Sequoia was hiking along a woodland trail in Fairmont Park, Philadelphia, leading a scraggly handful of sullen high school students through the park's soot-ravaged woodlands on a steaming August afternoon. They were dispiritedly picking up empty beer cans and gummy prophylactics—and keeping a wary eye out for muggers. Even full daylight was no protection against assault. And the school kids wouldn't help him, Sequoia knew. Half of them would jump in and join the fun.

Sequoia was broad-shouldered, almost burly. His rugged face

was seamed by weather and news conferences. He looked strong and fit, but lately his back had been giving him trouble and his old trick knee . . .

He heard someone pounding up the trail behind him.

"Mark! Mark!"

Sequoia turned to see Larry Helper, his oldest and therefore most trusted aide, running along the gravel path toward him, waving a copy of the *Daily News* over his head. Newspaper pages were slipping from his sweaty grasp and fluttering off into the bushes.

"Littering," Sequoia muttered in a tone sometimes used by archbishops when facing a case of heresy. "Some of you kids," he said in his most authoritative voice, "pick up those newspaper pages."

A couple of the students lackadaisically ambled after the fluttering sheets.

"Mark, look here!" Helper skidded to a gritty stop on the gravel and breathlessly waved the front page of the newspaper. "Look!"

Sequoia grabbed his aide's wrist and took what was left of the newspaper from him. He frowned at Helper, who cringed and stepped back.

"I . . . I thought you'd want to see . . ."

Satisfied that he had established his dominance, Sequoia turned his attention to the front page's blaring headline.

"Supersonic *zeppelin*?"

Two nights later, Sequoia was meeting with a half-dozen men and women in the basement of a prosperous downtown church that specialized in worthy causes capable of filling the pews upstairs.

Once Sequoia called his meeting I was informed by the mole I had planted in his pitiful little group of do-gooders. As a newcomer to the scene, I had no trouble joining Sequoia's Friends of the Planet organization, especially when I FedExed them a personal check for a thousand dollars—for which Anson Aerospace reimbursed me, of course.

So I was sitting on the floor like a good environmental activist while Sequoia paced across the little room. There was no table, just a few folding chairs scattered around, and a locked bookcase stuffed with tomes about sex and marriage. I could tell just from looking at Sequoia that the old activist flames were burning inside him again. He felt alive, strong, the center of attention.

"We can't just drive down to Washington and call a news conference," he exclaimed, pounding a fist into his open palm. "We've got to do something dramatic!"

"Automobiles pollute, anyway," said one of the women, a comely redhead whose dazzling green eyes never left Sequoia's broad, sturdy-looking figure.

"We could take the train; it's electric."

"Power stations pollute."

"Airplanes pollute, too."

"What about riding down to Washington on horseback! Like Paul Revere!"

"Horses pollute."

"They do?"

"Ever been around a stable?"

"Oh."

Sequoia pounded his fist again. "I've got it! It's perfect!"

"What?"

"A balloon! We'll ride down to Washington in a non-polluting balloon filled with helium. That's the dramatic way to emphasize our opposition to this SSZ monster."

"Fantastic!"

"Marvelous!"

The redhead was panting with excitement. "Oh, Mark, you're so clever. So dedicated." There were tears in her eyes.

Helper asked softly, "Uh . . . does anybody know where we can get a balloon? And how much they cost?"

"Money is no object," Sequoia snapped, pounding his fist again. Then he wrung his hand; he had pounded too hard.

When the meeting finally broke up, Helper had been given the task of finding a suitable balloon, preferably one donated by its owner. I had volunteered to assist him. Sequoia would spearhead the effort to raise money for a knockdown fight against the SSZ. The redhead volunteered to assist him. They left the meeting arm in arm.

I was learning the Washington lobbying business from the bottom up, but rising fast. Two weeks later I was in the White House, no less, jammed in among news reporters and West Wing staffers waiting for a presidential news conference to begin. TV lights were glaring at the empty podium. The reporters and camera crews shuffled their feet, coughed, talked to one another. Then:

"Ladies and gentlemen, the President of the United States."

We all stood up and applauded as she entered. I had been thrilled to be invited to the news conference. Well, actually it was Keene who'd been invited and he brought me with him, since I was the Washington rep for the SSZ project. The President strode to the podium and smiled at us in what some cynics had dubbed her rattlesnake mode. I thought she was being gracious.

"Before anything else, I have a statement to make about the tragic misfortune that has overtaken one of our finest public figures, Mark Sequoia. According to the latest report I have received from the Coast Guard—no more than ten minutes ago—there is still no trace of his party. Apparently the balloon they were riding in was blown out to sea two days ago, and nothing has been heard from them since.

"Now let me make this perfectly clear. Mr. Sequoia was frequently on the other side of the political fence from my administration. He was often a critic of my policies and actions, policies and actions that I believe in completely. He was on his way to Washington to protest our new supersonic zeppelin program when this unfortunate accident occurred.

"Mr. Sequoia opposed the SSZ program despite the fact that this project will employ thousands of aerospace engineers who are otherwise unemployed and untrainable. Despite the fact that the SSZ program will save the American dollar on the international market and salvage American prestige in the technological battleground of the world.

"And we should keep in mind that France and Russia have announced that they are studying the possibility of jointly starting their own SSZ effort, a clear technological challenge to America."

Gripping the edges of the podium tighter, the President went on, "Rumors that his balloon was blown off course by a flight of Air Force jets are completely unfounded, the Secretary of Defense assures me. I have dispatched every available military, Coast Guard, and Civil Air Patrol plane to search the entire coastline from Cape Cod to Cape Hatteras. We will find Mark Sequoia and his brave though misguided band of ecofr—er, activists—or their remains."

I knew perfectly well that Sequoia's balloon had not been blown out to sea by Air Force jets. They were private planes: executive jets, actually.

"Are there any questions?" the President asked.

The Associated Press reporter, a hickory-tough old man with thick glasses and a snow-white goatee, got to his feet and asked, "Is that a Versace dress you're wearing? It's quite becoming."

The President beamed. "Why, thank you. Yes, it is . . ."

Keene pulled me by the arm. "Let's go. We've got nothing to worry about here."

I was rising fast, in part because I was willing to do the legwork (and dirty work, like Sequoia) that Keene was too lazy or too squeamish to do. He was still head of our Washington office, in name. I was running the SSZ program, which was just about the only program Anson had going for itself, which meant that I was running the Washington office in reality.

Back in Phoenix, Bob Wisdom and the other guys had become the nucleus of the team that was designing the SSZ prototype. The program would take years, we all knew, years in which we had assured jobs. If the SSZ actually worked the way we designed it, we could spend the rest of our careers basking in its glory.

I was almost getting accustomed to being called over to the West Wing to deal with bureaucrats and politicians. Still, it was a genuine thrill when I was invited into the Oval Office itself.

The President's desk was cleared of papers. Nothing cluttered the broad expanse of rosewood except the telephone console, a black-framed photograph of her late husband (who had once also sat at that desk), and a gold-framed photograph of her daughter on her first day in the House of Representatives (D., Ark.).

She sat in her high-backed leather chair and fired instructions at her staff.

"I want the public to realize," she instructed her media consultant, "that although we are now in a race with the Russians and the French, we are building the SSZ for sound economic and social reasons, not because of competition from overseas."

"Yes, Ma'am," said the media consultant.

She turned to the woman in charge of Congressional liaison. "And you'd better make damned certain that the Senate appropriations committee okays the increased funding for the SSZ prototype. Tell them that if we don't get the extra funding we'll fall behind the Ivans and the Frogs.

"And I want you," she pointed a manicured finger at the research director of TURD, "to spend every nickel of your existing SSZ money as fast as you can. Otherwise we won't be able to get the additional appropriation out of Congress."

"Yes, Ma'am," said Roger K. Memo, with one of his rare smiles.

"But, Madam President," the head of the Budget Office started to object.

"I know what you're going to say," the President snapped at him. "I'm perfectly aware that money doesn't grow on trees. But we've *got* to get the SSZ prototype off the ground, and do it before next November. Take money from education, from the space program, from the environmental superfund—I don't care how you do it, just get it done. I want the SSZ prototype up and flying by next summer, when I'm scheduled to visit Paris and Moscow."

The whole staff gasped in sudden realization of the President's masterful plan.

"That right," she said, smiling slyly at them. "I intend to be the first Chief of State to cross the Atlantic in a supersonic zeppelin."

Although none of us realized its importance at the time, the crucial incident, we know now, happened months before the President's decision to fly the SSZ to Paris and Moscow. I've gone through every scrap of information we could beg, borrow or steal about that decisive day, reviewing it all time and again, trying to find some way to undo the damage.

It happened at the VA hospital in Hagerstown, a few days after Mark Sequoia had been rescued. The hospital had never seen so many reporters. There were news media people thronging the lobby, lounging in the halls, bribing nurses, sneaking into elevators and even surgical theaters (where several of them fainted). The parking lot was a jumble of cars bearing media stickers and huge TV vans studded with antennas.

Only two reporters were allowed to see Mark Sequoia on any given day, and they were required to share their interviews with all the others in the press corps. Today the two—picked by lot—were a crusty old veteran from Fox News and a perky young blonde from *Women's Wear Daily*.

"But I've told your colleagues what happened at least a dozen times," mumbled Sequoia from behind a swathing of bandages.

He was hanging by both arms and legs from four traction braces, his backside barely touching the crisply sheeted bed. Bandages covered eighty percent of his body and all of his face, except for tiny slits for his eyes, nostrils and mouth.

The Fox News reporter held his palm-sized video camera in one hand while he scratched at his stubbled chin with the other. On the opposite side of the bed, the blonde held a similar videocorder close to Sequoia's bandaged face.

She looked misty-eyed. "Are . . . are you in much pain?"

"Not really," Sequoia answered bravely, with a slight tremor in his voice.

"Why all the traction?" asked Fox News. "The medics said there weren't any broken bones."

"Splinters," Sequoia answered weakly.

"Bone splinters!" gasped the blonde. "Oh, how awful!"

"No," Sequoia corrected. "Splinters. Wood splinters. When the balloon finally came down we landed in a clump of trees just outside Hagerstown. I got thousands of splinters. It took most of the surgical staff three days to pick them all out of me. The chief of surgery said he was going to save the wood and build a scale model of the *Titanic* with it."

"Oh, how painful!" The blonde insisted on gasping. She gasped very well, Sequoia noted, watching her blouse.

"And what about your hair?" Fox News asked.

Sequoia felt himself blush underneath the bandages. "I . . . uh . . . I must have been very frightened. After all, we were aloft in that stupid balloon for six days, without food, without anything to drink except a six pack of Perrier. We went through a dozen different thunderstorms . . ."

"With lightning?" the blonde asked.

Nodding painfully, Sequioa replied, "We all thought we were going to die."

Fox News frowned. "So your hair turned white from fright. There was some talk that cosmic rays did it."

"Cosmic rays? We never got that high. Cosmic rays don't have any effect on you until you get really up there, isn't that right?"

"How high did you go?"

"I don't know," Sequoia answered. "Some of those updrafts in the thunderstorms pushed us pretty high. The air got kind of thin."

"But not high enough to cause cosmic ray damage."

"Well, I don't know . . . maybe . . ."

"It'd make a better story than just being scared," said Fox News. "Hair turned white by cosmic rays. Maybe even sterilized."

"Sterilized?" Sequoia yelped.

"Cosmic rays do that, too," Fox News said. "I checked."

"Well, we weren't *that* high."

"You're sure?"

"Yeah . . . well, I don't think we were that high. We didn't have an altimeter with us . . ."

"But you could have been."

Shrugging was sheer torture, Sequoia found.

"Okay, but those thunderstorms could've lifted you pretty damned high," Fox News persisted.

Before Sequoia could think of what to answer, the door to his private room opened and a horse-faced nurse said firmly, "That's all. Time's up. Mr. Sequoia must rest now. After his enema."

"Okay, I think I've got something to hang a story on," Fox News said with a satisfied grin. "Now to find a specialist in cosmic rays."

The blonde looked thoroughly shocked and terribly upset. "You . . . you don't think you were really sterilized, do you?"

Sequoia tried to make himself sound worried and brave at the same time. "I don't know. I just . . . don't know."

Late that night the blonde snuck back into his room, masquerading as a nurse. If she knew the difference between sterilization and impotence she didn't tell Sequoia about it. For his part, he forgot about his still-tender skin and the traction braces. The morning nurse found him unconscious, one shoulder dislocated, most of his bandages rubbed off, his skin terribly inflamed, and a goofy grin on his face.

I knew that the way up the corporate ladder was to somehow acquire a staff that reported to me. And, in truth, the SSZ project was getting so big that I truly needed more people to handle it. I mean, all the engineers had to do was build the damned thing and make it fly. I had to make certain that the money kept flowing, and that wasn't easy. An increasingly large part of my responsibilities as the *de facto* head of the Washington office consisted of putting out fires.

"Will you look at this!"

Senator Goodyear waved the morning *Post* at me. I had already read the electronic edition before I'd left my apartment that morning. Now, as I sat at Tracy Keene's former desk, the Senator's red face filled my phone screen.

"That Sequoia!" he grumbled. "He'll stop at nothing to destroy me. Just because the Ohio River melted his houseboat, all those years ago."

"It's just a scare headline," I said, trying to calm him down. "People won't be sterilized by flying in the supersonic zeppelin any more than they were by flying in the old *Concorde*."

"I know it's bullshit! And you know it's bullshit! But the goddamned news media are making a major story out of it! Sequoia's on every network talk show. I'm under pressure to call for hearings on the sterilization problem!"

"Good idea," I told him. "Have a Senate investigation. The scientists will prove that there's nothing to it."

That was my first mistake. I didn't get a chance to make another.

I hightailed it that morning to Memo's office. I wanted to see Pencilbeam and start building a defense against this sterilization story. The sky was gray and threatening. An inch or two of snow was forecast, and people were already leaving their offices for home, at ten o'clock in the morning. Dedicated government bureaucrats and corporate employees, taking the slightest excuse to knock off work.

The traffic was so bad that it had actually started to snow, softly, by the time I reached Memo's office. He was pacing across the thinly carpeted floor, his shoes squeaking unnervingly in the spacious room. Copies of *The Washington Post, The New York Times* and *Aviation Week* were spread across his usually immaculate desk, but his attention was focused on his window, where we could see fluffy snowflakes gently drifting down.

"Traffic's going to get worse as the day goes on," Memo muttered.

"They're saying it'll only be an inch or so," I told him.

"That's enough to paralyze this town."

Yeah, especially when everybody jumps in their cars and starts fleeing the town as if a terrorist nuke is about to go off, *I replied silently*.

Aloud, I asked, "What about this sterilization business? Is there any substance to the story?"

Memo glanced sharply at me. "They don't need substance as long as they can start a panic."

Dr. Pencilbeam sat at one of the unmatched conference chairs, all bony limbs and elbows and knees.

"Relax, Roger," Pencilbeam said calmly. "Congress isn't going to halt the SSZ program. It means too many jobs, too much international prestige. And besides, the President has staked her credibility on it."

"That's what worries me," Memo muttered.

"What?"

But Memo's eye was caught by movement outside his window. He waddled past his desk and looked down into the street below.

"Oh, my God."

"What's going on?" Pencilbeam unfolded like a pocket ruler into a six-foot-long human and hurried to the window. Outside, in the thin mushy snow, a line of somber men and women were filing along the street past the TURD building, bearing signs that screamed:

STOP THE SSZ!
DON'T STERILIZE THE HUMAN RACE
SSZ MURDERS UNBORN CHILDREN
ZEPPELINS GO HOME!

"Isn't that one with the sign about unborn children a priest?" Pencilbeam asked.

Memo shrugged. "Your eyes are better than mine."

"Ah-hah! And look at this!"

Pencilbeam pointed a long, bony finger farther down the street. Another swarm of people were advancing on the building. They also carried placards:

SSZ FOR ZPG
ZEPPELINS SI! BABIES NO!
ZEPPELINS FOR POPULATION CONTROL
UP THE SSZ

Memo sagged against the window. "This . . . this is awful."

The Zero Population Growth group marched through the thin snowfall straight at the environmentalists and anti-birth-control pickets. Instantly the silence was shattered by shouts and taunts. Shrill female voices battled against rumbling baritones and bassos. Placards wavered. Bodies pushed. Someone screamed. One sign struck a skull and then bloody war broke out.

Memo, Pencilbeam and I watched aghast until the helmeted TAC squad police doused the whole tangled mess of them with riot gas, impartially clubbed men and women alike and carted everyone off, including three bystanders and a homeless panhandler.

The Senate hearings were such a circus that Driver summoned me back to Phoenix for a strategy session with Anson's top management. I was glad to get outside the Beltway, and especially glad to see Lisa again. She even agreed to have dinner with me.

"You're doing a wonderful job there in Washington," she said, smiling with gleaming teeth and flashing eyes.

My knees went weak, but I found the courage to ask, "Would you consider transferring to the Washington office? I could use a sharp executive assistant—"

She didn't even let me finish. "I'd love to!"

I wanted to do handsprings. I wanted to grab her and kiss her hard enough to bruise our lips. I wanted to, but Driver came out of his office just at that moment, looking his jaw-jutting grimmest.

"Come on, kid. Time to meet the top brass."

The top brass was a mixture of bankers and former engineers. To my disgust, instead of trying to put together a strategy to defeat the environmentalists, they were already thinking about how many men and women they'd have to lay off when Washington pulled the plug on the SSZ program.

"But that's crazy!" I protested. "The program is solid. The President herself is behind it."

Driver fixed me with his steely stare. "With friends like that, who needs enemies?"

I left the meeting feeling very depressed, until I saw Lisa again. Her smile could light up the world.

Before heading back to Washington to fight Sequoia's sterilization propaganda, I looked up my old APT buddies. They were in the factory section where the SSZ was being fabricated.

The huge factory assembly bay was filled with the aluminum skeleton of the giant dirigible. Great gleaming metal ribs stretched from its titanium nosecap to the more intricate cagework of the tail fins. Tiny figures with flashing laser welders crawled along the ribbing like maggots cleaning the bones of some noble whale.

Even the jet engines sitting on their carrying pallets dwarfed human scale. Some of the welders held clandestine poker games inside their intake cowlings, Bob Wisdom told me. The cleaning crews kept quiet about the spills, crumbs and other detritus they found in them night after night. I stood with Bob, Ray Kurtz, Tommy Rohr and Richard Grand beside one of those huge engine pods, craning our necks to watch the construction work going on high overhead. The assembly bay rang to the shouts of working men and women, throbbed with the hum of machinery, clanged with the clatter of metal against metal.

"It's going to be some Christmas party if Congress cancels this project," Kurtz muttered gloomily.

"Oh, they wouldn't dare cancel it now that the Women's Movement is behind it," said Grand, with a sardonic little smile.

Kurtz glared at him from behind his beard. "You wish. Half those idiots in Congress will vote against us just to prove they're pro-environment."

"Actually, the scientific evidence is completely on our side," Grand said. "And in the long run, the weight of evidence prevails."

He always acts as if he knows more than anybody else, I thought. But he's dead wrong here. He hasn't the foggiest notion of how Washington works. But he sounds so damned sure of himself! It must be that phony accent of his.

"Well, just listen to me, pal," said Wisdom, jabbing a forefinger at Grand. "I've been working on that secretary of mine since the last Christmas party, and if this project falls through and the party is a bust that palpitating hunk of femininity is going to run home and cry instead of coming to the party!"

Grand blinked at him several times, obviously trying to think of the right thing to say. Finally he enunciated, "Pity."

But I was thinking about Lisa. If the SSZ is cancelled, Driver won't let her transfer to the Washington office. There'd be no need to hire more staff for me. There'd be no need for me!

I went back to Washington determined to save the SSZ from this stupid sterilization nonsense. But it was like trying to stop a tsunami with a floor mop. The women's movement, the environmental movement, the labor unions, even Leno and Letterman got into the act. The Senate hearings turned into a shambles; Pencilbeam and the other scientists were ignored while movie stars testified that they would never fly in an SSZ because of the dangers of radiation.

The final blow came when the President announced that she was not going to Paris and Moscow, after all. Urgent problems elsewhere. Instead, she flew to Hawaii for an economic summit of the Pacific nations. In her subsonic Air Force One.

The banner proclaiming *Happy Holidays!* drooped sadly across one wall of the company cafeteria. Outside in the late afternoon darkness, lights glimmered, cars were moving and a bright full moon shone down on a rapidly emptying parking lot.

Inside the Anson Aerospace cafeteria was nothing but gloom. The Christmas party had been a dismal flop, primarily because half the company's work force had received layoff notices that morning. The tables had been pushed to one side of the cafeteria to make room for a dance floor. Syrupy holiday music oozed out of the speakers built into the acoustic tiles of the ceiling. But no one was dancing.

Bob Wisdom sat at one of the tables, propping his aching head in his hands. Ray Kurtz and Tommy Rohr sat with him, equally dejected.

"Why the hell did they have to cancel the project two days before Christmas?" Rohr asked rhetorically.

"Makes for more pathos," Kurtz growled.

"It's pathetic, all right," Wisdom said. "I've never seen so many women crying at once. Or men, for that matter."

"Even Driver was crying, and he hasn't been laid off," Rohr said.

"Well," Kurtz said, staring at the half-finished drink in front of him, "Sequoia did it. He's a big media hero again."

"And we're on the bread line," said Rohr.

"You got laid off?" I asked.

"Not yet—but it's coming. This place will be closing its doors before the fiscal year ends."

"It's not that bad," said Wisdom. "We still have the Air Force work. As long as they're shooting off cruise missiles, we'll be in business."

Rohr grimaced. "You know what gets me? The way the whole project was scrapped, without giving us a chance to complete the big bird and show how it'd work. Without a goddamned chance."

Kurtz said, "Congressmen are scared of people getting sterilized."

"Not really," I said. "They're scared of not being on the right bandwagon."

All three of them turned toward me.

Rohr said, "Next time you dream up a project, pal, make it underground. Something in a lead mine. Or deeper still, a gold mine. Then Congress won't have to worry about cosmic rays."

Wisdom tried to laugh, but it wouldn't come.

"You know," I said slowly, "you just might have something there."

"What?"

"Where?"

"A supersonic transport—in a tunnel."

"Oh for Chri—"

But Wisdom sat up straighter in his chair. "You could make an air-cushion vehicle go supersonic. If you put it in a tunnel you get away from the sonic boom and the air pollution."

"The safety aspects would be better, too," Kurtz admitted. Then, more excitedly, "And pump the air out of the tunnel, like a pneumatic tube!"

Rohr shook his head. "You guys are crazy. Who the hell's going to build tunnels all over the country?"

"There's a lot of tunnels already built," I countered. "We could adapt them for the SSST."

"SSST?"

"Sure," I answered, grinning for the first time in weeks. "Supersonic subway train."

They stared at me. Rohr pulled out his PDA and started tapping on it. Wisdom got that faraway look in his eyes. Kurtz shrugged and said, "Why the hell not?"

I got up and headed for the door. Supersonic subway train. That's my ticket. I'm going back to Washington, I knew. And this time I'll bring Lisa with me.

THE SECRET LIFE OF HENRY K.

This is a pure romp, not to be taken seriously. Obviously, any relation between the characters in this story and real ex-Secretaries of State, movie stars, heiresses, et al. is purely . . . well, would you believe it's an alternate universe, maybe?

* 🌀 *

THIS LATE AT NIGHT, even the busiest corridors of the Pentagon were deserted. Dr. Young's footsteps echoed hollowly as he followed the mountainous, tight lipped, grim-faced man. Another equally large and steely-eyed man followed behind him, in lockstep with the first.

They were agents, Dr. Young knew that without being told. Their clothing bulged with muscles trained in murderous oriental arts, other bulges in unlikely places along their anatomy were various pieces of equipment: guns, two-way radios, stilettos, Bowie knives . . . Young decided his imagination wasn't rich enough to picture all the equipment these men might be carrying.

After what seemed like an hour's walk down a constantly curving corridor, the agent in front stopped abruptly before an inconspicuous, unmarked door.

"In here," he said, barely moving his lips.

The door opened by itself, and Dr. Young stepped into what seemed to be an ordinary receptionist's office. It was no bigger than a cubicle, and even in the dim lighting—from a single desk lamp, the overhead lights were off—Young could see that the walls were the same sallow depressing color as most Pentagon offices.

"The phone will ring," the agent said, glancing at a watch that looked absolutely dainty on his massive hairy wrist, "in exactly one minute and fifteen seconds. Sit at the desk. Answer when it rings."

With that, he shut the door firmly, leaving Dr. Young alone and bewildered in the tiny anteroom.

There was only one desk, cleared of papers. It was a standard government-issue battered metal desk. IN and OUT boxes stood empty atop it. Nothing else on it but a single black telephone. There were two creaky-looking straight-backed metal chairs in front of the desk, and a typist's swivel chair behind it. The only other things in the room were a pair of file cabinets, side by side, with huge padlocks and red SECURE signs on them, and a bulletin board that had been miraculously cleared of everything except the little faded fire-emergency instruction card.

Dr. Young found that his hands were trembling. He wished that he hadn't given up cigarettes: after all, oral eroticism isn't all that bad. He glanced at the closed hallway door and knew that both the burly agents were standing outside, probably with their arms folded across their chests in unconscious imitation of the eunuchs who guarded sultans' harems.

He took a deep breath and went around the desk and sat on the typist's chair.

The phone rang as soon as his butt touched the chair. He jumped, but grabbed the phone and settled himself before it could ring again.

"Dr. Canton Young speaking." His voice sounded an octave too high, and quavery, even to himself.

"Dr. Young, I thank you for accompanying the agents who brought you there without questioning their purpose. They were instructed to tell you who sent them, and nothing else."

He recognized the voice at once. "You—you're welcome, Mr. President."

"Please! No names! This is a matter of utmost security."

"Ye—yessir."

"Dr. Young, you have been recommended very highly for the special task I must ask of you. I know that, as a loyal, patriotic American, you will do your best to accomplish this task. And as the most competent man in your highly demanding and complex field, your efforts will be crowned with success. That's the American way, now isn't it?"

"Yessir. May I ask, just what is the task?"

"I'm glad you asked that. I have a personnel problem that you are uniquely qualified to solve. One of my closest and most valued aides—a man I depend on very heavily—has gone into a tailspin. I won't explain why or how. I must ask you merely to accept the bald statement. This aide is a man of great drive and talent, high moral purpose, and enormous energy. But at the moment, he's useless to himself, to this Administration, and to the nation. I need you to help him find himself."

"Me? But all I do is—"

"You run the best computer-dating service in the nation, I know. Your service has been checked out thoroughly by the FBI, the Secret Service, and the Defense Intelligence Agency—"

"Not the CIA?"

"I don't know, they won't tell me."

"Oh."

"This aide of mine—a very sincere and highly motivated man—needs a female companion. Not just any woman. The psychiatrists at Walter Reed tell me that he must find the woman who's perfect for him, his exact match, the one mate that can make him happy enough to get back to the important work he should be doing. As you know, I have a plan for stopping inflation, bridging the generation gap, and settling the Cold War. But to make everything perfectly clear, Dr. Young, none of these plans can be crowned with success unless this certain aide can do his part of the job, carry his share of the burden, pull his share of the load."

Dr. Young nodded in the semi-darkness. "I understand, sir. He needs a woman to make him happy. So many people do." A fleeting thought of the bins upon bins of punchcards that made up his files passed through Dr. Young's mind. "Even you, sir, even you need a woman."

"Dr. Young! I'm a married man!"

"I know—that's what I meant. You couldn't be doing the terrific job you're doing without your lovely wife, your lifetime mate, to support and inspire and you."

"Oh, I see what you mean. Yes, of course. Well, Dr. Young, my aide is in the office there with you, in the inner office. I want you to talk with him, help him, find him the woman he truly needs. Then we can end the war in Indochina, stop inflation, bridge—well, you know."

"Yes sir. I'll do my best."

"That will be adequate for the task, I'm sure. Good night, and God bless America!"

Dr. Young found that he was on his feet, standing at ramrod attention, a position he hadn't assumed since his last Boy Scout jamboree.

Carefully he replaced the phone in its cradle, then turned to face the door that led to the inner office. Who could be in there? The Vice President? No, Young told himself with a shake of his head; that didn't fit the description the President had given him.

Squaring his shoulders once again, Dr. Young took the three steps that carried him to the door and knocked on it sharply.

"Come in," said an equally sharp voice.

The office was kept as dark and shadowy as the anteroom, but Dr. Young recognized the man sitting rather tensely behind the desk.

"Dr. Kiss—!"

"No names! Please! Absolute security, Dr. Young."

"I under—no, come to think of it, I don't understand. Why keep the fact that you're using a computer-dating service *so* secret? What do the Russians and Chinese care—"

The man behind the desk cut him short with a gesture. "It's not the Russians or Chinese. It's the Democrats. If *they* find out—" He waggled both hands in the air—a Semitic gesture of impending doom.

Dr. Young took one of the plush chairs in front of the desk. "But Dr. K—"

"Just call me Henry," the other man said, "But don't get personal about it."

"All right, Henry. I still don't see what's so terrible about a man in your position using a computer-dating service. After all, some of the top Senators and Congressmen on the Democratic side of the aisle have been clients of mine."

"I know, I saw it all in the FBI report. Or was it the DIA report? Well, never mind." He fixed Dr. Young with a penetrating stare. "How would it look if the Dems knew that the President's most trusted and valued aide couldn't get a girl for himself? Eh?"

"Oh, I'm sure you could—"

"I can't!" The penetrating stare melted into something more pathetic. "I can't, the God of our forefathers knows I've tried. But I'm a failure, a flop. There are times when I can't even talk to a woman."

Dr. Young sat there in shocked silence. Even his advanced degrees in psychology might not be enough for this task, he began to realize.

"It's my mother's fault!" Henry all but sobbed. "My pushy mother! Why do you think I took this job in the White House? Because she pushed me into it, and because I thought it might help me to get girls. Well, it hasn't. I can tell the President when to invade Cambodia. I can eat shark's fin with Chou En-lai, but I get totally tongue-tied when I try to talk to an attractive woman! My momma—what can I do?"

Henry started to bury his head in his hands, then with an obvious effort of great willpower, he straightened up in his chair. "Sorry," he said. "I shouldn't get emotional like that."

"No, it's good for you," Dr. Young soothed. "You can't keep everything bottled up all the time."

"Well I have been," Henry retorted sourly, "and I'm getting very uptight about it."

Uptight? thought Dr. Young. *And everyone thinks he's a man of the world. I've got to help him.*

"Listen," he said, "you tell me the kind of woman you like, and I'll comb my computer files until I find her—"

Henry smiled faintly, stoically. "So what good will that do? I'll take one look at her and collapse like a pricked balloon, you should excuse the expression."

But Dr. Young expected that response and was ready for it. "You don't understand, Henry. The woman that I'll find for you will be special. She'll be anxious to make you happy: she'll know that the future of the nation—of the whole world—depends on her pleasing you."

"How can you be sure that she'll really want to?"

"Leave it to me," Dr. Young said, with his best professional smile of assurance. "Just tell me what you'd like, and I'll get my computer cracking on it before the sun comes up."

Henry gave a little shrug, as if he didn't really believe what he was hearing but was desperate enough to give it a try anyway.

"I've already taken the liberty," he said, "of coding my—" he smiled bashfully, "—my dream girl onto these punchcards. And you won't have to use your own computer. Too risky, security-wise, for one thing. Besides, the FBI computer has *everybody* on it."

Dr. Young gasped. "The FBI computer?"

Henry nodded.

Then it hit!

For the first time, it struck home to Dr. Young that he was really playing in the big leagues. Was he ready for it?

The room was sumptuous, with thick carpeting and rich drapes framing the full-length windows that looked out over Manhattan's glittering skyline. A thousand jewels gleamed in the skyscrapers and across the graceful bridges, outshining by far the smogged-over stars of heaven.

Henry swallowed his nervousness as he stood at the doorway with the famous movie star.

"Um, nice room you've got here," he managed to say.

She smiled at him and slid out of her coat. "The studio arranged it. It's mine until the premiere tomorrow night."

Her dress glittered more than the view outside. And showed more, too. Henry worked a finger into his shirt collar; it was starting to feel uncomfortably tight, and warm.

"Here, let me help you," she purred, still showing her perfectly capped teeth in a smile that earned a thousand letters per week, most of them obscene.

She undid his tie and popped the collar button open. "Make yourself comfortable and tell me all about those nasty Russians you outsmarted."

Taking him by the wrist, she led Henry to the plushest couch he had ever seen and pulled him down into it, right next to her lush, lascivious body.

"You're not going to be shy with me, are you? After all, I'm just a lonely little girl far from my home, and I need a big strong daddy to look after me."

He could smell her musky perfume, feel the brush of her beautiful plasticized hair against his cheek.

"I, uh, I've got to catch a plane for—for Ulan Bator in one hour!" As the words popped out of his mouth, Henry sat up stiffly on the edge of the couch. He looked at his wristwatch. "Yes. One hour, to Ulan Bator. That's in Mongolia, you know."

She stared at him, pouting. "But what about our date tomorrow night? The premiere of my new movie!"

"I'm sorry. You'll have to go with someone else. The President needs me in Mongolia. Top secret negotiations. You mustn't say a word about this—any of this! To any one!"

With a shrug that nearly popped her breasts out of the low-cut gown, she said, "Okay. Okay. But tell those creepy friends of yours that I've done my patriotic duty, and don't come around here looking for more!"

"But she liked you," Dr. Young said. He felt surprised and slightly hurt as he sat in the same dimly lit office in the Pentagon. Again it was late at night, and again Henry sat nervously behind the desk.

"It was all an act. She's an actress, you know."

"Of course, I know. But she genuinely liked you. It was no act. Take my word for it."

"How can you be sure?"

"Well—" Dr. Young hesitated, but then realized he'd find out anyway. "We had her room bugged. She cried for twenty minutes after you left."

Instead of getting angry, Henry looked suddenly guilty. "She did?"

A kaleidoscope of emotions played across Henry's face. Dr. Young saw surprise, guilt, pride, anxiety, and then he stopped watching.

At length Henry shook himself, as if getting rid of something unpleasant. "She was too—too flighty. A silly child."

"She was what you programmed into the computer," Dr. Young retorted. "I checked out the characteristics myself. Mathematically, of course."

"Well, the computer goofed!"

"No, Henry. That's not possible. You simply didn't give us a description of what you really want in a woman. You told us what you *think* you want, you gave us some idealizations. But that's not what your heart's really set on."

"You're trying to tell me I don't know what I want?"

"Not consciously, you don't. Now with a team of psychiatrists and possibly hypnosis therapy—"

"No!" Henry slammed a hand on the desktop. "Too risky! Remember our need for absolute security."

"But your conscious mind has only a very hazy idea of what your dream woman should be. The very term 'dream woman' indicates—"

"Never mind," Henry said firmly. "Just add a few points to the computer program. I want someone just like Jill, but tougher, more intelligent. Better able to stand on her own feet."

Dr. Young nodded. Another week of computer programming ahead.

"This is my pad, Hank. What do you think of it?"

Henry surveyed the crumbling plaster, the dirt-caked floor, the stacks of books strewn across the room covering the sink and the range, the desk, the drawing board, the sofa, the coffee table. The only piece of furniture in the filthy place that wasn't covered with books or papers of one sort or another was the bed. And *that* looked like something out of a Hong Kong brothel—a slimy, grimy, wrinkled mess that seemed to be writhing by itself even as he stared at it.

"It's efficient looking," he said. Actually, it looked like the storage room in the cellar of a Village tenement. Which it had been, until recently.

"Efficient, huh?' Gloria tossed her head slightly, a motion that spilled her long sun-bleached hair over one T-shirted shoulder.

"It's efficient, all right," she said. "This is where I do my writing, my illustrating, my editing, and my fucking."

Henry blinked. His glasses seemed to be getting steamed up. Or maybe it was dirt.

"You like to fuck. Hank?" she asked, grinning at him.

He squeezed his eyes shut and heard his voice utter a choked, "Yes."

"Good. Me too. But no sexual chauvinism. I get on top the same number of times you do," she said, starting toward the bed and pulling off the t-shirt. "No oral stuff unless we go together, and," she stepped out of her ragged jeans, "say, how many times can you pop off in one—"

She turned and saw that she was talking to the empty air. Henry had fled, and left the door open behind him.

* * *

"She was a monster!" Henry babbled to Dr. Young. "That computer is trying to destroy me. I'm going to have it investigated! And you too!"

"Now, now," Dr. Young said as soothingly as he could. "No one's tampered with anything. I've done all the programming myself, taken the printouts myself, done it *all* by myself. I haven't slept a full night since our first meeting. I'm losing business because of you."

"She was a monster," Henry repeated.

"If you'd only let the psychiatrists probe your subconscious—"

"No! I went through all that months ago. All they ever said was that it's all my mother's fault. I know that!"

Dr. Young made a helpless shrug. "But if you can't verbalize your real desires—can't tell me what you're really looking for—how can I help you?"

Clenching his hands into fists and frowning mightily Henry said, "Just find me the woman I'm looking for. Someone who's beautiful, intelligent, patient, patriotic—but not aggressive!"

Back to the computer, Dr. Young thought wearily. But something in the back of his mind made him smile inwardly. *There might be—yes, that might work.*

The Baroness's yacht rode easily at anchor in the soft swells of the sheltered cove. The coast of Maine was dark, just a jagged blackness against the softer stars scattered across the darkness of the sky.

"I've never seen the stars look so beautiful," Henry said. Then, sneaking a peek at the notes on his shirt cuff, he added, "They're almost as beautiful as you."

The Baroness smiled. And she was truly beautiful as she stood by the rail of the yacht, almost close enough to touch her warm and thrilling body to his. Her long midnight hair, always severely combed back and pinned up during the day, was now sweeping free and loose to her lovely bare shoulders.

"I would offer you another drink, Henri, but the servants have gone ashore."

"Oh?" He gripped the rail a bit tighter. "All of them?"

"Oui. I sent them away. I wanted to be alone with you. Totally alone."

Henry took a deep breath. All through the evening—the ballet recital, the dinner, the dizzying private jet ride to this cove, the dancing on the deck—he had been steeling himself for the supreme moment. He had no intention of muffing it this night.

"Maybe," he suggested slyly, "we can go back inside and find something for ourselves."

She put a hand to his close-shaven, lime-scented cheek. "What an admirable idea, Henri. No wonder your President depends on you so heavily."

Half an hour later they were sitting in the salon on a leather couch, discussing international relations. Gradually, Henry began to realize that the subject had drifted into the super romantic areas of spies and espionage.

She was leaning against him, as closely as her extensive bosom would allow. "You must have known many spies—clever, dangerous men and deceptive, beautiful women."

"Uh, well, yes," he lied. His hands were starting to tremble.

Suddenly she slid off the couch and kneeled at his feet.

"Pretend I'm a spy! Pretend you've caught me and have me at your mercy. Tie me up! Beat me! Torture me! Rape me!"

With a strangled scream, Henry leaped to his feet, dropped his glasses, bolted for the hatch, pounded up the ladder to the deck, and leaped into the water. For the first time since his last full summer at camp, he swam for his life. And his sanity.

"It's useless, it'll never work. It's just no good." Henry was muttering as Dr. Young led him down a long antiseptically white corridor.

"It might work. It could work."

For a moment the doctor thought he would have to take Henry by the hand and march him through the corridor like a stern schoolteacher with a recalcitrant child. Studying his "customer," Dr. Young realized that Henry was going down the drain. His physical condition was obviously deteriorating: his hands trembled, there were bags under his eyes, he had lost weight, and his face was starting to break out in acne. And his mental state! Poor Henry kept muttering things like, "Peeking—must get the Ping-Pong people to Peeking—"

Dr. Young felt desperate. And he knew that if *he* felt desperate, Henry must be on the verge of collapse.

Henry said, "You're sure nobody else knows—"

"It's two in the morning. This is my own building, my company owns it and occupies it exclusively. The guard couldn't possibly have recognized you with that false beard and the sunglasses. I laid off every known or suspected Democrat in my company weeks ago. Stop worrying."

They came at last to Room X. Dr. Young opened the door and motioned Henry to follow him inside.

The room was well lit, neat, and orderly. There was a comfortable couch along one wall, a modest desk of warm mahogany with a deep leather chair behind it, and a panel of lights and grillwork on the farthest wall. The panel was set into the wall so that someone reclining on the couch couldn't see it.

Henry balked at the doorway. "I'm not sure—"

"Come on," Dr. Young coaxed. "It won't hurt you. The President himself authorized nearly a million dollars to allow me to build this system. You wouldn't want him to feel that the money was wasted, would you?"

As he said that, Dr. Young almost laughed out loud. This system was going to make him the king of the computer selection business. And all built at government expense.

Henry took a hesitant step into the room. "What do I have to do?" he asked suspiciously.

"Just lie on the couch. I attach these two little electrodes to your head." Dr. Young pulled a small plastic bag from his jacket pocket. Inside was something that looked rather like the earphones that are handed out on airplanes for listening to the movie or stereo tapes.

"It won't hurt a bit," Dr. Young promised.

Henry just glared at him sullenly.

"I'll explain it again," Dr. Young said, as calmly as he could manage. It was like coaxing a four-year-old: "You don't want to talk to psychiatrists or anyone else—for security reasons. So I've programmed my own company's computer with the correlations determined by six of the nation's leading psychiatrists. All you have to do is answer a few questions that I'll ask you, and the computer will be able to translate your answers into an understanding of your subconscious desires— your real wishes, the dream girl that your conscious mind is too repressed to verbalize."

"I'm not sure I like this."

"It's harmless."

"What are the electrodes for?"

Dr. Young tried to make his reply sound casual, airy. "Oh, they're just something like lie detectors, not that you're consciously lying, of course. But they'll compare your brain's various electrical waves with your conscious words and allow the computer to determine what's really on your mind."

"A computer that can read minds?" Henry took a half-step back toward the door.

"Not at all," Dr. Young assured him and grabbed him by the shoulder of his jacket. "It doesn't read your mind. How could it? It's only a computer. It merely correlates your spoken words with your brain waves, that's all. Then it's up to a human being—me, in this case—to interpret those correlations."

As he half-dragged Henry to the couch, Dr. Young wondered if he should tell him that the computer did most of the correlation work itself. And thanks to the clandestine link between his company's computer here in this building and the FBI's monster machine, the correlations would come out as specific names and addresses.

"You really think this will work?" Henry asked as Dr. Young pushed him down onto the couch.

"Not only do I think it will work, but the President thinks it will. Now we wouldn't want to disappoint the President, would we?"

Henry lay back and closed his eyes. "No, I suppose not."

"Fine," said Dr. Young. He pulled the electrodes from the bag. "Now this isn't going to hurt at all." Henry jumped when the soft rubberized pads touched his temples.

"And if it doesn't work?" the President's voice sounded darkly troubled. "How can I get Chou to meet me at the airport if Henry isn't available to set things up?"

"It will work, Mr. Pre—uh, sir. I'm sure of it," Dr. Young said into the phone. *It better work*, he said to himself. *Tonight's the night. We'll find out for sure tonight.*

"I don't like it," growled the voice on the phone. "I want to make that perfectly clear. I don't like this one little bit."

"It's scientific, sir. You can't argue with science."

"It had better be worth the money we've spent," was the President's only reply.

Henry was strangely calm as he stepped out of the limousine and walked up the steps to the plain, red brick house in Georgetown. It was barely dusk, not dark enough to worry about muggers yet.

There was only one bell button at the door. Usually these homes were split into several apartments. This one was not. He and his dream girl would have it all to themselves.

He sighed. He had waited so long, been through so much. And now some computer-designated woman was waiting for him. Well, maybe it would work out all right. All he had ever wanted was a lovely, sweet woman to make him feel wanted and worthwhile.

He pressed the button. A buzzer sounded gratingly and he pushed the front door open and stepped inside.

The hallway led straight to the back of the house.

"In the kitchen!" a voice called out.

Briefly he wondered whether he should stop here and take off his topcoat. He was holding a bouquet of gladiolas in one hand, stiffly wrapped in green paper. Squaring his shoulders manfully, he strode down the hallway to the kitchen.

The lights were bright, the radio blaring, and the kitchen was filled with delicious warm aromas and sizzlings. The woman was standing at the range with her back to him.

Without turning, she said: "Put the flowers on the table and take off your coat. Then wash your hands and we'll eat."

With a thrill that surpassed understanding, Henry said, "Yes, Momma."

JOVIAN DREAMS

Why do human beings explore? Since long before history began to be written, humans have pushed themselves into new territories, sought new vistas, crossed deserts and oceans and chains of mountains. Why? Why have men deliberately gone into dangers that often killed them? For glory? For gain? For knowledge?

Here is an explorer who thinks he knows why he is risking his life in the globe-girdling ocean of our solar system's largest planet.

But he learns better.

FLOATING IN THE SUBMERSIBLE'S artificial womb, deep in Jupiter's planet-girdling ocean, Po Han dreamed of his martyred ancestor, Zheng He.

Forty years before Columbus was even born, Zheng He commanded the Ming emperor's mighty treasure fleets. He had sailed ships crewed by thousands of men across the wide Pacific and Indian Oceans, he had established trading posts among the primitives of North and South America and the kingdoms of Africa's east coast. He had explored Australia and the made the rulers of Indonesia kowtow to the Emperor. He had brought treasure and knowledge to China.

But when the old emperor died the Mandarins who supervised the newly crowned child on the throne forbade all exploratory voyages, burned the treasure fleets, castrated Zheng He far more cruelly than the Arab slave traders who had emasculated him in his youth.

In Po Han's dream, the Mandarins of the Chinese court and the bureaucrats of the International Astronautical Authority melted together into one stern, austere figure: Po Han's own father.

"Give up this madness," his father warned him. "There is nothing for you in Jupiter except pain and death."

Pain, yes. Po Han knew enough about pain now. He had run away from the safety of Beijing and the faculty post at the university that had been offered to him. He had flown to Jupiter to explore, to learn, to break the barriers of ignorance that lay between the humans of Earth and the gigantic Leviathans that swam the endless ocean of Jupiter.

"I'll show them," he swore to himself. "I'll make them all admit that I am the greatest explorer of them all."

He had to be surgically transformed. Not castrated, as Zheng He was, but altered to breathe the cold, slimy, high-pressure liquid that filled his submersible. There was no other way for fragile humans to stand the immense pressures of the deep Jovian ocean.

So Po Han floated in the cold liquid, his lungs, every cell of his body bathed in the thick, frigid, viscous fluid that filled the submersible. He was no longer a human being, he knew. Now he was a cyborg, part man, part machine, linked to the ship's systems by electronic connectors that allowed him to see what the sensors observed, feel the thrum of the ship's engines as his own heartbeat, hear the weird alien calls and cackles of the Jovian creatures that lived in the worldwide ocean.

An ocean ten times larger than the planet Earth. An ocean that had no land, no rocky shore, no sandy beach, nothing but chains of waves that surged unbroken for tens of thousands of kilometers, driven by storms that dwarfed entire worlds.

An ocean that was getting warmer as he sank deeper. Po Han felt the rising temperature of the acid-laced water beyond the sub's hull as heat against his own skin. He welcomed the warmth. Deeper, he directed his submersible. Deeper, into the realm of the Leviathans.

"I'll show them all," he muttered, his voice strangely deepened by the liquid in which he floated.

The first glimpses that automated probes had relayed back to the scientists in orbit around Jupiter were discounted as sensor errors. Living creatures as big as earthly cities? Impossible. But the cameras and sonars of the probes told the same story. Enormous Jovians swimming in that enormous ocean. Lordly beasts as huge as mountains.

The probes caught only glimpses of the Leviathans. The machines could not go deep enough, down to the depths where these creatures swam, because their communications systems blanked out at such tremendous depths and pressures. Humans had to go, but to do so meant that the humans had to be surgically altered, become more than human. Or perhaps less.

"There's no guarantee that we can return you to normal, once you've undergone the surgery," said the station's chief scientist.

Thinking of Zheng He and his own father, Po Han had agreed to the surgery.

"People have died down there," the chief scientist warned. "Others have returned crippled."

Po Han did not care. He had cut off the umbilical cord that connected him to home, to family, to Earth. "I am willing to accept the risks," he said simply.

Now, floating in this utterly alien man-made womb, he burned with eagerness to show the world the greatness of his courage, his daring. I will be famous! I'll show them all!

And then his heart leaped. Off in the distance, deeper than he was cruising, a shadowy shape glided through the ammoniated water. Blinking, Po Han calibrated the distance and size of the shape. It's enormous! Bigger than Beijing!

Deeper he pushed himself. The submersible groaned under the increasing pressure that Po Han felt squeezing him in a pitiless vise.

"I can stand the pain," he said to himself. "I'll show them . . . show them all."

The immense Jovian turned toward him, and Po Han saw that it was followed by others. Dozens more. He couldn't breathe; the pressure was crushing him. It took nearly half an hour for the gigantic beast to cruise past him. Po Han saw hundreds of eyes along that enormous flank turning toward him, focusing on him.

He shuddered.

And then the Leviathan's side lit up with a brilliant red display. Po Han goggled at it. A picture, an image of his own submersible. Down to the last sensor pod, every detail perfectly displayed.

All the other Leviathans flashed the same image.

"They're communicating!" Po Han realized. "They're trying to communicate with me!"

They are *intelligent*! Po Han knew it with undeniable certainty. An intelligent alien species.

For countless hours Po Han swam with these gentle giants in his pitifully tiny submersible. And his own fears, his own ambitions, his own resentment of his father and all the others faded into nothingness.

A new resolve filled him, a new dream. "You will show me, great ones," he whispered. "I will learn from you."

In the presence of the Leviathans, the humble dream of gaining new knowledge had taken hold of him and would never let go again.

BRILLO

by Harlan Ellison and Ben Bova

It all started with a pun.

For more than fifty years Harlan Ellison has been one of my cherished friends, even though he lives in California and I in Florida. For the first few years of our comradeship, Harlan occasionally sighed wistfully that he had never been published in the pages of Analog Science Fiction *magazine.*

Analog, *you see, was the most prestigious—and best-paying— magazine in the field of science fiction. It was (and still is) a bastion of "hard" science fiction, the kind of stuff that I write and Harlan does not. But Harlan saw his problem as deeper than that. He felt that the magazine's editor, John W. Campbell, Jr., would never publish a story written by Harlan Ellison—for personal reasons, including differences in personality, outlook, and foreskins.*

Campbell was the giant figure of the field in those days, and had been since he had become editor of the magazine in 1937, when it was called Astounding Stories.

It was now the late 1960s. Even though I assured Harlan that Campbell would buy any story he liked, no matter who wrote it, Harlan remained convinced that John would never publish a story he had written. So Harlan and I concocted a plot. We would write a story together, put a penname on it, and sell it to Campbell.

Since we lived so far apart, in those days before home computers and modems and fax machines, work on our story progressed slowly. We decided it would be about two police officers: one very human and one a robot that was programmed to know only the law and infractions thereof.

The robot would have no human traits such as mercy or judgment. Casting about for a name for the robot, I punned:

"Brillo—that's what we should call metal fuzz." (In those days "fuzz" was a slang term for "police.")

Although he denies it vigorously to this very day, Harlan laughed uproariously at my pun, and we agreed to title the story "Brillo."

Then came the writing. I flew out to the West Coast on other business, and Harlan and I arranged to meet one evening to start writing the story. We had already exchanged notes about the major characters and the background setting. This one evening would be devoted to writing as much of the story's first draft as we could.

I finished my day's work and arrived at Harlan's home in Sherman Oaks near sunset, ready to work. But Harlan was ready for dinner, instead.

He took me, and his current girlfriend, to a Cecil B. DeMille-type restaurant somewhere deep in Beverly Hills. The place was jammed. It looked like a mob scene out of The Ten Commandments. *Not to worry. The maitre d' spotted Harlan in the crowd and personally ushered us to the best table in the place. No waiting. He even sent over a complimentary bottle of fine red wine.*

It was nearly ten o'clock by the time we got back to Harlan's place and down to work. Only to discover that we both had the runs. Something in the food had afflicted us sorely.

But we are professional writers. We wrote the first draft of our story, one painful paragraph at a time. One paragraph was about as long as either one of us could stay out of the bathroom. We would meet each other in the hallway between the john and the typewriter.

By dawn's bleary light we were exhausted, in more ways than one. And we had roughly five thousand words of first draft on paper.

I flew back home to Massachusetts, where I lived at the time. Months passed.

At the Cleveland airport, as I was waiting for my plane home after another business trip, I was paged. None other than Harlan, who excitedly read me the fifteen-thousand-word second draft of "Brillo," while my plane was loaded up and taxied off without me.

It was beautiful and I told Harlan so. It is essentially the story you will read here.

"Campbell will love it!" I said.

"It's too good for Campbell!" Harlan replied. "Let's send it to Playboy!"

Playboy *paid ten times what Analog did. We are, as I pointed out earlier, professional writers. So we instructed our mutual agent to send "Brillo" to Playboy.*

More months passed. It is now Christmas Eve. I am sitting in my office at the laboratory, where I worked as the manager of the marketing department (i.e., resident science-fiction writer). Four p.m. and already pitch dark outside. Snow is sifting past my window. The office Christmas party is about to begin.

My phone rings. Harlan.

Not only has Playboy *rejected our story (they had published a story about a robot the year before, and felt that was as far out as they could go then), but our mutual agent automatically sent the manuscript to the next best market—John C. Campbell, Jr.—with Harlan's name still on it! (And mine too, of course.)*

Harlan was in despair. He knew Campbell would tear the manuscript into tiny pieces and dance a Highland fling on the scraps. Would I pu-leeze call John and put in a personal word for the story? I told Harlan that John Campbell would never be swayed by pleading; either he liked the story or he didn't.

But Harlan pleaded with me, so I reluctantly phoned Campbell's office, hoping deep in my heart that he would not be there.

He was there. "Oh, it's you," he said. My heart sank.

But then John proceeded to tell me that he had just read "Brillo" and wanted to buy it. He even explained what the story was really about, something that he was certain its authors did not understand. (John was like that. Often he was right.) He asked for a couple of very minor revisions, but he wanted to publish "Brillo"!

I got off the phone as gracefully as I could and quickly dialed Harlan. For some devilish reason I decided to give Harlan somewhat the same treatment Campbell had just given me.

"Harlan, it's me, Ben."

A dull, dispirited grunt.

"I . . . uh, I talked with John."

A moan.

"And he . . . well, he's read the story . . ."

A groan.

"And, uh . . . well, what can I say, Harlan? He wants to buy it."

For several seconds, there was no sound whatever from Harlan's end of the phone. Then a squawk that could have shattered a diamond.

"He's buying it?" All sorts of screeching and howling noises that might have been some exotic form of merriment. "He's buying it?"

So we had a happy Christmas and "Brillo" was published in the August 1970 issue of Analog.

Harlan still thinks that Campbell thought I had done most of the writing. As you will clearly be able to see, "Brillo" is written in Harlan's style, not mine. John Campbell was smart enough to know the difference—and not care.

Like several other tales in this book, "Brillo" deals with the differences between what we say we want from the criminal justice system and what we really want. The differences between the everyday pieties that we all give lip service to, and the realities of how we actually behave toward the police.

Oh, yes! After the story was published, Harlan and I were approached by certain parties who wanted to turn "Brillo" into a TV series. That project ended in a plagiarism suit that terminated only after four years of lawyers and a month-long trial in a Federal District courtroom in Los Angeles. I can't tell you much about the case, because one of the terms of the eventual settlement was that neither Harlan nor I can write or speak about it—unless we are asked direct questions.

So read "Brillo." And ask me questions.

CRAZY SEASON FOR COPS is August. In August the riots start. Not just to get the pigs off campus (where they don't even happen to be, because school is out) or to rid the railroad flats of *Rattus norvegicus*, but they start for no reason at all. Some bunch of sweat-stinking kids get a hydrant spouting and it drenches the storefront of a shylock who lives most of his time in Kipps Bay when he's not sticking it to his Spanish Harlem customers, and he comes out of the pawnshop with a Louisville Slugger somebody hocked once, and he takes a swing at a mestizo urchin, and the next thing the precinct knows, they've got a three-star riot going on two full city blocks; then they call in the cop choppers from Governor's Island and spray the neighborhood with quiescent, and after a while the beat cops go in with breathers, in threes, and they start pulling in the bash-head cases. Why did it get going? A little water on a store window that hadn't been squeegee'd since 1974? A short temper? Some kid flipping some guy the bird? No.

Crazy season is August.

Housewives take their steam irons to their old men's heads. Basset hound salesmen who trundle display suitcases full of ready-to-wear for eleven months, without squeaking at their bosses, suddenly pull twine knives and carve up taxi drivers. Suicides go out tenth storey windows and off the Verrazano-Narrows Bridge like confetti at an astronaut's parade down Fifth Avenue. Teenaged rat packs steal half a dozen cars and drag-race them three abreast against traffic up White Plains Road till they run them through the show windows of supermarkets. No reason. Just August. Crazy season.

It was August, that special heat of August when the temperature keeps going till it reaches the secret kill-crazy mugginess at which point eyeballs roll up white in florid faces and gravity knives appear as if by magic. It was that time of August, when Brillo arrived in the precinct.

Buzzing softly (the sort of sound an electric watch makes), it stood inert in the center of the precinct station's bullpen, its bright blue-anodized metal a gleaming contrast to the paintless worn floorboards. It stood in the middle of momentary activity, and no one who passed it seemed to be able to pay attention to anything but it:

Not the two plainclothes officers duckwalking between them a sixty-two-year-old pervert whose specialty was flashing just before the subway doors closed.

Not the traffic cop being berated by his Sergeant for having allowed his parking ticket receipts to get waterlogged in a plastic bag bombardment initiated by the last few residents of a condemned building.

Not the tac/squad macers reloading their weapons from the supply dispensers.

Not the line of beat cops forming up in ranks for their shift on the street.

Not the Desk Sergeant trying to book three hookers who had been arrested soliciting men queued up in front of NBC for a network game show called "Sell A Sin."

Not the fuzzette using a wrist bringalong on the mugger who had tried to snip a cutpurse on her as she patrolled Riverside Drive.

None of them, even engaged in the hardly ordinary business of sweeping up felons, could avoid staring at it. All eyes kept returning to the robot: a squat cylinder resting on tiny trunnions. Brillo's optical sensors, up in his dome-shaped head, bulged like the eyes of an arcromegalic insect. The eyes caught the glint of the overhead neons.

The eyes, particularly, made the crowd in the muster room nervous. The crowd milled and thronged, but did not clear until the Chief of Police spread his hands in a typically Semitic gesture of impatience and yelled, "All right, already, can you clear this room!"

There was suddenly a great deal of unoccupied space.

Chief Santorini turned back to the robot. And to Reardon.

Frank Reardon shifted his weight uneasily from one foot to the other. He absorbed the Police Chief's look and tracked it out around the muster room, watching the men who were watching the robot. His robot. Not that he owned it any longer, but he still thought of it as his. He understood how Dr. Victor Frankenstein could feel paternal about a congeries of old spare body parts.

He watched them as they sniffed around the robot like bulldogs delighted with the discovery of a new fire hydrant. Even beefy Sergeant Loyo, the Desk Sergeant, up in his perch at the far end of the shabby room, looked clearly suspicious of the robot.

Santorini had brought two uniformed Lieutenants with him. Administrative assistants. Donkeywork protocol guardians. By-the-book civil service types, lamps lit against any evil encroachment of dat ole debbil machine into the paydirt of human beings' job security. They looked grim.

The FBI man sat impassively on a stout wooden bench that ran the length of the room. He sat under posters for the Police Athletic League, the 4th War Bond Offensive, Driver Training Courses and an advertisement for *The Christian Science Monitor* with a FREE—TAKE ONE pocket attached. He had not said a word since being introduced to Reardon. And Reardon had even forgotten his name. Was that part of the camouflage of FBI agents? He sat there looking steely-eyed and jut-jawed. He looked grim, too.

Only the whiz kid from the Mayor's office was smiling as he stepped once again through the grilled door into the bullpen. He smiled as he walked slowly all around the robot. He smiled as he touched the matte-finish of the machine, and he smiled as he made pleasure noises: as if he was inspecting a new car on a showroom floor, on the verge of saying, "I'll take it. What terms can I get?"

He looked out through the wirework of the bullpen at Reardon. "Why do you call it Brillo?"

Reardon hesitated a moment, trying desperately to remember the whiz kid's first name. He was an engineer, not a public relations man. Universal Electronics should have sent Wendell down with Brillo. He knew how to talk to these image-happy clowns from City Hall. Knew how to butter and baste them so they put ink to contract. But part of the deal when he'd been forced to sell Reardon Electronics into merger with UE (after the stock raid and the power grab, which he'd lost) was that he stay on with projects like Brillo. Stay with them all the way to the bottom line.

It was as pleasant as clapping time while your wife made love to another man.

"It's . . . a nickname. Somebody at UE thought it up. Thought it was funny."

The whiz kid looked blank. "What's funny about Brillo?"

"Metal fuzz," the Police Chief rasped.

Light dawned on the whiz kid's face, and he began to chuckle; Reardon nodded, then caught the look of animosity on the Police Chief's face. Reardon looked away quickly from the old man's fiercely seamed features. It was getting more grim, much tenser.

Captain Summit came slowly down the stairs to join them. He was close to Reardon's age, but much grayer. He moved with one hand on the banister, like an old man.

Why do they all look so tired? Reardon wondered. *And why do they seem to look wearier, more frightened, every time they look at the robot? Are they afraid it's come around their turn to be replaced? Is that the way I looked when they forced me out of the company I created?*

Summit eyed the robot briefly, walked over and sat down on the bench several feet apart from the silent FBI man. The whiz kid came out of the bullpen. They all looked at Summit.

"Okay, I've picked a man to work with him . . . it, I mean." He was looking at Reardon. "Mike Polchik. He's a good cop; young and alert. Good record. Nothing extraordinary, no showboater, just a solid cop. He'll give your machine a fair trial."

"That's fine. Thank you, Captain," Reardon said.

"He'll be right down. I pulled him out of the formation. He's getting his gear. He'll be right down."

The whiz kid cleared his throat. Reardon looked at him. He wasn't tired. But then, he didn't wear a uniform. He wasn't pushed up against what these men found in the streets every day. He lives in Darien, probably, Frank Reardon thought, and buys those suits in quiet little shops where there are never more than three customers at a time.

"How many of these machines can your company make in a year?" the whiz kid asked.

"It's not my company any more."

"I mean the company you work for—Universal."

"Inside a year: we can have them coming out at a rate of a hundred a month." Reardon paused. "Maybe more."

The whiz kid grinned. "We could replace every beat patrolman—"

A spark-gap was leaped. The temperature dropped. Reardon saw the uniformed men stiffen. Quickly, he said, "Police robots are intended to augment the existing force." Even more firmly he said, "Not replace it. We're trying to help the policeman, not get rid of him."

"Oh, hey, sure. Of course!" the whiz kid said, glancing around the room.

"That's what I meant," he added unnecessarily. Everyone knew what he meant.

The silence at the bottom of the Marianas Trench.

And in that silence: heavy footsteps, coming down the stairs from the second-floor locker rooms.

He stopped at the foot of the stairs, one shoe tipped up on the final step; he stared at the robot in the bullpen for a long moment. Then the patrolman walked over to Captain Summit, only once more casting a glance into the bullpen. Summit smiled reassuringly at the patrolman and then gestured toward Reardon.

"Mike, this is Mr. Reardon. He designed—the robot. Mr. Reardon, Patrolman Polchik."

Reardon extended his hand and Polchik exerted enough pressure to make him wince.

Polchik was two inches over six feet tall, and weighty. Muscular, thick forearms; the kind found on men who work in foundries. Light, crewcut hair. Square face, wide open; strong jaw, hard eyes under heavy brow ridges. Even his smile looked hard. He was ready for work, with a .32 Needle Positive tilt-stuck on its velcro fastener at mid-thigh and an armament bandolier slanted across his broad chest. His aura keyed one word: cop.

"The Captain tells me I'm gonna be walkin' with your machine t'night."

Nodding, flexing his fingers, Reardon said, "Yes, that's right. The Captain probably told you, we want to test Brillo under actual foot patrol conditions. That's what he was designed for: foot patrol."

"Been a long time since I done foot patrol," Polchik said. "Work a growler, usually."

"Beg pardon?"

Summit translated. "Growler: prowl car."

"Oh. Oh, I see," Reardon said, trying to be friendly. "It's only for tonight, Mike," the Captain said. "Just a test."

Polchik nodded as though he understood far more than either Reardon or Summit had told him. He did not turn his big body, but his eyes went to the robot. Through the grillwork Brillo (with the sort of sound an electric watch makes) buzzed softly, staring at nothing. Polchik looked it up and down, slowly, very carefully. Finally he said, "Looks okay to me."

"Preliminary tests," Reardon said, "everything short of actual field runs . . . everything's been tested out. You won't have any trouble."

Polchik murmured something.

"I beg your pardon?" Frank Reardon said.

"On-the-job-training," Polchik repeated. He did not smile. But a sound ran through the rest of the station house crew.

"Well, whenever you're ready, Officer Polchik," the whiz kid said suddenly. Reardon winced. The kid had a storm-window salesman's tone even when he was trying to be disarming.

"Yeah. Right." Polchik moved toward the front door. The robot did not move. Polchik stopped and turned around. Everyone was watching.

"I thought he went on his own, uh, independent?"

They were all watching Reardon now.

"He's been voice-keyed to me since the plant," Reardon said. "To shift command, I'll have to prime him with your voice." He turned to the robot. "Brillo, come here, please."

The word *please*.

The buzzing became more distinct for a moment as the trunnions withdrew inside the metal skin. Then the sound diminished, became barely audible, and the robot stepped forward smoothly. He walked to Reardon and stopped.

"Brillo, this is Officer Mike Polchik. You'll be working with him tonight. He'll be your superior and you'll be under his immediate orders."

Reardon waved Polchik over. "Would you say a few words, so he can program your voice-print?"

Polchik looked at Reardon. Then he looked at the robot. Then he looked around the muster room. Desk Sergeant Loyo was grinning. "Whattaya want me to say?"

"Anything."

One of the detectives had come down the stairs. No one had noticed before. Lounging against the railing leading to the squad room upstairs, he giggled. "Tell him some'a your best friends are can openers, Mike."

The whiz kid and the Chief of Police threw him a look. Summit said, "Bratten!" He shut up. After a moment he went back upstairs. Quietly.

"Go ahead. Anything," Reardon urged Polchik.

The patrolman drew a deep breath, took another step forward and said, self-consciously, "Come on, let's go. It's gettin' late."

The soft buzzing (the sort of sound an electric watch makes) came once again from somewhere deep inside the robot. "Yes, sir," he said, in the voice of Frank Reardon, and moved very smoothly, very quickly, toward Polchik. The patrolman stepped back quickly, tried to look casual, turned and started toward the door of the station house once more. The robot followed.

When they had gone, the whiz kid drywashed his hands, smiled at everyone and said, "Now it begins."

Reardon winced again. The Desk Sergeant, Loyo, rattled pencils, tapped them even, dumped them into an empty jelly jar on the blotter desk. Everyone else looked away. The FBI man smiled.

From outside the precinct house the sounds of the city seemed to grow louder in the awkward silence. In all that noise no one even imagined he could hear the sound of the robot.

Polchik was trying the locks on the burglarproof gates of the shops lining Amsterdam between 82nd and 83rd. The robot was following him, doing the same thing. Polchik was getting burned up. He turned up 83rd and entered the alley behind the shops, retracing his steps back toward 82nd. The robot followed him.

Polchik didn't like being followed. It made him feel uneasy. *Damned piece of junk!* he thought. *He rips one of them gates off the hinges, there'll be hell to pay down at the precinct.*

Polchik rattled a gate. He moved on. The robot followed. (*Like a little kid,* Polchik thought.) The robot grabbed the gate and clanged it back and forth. Polchik spun on him. "Listen, dammit, stop makin' all that racket! Y'wanna wake everybody? You know what time it is?"

"1:37 a.m.," the robot replied, in Reardon's voice.

Polchik looked heavenward.

Shaking his head he moved on. The robot stopped. "Officer Polchik."

Mike Polchik turned, exasperated. What now?

"I detect a short circuit in this alarm system," the robot said. He was standing directly under the Morse Dictograph Security panel. "If it is not repaired, it will cancel the fail-safe circuits."

"I'll call it in," Polchik said, pulling the pin-mike on its spring-return wire from his callbox. He was about to thumb on the wristband callbox, when the robot extruded an articulated arm from its chest. "I am equipped to repair the unit without assistance," the robot said, and a light-beam began to pulse at the end of the now-goosenecked arm.

"Leave it alone!"

"A simple 155-0 system," the robot said. "Fixed temperature unit with heat detectors, only barely exceeding NFPA standard 74 and NFPA 72-A requirements." The arm snaked up to the panel and followed the break line around the outside.

"Don't screw with it! It'll set it—"

The panel accordion-folded back. Polchik's mouth fell open. "Oh my God," he mumbled.

The robot's extruded arm worked inside for a long moment, then withdrew. "It is fully operable now." The panel folded back into place.

Polchik let the pin-mike slip from his fingers and it zzzzz'd back into the wristband. He walked away down the alley, looking haunted.

Down at the corner, the Amsterdam Inn's lights shone weakly, reflecting dully in the street oil slick. Polchik paused at the mouth of the alley and pulled out the pin-mike again. He thumbed the callbox on his wrist, feeling the heavy shadow of the robot behind him.

"Polchik," he said into the mike.

"Okay, Mike?" crackled the reply. "How's yer partner doing?"

Glancing over his shoulder, Polchik saw the robot standing impassively, gooseneck arm vanished, ten feet behind him. Respectfully.

"Don't call it my partner."

Laughter on the other end of the line. "What's'a'matter, Mike? 'Fraid of him?"

"Ahhh . . . cut the clownin'. Everything quiet here, Eighty-two and Amsterdam."

"Okay. Oh, hey, Mike, remember . . . if it starts to rain, get yer partner under an awning before he starts t'rust!"

He was still laughing like a jackass as Polchik let the spring-wire zzzzz back into the callbox.

"Hey, Mike! What you got there?"

Polchik looked toward the corner. It was Rico, the bartender from the Amsterdam Inn.

"It's a robot," Polchik said. He kept his voice very flat. He was in no mood for further ribbing.

"Real he is, yeah? No kidding?" Rico's face always looked to Polchik like a brass artichoke, ready to be peeled. But he was friendly enough. And cooperative.

It was a dunky neighborhood and Polchik had found Rico useful more than once.

"What's he supposed to do, eh?"

"He's supposed to be a cop." Glum.

Rico shook his vegetable head. "What they gonna do next? Robots. So what happens t'you, Mike? They make you a detective?"

"Sure. And the week after that they make me Captain."

Rico looked uncertain, didn't know whether he should laugh or sympathize. Finally, he said, "Hey, I got a bottle for ya," feeling it would serve, whatever his reaction should properly have been. "Betcha your wife likes it. From Poland, imported stuff. Got grass or weeds or some kinda stuff in it. S'possed to be really sensational."

For just a second, peripherally seen, Polchik thought the robot had stirred.

"*Escuchar!* I'll get it for you."

Rico disappeared inside the bar before Polchik could stop him. The robot *did* move. It trembled . . .

Rico came out with a paper bag, its neck twisted close around what was obviously a bottle of liquor.

"I'll have to pick it up tomorrow," Polchik said. "I don't have the car tonight."

"I'll keep it for you. If I'm on relief when you come by, ask Maldonado."

The robot was definitely humming. Polchik could hear it. (The sort of sound an electric watch makes.) It suddenly moved, closing the distance, ten feet between them, till it passed Polchik, swiveled to face Rico—who stumbled backward halfway to the entrance to the Amsterdam Inn—then swiveled back to face Polchik.

"Visual and audio data indicate a one-to-one extrapolation of same would result in a conclusion that a gratuity has been offered to you, Officer Polchik. Further, logic indicates that you intend to accept said gratuity. Such behavior is a programmed infraction of the law. It is—"

"Shut up!"

Rico stood very close to the door, wide-eyed.

"I'll see you tomorrow night," Polchik said to him.

"Officer Polchik," the robot went on as though there had been no interruption, "it is clear if you intend to accept a gratuity, you will be breaking the law and liable to arrest and prosecution under Law Officer Statutes number—"

"I said shuddup, dammit!" Polchik said, louder. "I don't even know what the hell you're talkin' about, but I said shuddup, and that's an order!"

"Yes, sir," the robot replied instantly. "However, my data tapes will record this conversation in its entirety and it will be transcribed into a written report at the conclusion of our patrol."

"What?" Polchik felt gears gnashing inside his head, thought of gears, thought of the robot, rejected gears and thought about Captain Summit. Then he thought about gears again . . . crushing him.

Rico's voice intruded, sounding scared. "What's he saying? What's that about a report?"

"Now wait a minute, Brillo," Polchik said, walking up to the robot. "Nothin's happened here you can write a report on."

The robot's voice—Reardon's voice, Polchik thought irritatedly—was very firm. "Logic indicates a high probability that a gratuity has been accepted in the past, and another will be accepted in the future."

Polchik felt chili peppers in his gut. Hooking his thumbs in his belt—a pose he automatically assumed when he was trying to avert trouble—he deliberately toned down his voice. "Listen, Brillo, you forget the whole thing, you understand. You just forget it."

"Am I to understand you desire my tapes to be erased?"

"Yeah, that's right. Erase it."

"Is that an order?"

"It's an order!"

The robot hummed to itself for a heartbeat, then, "Primary programming does not allow erasure of data tapes. Tapes can be erased only post-transcription or by physically removing same from my memory bank."

"Listen—" Rico started, "—I don't wan' no trub—"

Polchik impatiently waved him to silence. He didn't need any complications right now. "Listen, Brillo . . ."

"Yes. I hear it."

Polchik was about to continue speaking. He stopped. I hear it? This damned thing's gone bananas. "I didn't say anything yet."

"Oh. I'm sorry, sir. I thought you were referring to the sound of a female human screaming on 84th Street, third-floor front apartment."

Polchik looked every whichway. "What are you talkin' about? You crazy or something?"

"No, sir. I am a model X-44. Though under certain special conditions my circuits can malfunction, conceivably, nothing in my repair programming parameters approximates 'crazy.'"

"Then just shuddup and let's get this thing straightened out. Now, try'n understand this. You're just a robot, see. You don't understand the way real people do things. Like, for instance, when Rico here offers me a bottle of—"

"If you'll pardon me, sir, the female human is now screaming in the 17,000 cycle-per-second range. My tapes are programmed to value-judge such a range as concomitant with fear and possibly extreme pain. I suggest we act at once."

"Hey, Polchik," Rico began.

"No, shuddup, Rico. Hey, listen, robot, Brillo, whatever: you mean you can hear some woman screaming, two blocks away and up three flights? Is the window open?" Then he stopped. "What'm I doin'? Talking to this thing!" He remembered the briefing he'd been given by Captain Summit. "Okay. You say you can hear her . . . let's find her."

The robot took off at top speed. Back into the alley behind the Amsterdam Inn, across the 82nd-83rd block, across the 83rd-84th block, full-out with no clanking or clattering. Polchik found himself pounding along ten feet behind the robot, then twenty feet, then thirty feet; suddenly he was puffing, his chest heavy, the armament bandolier banging the mace cans and the riot-prod and the bullhorn and the peppergas shpritzers and the extra clips of needler ammunition against his chest and back.

The robot emerged from the alley, turned a ninty-degree angle with the sharpest cut Polchik had ever seen, and jogged up 84th Street. Brillo was caught for a moment in the glare of a neon streetlamp, then was taking the steps of a crippled old brownstone three at a time.

Troglodytes with punch-presses were berkeleying Polchik's lungs and stomach. His head was a dissenter's punchboard. But he followed. More slowly now; and had trouble negotiating the last flight of stairs to the third floor. As he gained the landing, he was hauling himself hand-over-hand up the banister. If God'd wanted cops to walk beats he wouldn't 'a created the growler!

The robot, Brillo, X-44, was standing in front of the door marked 3-A. He was quivering like a hound on point. (Buzzing softly with the sort of sound an electric watch makes.)

Now Polchik could hear the woman himself, above the roar of blood in his temples.

"Open up in there!" Polchik bellowed. He ripped the .32 Needle Positive off its Velcro fastener and banged on the door with the butt. The lanyard was twisted; he untwisted it. "This's the police. I'm demanding entrance to a private domicile under Public Law 22-809, allowing for superced'nce of the 'home-castle' rule under emergency conditions. I said open up in there!"

The screaming went up and plateau'd a few hundred cycles higher, and Polchik snapped at the robot, "Get outta my way."

Brillo obediently moved back a pace, and in the narrow hallway Polchik braced himself against the wall, locked the exoskeletal rods on his boots, dropped his crash-hat visor, jacked up his leg and delivered a powerful savate kick at the door.

It was a pre-SlumClear apartment. The door bowed and dust spurted from the seams, but it held. Despite the rods, Polchik felt a searing pain gash up through his leg. He fell back, hopping about painfully, hearing himself going, "oo-oo-oo" and then prepared himself to have to do it again. The robot moved up in front of him, said, "Excuse me, sir," and smoothly cleaved the door down the center with the edge of a metal hand that had somehow suddenly developed a cutting edge. He reached in, grasped both sliced edges of the hardwood, and ripped the door outward in two even halves.

"Oh." Polchik stared open-mouthed for only an instant. Then they were inside.

The unshaven man with the beer gut protruding from beneath his olive drab skivvy undershirt was slapping the hell out of his wife. He had thick black tufts of hair that bunched like weed corsages in his armpits. She was half-lying over the back of a sofa with the springs showing. Her eyes were swollen and blue-black as dried prunes. One massive bruise was already draining down her cheek into her neck. She was weakly trying to fend off her husbands blows with ineffectual wrist-blocks.

"Okay! That's it!" Polchik yelled.

The sound of another voice, in the room with them, brought the man and his wife to a halt. He turned his head, his left hand still tangled in her long black hair, and he stared at the two intruders.

He began cursing in Spanish. Then he burst into a guttural combination of English and Spanish, and finally slowed in his own spittle to a ragged English. " . . . won't let me alone . . . go out my house . . . always botherin' won't let me alone . . . damn . . ." and he went back to Spanish as he pushed the woman from him and started across the room.

The woman tumbled, squealing, out of sight behind the sofa.

The man stumbled crossing the room, and Polchik's needler tracked him. Behind him he heard the robot softly humming, and then it said, "Sir, analysis indicates psychotic glaze over subject's eyes."

The man grabbed a half-filled quart bottle of beer off the television set, smashed it against the leading edge of the TV, giving it a half-twist (which registered instantly in Polchik's mind: this guy knew how to get a ragged edge on the weapon; he was an experienced barroom brawler) and suddenly lurched toward Polchik with the jagged stump in his hand.

Abruptly, before Polchik could even thumb the needler to stun (it was on dismember), a metal blur passed him, swept into the man, lifted him high in the air with one hand, turned him upside-down so the bottle, small plastic change and an unzipped shoe showered down onto the threadbare rug. Arms and legs fluttered helplessly.

"Aieeee!" the man screamed, his hair hanging down, his face plugged red with blood. "Madre de dios!"

"Leave him alone!" It was the wife screaming, charging—if it could be called that, on hands and knees—from behind the sofa. She clambered to her feet and ran at the robot, screeching and cursing, pounding her daywork-reddened fists against his gleaming hide.

"Okay, okay," Polchik said, his voice lower but strong enough to get through to her. Pulling her and her hysteria away from the robot, he ordered, "Brillo, put him down."

"You goddam cops got no right bustin' in here," the man started complaining the moment he was on his feet again. "Goddam cops don't let a man'n his wife alone for nothin' no more. You got a warrant? Huh? You gonna get in trouble, plenty trouble. This my home, cop, 'home is a man's castle,' hah? Right? Right? An' you an' this tin can." He was waving his arms wildly.

Brillo wheeled a few inches toward the man. The stream of abuse cut off instantly, the man's face went pale, and he threw up his hands to protect himself.

"This man can be arrested for assault and battery, failure to heed a legitimate police order, attempted assault on a police officer with a deadly weapon, and disturbing the peace," Brillo said. His flat, calm voice seemed to echo off the grimy walls.

"It . . . it's talkin'! Flavio! Demonio!" The wife spiraled toward hysteria again.

"Shall I inform him of his rights under the Public Laws, sir?" Brillo asked Polchik.

"You gon' arrest me? Whu'for?"

"Brillo . . ." Polchik began.

Brillo started again, "Assault and battery, failure to—"

Polchik looked annoyed. "Shuddup, I wasn't asking you to run it again. Just shuddup."

"I din't do nothin'! You come bust t'rough my door when me an' my wife wass arguin', an' you beat me up. Look'a the bruise on my arm."

The arm was slightly inflamed where Brillo had grabbed him.

"Flavio!" the woman whimpered.

"Isabel, cállete la boca!"

"I live right downstairs," a voice said from behind them. "He's always beating her up, and he drinks all the time and then he pisses out the window!" Polchik spun and a man in Levi's and striped pajama tops was standing in the ruined doorway. "Sometimes it looks like it's raining on half my window. Once I put my hand out to see—"

"Get outta here!" Polchik bellowed, and the man vanished.

"I din't do nothin'!" Flavio said again, semi-surly.

"My data tapes," Brillo replied evenly, "will clearly show your actions."

"Day to tapes? Whass he talkin 'bout?" Flavio turned to Polchik, an unaccustomed ally against the hulking machine. Polchik felt a sense of camaraderie with the man.

"He's got everything down, recorded . . . like on TV. And sound tapes, too." Polchik looked back at him and recognized something in the dismay on the man's fleshy face.

Brillo asked again, "Shall I inform him of his rights, sir?"

"Officer, sir, you ain't gonna' 'rrest him?" the woman half-asked, half-pleaded, her eyes swollen almost closed, barely open, but tearful.

"He came after me with a bottle," Polchik said. "And he didn't do you much good, neither."

"He wass work up. Iss allright. He's okay now. It wass joss a'argumen'. Nobody got hort."

Brillo's hum got momentarily higher. "Madam, you should inspect your face in my mirror." He hummed and his skin became smoothly reflective. "My sensors detect several contusions and abrasions, particularly . . ."

"Skip it," Polchik said abruptly. "Come on, Brillo, let's go."

Brillo's metal hide went blank again. "I have not informed the prisoner—"

"No prisoner," Polchik said. "No arrest. Let's go."

"But the data clearly shows—"

"Forget it!" Polchik turned to face the man; he was standing there looking uncertain, rubbing his arm. "And you, strongarm . . . lemme hear one more peep outta this apartment and you'll be in jail so fast it'll make your head swim and for a helluva long time, too. If you get there at all. We don't like guys like you. So I'm puttin' the word out on you . . . I don't like guys comin' at me with bottles."

"Sir . . . I . . ."

"Come on!"

The robot followed the cop and the apartment was suddenly silent. Flavio and Isabel looked at each other sheepishly, then he began to cry, went to her and touched her bruises with the gentlest fingers.

They went downstairs, Polchik staring and trying to figure out how it was such a massive machine could navigate the steps so smoothly. Something was going on at the base of the robot, but Polchik couldn't get a good view of it. Dust puffed out from beneath the machine. And something sparkled.

Once on the sidewalk, Brillo said, "Sir, that man should have been arrested. He was clearly violating several statutes."

Polchik made a sour face. "His wife wouldn't of pressed the charge."

"He attacked a police officer with a deadly weapon."

"So that makes him Mad Dog Coil? He's scared shitless, in the future he'll watch it. For a while, at least."

Brillo was hardly satisfied at this noncomputable conclusion. "A police officer's duty is to arrest persons who are suspected of having broken the law. Civil or criminal courts have the legal jurisdiction to decide the suspect's guilt or innocence. Your duty, sir, was to arrest that man."

"Sure, sure. Have it your way, half the damn city'll be in jail, and the other half'll be springin' 'em out."

Brillo said nothing, but Polchik thought the robot's humming sounded sullen. He had a strong suspicion the machine wouldn't forget it. Or Rico, either.

And farther up the street, to cinch Polchik's suspicion, the robot once more tried to reinforce his position. "According to the Peace Officer Responsibility Act of 1975, failure of an officer to take into custody person or persons indisputably engaged in acts that contravene . . ."

"Awright, dammit, knock it off. I tole you why I didn't arrest that poor jughead, so stop bustin' my chops with it. You ain't happy, you don't like it, tell my Sergeant!"

Sergeant, hell, Polchik thought. *This stuff goes right to Captain Summit, Santorini and the Commissioner. Probably the Mayor. Maybe the President. Who the hell knows?*

Petulantly (it seemed to Polchik), the robot resumed, "Reviewing my tapes, I find the matter of the bottle of liquor offered as a gratuity still unresolved. If I am to—"

Polchik spun left and kicked with all his might at a garbage can bolted to an iron fence. The lid sprang off and clanged against the fence at the end of its short chain. "I've had it with you . . . you nonreturnable piece of scrap crap!" He wanted very much to go on, but he didn't know what to say. All he knew for certain was that he'd never had such a crummy night in all his life. It couldn't just be this goddammed robot, staring back blankly. It was everything. The mortgage payment was due; Benjy had to go in to the orthodontist and where the hell was the money going to come from for that; Dorothy had called the precinct just before he'd come down to tell him the hot water heater had split and drowned the carpets in the kid's bedroom; and to top it all off, he'd been assigned this buzzing pain in the ass and got caught with a little juice passed by that nitwit Rico; he'd had to have this Brillo pain tell him there was a hassle two blocks away; he was sure as God made little green apples going to get a bad report out of this, maybe get set down, maybe get reprimanded, maybe get censured . . . he didn't know what all.

But one thing was certain: this metal bird-dog, this stuffed shirt barracks lawyer with the trailalong of a ten-year-old kid behind his big brother, this nuisance in metal underwear, this . . . this . . . thing was of no damned earthly use to a working cop pulling a foot beat!

On the other hand, a voice that spoke with the voice of Mike Polchik said, *he did keep that jughead from using a broken bottle on you.*

"Shuddup!" Polchik said.

"I beg your pardon?" answered the robot.

Ingrate! said the inner voice.

It was verging on that chalky hour before dawn, when the light filtering out of the sky had a leprous, sickly look. Mike Polchik was a much older man.

Brillo had interfered in the apprehension of Milky Kyser, a well-known car thief. Mike had spotted him walking slowly and contemplatively along a line of parked cars on Columbus Avenue, carrying a tightly rolled copy of the current issue of *Life* magazine.

When he had collared Milky, the robot had buzzed up to them and politely inquired precisely what in the carborundum Polchik thought he was doing. Polchik had responded with what was becoming an hysterical reaction-formation to anything the metal cop said. "Shuddup!"

Brillo had persisted, saying he was programmed to protect the civil rights of the members of the community, and as far as he could tell, having "scanned all data relevant to the situation at hand," the gentleman now dangling from Polchik's grip was spotlessly blameless of even the remotest scintilla of wrongdoing. Polchik had held Milky with one hand and with the other gesticulated wildly as he explained, "Look, dimdumb, this is Milky Kyser, AKA Irwin Kayser, AKA Clarence Irwin, AKA Jack Milk, AKA God Knows Who All. He is a well-known dip and car thief, and he will use that rolled-up copy of the magazine to jack-and-snap the door handle of the proper model car, any number of which is currently parked, you will note, along this street . . . unless I arrest him! Now will you kindly get the hell outta my hair and back off?"

But it was no use. By the time Brillo had patiently repeated the civil rights story, reiterated pertinent sections of the Peace Officer Responsibility Act of 1975 and topped it off with a précis of Miranda-Escobedo Baum Supreme Court decisions so adroit and simplified even a confirmed tautologist would have applauded, Milky himself—eyes glittering and a sneer that was hardly a smile on his ferret face—was echoing it, word for word.

The robot had given Milky a thorough course in legal cop-outs, before Polchik's dazed eyes.

"Besides," Milky told Polchik with as much dignity as he could muster, hanging as he was from the cop's meaty fist, "I ain't done nuthin', and just because I been busted once or twice—"

"Once or twice!?" Polchik yanked the rolled-up magazine out of Milky's hand and raised it to clobber him. Milky pulled in his head like a turtle, wincing.

But in that fraction of a second, Polchik suddenly saw a picture flashed on the wall of his mind. A picture of Desk Sergeant Loyo and Captain Summit and Chief Santorini and the Mayor's toady and that silent FBI man, all watching a TV screen. And on the screen, there was the pride of the Force, Officer Mike Polchik, beaning Milky Kyser with a semi-lethal copy of *Life* magazine.

Polchik held the magazine poised, trembling with the arrested movement. Milky, head now barely visible from between his shoulders, peeped up from behind his upraised hands. He looked like a mole.

"Beat it," Polchik growlled. "Get the hell out of this precinct, Milky. If you're spotted around here again, you're gonna get busted. And don't stop to buy no magazines."

He let Milky loose.

The mole metamorphosed into a ferret once more. And straightening himself, he said, "An' don't call me 'Milky' any more. My given name is Irwin."

"You got three seconds t'vanish from my sight!"

Milky, neé Irwin, hustled off down the street. At the corner he stopped and turned around. He cupped his hands and yelled back, "Hey, robot, thanks!"

Brillo was about to reply when Polchik bellowed, "Will you please!"

The robot turned and said, very softly in Reardon's voice, "You are still holding Mr. Kyser's magazine."

Polchik was weary. Infinitely weary. "You hear him askin' for it?" He walked away from the robot and, as he passed a sidewalk dispenser, stepped on the dispodpedal, and flipped the magazine into the receptacle.

"I saved a piece of cherry pie for you, Mike," the waitress said.

Polchik looked up from his uneaten hot (now cold) roast beef and french fries. He shook his head.

"Thanks anyway. Just another cuppa coffee."

The waitress had lost her way somewhere beyond twenty-seven. She was a nice person. She went home to her husband every morning. She didn't fool around. Extra mates under the new lottery were not her interest; she just didn't fool around. But she liked Mike Polchik. He, like she, was a very nice person.

"What's the matter, Mike?"

Polchik looked out the window of the diner. Brillo was standing directly under a neon streetlamp. He couldn't hear it from here, but he was sure the thing was buzzing softly to itself (with the sort of sound an electric watch makes).

"Him."

"That?" The waitress looked past him.

"Uh-uh. Him."

"What is it?"

"My shadow."

"Mike, you okay? Try the pie, huh? Maybe a scoop of nice vanilla ice cream on top."

"Onita, please. Just a cuppa coffee. I'm fine. I got problems." He stared down at his plate again.

She looked at him for a moment longer, worried, then turned and returned the pie on its plate to the empty space behind the smudged glass of the display case. "You want fresh?" she asked.

When he didn't answer, she shrugged and came back, using the coffee siphon on the portable cart to refill his cup.

She lounged behind the counter, watching her friend, Mike Polchik, as he slowly drank his coffee; and every few minutes he'd look out at that metal thing on the corner under the streetlamp.

She was a nice person.

When he rose from the booth and came to the counter, she thought he was going to apologize, or speak to her, or something, but all he said was, "You got my check?"

"What check?"

"Come on."

"Oh, Mike, for Christ's sake, what's wrong with you?"

"I want to pay the check; you mind?"

"Mike, almost—what—five years you been eating here, you ever been asked to pay a check?"

Polchik looked very tired. "Tonight I pay the check. Come on . . . I gotta get back on the street. He's waiting."

There was a strange look in his eyes, and she didn't want to ask which "he" Polchik meant. She was afraid he meant the metal thing out there. Onita, a very nice person, didn't like strange new things that waited under neon streetlamps. She hastily wrote out a check and slid it across the counter to him. He pulled change from a pocket, paid her, turned back, added a tip, then swiftly left the diner.

She watched through the glass as he went up to the metal thing. Then the two of them walked away, Mike leading, the thing following.

Onita made fresh. It was a good thing she had done it so many times she could do it by reflex, without thinking. Hot coffee scalds are very painful.

At the corner, Polchik saw a car weaving toward the intercection. A Ford electric, convertible, four years old. Still looked flashy. Top down. He could see a bunch of long-haired kids inside. He couldn't tell the girls from the boys. It bothered him.

Polchik stopped. They weren't going too fast, but the car was definitely weaving as it approached the intersection. *The warrior-lizard,* he thought. It was almost an unconscious directive. He'd been a cop long enough to react to the little hints, the flutters, the inclinations. The hunches.

Polchik stepped out from the curb, unshipped his gumball from the bandolier and flashed the red light at the driver. The car slowed even more; now it was crawling.

"Pull it over, kid!" he shouted.

For a moment he thought they were ignoring him, that the driver might not have heard him, that they'd try and make a break for it . . . that they'd speed up and sideswipe him. But the driver eased the car to the curb and stopped. Then he slid sidewise, pulled up his legs and crossed them neatly at the ankles. On the top of the dashboard.

Polchik walked around to the driver's side. "Turn it off. Everybody out."

There were six of them. None of them moved. The driver closed his eyes slowly, then tipped his Irkutsk fur hat over his eyes till it rested on the bridge of his nose. Polchik reached into the car and turned it off. He pulled the keys.

"Hey! Whuzzis allabout?" one of the kids in the back seat—a boy with terminal acne—complained. His voice began and ended on a whine. Polchik re-stuck the gumball.

The driver looked up from under the fur. "Wasn't breaking any laws." He said each word very slowly, very distinctly, as though each one was on a printout.

And Polchik knew he'd been right. They were on the lizard.

He opened the door, free hand hanging at the needler. "Out. All of you, out."

Then he sensed Brillo lurking behind him, in the middle of the street. *Good. Hope a damned garbage truck hits him.*

He was getting mad. That wasn't smart. Carefully, he said, "Don't make me say it again. Move it!"

He lined them up on the sidewalk beside the car, in plain sight. Three girls, three guys. Two of the guys with long, stringy hair and the third with a scalplock. The three girls wearing tammy cuts. All six sullen- faced, drawn, dark smudges under the eyes. The lizard. But good clothes, fairly new. He couldn't just hustle them, he had to be careful.

"Okay, one at a time, empty your pockets and pouches onto the hood of the car."

"Hey, we don't haveta do that just because . . ."

"Do it!"

"Don't argue with the pig," one of the girls said, lizard-spacing her words carefully. "He's probably trigger-happy."

Brillo rolled up to Polchik. "It is necessary to have a probable cause clearance from the precinct in order to search, sir."

"Not on a stop'n'frisk," Polchik snapped, not taking his eyes off them. He had no time for nonsense with the can of cogs. He kept his eyes on the growing collection of chits, change, code-keys, combs, nail files, toke pipes and miscellanea being dumped on the Ford's hood.

"There must be grounds for suspicion even in a spot search action, sir," Brillo said.

"There's grounds. Narcotics."

"Nar . . . you must be outtayer mind," said the one boy who slurred his words. He was working something other than the lizard.

"That's a pig for you," said the girl who had made the trigger-happy remark.

"Look," Polchik said, "you snots aren't from around here. Odds are good if I run h&b tests on you, we'll find you're under the influence of the lizard."

"Heyyyy!" the driver said. "The what?"

"Warrior-lizard," Polchik said.

"Oh, ain't he the jive thug," the smartmouth girl said. "He's a word user. I'll bet he knows all the current rage phrases. A philologist. I'll bet he knows all the solecisms and colloquialisms, catch phrases, catachreses, nicknames and vulgarisms. The 'warrior-lizard,' indeed."

Damned college kids, Polchik fumed inwardly. They always try to make you feel stupid; I coulda gone to college—if I didn't have to work. Money, they probably always had money. The little bitch.

The driver giggled. "Are you trying to tell me, Mella, my dear, that this Peace Officer is accusing us of being under the influence of the illegal Bolivian drug commonly called Guerrera-Tuera?" He said it with pinpointed scorn, pronouncing the Spanish broadly: gwuhr are-uh too-err-uh.

Brillo said, "Reviewing my semantic tapes, sir, I find no analogs for 'Guerrera-Tuera' as 'warrior-lizard.' True, guerrero in Spanish means warrior, but the closest spelling I find is the feminine noun guerra, which translates as war. Neither guerrera nor tuera appear in the Spanish language. If tuera is a species of lizard, I don't seem to find it—"

Polchik had listened dumbly. The weight on his shoulders was monstrous. All of them were on him. The kids, that lousy stinking robot—they were making fun, such fun, such damned fun of him! "Keep digging," he directed them. He was surprised to hear his words emerge as a series of croaks.

"And blood and breath tests must be administered, sir—"

"Stay the hell outta this!"

"We're on our way home from a party," said the boy with the scalplock, who had been silent till then. "We took a shortcut and got lost."

"Sure," Polchik said. "In the middle of Manhattan, you got lost." He saw a small green bottle dumped out of the last girl's pouch. She was trying to push it under other items. "What's that?"

"Medicine," she said. Quickly. Very quickly.

Everyone tensed.

"Let me see it." His voice was even.

He put out his hand for the bottle but all six watched his other hand, hanging beside the needler. Hesitantly, the girl picked the bottle out of the mass of goods on the car's hood, and handed him the plastic container.

Brillo said, "I am equipped with chemical sensors and reference tapes in my memory bank enumerating common narcotics. I can analyze the suspected medicine."

The six stared wordlessly at the robot. They seemed almost afraid to acknowledge its presence.

Polchik handed the plastic bottle to the robot.

Brillo depressed a color-coded key on a bank set flush into his left forearm, and a panel that hadn't seemed to be there a moment before slid down in the robot's chest. He dropped the plastic bottle into the opening and the panel slid up. He stood and buzzed.

"You don't have to open the bottle?" Polchik asked.

"No, sir."

"Oh."

The robot continued buzzing. Polchik felt stupid, just standing and watching. After a few moments the kids began to smirk, then to grin, then to chuckle openly, whispering among themselves. The smartmouthed girl giggled viciously. Polchik felt fifteen years old again; awkward, pimply, the butt of secret jokes among the long-legged high school girls in their miniskirts who had been so terrifyingly aloof he had never even considered asking them out. He realized with some shame that he despised these kids with their money, their cars, their flashy clothes, their dope. And most of all, their assurance. He, Mike Polchik, had been working hauling sides of beef from the delivery trucks to his old man's butcher shop while others were tooling around in their Electrics. He forced the memories from his mind and took out his anger and frustration on the metal idiot still buzzing beside him.

"Okay, okay, how long does it take you?"

"Tsk, tsk," said the driver, and went cross-eyed. Polchik ignored him. But not very well.

"I am a mobile Unit, sir. Experimental model 44. My parent mechanism—the Master Unit AA—at Universal Electronics

Laboratories is equipped to perform this function in under one minute."

"Well, hurry it up. I wanna run these hairies in."

"Gwuh-rare-uh too-err-uh," the scalplock said in a nasty undertone.

There was a soft musical tone from inside the chest compartment, the plate slid down again, and the robot withdrew the plastic bottle. He handed it to the girl.

"Now whaddaya think you're doing?"

"Analysis confirms what the young lady attested, sir. This is a commonly prescribed nosedrop for nasal congestion and certain primary allergies."

Polchik was speechless.

"You are free to go," the robot said. "With our apologies. We are merely doing our jobs. Thank you."

Polchik started to protest—he knew he was right—but the kids were already gathering up their belongings. He hadn't even ripped the car, which was probably where they had it locked away. But he knew it was useless. He was the guinea pig in this experiment, not the robot. It was all painfully clear. He knew if he interfered, if he overrode the robot's decision, it would only add to the cloud under which the robot had put him: short temper, taking a gift from a neighborhood merchant, letting the robot outmaneuver him in the apartment, false stop on Kyser . . . and now this. Suddenly, all Mike Polchik wanted was to go back, get out of harness, sign out, and go home to bed. Wet carpets and all. Just to bed.

Because if these metal things were what was coming, he was simply too tired to buck it.

He watched as the kids—hooting and ridiculing his impotency—piled back in the car, the girls showing their legs as they clambered over the side. The driver burned polyglas speeding up Amsterdam Avenue. In a moment they were gone.

"You see, Officer Polchik," Brillo said, "false arrest would make us both liable for serious—" But Polchik was already walking away, his shoulders slumped, the weight of his bandolier and five years on the Force too much for him.

The robot (making the sort of sound an electric watch makes) hummed after him, keeping stern vigil on the darkened neighborhood in the encroaching dawn. He could not compute despair. But he had been built to serve. He was programmed to protect, and he did it, all the way back to the precinct house.

Polchik was sitting at a scarred desk in the squad room, laboriously typing out his report on a weary IBM Selectric afflicted with grand mal. Across the room Reardon poked at the now-inert metal bulk of Brillo, using some sort of power tool with a teardrop-shaped lamp on top of it. The Mayor's whiz kid definitely looked sandbagged. *He doesn't go without sleep very often,* Polchik thought with grim satisfaction.

The door to Captain Summit's office opened, and the Captain, looking oceanic and faraway, waved him in.

"Here it comes," Polchik whispered to himself.

Summit let Polchik pass him in the doorway. He closed the door and indicated the worn plastic chair in front of the desk. Polchik sat down.

"I'm not done typin' the beat report yet, Capt'n."

Summit ignored the comment. He moved over to the desk, picked up a yellow printout flimsy, and stood silently for a moment in front of Polchik, considering it.

"Accident report out of the 86th precinct uptown. Six kids in a Ford Electric convertible went out of control, smashed down a pedestrian and totaled against the bridge abutment. Three dead, three critical— not expected to live. Fifteen minutes after you let them go."

Dust.

Dried out.

Ashes.

Gray. Final.

Polchik couldn't think. Tired. Confused. Sick. Six kids. Now they were kids, just kids, nothing else made out of old bad memories.

"One of the girls went through the windshield, D.O.A. Driver got the steering column punched out through his back. Another girl with a snapped neck. Another girl—"

He couldn't hear him. He was somewhere else, far away. Kids. Laughing, smartmouth kids having a good time. Benjy would be that age some day. The carpets were all wet.

"Mike!"

He didn't hear.

"Mike! Polchik!"

He looked up. There was a stranger standing in front of him holding a yellow flimsy.

"Well, don't just sit there, Polchik. You had them! Why'd you let them go?"

"The . . . lizard . . ."

"That's right, that's what five of them were using. Three beakers of it in the car. And a dead cat on the floor and all the makings wrapped in foam-bead bags. You'd have had to be blind to miss it all!"

"The robot . . ."

Summit turned away with disgust, slamming the report onto the desktop. He thumbed the call-button.

When Desk Sergeant Loyo came in, he said, "Take him upstairs and give him a breather of straightener, let him lie down for half an hour, then bring him back to me."

Loyo got Polchik under the arms and took him out. Then the Captain turned off the office lights and sat silently in his desk chair, watching the night die just beyond the filthy windows.

"Feel better?"

"Yeah; thank you, Capt'n. I'm fine."

"You're back with me all the way? You understand what I'm saying?"

"Yeah, sure, I'm just fine, sir. It was just . . . those kids . . . I felt . . ."

"So why'd you let them go? I've got no time to baby you, Polchik. You're five years a cop and I've got all the brass in town outside that door waiting. So get right."

"I'm right, Capt'n. I let them go because the robot took the stuff the girl was carrying, and he dumped it in his thing there, and told me it was nosedrops."

"Not good enough, Mike."

"What can I say besides that?"

"Well, dammit Officer Polchik, you damned well better say something besides that. You know they run that stuff right into the skull, you've been a cop long enough to see it, to hear it the way they talk! Why'd you let them custer you?"

"What was I going to run them in for? Carrying nosedrops? With that motherin' robot reciting civil rights chapter-an'-verse at me every step of the way? Okay, so I tell the robot to go screw off, and I bust 'em and bring 'em in. In an hour they're out again and I've got a false arrest lug dropped on me. Even if it ain't nosedrops. And they can use the robot's goddam tapes to hang me up by the thumbs!"

Summit dropped back into his chair, sack weight. His face was a burned-out pudding. "So we've got three, maybe six kids dead. Jesus, Jesus, Jesus." He shook his head.

Polchik wanted to make him feel better. But how did you do that? "Listen, Capt'n, you know I would of had those kids in here so fast it'd made their heads swim, if I'd've been on my own. That damned robot. Well, it just didn't work out. Capt'n, listen, I'm not trying to alibi, it was godawful out there, but you were a beat cop . . . you know a cop ain't a set of rules and a pile of wires. Guys like me just can't work with things like that Brillo. It won't work, Capt'n. A guy's gotta be free to use his judgment, to feel like he's worth something', not just a piece of sh—"

Summit's head came up sharply. "Judgment?!" He looked as though he wanted to vomit. "What kind of judgment are you showing with that Rico over at the Amsterdam Inn? And all of it on the tapes, sound, pictures, everything?"

"Oh. That."

"Yes, that. You're damned lucky I insisted those tapes get held strictly private, for the use of the Force only. I had to invoke privileged data. Do you have any idea how many strings that puts on me, on this office now, with the Chief, with the Commissioner, with the goddam Mayor? Do you have any idea, Polchik?"

"No, sir. I'm sorry." Chagrin.

"Sorry doesn't buy it, goddammit! I don't want you taking any juice from anywhere. No bottles, no gifts, no nothing, not from anybody. Have you got that?"

"Yessir."

Wearily, Summit persisted. "It's tough enough to do a job here without having special graft investigations and the D.A.'s squad sniffing all over the precinct. Jesus, Polchik, do you have any idea . . . !" He stopped, looked levelly at the patrolman and said, "One more time and you're out on your ass. Not set down, not reprimanded, not docked— out. All the way out. Kapish?"

Polchik nodded; his back was broken.

"I've got to set it right."

"What, sir?"

"You, that's what."

Polchik waited. A pendulum was swinging.

"I'll have to think about it. But if it hadn't been for the five good years you've given me here, Polchik, well, you'll be getting punishment, but I don't know just what yet."

"Uh, what's gonna happen with the robot?"

Summit got to his feet slowly; mooring a dirigible. "Come on outside and you'll see."

Polchik followed him to the door, where the Captain paused. He looked closely into Polchik's face and said, "Tonight has been an education, Mike."

There was no answer to that one.

They went into the front desk room. Reardon still had his head stuck into Brillo's open torso cavity, and the whiz kid was standing tiptoed behind him, peering over the engineer's shoulder. As they entered the ready room, Reardon straightened and clicked off the lamp on the power tool. He watched Summit and Polchik as they walked over to Chief Santorini. Summit murmured to the Chief for a moment. Then Santorini nodded and said, "We'll talk tomorrow, then."

He started toward the front door, stopped and said, "Good night, gentlemen. It's been a long night. I'll be in touch with your offices tomorrow." He didn't wait for acknowledgment; he simply went.

Reardon turned around to face Summit. He was waiting for words. Even the whiz kid was starting to come alive again. The silent FBI man rose from the bench (as far as Polchik could tell, he hadn't changed position all the time they'd been gone on patrol) and walked toward the group.

Reardon said, "Well . . ." His voice trailed off.

The pendulum was swinging.

"Gentlemen," said the Captain, "I've advised Chief Santorini I'll be writing out a full report to be sent downtown. My recommendations will more than likely decide whether or not these robots will be added to our Force."

"Grass-roots-level opinion, very good, Captain, very good," said the whiz kid. Summit ignored him.

"But I suppose I ought to tell you right now my recommendations will be negative. As far as I'm concerned, Mr. Reardon, you still have a long way to go with your machine."

"But, I thought—"

"It did very well," Summit said, "don't get me wrong. But I think it's going to need a lot more flexibility and more knowledge of the police officer's duties before it can be of any real aid in our work."

Reardon was angry, but trying to control it. "I programmed the entire patrolman's manual, and all the City codes, and the Supreme Court—"

Summit stopped him with a raised hand. "Mr. Reardon, that's the least of a police officer's knowledge. Anybody can read a rule book. But how to use those rules, how to make those rules work in the street, that takes more than programming. It takes, well, it takes training. And experience. It doesn't come easily. A cop isn't a set of rules and a pile of wires."

Polchik was startled to hear his words. He knew it would be okay. Not as good as before, but at least okay.

Reardon was furious now. And he refused to be convinced. Or perhaps he refused to allow the Mayor's whiz kid and the FBI man to be so easily convinced. He had worked too long and at too much personal cost to his career to let it go that easily. He hung onto it.

"But merely training shouldn't put you off the X-44 completely!"

The Captain's face tensed around the mouth. "Look, Mr. Reardon, I'm not very good at being, politic—which is why I'm still a Captain, I suppose—"

The whiz kid gave him a be-careful look, but the Captain went on. "But it isn't merely training. This officer is a good one. He's bright, he's on his toes, he maybe isn't Sherlock Holmes but he knows the feel of a neighborhood, the smell of it, the heat level. He knows every August we're going to get the leapers and the riots and some woman's head cut off and dumped in a mailbox mailed C.O.D. to Columbus, Ohio. He knows when there's racial tension in our streets. He knows when those poor slobs in the tenements have just had it. He knows when some new kind of vice has moved in. But he made more mistakes out there tonight than a rookie. Five years walking and riding that beat, he's never foulballed the way he did tonight. Why? I've got to ask why? The only thing different was that machine of yours. Why? Why did Mike Polchik foulball so bad? He knew those kids in that car should have been run in for h&b or naline tests. So why, Mr. Reardon . . . why?"

Polchik felt lousy. The Captain was more worked up than he'd ever seen him. But Polchik stood silently, listening; standing beside the silent, listening FBI man.

Brillo merely stood silently. Turned off.

Then why did he still hear that robot buzzing?

"It isn't rules and regs, Mr. Reardon." The Captain seemed to have a lot more to come. "A moron can learn those. But how do you evaluate the look on a man's face that tells you he needs a fix? How do you gauge the cultural change in words like 'custer' or 'grass' or 'high' or 'pig'? How do you know when not to bust a bunch of kids who've popped a hydrant so they can cool off? How do you program all of that into a robot . . . and know that it's going to change from hour to hour?"

"We can do it! It'll take time, but we can do it."

The Captain nodded slowly. "Maybe you can."

"I know we can."

"Okay, I'll even go for that. Let's say you can. Let's say you can get a robot that'll act like a human being and still be a robot . . . because that's what we're talking about here. There's still something else."

"Which is?"

"People, Mr. Reardon. People like Polchik here. I asked you why Polchik foulballed, why he made such a bum patrol tonight that I'm going to have to take disciplinary action against him for the first time in five years . . . so I'll tell you why, Mr. Reardon, about people like Polchik here. They're still afraid of machines, you know. We've pushed them and shoved them and lumbered them with machines till they're afraid the next clanking item down the pike is going to put them on the bread line. So they don't want to cooperate. They don't do it on purpose. They may not even know they're doing it, hell, I don't think Polchik knew what was happening, why he was falling over his feet tonight. You can get a robot to act like a human being, Mr. Reardon. Maybe you're right and you can do it, just like you said. But how the hell are you going to get humans to act like robots and not be afraid of machines?"

Reardon looked as whipped as Polchik felt.

"May I leave Brillo here till morning? I'll have a crew come over from the labs and pick him up."

"Sure," the Captain said, "he'll be fine right there against the wall. The Desk Sergeant'll keep an eye on him." To Loyo he said, "Sergeant, instruct your relief."

Loyo smiled and said, "Yessir."

Summit looked back at Reardon and said, "I'm sorry."

Reardon smiled wanly, and walked out. The whiz kid wanted to say something, but too much had already been said, and the Captain looked through him.

"I'm pretty tired, Mr. Kenzie. How about we discuss it tomorrow after I've seen the Chief?"

The whiz kid scowled, turned and stalked out.

The Captain sighed heavily. "Mike, go get signed out and go home. Come see me tomorrow. Late." He nodded to the FBI man, who still had not spoken; then he went away.

The robot stood where Reardon had left him. Silent. Polchik went upstairs to the locker room to change.

Something was bothering him. But he couldn't nail it down.

When he came back down into the muster room, the FBI man was just racking the receiver on the desk blotter phone. "Leaving?" he asked. It was the first thing Polchik had heard him say. It was a warm brown voice.

"Yeah. Gotta go home. I'm whacked out."

"Can't say I blame you. I'm a little tired myself. Need a lift?"

"No, thanks," Polchik said. "I take the subway. Two blocks from the house." They walked out together. Polchik thought about wet carpets waiting. They stood on the front steps for a minute, breathing in the chill morning air, and Polchik said, "I feel kinda sorry for that chunk of scrap now. He did a pretty good job."

"But not good enough," the FBI man added.

Polchik felt suddenly very protective about the inert form against the wall in the precinct house. "Oh, I dunno. He saved me from getting clobbered, you wanna know the truth. Tell me . . . you think they'll ever build a robot that'll cut it?"

The FBI man lit a cigarette, blew smoke in a thin stream, and nodded. "Yeah. Probably. But it'll have to be a lot more sophisticated than old Brillo in there."

Polchik looked back through the doorway. The robot stood alone, looking somehow helpless. Waiting for rust. Polchik thought of kids, all kinds of kids, and when he was a kid. It must be hell, he thought, being a robot. Getting turned off when they don't need you no more.

Then he realized he could still hear that faint electrical buzzing. The kind a watch makes. He cast a quick glance at the FBI man but, trailing cigarette smoke, he was already moving toward his car, parked directly in front of the precinct house. Polchik couldn't tell if he was wearing a watch or not.

He followed the government man.

"The trouble with Brillo," the FBI man said, "is that Reardon's facilities were too limited. But I'm sure there are other agencies working on it. They'll lick it one day." He snapped the cigarette into the gutter.

"Yeah, sure," Polchik said. The FBI man unlocked the car door and pulled it. It didn't open.

"Damn it!" he said. "Government pool issue. Damned door always sticks." Bunching his muscles, he suddenly wrenched at it with enough force to pop it open. Polchik stared. Metal had ripped.

"You take care of yourself now, y'hear?" the FBI man said, getting into the car. He flipped up the visor with its OFFICIAL GOVERNMENT BUSINESS card tacked to it, and slid behind the steering wheel

The car settled heavily on its springs, as though a ton of load had just been dumped on the front seat. He slammed the door. It was badly sprung.

"Too bad we couldn't use him." the FBI man said, staring out of the car at Brillo, illuminated through the precinct house doorway. "But . . . too crude."

"Yeah, sure, I'll take care of myself," Polchik replied, one exchange too late. He felt his mouth hanging open.

The FBI man grinned, started the car, and pulled away. Polchik stood in the street, for a while.

Sometimes he stared down the early morning street in the direction the FBI man had taken.

Sometimes he stared at the metal cop immobile in the muster room.

And even as the sounds of the city's new day rose around him, he was not at all certain he did not still hear the sound of an electric watch. Getting louder.

ANSWER, PLEASE ANSWER

The Cold War is over, and good riddance to it. "Answer, Please Answer,"
however, was written when the Cold War was at its bitterest and most
dangerous: in 1961, when the Soviet Union and the U.S. were building
hydrogen bombs and missiles as fast as they could, the Berlin Wall was
going up, the Bay of Pigs was going down, and the Cuban Missile Crisis
was on its way.

You might think that a fifty-some-year-old story would be dated, but
I believe that the basic message of "Answer, Please Answer" is more
relevant today than ever. The knowledge of how to build terrible weapons
of mass destruction has not evaporated with the end of the Cold War.
While the former Soviet Union and the U.S. are presently scrapping most
of their missiles and H-bombs, other nations are building missiles and
developing nuclear, chemical, and biological weaponry. The ability to
destroy ourselves utterly is now part of the human store of knowledge: it
will never go away. We will have to police our destructive impulses
forever.

Science fiction is uniquely qualified to make points like that. Only in
science fiction can we use an extraterrestrial civilization from a distant
star to show how permanently dangerous is the world we have created for
ourselves.

To make that point as strong as possible, it was necessary to strip the story of everything else. Every possible distraction had to be removed. So the characters are the bare minimum: two. The setting is as uncomplicated as possible: the two characters are alone in a remote Antarctic base. There is a good deal of astronomy thrown at the reader, for two reasons: one, to help the reader to understand what the characters are trying to do; two, to mask the approach of the final denouement.

A simple story, with no frills. But some depth, I think.

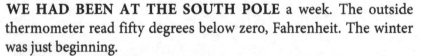

WE HAD BEEN AT THE SOUTH POLE a week. The outside thermometer read fifty degrees below zero, Fahrenheit. The winter was just beginning.

"What do you think we should transmit to McMurdo?" I asked Rizzo.

He put down his magazine and half-sat up on his bunk. For a moment there was silence, except for the nearly inaudible hum of the machinery that jammed our tiny dome, and the muffled shrieking of the ever-present wind, above us.

Rizzo looked at the semicircle of control consoles, computers, and meteorological sensors with an expression of disgust that could be produced only by a drafted soldier.

"Tell 'em it's cold, it's gonna get colder, and we've both got appendicitis and need replacing immediately."

"Very clever," I said, and started touching the buttons that would automatically transmit the sensors' memory files.

Rizzo sagged back into his bunk. "Why?" he asked the curved ceiling of our cramped quarters. "Why me? Why here? What did I ever do to deserve spending the whole goddamned winter at the goddamned South Pole?"

"It's strictly impersonal," I assured him. "Some bright young meteorologist back in Washington has convinced the Pentagon that the South Pole is the key to the world's weather patterns. So here we are."

"It doesn't make sense," Rizzo continued, unhearing. His dark, broad-boned face was a picture of wronged humanity. "Everybody knows that when the missiles start flying, they'll be coming over the *North* Pole. The goddamned Army is a hundred and eighty degrees off base."

"That's about normal for the Army, isn't it?" I was a drafted soldier, too.

Rizzo swung out of the bunk and paced across the dimly lit room. It only took a half-dozen paces; the dome was small and most of it was devoted to machinery.

"Don't start acting like a caged lion," I warned. "It's going to be a long winter."

"Yeah, guess so." He sat down next to me at the radio console and pulled a pack of cigarettes from his shirt pocket. He offered one to me, and we both smoked in silence for a minute or two.

"Got anything to read?"

I grinned. "Some microspool catalogues of stars."

"Stars?"

"I'm an astronomer . . . at least, I *was* an astronomer, before the National Emergency was proclaimed."

Rizzo looked puzzled. "But I never heard of you."

"Why should you?"

"I'm an astronomer, too."

"I thought you were an electronicist."

He pumped his head up and down. "Yeah . . . at the radio astronomy observatory at Greenbelt. Project OZMA. Where do you work?"

"Lick Observatory . . . with the hundred-and-twenty-inch reflector."

"Oh . . . an optical astronomer."

"Certainly."

"You're the first optical man I've met." He looked at me a trifle queerly.

I shrugged. "Well, we've been around a few millennia longer than you static-scanners."

"Yeah, guess so."

"I didn't realize that Project OZMA was still going on. Find anything yet?"

It was Rizzo's turn to shrug. "Nothing yet. The project's been shelved for the duration of the emergency, of course. If there's no war, and the dish doesn't get bombed out, we'll try again."

"Still listening to the same two stars?"

"Yeah ... Tau Ceti and Epsilon Eridani. They're the only two Sun-type stars within reasonable range that might have planets like Earth."

"And you expect to pick up radio signals from an intelligent race."

"Hope to."

I flicked the ash off my cigarette. "You know, it always struck me as rather hopeless . . . trying to find radio signals from intelligent creatures."

"Whattaya mean, hopeless?"

"Why should an intelligent race send radio signals out into interstellar space?" I asked. "Think of the power it requires, and the likelihood that it's all wasted effort, because there's no one within range to talk to."

"Well . . . it's worth a try, isn't it? If you think there could be intelligent creatures somewhere else, on a planet of another star."

"Hmph. We're trying to find another intelligent race; are we transmitting radio signals?"

"No," he admitted. "Congress wouldn't vote the money we needed for a dedicated transmitter."

"Exactly," I said. "We're listening, but not transmitting."

Rizzo wasn't discouraged. "Listen, the chances—just on statistical figuring alone—the chances are that there're millions of other solar systems with intelligent life. We've got to try contacting them! They might have knowledge that we don't have, answers to questions that we can't solve yet."

"I completely agree," I said. "But listening for radio signals is the wrong way to do it."

"Huh?"

"Radio broadcasting requires too much power to cover interstellar distances efficiently. We should be looking for signals, not listening for them."

"Looking?"

"Lasers," I said, pointing to the low-key lights over the consoles. "Optical lasers. Superlamps shining out in the darkness of the void. Pump in a modest amount of electrical power, excite a few trillion atoms, and out comes a coherent, pencil-thin beam of light that can be seen for millions of miles."

"Millions of miles aren't lightyears," Rizzo muttered.

"We're rapidly approaching the point where we'll have lasers capable of lightyear ranges. I'm sure that some intelligent race somewhere in this galaxy has achieved the necessary technology to signal from star to star by light beams."

"Then how come we haven't seen any?" Rizzo demanded.

"Perhaps we already have."

"What?"

"We've observed all sorts of variable stars—Cepheids, RR Lyraes, T Tauris. We assume that what we see are stars that are pulsating and changing brightness for reasons that are natural, but unexplainable to us. Now, suppose what we are really viewing are laser beams, signaling from planets that circle stars too faint to be seen from Earth."

In spite of himself, Rizzo looked intrigued.

"It would be fairly simple to examine the spectra of such light sources and determine whether they're natural stars or artificial laser beams."

"Have you tried it?"

I nodded.

"And?"

I hesitated long enough to make him hold his breath, waiting for my answer. "No soap. Every variable star I've examined is a real star."

He let out his breath in a long disgusted puff. "Ahhh, you were kidding all along. I thought so."

"Yes," I said. "I suppose I was."

Time dragged along in the weather dome. I had managed to smuggle a small portable telescope along with me, and tried to make observations whenever possible. But the weather was unusually poor. Rizzo, almost in desperation for something to do, started to build an electronic image-amplifier for me.

Our one link with the rest of the world was our weekly radio message from McMurdo. The times for the messages were randomly scrambled, so that the chances of being intercepted or jammed were lessened. And we were ordered to maintain strict radio silence.

As the weeks sloughed on, we learned that one of our manned satellites had been boarded by the Reds at gunpoint. Our space crews had put two Red automated spy satellites out of commission. Shots had been exchanged on an ice-island in the Arctic. And six different nations were testing nuclear bombs.

We didn't get any mail of course. Our letters would be waiting for us at McMurdo when we were relieved. I thought about Gloria and our two children quite a bit, and tried not to think about the blast and fallout patterns in the San Francisco area, where they were.

"My wife hounded me until I spent pretty nearly every damned cent I had on a shelter, under the house," Rizzo told me. "Damned shelter is fancier than the house. She's the social leader of the disaster set. If we don't have a war, she's gonna feel damned silly."

I said nothing.

The weather cleared and steadied for a while (there was no daylight during the long Antarctic winter) and I split my time evenly between monitoring the meteorological sensors and observing the stars. The snow covered the dome completely, of course, but our "snorkel" burrowed through it and out into the air.

"This dome's just like a submarine, only we're submerged in snow instead of water," Rizzo observed. "I just hope we don't sink to the bottom."

"The calculations say that we'll be all right."

He made a sour face. "Calculations proved that airplanes would never get off the ground."

The storms closed in again, but by the time they cleared once more, Rizzo had completed the image-amplifier for me. Now, with the tiny telescope I had, I could see almost as far as a professional instrument would allow. I could even lie comfortably in my bunk, watch the amplifier's viewscreen, and control the entire setup remotely.

Then it happened.

At first it was simply a curiosity. An oddity.

I happened to be studying a Cepheid variable star—one of the huge, very bright stars that pulsate so regularly that you can set your watch by them. It had attracted my attention because it seemed to be unusually close for a Cepheid, only seven hundred lightyears away. The distance could be easily gauged by timing the star's pulsations.

I talked Rizzo into helping me set up a spectrometer. We scavenged shamelessly from the dome's spare-parts bin and finally produced an instrument that would break up the light of the star into its component wavelengths, and thereby tell us much about the star's chemical composition and surface temperature.

At first I didn't believe what I saw.

The star's spectrum—a broad rainbow of colors—was crisscrossed with narrow dark lines. That was all right. They're called absorption lines; the Sun has thousands of them in its spectrum. But one line—one—was an insolently bright emission line. All the laws of physics and chemistry said it shouldn't be there.

But it was.

We photographed the star dozens of times. We checked our instruments ceaselessly. I spent hours scanning the star's "official" spectrum, as published in the standard star catalogues. There was nothing wrong with our instruments.

Yet the bright line showed up. It was real.

"I don't understand it," I admitted. "I've seen stars with bright emission spectra before, but a single bright line in an absorption spectrum! It's unheard of. One single wavelength . . . one particular type of atom at one precise energy level . . . why? Why is it emitting energy when the other wavelengths aren't?"

Rizzo was sitting on his bunk, puffing a cigarette. He blew a cloud of smoke at the low ceiling. "Maybe it's one of those laser signals you were telling me about a couple of weeks ago."

I scowled at him. "Come on, now. I'm serious. This thing has me puzzled."

"Now wait a minute. You're the one who said radio astronomers were straining their ears for nothing. You're the one who said we ought to be looking. So look!" He was enjoying his revenge.

I shook my head, and turned back to the meteorological equipment.

But Rizzo wouldn't let up. "Suppose there's an intelligent race living on a planet near a Cepheid variable star. They figure that any other intelligent creatures would have astronomers who'd be curious about their star, right? So they send out a laser signal that matches the star's pulsations. When you look at the star, you see their signal. What's more logical?"

"All right," I groused. "You've had your joke . . ."

"Tell you what," he insisted. "Let's put that one wavelength into an oscilloscope and see if a definite signal comes out. Maybe it'll spell out 'Take me to your leader' or something."

I ignored him and turned my attention to Army business. The meteorological equipment was functioning perfectly, but our orders read that one of us had to check it every twelve hours. So I checked and tried to keep my eyes from wandering as Rizzo tinkered with a photocell and oscilloscope.

"There we are," he said, at length. "Now let's see what they're telling us."

In spite of myself I looked up at the face of the oscilloscope. A steady, gradually sloping greenish line was traced across the screen.

"No message," I said.

Rizzo shrugged elaborately.

"If you leave the 'scope on for two days, you'll find that the line makes a full swing from peak to null," I informed him. "The star pulsates every two days, bright to dim."

"Let's turn up the gain," he said, and he flicked a few knobs on the front of the 'scope.

The line didn't change at all.

"What's the sweep speed?" I asked.

"One nanosecond per centimeter." That meant that each centimeter-wide square on the screen's face represented one billionth of a second. There are as many nanoseconds in one second as there are seconds in thirty-two years.

"Well, if you don't get a signal at that sensitivity, there just isn't any signal there," I said.

Rizzo nodded. He seemed slightly disappointed that his joke was at an end. I turned back to the meteorological instruments, but I couldn't concentrate on them. Somehow I felt disappointed, too. Subconsciously, I suppose, I had been hoping that Rizzo actually would detect a signal from the star. Fool! I told myself. But what could explain that bright emission line? I glanced up at the oscilloscope again.

And suddenly the smooth, steady line broke into a jagged series of millions of peaks and nulls!

I stared at it.

Rizzo was back on his bunk again, reading one of his magazines. I tried to call him, but the words froze in my throat. Without taking my eyes from the flickering 'scope, I reached out and touched his arm.

He looked up.

"Holy Mother of God," Rizzo whispered.

For a long time we stared silently at the fluttering line dancing across the oscilloscope screen, bathing our tiny dome in its weird greenish light. It was eerily fascinating, hypnotic. The line never stood still; it jabbered and stuttered, a series of little peaks and nulls, changing almost too fast for the eye to follow, up and down, calling to us, up, down, never still, never quiet, constantly flickering its unknown message to us.

"Can it be . . . people?" Rizzo wondered. His face, bathed in the greenish light, was suddenly furrowed, withered, ancient: a mixture of disbelief and fear.

"What else could it be?" I heard my own voice answer. "There's no other explanation possible."

We sat mutely for God knows how long.

Finally Rizzo asked, "What do we do now?"

The question broke our entranced mood. What do we do? What action do we take? We're thinking men, and we've been contacted by other creatures that can think, reason, send a signal across seven hundred lightyears of space. So don't just sit there in stupefied awe. Use your brain, prove that you're worthy of the tag *sapiens.*

"We decode the message," I announced. Then, as an afterthought, "But don't ask me how."

We should have called McMurdo, or Washington. Or perhaps we should have attempted to get a message through to the United Nations. But we never even thought of it. This was our problem. Perhaps it was the sheer isolation of our dome that kept us from thinking about the rest of the world. Perhaps it was sheer luck.

"If they're using lasers," Rizzo reasoned, "they must have a technology something like ours."

"They must have had," I corrected. "That message is seven hundred years old, remember. They were playing with lasers when King John was signing the Magna Carta and Genghis Khan owned most of Asia. Lord knows what they have now."

Rizzo blanched and reached for another cigarette.

I turned back to the oscilloscope. The signal was still flashing across its face.

"They're sending out a signal," I mused, "probably at random. Just beaming it out into space, hoping that someone, somewhere, will pick it up. It must be in some form of code, but a code that they feel can be easily cracked by anyone with enough intelligence to realize that there's a message there."

"Sort of an interstellar Morse code."

I shook my head. "Morse code depends on both sides knowing the code. We've got no key."

"Cryptographers crack codes."

"Sure. If they know what language is being used. We don't know the language, we don't know the alphabet, the thought process . . . nothing."

"But it's a code that can be cracked easily," Rizzo muttered.

"Yes," I agreed. "Now what the hell kind of code can they assume will be known to another race that they've never seen?"

Rizzo leaned back on his bunk and his face was lost in shadows.

"An interstellar code," I rambled on. "Some form of presenting information that would be known to almost any race intelligent enough to understand lasers."

"Binary!" Rizzo snapped, sitting up on the bunk.

"What?"

"Binary code. To send a signal like this, they've gotta be able to write a message in units that're only a billionth of a second long. That takes computers. Right? Well, if they have computers, they must figure that we have computers. Digital computers run on binary code. Off or on, go or no go. It's simple. I'll bet we can run that signal through our computer here."

"To assume that they use computers exactly like ours . . ."

"Maybe the computers are completely different," Rizzo said excitedly, "but the binary code is basic to them all. I'll bet on that! And this computer we've got here—this transistorized baby—she can handle more information than the whole army could feed into her. I'll bet nothing's been developed anywhere that's better for handling simple one-plus-one types of operations."

I shrugged. "All right. It's worth a trial."

It took Rizzo a few hours to get everything properly set up. I did some arithmetic while he worked. If the message was in binary code, that meant that every cycle of the signal—every flick of the dancing line on our screen—carried a bit of information. The signal's wavelength was five thousand angstroms. There are a hundred million angstrom units to the centimeter; figuring the speed of light, the signal could carry something like six hundred trillion bits of information per second.

I told Rizzo.

"Yeah, I know. I've been going over the same numbers in my head." He set a few switches on the computer control board. "Now let's see how many of the six hundred trillion we can pick up." He sat down before the board and pressed a series of buttons.

We watched, hardly breathing, as the computer's spools began spinning and the indicator lights flashed across the control board. Within a few minutes, the printer chugged to life.

Rizzo swiveled his chair over to the printer and held up the unrolling sheet in a trembling hand. Numbers. Six-digit numbers. Completely meaningless.

"Gibberish," Rizzo snapped.

It was peculiar. I felt relieved and disappointed at the same time.

"Something's screwy," Rizzo said. "Maybe I fouled up the circuits . . ."

"I don't think so," I answered. "After all, what did you expect to come out of the computer? Shakespearean poetry?"

"No, but I expected numbers that would make some kind of sense. One and one, maybe. Something that means something. This stuff is nowhere."

Our nerves must have really been wound up tight, because before we knew it we were in the middle of a nasty argument—and it was over nothing, really. But in the middle of it:

"Hey, look!" Rizzo shouted, pointing to the oscilloscope.

The message had stopped. The 'scope showed only the calm, steady line of the star's basic two-day-long pulsation.

It suddenly occurred to us that we hadn't slept for more than thirty-six hours, and we were both exhausted. We forgot the senseless argument. The message was ended. Perhaps there would be another; perhaps not. We had the telescope, spectrometer, photocell, oscilloscope, and computer set to record automatically. We collapsed into our bunks. I suppose I should have had monumental dreams. I didn't. I slept like a dead man.

When we woke up, the oscilloscope trace was still quiet.

"Y'know," Rizzo muttered, "it might just be a fluke. I mean, maybe the signals don't mean a damned thing. The computer is probably translating nonsense into numbers just because it's built to print out numbers and nothing else."

"Not likely," I said. "There are too many coincidences to be explained. We're receiving a message, I'm sure of it. Now we've got to crack the code."

As if to reinforce my words, the oscilloscope trace suddenly erupted into the same flickering pattern. The message was being sent again.

We went through two weeks of it. The message would run for seven hours, then stop for seven. We transcribed it on tape forty-eight times and ran it through the computer constantly. Always the same result: six-digit numbers, millions of them. There were six different seven-hour-long messages, being repeated one after the other, constantly.

We forgot the meteorological equipment. We ignored the weekly messages from McMurdo. The rest of the world became meaningless fiction to us. There was nothing but the confounded, tantalizing, infuriating, enthralling message. The National Emergency, the bomb tests, families, duties—all transcended, all forgotten. We ate when we thought of it and slept when we couldn't keep our eyes open any longer. The message. What was it? What was the key to unlock its meaning?

"It's got to be something universal," I told Rizzo. "Something universal, in the widest sense of the term."

He looked up from his desk, which was wedged in between the end of his bunk and the curving dome wall. The desk was littered with printout sheets from the computer, each one of them part of the message.

"You've only said that a half a million times in the past couple of weeks. What the hell is universal? If you can figure that out, you're damned good!"

What is universal? I wondered. You're an astronomer. You look out at the universe. What do you see? I thought about it. What do I see? Stars, gas, dust clouds, planets . . . what's universal about them? What do they all have that—

"Atoms!" I blurted.

Rizzo cocked a weary eye at me. "Atoms?"

"Atoms. Elements. Look . . ."

I grabbed a fistful of the sheets and thumbed through them. "Look . . . each message starts with a list of numbers. Then there's a long blank to separate the opening list from the rest of the message. See? Every time, the same-length list."

"So?"

"The periodic table of elements!" I shouted into his ear. "That's the key!"

Rizzo shook his head. "I thought of that two days ago. No soap. In the first place, the list that starts each message isn't always the same. It's the same length, all right, but the numbers change. In the second place, it always begins with 100000. I looked up the atomic weight of hydrogen—it's 1.008, something."

That stopped me for a moment. But then something clicked into place in my mind.

"Why is the hydrogen weight 1.008?" Before Rizzo could answer, I went on, "For two reasons. The system we use arbitrarily rates oxygen as sixteen even. Right? All the other weights are calculated from oxygen's. And we also give the average weight of an element, counting all its isotopes, right? Our weight for hydrogen also includes an adjustment for tiny amounts of deuterium and tritium. Right? Well, suppose they have a system that rates hydrogen as a flat one: 1.00000. Doesn't that make sense?"

"You're getting punchy," Rizzo grumbled. "What about the isotopes? How can they expect us to handle decimal points if they don't tell us about them—mental telepathy? What about—"

"Stop arguing and start calculating," I snapped. "Change that list of numbers to agree with our periodic table. Change 1.0000 to 1.008-whatever-it-is and tackle the next few elements. The decimals shouldn't be so hard to figure out."

Rizzo grumbled to himself, but started working out the calculations. I stepped over to the dome's microspool library and found an elementary physics text. Within a few minutes, Rizzo had some numbers and I had the periodic table focused on the microspool reading machine.

"Nothing," Rizzo said, leaning over my shoulder and looking at the screen. "They don't match at all."

"Try another list. They're not all the same."

He shrugged and returned to his desk. After a while he called out, "Their second number is 3.97123; that works out to 4.003-something."

It checked! "Good. That's helium. What about the next one, lithium?"

"That's 6.940."

"Right!"

Rizzo went to work furiously after that. I pushed a chair to the desk and began working up from the end of the list. It all checked out, from hydrogen to a few elements beyond the artificial ones that had been created in the laboratories here on Earth.

"That's it," I said. "That's the key. That's our Rosetta Stone . . . the periodic table."

Rizzo stared at the scribbled numbers and the jumble of papers. "I bet I know what the other lists are . . . the ones that don't make sense."

"Oh?"

"There are always other ways to identify the elements: vibration resonances, quantum wavelengths . . . somebody named Lewis came out a couple of years ago with a Quantum Periodic Table . . ."

"They're covering all the possibilities! There are messages for many different levels of understanding. We just decoded the simplest one."

"Yeah."

I noticed that as he spoke, Rizzo's hand, still tightly clutching the pencil, was trembling and white with tension.

"Well?"

Rizzo licked his lips. "Let's get to work."

We were like two men possessed. Eating, sleeping, even talking was ignored completely as we waded through the hundreds of sheets of paper. We could decode only a small percentage of them, but they still represented many hours of communication. The sheets that we couldn't decode we suspected were repetitions of the same message that we were working on.

We lost all concept of time. We must have slept, more than once, but I simply don't remember. All I can recall is thousands of numbers, row upon row, sheet after sheet of numbers . . . and my pencil scratching symbols of the various chemical elements over them until my hand was so cramped I could no longer open the fingers.

The message consisted of a long series of formulas; that much was certain. But, without punctuation, with no knowledge of the symbols that denoted even such simple things as "plus" or "equals" or "yields," it took us more weeks of hard work to unravel the sense of each equation. And even then, there was more to the message than met the eye:

"Just what the hell are they driving at?" Rizzo wondered aloud. His face had changed: it was thinner, hollow-eyed, weary, covered with a scraggly beard.

"Then you think there's a meaning behind all these equations, too?"

He nodded. "It's a message, not just a contact. They're going to an awful lot of trouble to beam out this message, and they're repeating it every seven hours. They haven't added anything new in the weeks we've been watching."

"I wonder how many years or centuries they've been sending out this message, waiting for someone to pick it up, looking for someone to answer them."

"Maybe we should call Washington . . ."

"No!"

Rizzo grinned. "Afraid of breaking radio silence?"

"Hell no. I just want to wait until we're relieved, so we can make this announcement in person. I'm not going to let some old wheezer in Washington get credit for this. Besides, I want to know just what they're trying to tell us."

It was agonizing, painstaking work. Most of the formulas meant nothing to either one of us. We had to ransack the dome's meager library of microspools to piece them together. They started simply enough—basic chemical combinations: a carbon and two oxygens yield CO_2; two hydrogens and one oxygen give water. A primer, not of words, but of equations.

The equations became steadily longer and more complex. Then, abruptly, they simplified, only to begin a new deepening, simplify again, and finally became very complicated just at the end. The last few lines were obviously repetitious.

Gradually, their meaning became clear to us.

The first set of equations started off with simple, naturally occurring energy-yielding formulas. The oxidation of cellulose (we found the formula for that in an organic chemistry text left behind by one of the dome's previous occupants), which probably referred to the burning of plants and vegetation. A string of formulas that had groupings in them that I dimly recognized as amino acids—no doubt something to do with digesting food. There were many others, including a few that Rizzo claimed had the expression for chlorophyll in them.

"Naturally occurring, energy-yielding reactions," Rizzo summarized. "They're probably trying to describe the biological setup on their planet."

It seemed an inspired guess.

The second set of equations again began with simple formulas. The cellulose-burning reaction appeared again, but this time it was followed by equations dealing with the oxidation of hydrocarbons: coal and oil burning? A long series of equations that bore repeatedly the symbols for many different metals came up next, followed by more on hydrocarbons, and then a string of formulas that we couldn't decipher at all.

This time it was my guess: "These look like the energy-yielding reactions, too. At least in the beginning. But they don't seem to be naturally occurring types. Then comes a long story about metals. They're trying to tell us the history of their technological development— burning wood, coal, and eventually oil; smelting metals. They're showing us how they developed their technology."

The final set of equations began with an ominous simplicity: a short series of very brief symbols that had the net result of four hydrogen atoms building into a helium atom. Nuclear fusion.

"That's the proton-proton reaction," I explained to Rizzo. "The type of fusion that goes on in the Sun."

The next series of equations spelled out the more complex carbon-nitrogen cycle of nuclear fusion, which was probably the primary energy source of their own Cepheid variable star. Then came a long series of equations that we couldn't decode at all in any detail, but the symbols for uranium and plutonium, and some of the even heavier elements, kept cropping up.

Then came one line that told us the whole story: the lithium-hydride equation: nuclear fusion bombs.

The equations went on to more complex reactions, formulas that no man on Earth had ever seen before. They were showing us the summation of their knowledge, and they had obviously been dealing with nuclear energy for much longer than we have on Earth.

But interspersed among the new equations, they repeated a set of formulas that always began with the lithium-hydride fusion reaction. The message ended in a way that wrenched my stomach: the fusion bomb reaction and its cohorts were repeated ten straight times.

I'm not sure what day it was on the calendar, but the clock on the master control console said it was well past eleven.

Rizzo rubbed a weary hand across his eyes. "Well, what do you think?"

"It's pretty obvious," I said. "They have the bombs. They've had them for quite some time. They must have a lot of other weapons, too—more . . . advanced. They're trying to tell us their history with the equations. First they depended on natural resources of energy, plants, and animals; then they developed artificial energy sources and built up a technology; finally they discovered nuclear energy."

"How long do you think they've had the bombs?"

"Hard to tell. A generation, a century. What difference does it make? They have them. They probably thought, at first, that they could learn to live with them. But imagine what it must be like to have those weapons at your fingertips for a century. Forever. Now they're so scared of them that they're beaming their whole history out into space, looking for someone to tell them how to live with the bombs, how to avoid using them."

"You could be wrong," Rizzo said. "They could be boasting about their arsenal."

"Why? For what reason? No . . . the way they keep repeating those last equations. They're pleading for help."

Rizzo turned to the oscilloscope. It was flickering again.

"Think it's the same thing?"

"No doubt. You're recording it anyway, aren't you?"

"Yeah, sure. Automatically."

Suddenly, in midflight, the signal winked off. The pulsations didn't simply smooth out into a steady line, as they had before. The screen simply went dead.

"That's funny," Rizzo said, puzzled. He checked the oscilloscope. "Nothing wrong here. Something must've happened to the telescope."

Suddenly I knew what had happened. "Take the spectrometer off and turn on the image amplifier," I told him.

I knew what we would see. I knew why the oscilloscope beam had suddenly gone off scale. And the knowledge was making me sick.

Rizzo removed the spectrometer setup and flicked the switch that energized the image-amplifier's viewscreen.

"Holy God!"

The dome was flooded with light. The star had exploded.

"They had the bombs all right," I heard myself saying. "And they couldn't prevent themselves from using them. And they had a lot more, too. Enough to push their star past its natural limits."

Rizzo's face was etched in the harsh light.

"I've got to get out of here," he muttered, looking all around the cramped dome. "I've gotta get back to my wife and find someplace where it's safe . . ."

"Someplace safe?" I asked, staring at the screen. "Where?"

THE MAN WHO SAW "GUNGA DIN" THIRTY TIMES

I've seen the movie Gunga Din *more than thirty times, and I have the feeling that unless you've seen the film often enough, or recently enough, to remember it well, this story may not hit you as hard as it could. But it says something to me about the Zarathustrian dichotomy between the Forces of Light and the Forces of Darkness, a conflict that was very much in evidence when you worked for a military-oriented research laboratory during the strife-torn Sixties.*

NOSING THE CAR through the growling traffic down Memorial Drive, autos clustered thick and sullen as Bombay thieves, the Charles River looking clear in the morning sunlight, the golden dome of the Capitol sparkling up on Beacon Hill, the sky a perfect Indian blue.

The temple of gold.

—What?—

Charlie's a perfect Higgenbottom type: capable in a limited way, self-centered, basically stupid.

The golden temple, I repeat.

— Oh, the Capitol. It's a wonder the goddam politicians haven't stolen *that* yet.—

A Fiat bulging with bearded Harvard Square types cuts in front of us. I hit the brakes and Charles lurches and grumbles.

— Goddam hippies. They oughtta get a job.—

They're in the morning traffic. Maybe they have jobs. Maybe they're driving to work.

— Yeah. Undercutting some guy who's been working twenty years and has a family to support.—

It was on the Late Show again last night, did you see it?

— See what?—

Gunga Din. The movie. Cary Grant. Doug Fairbanks, Jr., Victor McLaglen.

— What? They have that on again?—

It's the best movie Hollywood ever made. It has everything: golden temple, elephants, cavalry charges, real heroes. They don't make movies like that anymore. Can't.

— They must have it on the Late Show every week.—

No, it's been months since they showed it. I check *TV Guide* every week to make sure.

Charlie looks a little surprised, startled. Just like Higgenbottom when Cary Grant dropped that kilted Scottie corporal out the window.

I'll bet I've seen that movie thirty times, at least. I know every line of it, just about. They cut it terribly on television. Next time there's a Cary Grant film festival in New York I'm going down to see it. All of it. Without cuts.

Charlie says nothing.

We inch along, crawling down the Drive as slowly as the waterboy himself. I can seen him, old Sam Jaffe all blacked over, heavy goatskin waterbag pulling one shoulder down, twisting his whole skinny body. White turban, white breechcloth. Staggering down the grassy walk alongside the drive, keeping pace with us. If they made the movie now, they'd have to use a real Negro for the part. Or an Indian. For the guru's part, too. No Eduardo Ciannelli.

We turn off at the lab. There are guards at the gates and more guards standing around in the parking lot. The lab building is white and square and looming, like Army headquarters—an oasis of science and civilization in the midst of the Cambridge slum jungles.

Even in uniform the guards look sloppy. They ought to take more pride in themselves. We drive past them slowly, like the colonel reviewing the regiment. The regimental band is playing "Bonnie Charlie." The wind is coming down crisply off the mountains, making all the pennants flutter.

— Stockholders' meeting today. They're worried about some of these hippie students kicking up a rumpus.—

McLaglen would straighten them out. That's what they need, a tough sergeant major.

This time Charlie really looks sour.

— McLaglen! You'd better come back into the real world. It's going to be a long day.—

For you, I say to myself. Accountant, paper shuffler, money juggler. The stockholders will be after you. Not me. They don't care what I do, as long as it makes money. They don't care who it kills, as long as it works right and puts number in the right columns of your balance sheets.

The air-conditioning in my office howls like a wind tunnel. It's too cold. Be nice to have one of those big lazy fans up on the ceiling.

— Got a minute?—

Come on in, Elmer. What's the matter, something go wrong downstairs?

— Naw, the lab's fine. Everything almost set up for the final series. Just got to calibrate the spectrometer.—

But something's bothering you.

— I was wondering if I could have some time off to attend the stockholders meeting.—

Today? I didn't know you were a stockholder.

— Five shares.—

Elmer is black. He's always seemed like a good lab technician, a reasonable man. But could he be one of them?

— I never been to a stockholders' meeting.—

Oh sure. You can go. But . . . we're not allowed to talk about PMD. Understand?

— Yeah, I know.—

Not that it's anything we're ashamed of—military security.

— Yeah. I know.—

Good military form. Good regimental attitude. We've got to stand together against the darkness.

Elmer nods as he leaves, but I don't think he really understands. When the time comes, when the Thugees rise in rebellion, which side will he join?

I wonder how I'd look in uniform? With one of those stiff collars and a sergeant's stripes on my sleeves. I'm about as tall as Grant, almost. Don't have his shoulders, though. And this flabby middle— ought to exercise more.

Through my office window I can see the world's ugliest water tower, one of Cambridge's distinguishing landmarks. Mountains, that's what should be out there. The solid rock walls of the Himalayas. And the temple of gold is tucked in them somewhere. Pure gold! Din was telling the truth. It's all gold. And I'm stuck here, like Cary Grant in the stockade. Get me out of here, Din. Get me out.

— Please, sahib, don't take away bugle. Bugle only joy for poor *bhisti.*—

He only wants to be one of us. Wants to be a soldier, like the rest of us. A bugler. McLagen would laugh at him. Fairbanks would be sympathetic. Let him keep the bugle. He's going to need it.

— Tonight, when everyone sleeping. I go back to temple.—

Not now, Din, Not now. Got some soldiering to do. Down in the lab. Test out the new batch of PMD. A soldier's got to do his duty.

The phone. Don't answer it. It's only some civilian who wants to make trouble. Leave it ringing and get down to the lab. Wife, sister, mother, they're all alike. Yes, I'm a man, but I'm a soldier first. You don't want a man, you want a coward who'd run out on his friends. Well, that's not me and never was . . . No, wait—that's Fairbanks' speech. He's Ballantine. And who was the girl? Olivia de Havilland or her sister?

The halls are crawling with stockholders. Fat and old. Civilians. Visiting the frontier, inspecting the troops. We're the only thing standing between you and the darkness, but you don't know it. Or if you do, you wouldn't dare admit it.

The lab's always cold as ice. Got to keep it chilled clown. If even a whiff of PMD gets out . . .

Elmer, hey, why isn't the spectrometer ready to go?

— You said I could go to the stockholders' meeting.—

Yes, but *we've* still got work to do. When does the meeting start?

— Ten sharp.—

Well, we've still got lots of time.

— It's ten to ten.—

What? Can't be . . . Is that clock right?

— Yep.—

He wouldn't have tampered with the clock; stop being so suspicious. Okay, go on to the meeting. I'll set it up myself.

— Okay. Thanks!—

But I'm not by myself, of course. Good old grinnin' gruntin' Gunga Din. You lazarushin leather Gunga Din. He's not much help, naturally. What does an actor know about biochemistry? But he talks, and I talk, and the work gets done.

— Satisfactory, sahib?—

Very regimental, Din. Very regimental.

He glows with pride. White teeth against black skin. He'll die for us. They'll kill him, up there atop the temple of gold. The Thugees, the wild ones. The cult of death, worshippers of heathen idols. Kali, the goddess of blood.

Up to the roof for lunch. The stockholders are using the cafeteria. Let them. It's better up here, alone. Get the sun into your skin. Let the heat sink in and the glare dazzle your eyes.

My god, there they are! The heathens, the Thugees. Swarms of them grumbling outside the gate. Dirty, unkempt. Stranglers and murderers. Already our graves are dug. Their leader, he's too young to be Ciannelli. And he's bearded; the guru should be clean-shaven. The guards look scared. He's got a bullhorn, he's black enough to be the guru, all right. What's he telling the crowd? I know what he's saying, even though lie tries to disguise the words. Ciannelli didn't hide it, he said it straight out: Kill lest you be killed yourselves. Kill for the love of killing. Kill for the love of Kali. Kill! Kill! Kill!

They howl and rush the gate. The guards are bowled over. Not a chance for them. The swarming heathen boil across the parking lot and right into the lab building itself. They're all over the place, Savages. I can smell smoke. Glass is shattering somewhere down there. People screaming.

One of the guards comes puffing up here. Uniform torn and sweaty, face red.

— Hey, Doc, better get down the emergency stairs right away. It ain't safe up here. They're burning your lab.—

I'm a soldier of her Majesty the Queen. I don't bow before no heathen!

His eyes go wide. He's scared. Scared of rabble, of heathen rabble.

— I'll . . . I'll get somebody to help you, Doc. The fire engines oughtta be here any minute.—

Let him run. We can handle it. The Scotties will be here soon. I can hear their bagpipes now, or is it just the blooming heat singing in my ears?

They'll be here. Get up on top of the temple dome, Din. Warn them. Sound your trumpet. The colonel's got to know! These dark incoherent forces of evil can't be allowed to win. You know that. Snake worshippers, formless, nameless shadows of death. The Forces of Light and Order have to win out in the end. Western organization and military precision always triumph. It will kill you, Din, I know. But that's the price of admission. We'll make you an honorary corporal in the regiment, Din. Your name will be written on the rolls of our honored dead.

They're coming; I know they're coming. The whole bloomin' regiment! Climb the golden dome and warn them. Warn them. Warn them!

OUT OF TIME

As my old Armenian boss often told me, "Figures don't lie, but liars sure can figure."

THE FIRST DAY OF THE TRIAL, the courtroom had been as hectic as a television studio, what with four camera crews and all their lights, dozens of reporters, all the extra cops for security, and just plain gawkers. But after eight months, hardly any onlookers were there when Don Carmine Lombardo had his heart attack.

The *cappo di tutti cappi* for the whole New England region clawed at his chest and made a few gasping, gargling noises in the middle of his brother-in-law's incredibly perjured testimony, struggled halfway out of his chair, then collapsed across the table in front of him, scattering the notes and depositions neatly laid out by his quartet of lawyers as he slid to the floor like a limp sack of overcooked spaghetti.

The rumor immediately sprang up that his brother-in-law's testimony, in which he described the Don as a God-fearing family man who had become immensely wealthy merely by hard work and frugality, brought down the vengeance of the Lord upon the old man. This is probably not true. The heart attack was no great surprise. Don

Carmine was almost eighty, grossly overweight, and given to smoking horrible little Sicilian rum-soaked cigars by the boxful.

The most gifted and expensive physicians in the Western world were flown to Rhode Island in the valiant attempt to save the Don's life. Tenaciously, the old man hung on for six days, then, like the God he was said to have feared, he relaxed on the seventh. He was declared dead jointly by the medical team, no single one of them wishing to take the responsibility of making the announcement to the stony-eyed men in their perfectly tailored silk suits who waited out in the hospital's corridors, eating pizzas brought in by muscular errand boys and conversing in whispered mixtures of Italian and English.

But Don Carmine did not die before issuing orders that his body be preserved in liquid nitrogen. Perhaps he truly did fear God. If there was any chance that he could survive death, he was willing to spend the money and take the risk.

"What is this cryo . . . cryology or whatever the hell they call it?" snarled Angelo Marchetti. He was not angry. Snarling was his normal mode of conversation, except when he did get angry. Then he bellowed.

"Cryonics," said his lawyer, Pat del Vecchio.

"They froze him in that stuff," Marchetti said. "Like he was a popsickle."

Del Vecchio was a youngster, one of the new breed of university-trained legal talents that was slowly, patiently turning the Mob away from its brutal old ways and toward the much more profitable pursuits of computer crime and semi-legitimate business. There was far more money to be made, at far less risk, in toxic waste disposal than in narcotics. Let the Latinos cut each other up over the drug trade. Let one state after another legalize gambling. Del Vecchio knew the wave of the future: more money was stolen with a few touches of the fingers on the right computer keyboard than with all the guns the old-timers liked to carry.

Marchetti was one of the last surviving old-timers among the New England families. Bald, built like a squat little fireplug with a glistening, narrow-eyed bullet head stuck atop it, he had been a bully all his life. Once he cowed men with his fists. Now he used the threat of his powerful voice, and the organization behind him, to make men do his will. He had inherited Don Carmine's empire, but the thought that the Don might come back some day bothered him.

He sat on the patio of his luxurious home in Newport, gazing out at the lovely seascape formed by Narragansett Bay. The blue waters were dotted by dozens of white sails; the blue sky, by puffy white clouds. Marchetti often spent the afternoon out here, relaxing on his lounge chair, ogling the girls in their bikinis through a powerful pair of binoculars. He was not oblivious to the fact that the great robber barons of the previous century had built their summer retreats nearby. The thought pleased him. But today he was worried about this scientific miracle called cryonics.

"I mean, is the old Don dead or ain't he?"

Del Vecchio, lean and dapper in a sharply cut double-breasted ivory blazer and dark blue slacks, assured Marchetti, "He's legally, medically, and really dead."

Marchetti scowled suspiciously. "Then why didn't he wanna be buried?"

With great patience, del Vecchio explained that while the old man was clinically dead, there were some scientists who believed that perhaps in some far-distant future it might be possible to cure the heart problem that caused the death. So Don Carmine had himself frozen, preserved in liquid nitrogen at the temperature of 346 degrees below zero Fahrenheit.

"Christ, that's cold!" Marchetti growled.

At that temperature, del Vecchio said, the old man's body would be perfectly preserved for eternity. As long as the refrigerator wasn't turned off.

"And if the scientists ever find a way to fix what killed him, they can thaw him out and bring him back to life," the young lawyer concluded.

Marchetti squinted in the sunlight, his interest in the sailboats and even the bathing beauties totally gone now.

"Maybe," he said slowly, "somebody oughtta pull the plug out of that icebox." He pronounced the word in the old neighborhood dialect: *i-sa-bocks*.

Del Vecchio smiled, understanding his boss's reluctance to return the New England empire to a newly arisen Don Carmine.

"Don't worry," he soothed. "There's one great big loophole in the situation."

"Yeah? What?"

"Nobody knows how to defrost a corpse, once it's been frozen. Can't be done without breaking up the body cells. Try to defrost Don Carmine and you'll kill him."

Marchetti burst into laughter, a hearty, loud, blood-chilling roar. "Then he'll be twice as dead!" He laughed until tears streamed down his cheeks.

The years passed swiftly, too swiftly and too few for Angelo Marchetti. Despite del Vecchio's often-repeated advice that he get into the profits that can be skimmed from legalized casino gambling and banking, Marchetti could not change his ways. But the law enforcement agencies of the federal government were constantly improving their techniques, too, and inevitably they caught up with him. Marchetti (he never thought to have himself styled "Don Angelo") was brought to trial to face charges of loan sharking, tax evasion, and—most embarrassing of all—endangering the public health by improperly disposing of toxic wastes. One of the companies that del Vecchio had urged him to buy through a dummy corporation had gotten caught dumping chemical sludge into a public storm sewer.

Thirty pounds heavier than he had been the year that Don Carmine died, Marchetti sat once again on the patio behind his mansion. The binoculars rested on the flagstones beside his lounge chair; they had not been used all summer. Marchetti's eyesight was not what it once was, nor was his interest in scantily clad young women. He lay on the lounge chair like a beached white whale in size 52 plaid bathing trunks.

"They've got the goods," del Vecchio was saying, gloomily.

"Ain't there nothin' we can do?"

Standing over his boss's prostrate blubber, the lawyer looked even more elegant that he had a few years earlier. Still lean and trim, there were a few lines in his face now that might have been wisdom, or debauchery, or both. He was deeply tanned, spending almost all his time under the sun, either during the New England summer or the Arizona and California winter. He even had a sunlamp system installed over his bed, encircling the smoked mirror on the ceiling.

"We've tried everything from change-of-venue to bribery," del Vecchio said. "Nothing doing. Uncle Sam's got your balls in a vise."

"How about putting some pressure on the witnesses?" Marchetti growled. "Knock off one or two and the rest'll clam up."

Del Vecchio shook his head. "Most of the 'witnesses' against you are computer records, tapes, CD ROM disks. The FBI has them under tight security, and they've made copies of them, besides."

Marchetti peered up at his lawyer. "There's gotta be *something* you can do. I ain't goin' to jail—not while you're alive."

A hint of surprise flashed in del Vecchio's dark eyes for a moment, but Marchetti never saw it, hidden behind the lawyer's stylish sunglasses. Del Vecchio recognized the threat in his employer's words, but what shocked him was that the old man was getting desperate enough to make such a threat. Soon he would be lashing out in blind anger, destroying everything and everyone around him.

"There is one thing," he said slowly.

"What? What is it?"

"You won't like it. I know you won't."

"What the hell is it?" Marchetti bellowed. "Tell me!"

"Freezing."

"What?"

"Have yourself frozen."

"Are you nuts? I ain't dead!"

Del Vecchio allowed a slight smile to cross, his lips. "No, but you could be."

Actually, the plan had been forming in his mind since Don Carmine's immersion in the gleaming stainless steel tank full of liquid nitrogen. Even then, del Vecchio had thought back to his college days when, as an agile young undergraduate, he had been a star on the school's fencing team. He remembered that there were strict rules of procedure in foil fencing, almost like the fussy rules of procedure in a criminal court. It was possible for a fencer to score a hit on his opponent, but have the score thrown out because he had not followed the proper procedure.

"Out of time!" he remembered his fencing coach screaming at him. "You can't just stab your opponent whenever the hell you feel like it! You've got to establish the proper right-of-way, the proper timing. You're out of time, del Vecchio!"

He realized that Marchetti was glowering at him. "Whattaya mean I could be dead?"

With a patient sigh, del Vecchio explained, "We've gotten your case postponed three times because of medical excuses. Dr. Brunelli has testified that you've got heart and liver problems."

"Fat lot of good that's done," Marchetti grumbled.

"Yeah, but suppose Brunelli makes out a death certificate for you, says you died of a heart attack, just like old Don Carmine."

"And they put somebody else into the ground while I take a vacation in the old country?" Marchetti's face brightened a little.

"No, that won't work. The law enforcement agencies are too smart for that. You'd be spotted and sent back here."

"Then what?"

"We make you clinically dead. Brunelli gives you an injection—"

"And kills me?" Marchetti roared.

Del Vecchio put his hands up, as if to defend himself. "Wait. Hear me out. You'll be clinically dead. We'll freeze you for a while. Then we'll bring you back and you'll be as good as ever!"

Marchetti scowled. "How do I know I can trust you to bring me back?"

"For God's sake, Angelo, you've been like a father to me ever since my real father died. You can trust me! Besides, you can arrange for a dozen different guys to see to it that you're revived. And a dozen more to knock me off if I try to keep you frozen."

"Yeah . . . maybe."

"You won't only be clinically dead," del Vecchio pointed out. "You'll be *legally* dead. Any and all charges against you will be wiped out. When you come back, legally you'll be a new person. Just like a baby!"

"Yeah?" The old man broke into a barking, sandpaper laugh.

"Sure. And just to make sure, we'll keep you frozen long enough so that the statute of limitations runs out on all the charges against you. You'll come out of that freezer free and clear!"

Marchetti's laughter grew louder, heartier. But then it abruptly stopped. "Hey, wait. Didn't you tell me that nobody knows how to defrost a corpse? If they try to thaw me out it'll kill me all over again!"

"That's all changed in the past six months," del Vecchio said. "Some bright kid down at Johns Hopkins thawed out some mice and rabbits. Then a couple weeks ago a team at Pepperdine brought back three people, two men and a woman. I hear they're going to thaw Walt Disney and bring him back pretty soon."

"What about Don Carmine?" asked Marchetti.

The lawyer shrugged. "That's up to you."

Without an instant's hesitation, Marchetti ran a stubby forefinger across his throat.

Del Vecchio had every intention of honoring his commitment to Marchetti. He really did. The fireplug-shaped old terror had truly been like a father to the younger man, paying his way through college and even law school after del Vecchio's father had been cut down in the line of duty one rainy night on the street outside a warehouse full of Japanese stereos and television sets.

But one thing led to another as the years rolled along. Del Vecchio finally married and started to raise a family. More and more of the Mob business came under his hands, and he made it prosper better than ever before. The organization now owned banks, resort hotels and other legitimate businesses, as well as state legislators, judges, and half a dozen Congressmen. Violent crime was left to the disorganized fools. Del Vecchio's regime was marked by peace, order, and upwardly spiraling profits.

One after another, Marchetti's lieutenants came to depend on him. Del Vecchio never demanded anything as archaic and embarrassing as an oath of fealty, kissing the hand, or other ancient prostrations. But the lieutenants, some of them heavily built narrow-eyed thugs, others more lean and stylish and modern, all let it be known, one way or the other, that to revive Marchetti from his cryonic slumber would be a terrible mistake.

So Marchetti slept. And del Vecchio saw his empire grow more prosperous.

But owning legitimate banks and businesses does not make one necessarily honest. Del Vecchio's banks often made highly irregular loans, and sometimes collected much higher interest than permitted by law. On rare occasions, the interest was collected only after brutal demonstrations of force. There were also some stock manipulations that finally attracted the attention of the Securities and Exchange Commission, and a string of disastrous fires in Mob-owned hotels that were on the verge of bankruptcy.

And even the lackadaisical state gambling commission roused itself when the federal income tax people started investigating the strange phenomenon of certain gambling casinos that took in customers by the millions, yet somehow failed to show a profit on their books.

Once he realized that there was no way out of the mounting legal troubles facing him, del Vecchio decided to take his own advice. Carefully, he began to create a medical history for himself that would end in clinical death and cryonic immersion. He explained what he was doing to his most trusted lieutenants, told them that he would personally take the blame and the legal punishment for them all, allowing them to elect a new leader and go on operating as before once he was declared dead. They expressed eternal gratitude.

But del Vecchio knew perfectly well how long eternal gratitude lasted. So he sent his wife and their teenaged children to live in Switzerland, where most of his personal fortune had been cached with the gnomes of Zurich. He gave his wife painfully detailed instructions on when and how to revive him.

"Fifteen years will do it," he told her. "Can you wait for me that long?"

She smiled limpidly at him, threw her arms around his neck and kissed him passionately. But she said, "I'll only be fifty-eight when you get out."

Del Vecchio wondered if she knew about his playmates in Boston. He realized he would still be his current age, forty-seven, when he was thawed back to life. There would be plenty of other women to play with. But would his wife remain faithful enough to have him revived? To make doubly certain of his future, he flew to Zurich and had a very tight legal contract drawn by the bank which held his personal fortune. The gnomes would free him, if no one else would. Otherwise his money would be donated to charity and the bank would lose control of it.

"What you're doing may be legal, Del, but it's damned immoral."

Del Vecchio was having dinner with one of the federal district attorneys who was prosecuting one of the innumerable current cases against him. They were old friends, had been classmates at law school. The fact that they were on opposite sides of the case did not bother either of them: they were too professional to allow such trivialities to get in the way of their social lives.

"Immoral?" Del Vecchio shot back. "What do I care about that? Morality's for little guys, for people who've got no muscle, no backbone. You worry about morality, I'm worrying about spending the rest of my life in jail."

They were sitting at a small corner table in a quiet little restaurant in downtown Providence, barely a block from the federal courthouse, a place frequented almost exclusively by lawyers who never lifted an eyebrow at a defendant buying dinner for a prosecuting attorney. After all, prosecuting attorneys rarely made enough money to afford such an elegant restaurant: candlelight and leather-covered wine lists were not for the protectors of the public, not on the salaries the public allowed them.

"If the jury finds you guilty, the judge has to impose the penalty," the district attorney said, very seriously.

"Jury," del Vecchio almost spat. "Those twelve *chidrools!* I'm supposed to be tried by a jury of my peers, right? That means my equals, doesn't it?"

The district attorney frowned slightly. "They are your equals, Del. What makes you think—"

"My equals?" del Vecchio laughed. "Do you really think those unemployed bums and screwy housewives are my equals? I mean, how smart can they be if they let themselves get stuck with jury duty?"

The attorney's frown deepened. His name was Christopher Scarpato. He had gone into the profession of law because his father, a small shopkeeper continually in debt to bookmakers, had insisted that his son learn how to outwit the rest of the world. While Chris was working his way through law school, his father was beaten to death by a pair of overly zealous collection agents. More of a plodder than a brilliant student, Chris was recruited by the Department of Justice, where careful, thorough groundwork is more important than flashy public relations and passionate rhetoric. Despite many opportunities, he had remained honest and dedicated. Del Vecchio found that charming, even noteworthy, and felt quite superior to his friend.

"And what makes you think they'll find me guilty?" asked del Vecchio, just a trifle smugly. "They're stupid, all right, but can they be *that* stupid?"

Scarpato finally realized he was being baited. He smiled one of his rare smiles, but it was a sad one. "They'll find you guilty, Del. They've got no choice."

Del Vecchio's grin faded. He looked down at his plate of pasta, then placed his fork on the damask tablecloth alongside it. "I got no appetite. Haven't been feeling so good."

With a weary shake of his head, Chris replied. "You don't have to put on the act for me, Del. I know what you're going to do."

"What do you mean?"

"You're going to get some tame doctor to pronounce you dead and then have yourself frozen. Just like Marchetti."

Del Vecchio tried to look shocked, but instead he broke into a grin. "Is there anything illegal about dying? Or being frozen?"

"The doctor will be committing a homicide."

"You'll have to prove that."

Scarpato said, "It's an attempt to evade the law. That's immoral, even if it's not illegal—yet."

"Let the priests worry about morality," del Vecchio advised his old friend.

"You should worry about it," said Scarpato. "You've turned into an asocial menace, Del. When we were in school, you were an okay kind of guy. But now—"

"What, I'm going to lose my soul?"

"Maybe you've already lost it. Maybe you ought to be thinking about how you can get it back."

Del Vecchio grinned at him. "Listen, Chris, I don't give a damn about souls. But I'm going to protect my body, you can bet. You won't see me in jail, old buddy. I'm going to take a step out of time, and when I come back, you'll be an old man and I'll still be young."

Scarpato said nothing, and del Vecchio knew that he had silenced his friend's attempts at conscience.

Still, that little hint of "yet" that Scarpato had dropped bothered del Vecchio as the days swiftly raced by. He checked every aspect of his plan while his health appeared to deteriorate rapidly: the doctors played their part to perfection, his wife was already comfortably ensconced in Switzerland, the bankers in Zurich understood exactly what they had to do.

Yet as he lay on the clinic table with the gleaming stainless steel cylinder waiting beside him like a mechanical whale that was going to swallow him in darkness, del Vecchio could feel his pulse racing with fear. The last thing he saw was the green-gowned doctor, masked, approaching him with the hypodermic syringe. That, and frigid wisps of vapor wafting up from the tanks of liquid nitrogen. The needle felt sharp and cold. He remembered that parts of Dante's hell were frozen in ice.

When they awoke him, there was a long period of confusion and disorientation. They told him later that it lasted only a day or so, but to del Vecchio it seemed like weeks, even months.

At first he thought something had gone wrong, and they had never put him under. But the doctors were all different, and the room he was in was not the clinic he had known. They kept him in bed most of the time, except when two husky young men came in to force him to get up and walk around the room. Four times around the little hospital room exhausted him. Then they flopped him back on the bed, gave him a mercilessly efficient massage, and left.

A female nurse wheeled in his first meal and spoon-fed him; he was too weak to lift his arms.

The second day (or week, or month), Scarpato came in to visit him.

"How do you feel, Del?"

Strangely, the attorney seemed barely to have aged at all. There was a hint of gray at his temples, perhaps a line or two in his face that had not been there before, but otherwise the years had treated him very kindly.

"Kind of weak," del Vecchio answered truthfully.

Scarpato nodded. "That's to be expected, from what the medics tell me. Your heart is good, circulation strong. Everything is okay, physically."

A thought suddenly flashed into del Vecchio's thawing mind. "What are you doing in Switzerland?"

The attorney's face grew somber. "You're not in Switzerland, Del. We had your vat flown back here. You're in New York."

"Wh . . . how . . . ?"

"And you haven't been under for fifteen years, either. It's only three years."

Del Vecchio tried to sit up in the bed, but he was too weak to make it. His head sank back onto the pillows. He could hear his pulse thudding in his ears.

"I tried to warn you," Scarpato said, "that night at dinner in Providence. You thought you were outsmarting the law, outsmarting the people who make up the law, who *are* the law. But you can't outwit the people for long, Del."

Out of the corner of his eye, del Vecchio saw that the room's only window was covered with a heavy wire mesh, like bars on a jail cell's window. He choked back a shocked gasp.

Scarpato spoke quietly, without malice. "Your cute little cryonics trick forced the people to take a fresh look at things. There've been a few new laws passed since you had yourself frozen."

"Such as?"

"Such as the state has the right to revive a frozen corpse if and when a grand jury feels he's had himself frozen specifically to evade the law."

Del Vecchio felt his heart sink in his chest.

"But once they got that one passed, they went one step further."

"What?"

"Well, you know how the country's been divided about the death penalty. Some people think it's cruel and unusual punishment; others think it's a necessary deterrent to crime, especially violent crime. Even the Supreme Court has been split on the issue."

Del Vecchio couldn't catch his breath. He realized what was coming.

"And there's been the other problem," Scarpato went on, "of overcrowding in the jails. Some judges—I'm sure you know who— even let criminals go free because they claim that putting them in overcrowded jails is cruel and unusual punishment."

"Oh my God in heaven," del Vecchio gasped.

"So . . ." Scarpato hesitated. Del Vecchio had never seen his old friend look so grim, so purposeful. "So they've passed laws in just about every state in the union to freeze criminals, just store them in vats of liquid nitrogen. Dewars, they call them. We're emptying the jails, Del, and filling them up again with Dewars. They're starting to look like mortuaries, all those stainless steel caskets piled up, one on top of another."

"But you can't do that!"

"It's done. The laws have been passed. The Supreme Court has ruled on it."

"But that's murder!"

"No. The convicts are clinically dead, but not legally. They can be revived. And since the psychologists and sociologists have been yelling for years that crime is a social maladjustment, and not really the fault of the criminal, we've found a way to make them happy."

"I don't see . . ."

Scarpato almost smiled. "Well, look. If you can have yourself frozen because you've just died of a heart ailment or a cancer that medical science can't cure, in the hopes that science will find a cure in the future and thaw you out and make you well again . . . well, why not use the same approach to social and psychological illnesses?"

"Huh?"

"You're a criminal because of some psychological maladjustment," Scarpato said. "At least, that's what the head-shrinkers claim. So we freeze you and keep you frozen until science figures out a way to cure you. That way, we're not punishing you; we're *rehabilitating* you."

"You can't do that! I got civil rights . . ."

"Your civil rights are not being infringed. Once you're found guilty by a jury of your peers you will be frozen. You will not age a single day while in the liquid nitrogen. When medical science learns how to cure your psychological unbalance, you will be thawed, cured, and returned to society as a healthy, productive citizen. We even start a small bank account for you which accrues compound interest, so that you'll have some money when you're rehabilitated."

"But that could be a thousand years in the future!" del Vecchio screamed.

"So what?"

"The whole world could be completely changed by then! They could revive me to make a slave out of me! They could use me for meat, for Chrissakes! Or spare parts!" He was screeching now, in absolute terror.

Scarpato shrugged. "We have no control over that, unfortunately. But we're doing our best for you. In earlier societies you might have been tortured, or mutilated, or even put to death. Up until a few years ago, you would have been sentenced to years and years in prison; a degrading life, filled with violence and drugs and danger. Now—you just take a nap and then someday someone will wake you up in a wonderful new world, completely rehabilitated, with enough money to start a new life for yourself."

Del Vecchio broke into uncontrollable sobs. "Don't. For God's mercy, Chris, don't do this to me. My wife, my kids . . ."

Scarpato shook his head. "It's done. Believe me, there's no way I could get you out of it, even if I wanted to. Your wife has found herself a boyfriend in Switzerland, some penniless count or duke or something. Your kids are getting along fine. Your girlfriends miss you, though, from what I hear."

"You sonofabitch! You dirty, scheming—"

"You did this to yourself, Del!" Scarpato snapped, with enough power in his voice to silence del Vecchio. "You thought you had found a nice fat loophole in the law, so you could get away with almost anything. You thought the rest of us were stupid fools. Well, you made a loophole, all right. But the people—those shopkeepers and unemployed bums and screwy housewives that you've walked over all your life—they've turned your loophole into a noose. And your neck is in it. Don't blame me. Blame yourself."

His eyes still flowing tears, del Vecchio pleaded, "Don't do it to me, Chris. Please don't do it. They'll never wake me up. They'll pull the plug on me . . ."

"Don't think that everyone's as dishonest as you are. The convicts will be kept frozen. It only costs a thousandth of what it costs to keep a man in jail. You'll be safe enough."

"But they'll thaw me out sometime in the future. I'll be all alone in the world. I won't know anybody. It'll be all strange to me. I'll be a total stranger."

"No you won't," Scarpato said, his face grim. "It's practically certain that Marchetti and Don Carmine will both be thawed out when you are. After all, you're all three suffering from the same dysfunction, aren't you?"

That's when the capillary in del Vecchio's brain ballooned and burst. Scarpato saw his friend's eyes roll up into his head, his body stiffen. He slammed the emergency call button beside the bed and a team of medics rushed in. While Scarpato watched, they declared del Vecchio clinically dead. Within an hour they slid his corpse into a waiting stainless steel cylinder where it would repose until some happier day in the distant future.

"You're out of time now, Del," Scarpato whispered as a technician sealed the end of the gleaming Dewar. "Really out of time."

BÉISBOL

There are other (better!) ways for nations to compete than by going to war. The Greeks figured that out more than two thousand years ago.

I got this crazy idea one day—if the United States began its rapprochement with Communist China by sending Ping-Pong players to Beijing, maybe someday we would start to make up with Castro's Cuba by sending a baseball team to Havana. As I mulled it over in my mind, a certain Mr. Lucius J. Riccio, of New York City, suggested the same thing in a letter to The New York Times *of March 3, 1985.*

I realized that I could not waste time mulling. The idea would slip away from me if I didn't get the story onto paper.

The first draft of the tale was pretty dull. Thank heaven, I was smart enough to look up Alfred Bester, one of the great talents of our age—especially when it comes to sparking up a story idea. Alfie's mind worked in leaps and bounds, and after an evening of swapping ideas and swilling booze, "Béisbol" just about wrote itself.

So thank you, Alfie. See you at the big game Up There.

RICHARD NIXON sat scowling in the dugout, his dark chin down on the letters of his baseball uniform, his eyes glaring. It wasn't us he was mad at, it was Castro.

Across the infield, the Cubans were passing out cigars in their dugout. Top of the ninth inning and they were ahead, 1-0. We had three more chances at their robot pitcher. So far, all the mechanical monster had done was strike out fourteen of us USA All-Stars and not allow a runner past first base.

Castro looked a lot older than I thought he'd be. His beard was all gray. But he was laughing and puffing on a big cigar as his team took the field and that damned robot rolled itself up to the mound.

Nixon jumped to his feet. He looked kind of funny in a baseball uniform, like, out of place.

"Men," he said to us, "this is more than a game. I'm sure you know that."

We all kind of muttered and mumbled and nodded our heads.

"If they win this series, they'll take over all of the Caribbean. All of Central America. The United States will be humiliated."

Yeah, maybe so, I thought. And you'll be a bum again, instead of a hero. But he didn't have to go up and try to bat against that Commie robot. From what we heard, they had built it in Czechoslovakia or someplace like that to throw hand grenades at tanks. Now it was throwing baseballs right past us, like a blur.

"We've got to win this game," Nixon said, his voice trembling. "We've got to!"

It had seemed like a good idea. Use baseball to reestablish friendly relations with Cuba, just like they had used Ping-Pong to make friends with Red China. So the commissioner personally picked an All-Star team and Washington picked Nixon to manage us. It would be a pushover, we all thought. I mean, the Cubans like baseball, but they couldn't come anywhere near matching us.

Well, pitching may be eighty percent of the game, but scouting is two hundred percent more. We waltzed into Havana and found ourselves playing guys who were just about as good as we were. According to a CIA report, their guys were pumped up on steroids and accelerators and God knows what else. They'd never pass an Olympic Games saliva test, but nobody on our side had thought to include drug testing in the ground rules.

Oh, we won the first two games okay. But it wasn't easy.

And then the Commies used their first secret weapon on us. Women. It was like our hotel was all of a sudden invaded by them. Tall show-girl types, short little senioritis, redheads, blondes, dark flashing eyes and luscious lips that smiled and laughed. And boobs. Never saw so many bouncing, jiggling, low-cut bosoms in my life.

What could we do? Our third baseman hurt his back swinging by his knees from the chandelier in his room with a broad in one arm and a bottle of champagne in the other. Two of our best pitchers were so hung over that they couldn't see their catchers the next morning. And our center fielder, who usually batted cleanup, was found under his bed in a coma that lasted three days. But there was a big smile on his face the whole time.

By the time the Cubans had pulled ahead, three games to two, Nixon called a team meeting and put it to us but good.

"This has got to stop," he said, pacing back and forth across the locker room, hands locked behind his stooped back, jowls quivering with anger. "These women are trained Communist agents," he warned us. "I've been getting intelligence reports from Washington. Castro has no intentions of establishing friendly relations with us."

Somebody snickered at the words *friendly relations,* but quickly choked it off as Nixon whirled around, searching for the culprit like a schoolteacher dealing with a bunch of unruly kids.

"This isn't funny! If the Commies win this series, they'll go all through Latin America crowing about how weak the United States is. We'll lose the whole Caribbean, Central America, the Panama Canal— everything!"

We promised to behave ourselves. Hell, he was worried about Latin America, but most of us had more important problems. I could just imagine my next salary negotiation: "Why, you couldn't even beat a bunch of third-rate Cubans," the general manager would tell my agent.

More than that, I could see my father's face. He had spent many years teaching me how to play baseball. He had always told me that I could be a big leaguer. And he had always asked nothing more of me than that I gave my best out on the field. I wouldn't be able to face him, knowing that we had lost to Castro because we had screwed around.

We went out there that afternoon and tore them apart, 11-2. That tied the series. The seventh and final game would decide it all.

That's when they brought out their second secret weapon: Raoul the Robot, the mechanical monster, the Czechoslovak chucker, the machine that threw supersonic fastballs.

I thought Nixon would have apoplexy when the little robot rolled itself up to the pitcher's mound to start the game. It looked sort of like a water cooler, a squat metal cylinder with a glass dome on top. It had two "arms": curved metal chutes that wound around and around several times and then fired the ball at you. Fast. Very fast.

Nixon went screaming out onto the field before our leadoff batter got to the plate. Castro ambled out, grinning and puffing his cigar. The huge crowd—the Havana stadium was absolutely jammed—gave him the kind of roar that American fans reserve for pitchers who throw no-hitters in the seventh game of the World Series.

Castro turned, doffed his cap just like any big leaguer would, and then joined the argument raging at the mound.

Nixon did us proud. He jumped up and down. He threw his cap on the dirt and kicked it. He turned red in the face. He raged and shouted at the umpires—two of them from the States, two from Cuba.

The crowd loved it. They started shouting *"Ole!"* every time Nixon kicked up some dirt.

The umpires went through the rule hook. There's no rule that says all the players have to be human beings. So Raoul the Robot stayed on the mound.

He struck out the side in the first inning. Leading off the second inning, our cleanup hitter, well rested after his three-day coma, managed to pop a fly to center field. But the next two guys struck out.

And so it went. Raoul had three basic pitches: fast, faster, and fastest. No curve, no slider, no change-up. His fastballs were pretty straight, too. Not much of a hop or dip to them. They just blazed past you before you could get your bat around. And he could throw either right-handed or left-handed, depending on the batter.

He couldn't catch the ball at all. After each pitch the catcher would toss the ball to the shortstop, who would come over to the mound and stick the ball in a round opening at the top of the robot's glassed-in head. Then the machine would be ready to wind up and throw.

"Hit him in the head," Nixon advised us. "Break that glass top and knock him the hell out of there."

Easy to say. Through the first four innings we got exactly one man on base, a walk. Their catcher adjusted the little gizmo he had clipped to his chest protector, and the mechanical monster started throwing strikes again.

By the time the ninth inning came around, we had collected two hits, both of them bloop pop-ups that just happened to fall in between fielders. Raoul had struck out fourteen. Nixon was glaring pure hatred across the infield. Castro was laughing and passing out cigars in the Cubans' dugout.

Our own pitcher had done almost as well as the robot. But an error by our substitute third baseman, a sacrifice fly, and a squeeze bunt had given the Cubans a 1-0 lead. That one run looked as big as a million.

Our shortstop led off the ninth inning and managed to get his bat on the ball. A grounder. He was out by half a step. The next guy popped up—not bad after three strikeouts.

I breathed a sigh of relief. The next man up, Harry Bates, would end the game, and that would be that. I was next after him, and I sure didn't want to be the guy who made the last out. I went out to the on-deck circle, kneeled on one knee, and watched the final moment of the game.

"Get it over with, Harry," I said inside my head. "Don't put me on the spot." I was kind of ashamed of myself for feeling that way, but that's how I felt.

Raoul cranked his metal slingshot arm once, twice, and then fired the ball. It blurred past the batter. Strike one. The crowd roared *"Ole!"* The catcher flipped the ball to the shortstop, who trotted over to the mound and popped the ball into the robot's slot like a guy putting money into a video game.

The curved metal arm cranked again. The ball came whizzing to the plate. Strike two. *"Ole!"* Louder this time. Castro leaned back on the dugout bench and clasped his hands behind his head. His grin was as wide as a superhighway.

But on the third pitch Harry managed to get his bat around and cracked a solid single, over their shortstop's head. The first real hit of the day for us.

The crowd went absolutely silent.

Castro looked up and down his bench, then made a big shrug. He wasn't worried.

I was. It was my turn at bat. All I had to show for three previous trips to the plate was a strikeout and two pop flies.

Automatically, I looked down to our third-base coach. He was staring into the dugout. Nixon scratched his nose, tugged at the bill of his cap, and ran a hand across the letters on the front of his shirt. The coach's eyes goggled. But he scratched his nose, tugged at his cap, and ran his hand across the letters.

Hit and run.

Damn! I'm supposed to poke the first pitch into right field while Harry breaks for second as soon as the pitcher starts his—its—delivery. Terrific strategy, when the chances are the damned ball will be in the catcher's mitt before I can get the bat off my shoulder. Nixon's trying to be a genius. Well, at least when they throw Harry out at second, the game'll be over and I won't have to make the final out.

The mechanical monster starts its windup, Harry breaks from first, and *wham!* the ball's past me. I wave my bat kind of feebly, just to make the catcher's job a little bit tougher.

But his throw is late. Raoul's windup took so much time that Harry made it to second easy. I look down to the third-base coach again.

Same sign. Hit and run. Sweet Jesus! Now he wants Harry to head for third. I grit my teeth and pound the bat on the plate. Stealing second is a lot easier than stealing third.

Raoul swings his mechanical arm around. Harry breaks for third, and the ball comes whizzing at me. I swing at it but it's already in the catcher's mitt and he's throwing to third. Harry dives in headfirst and the umpire calls him safe. By a fingernail.

The crowd is muttering now, rumbling like a dark thundercloud. The tying run's on third.

And I've got two strikes on me.

Nixon slumps deeper on the bench in the dugout, his face lost in shadow. Both Harry and our third-base coach are staring in at him. He twitches and fidgets. The coach turns to me and rubs his jaw.

Hit away. I'm on my own.

No, my whole life didn't flash before my eyes, but it might as well have. Old Raoul out there on the mound hadn't thrown anything but strikes since the fourth inning. One more strike and I'm out and the game's over and we've lost. The only time I got any wood on the ball I produced a feeble pop fly. There was only one thing I could think of that had any chance.

You can throw, you goddamned Commie tin can, I said silently to the robot. But can you field?

Raoul cranked up his metal arm again, and I squared away and slid my hand halfway up the bat. Out of the corners of my eyes I could see the Cuban infielders suddenly reacting to the idea that I was going to bunt. The first and third basemen started rushing in toward me. But too late. The pitch was already on its way.

Harry saw it, too, and started galloping for home. I just stuck my bat in front of the ball, holding it limply to deaden the impact. I had always been a good bunter, and this one had to be perfect.

It damned near was. I nudged the ball right back toward the mound. It trickled along the grass as I lit out for first, thinking, "Let's see you handle that, Raoul."

Sonofabitch if the mechanical monster didn't roll itself down off the mound and scoop up the ball as neatly as a vacuum cleaner picking up a fuzzball. I was less than halfway to first and I knew that I had goofed. I was dead meat.

Raoul the Robot sucked up the ball, spun itself around to face first base, and fired the baseball like a bullet to the guy covering the bag. It got there ten strides ahead of me, tore the glove off the fielder's hand, and kept on going deep into right field, past the foul line.

My heart bounced from my throat to my stomach and then back again. Raoul had only three pitches: fast, faster, and fastest. The poor sucker covering first base had never been shot at so hard. He never had a chance to hold on to the ball.

Harry scored, of course, and I must have broken the world record for going from first to third. I slid into the bag in a storm of dust and dirt, an eyelash ahead of the throw.

The game was tied. The winning run—me!—was on third base, ninety feet away from home.

And the stadium was dead quiet again. Castro came out to the mound and they didn't even applaud him. The catcher and the whole infield clustered around him and the robot. Castro, taller than all his players, turned and pointed at somebody in the dugout.

"He's bringin' in a relief pitcher!" our third-base coach said.

No such luck. A stumpy little guy who was built kind of like the robot himself, thick and solid, like a fireplug, came trudging out of the dugout with something like a tool kit in one hand. He was wearing a mechanic's coveralls, not a baseball uniform.

They tinkered with Raoul for about ten minutes, while the crowd got restless and Nixon shambled out of our dugout to tell the umpires that the Cubans should be penalized for delaying the game.

"This ain't football, Mr. President," said the chief umpire.

Nixon grumbled and mumbled and went back inside the dugout.

Finally, the repair job at the mound was finished. The infielders dispersed and the repairman trotted off the field. Castro stayed at the mound while Raoul made a few practice pitches.

Kee-rist! Now he didn't wind up at all. He just swung the arm around once and fired the ball to the catcher. Faster than ever.

And our batter, Pedro Valencia, had struck out three straight times. Never even managed to tick the ball foul. Not once. Nine pitches, nine strikes, three strikeouts.

I looked at the coach, a couple of feet away from me. No sign. No strategy. I was on my own.

Pedro stepped into the batter's box. Raoul stood up on the mound. His mechanical arm swung around and something that looked like an aspirin tablet whizzed into the catcher's mitt. *"Ole!"* Strike one.

I took a good-sized lead off third base. Home plate was only a couple dozen strides away. The shortstop took the catcher's toss and popped the ball into the robot's slot.

If I stole home, we would win. If I got thrown out, we would lose for sure. Raoul could keep pitching like that all day, all night, all week. Sooner or later we'd tire out and they'd beat us. We'd never get another runner to third base. It was up to me. Now.

I didn't wait for the damned robot to start his pitch. He had the ball, he was on the mound, nobody had called time out. I broke for the plate.

Everything seemed to happen in slow motion. I could see the surprised expression on Pedro's face. But he was a pro; he hung in there and swung at the pitch. Missed it. The catcher had the ball in his mitt and I was still three strides up the line. I started a slide away from him, toward the pitcher's side of the plate. He lunged at me, the ball in his bare hand.

I felt him tag my leg. And I heard the umpire yell, "Out . . . no, *safe!*"

I was sitting on the ground. The catcher was on top of me, grabbing for the ball as it rolled away from us both. He had dropped it.

Before I could recover from the shock, he whispered from behind his mask, "You ween. Now we have to play another series. In the States, no?"

I spit dust from my mouth. He got to his feet. "See you in Peetsborgh, no?"

He had dropped the damned ball on purpose. He wanted to come to the States and play for my team, the Pirates.

By now the whole USA team was grabbing me and hiking me up on their shoulders. Nixon was already riding along, his arms upraised in his old familiar victory gesture. The fans were giving us a grudging round of applause. We had won—even if it took a deliberate error by a would-be defector.

In the locker room, news correspondents from all the Latin American nations descended on us. Fortunately, my Spanish was up to the task. They crowded around me, and I told them what it was like to live in Miami and get the chance to play big-league baseball. I told them about my father, and how he had fled from Cuba with nothing but his wife and infant son—me—twenty-three years ago. I knew we had won on a fluke, but I still felt damned good about winning.

Finally the reporters and photographers were cleared out of the locker room, and Nixon stood on one of the benches, a telegram in his hand, tears in his eyes.

"Men," he said, "I have good news and bad news."

We clustered around him.

"The good news is that the President of the United States," his voice quavered a little, "has invited all of us to the White House. You're all going to receive medals from the President himself."

Smiles all around.

"And now the bad news," he went on. "The President has agreed to a series against a Japanese team—the Mitsubishi Marvels. They're all robots. Each and every one of them."

RE-ENTRY SHOCK

Normally I write my stories from a male point of view. My protagonists are almost always men. Caucasian men, at that. Chet Kinsman. Keith Stoner, of the Voyagers *novels. Jamie Waterman, the protagonist of* Mars.

I have written about male characters who are black or Asian; Jamie Waterman is half-Navaho, although his Navaho heritage is pretty deeply submerged beneath his white Western upbringing. I have written about women characters, some of them quite strong enough to be the protagonists of their stories.

But I've always found it difficult to see women characters (or non-Caucasian male characters, for that matter) from the inside. That's what I need to be able to do, for my protagonists. I have to be able to get inside their heads, deep into their souls, to make them work as protagonists.

So when I started writing "Re-Entry Shock," the protagonist was male. And the story wasn't working. Something in my subconscious mind was resisting the story as I was trying to write it.

Then a very conscious thought struck me. The Magazine of Fantasy & Science Fiction, the most literate market in the field, had just acquired a new editor: Kristine Kathryn Rusch. I knew Kristine slightly; she was a fellow writer, and practically every writer in the field knows every other writer, at least slightly. It occurred to the business side of my brain that Kris might prefer stories with women protagonists. Hmm.

Purely as an exercise in writing—and marketing—I went back to "Re-Entry Shock" and changed the protagonist to a woman. To my

229

somewhat surprised delight, Dolores Anna Maria Alvarez de Montoya
stepped onto the center of the stage and took over the story as if she had
been meant to be its protagonist from the beginning of time.

Which, of course, she had been.

＊ 🌑 ＊

"**THE TESTS** are for your own protection," he said. "Surely you can
understand that."

"I can understand that you are trying to prevent me from returning
to my home," Dolores flared angrily. And immediately regretted her
outburst. It would do her no good to lose her temper with this little
man.

The two of them were sitting in a low-ceilinged windowless room
that might have been anywhere on Earth or the Moon. In fact, it was
on the space station that served as the major transfer point for those
few special people allowed to travel from the Moon to Earth or vice
versa.

"It's nothing personal," the interviewer said, looking at the display
screen on his desk instead of at Dolores. "We simply cannot allow
someone to return just because they announce that they want to."

"So you say," she replied.

"The tests are for your own protection," he repeated, weakly.

"Yes. Of course." She had been through the whole grueling routine
for more than a week now. "I have passed all the tests. I can handle the
gravity. The difference in air pressure. I am not carrying any diseases.
There is no physical reason to keep me from returning."

"But you've been away nearly ten years. The cultural shock, the
readjustment, the psychological problems often outweigh the physical
ones. It's not simply a matter of buying a return ticket and boarding a
shuttle."

"I know. I have been told time and again that it is a privilege, not a
right."

The interviewer lifted his eyes from his display screen and looked
directly at her for the first time. "Are you absolutely certain you want
to do this?" he asked. "After ten years—are you willing to give up your
whole life, your friends and all, just to come back?"

Dolores glanced at the nameplate on his desk. "Yes, Mr. Briem," she said icily. "That is precisely what I want to do."

"But why?"

Dolores Anna Maria Alvarez de Montoya leaned back in the spindly plastic chair. It creaked in complaint. She was a solidly built woman in her early forties, with a strong-boned deeply tanned face. Her dark straight hair, graying prematurely, was tied back in a single long braid. To the interviewer she looked exactly like what the computer files said she was: a journeyman construction worker with a questionable political background. A problem.

"I want to be able to breathe freely again," Dolores answered slowly. "I've lived like an ant in a hive long enough. Hemmed in by their laws and regulations. People weren't meant to live like that. I want to come back home."

For a long moment the interviewer stared at Dolores, his Nordic blue eyes locked on her deep onyx pools. Then he turned back toward the display screen on his desk as if he could see more of her through her records than by watching the woman herself.

"You say 'home.' You've been away nearly ten years."

"It is still my home," Dolores said firmly. "I was born there. My roots are there."

"Your son is there."

She had expected that. Yet she still drew in her breath at the pain. "Yes," she conceded. "My son is there."

"You left of your own volition. You declared that you never wanted to come back. You renounced your citizenship."

"That was ten years ago."

"You've changed your mind—after ten years."

"I was very foolish then. I was under great emotional stress. A divorce . . ." She let her voice trail off. She did not mention the fierce political passions that had burned within her back in those days.

"Yes," said the interviewer. "Very foolish."

C. Briem: that was all his nameplate said. He did not seem to Dolores to be a really nasty man. Not very sympathetic, naturally. But not the totally cold inhuman kind of bureaucrat she had seen so often over the years. He was quite young, she thought, for a position of such power. Young and rather attractive, with hair the color of afternoon sunshine cropped short and neat. And good shoulders beneath his severely tailored one-piece suit. It was spotless white, of course. Dolores wore her one and only business suit, gray and shabby after all the years of hanging in closets or being folded in a tight travel bag. She had worn it only at the rallies and late-night meetings she had attended; fewer and fewer, as the years passed by.

Over the past week Dolores had gone through a dozen interviews like this one. And the complete battery of physical tests. This man behind the desk had the power to recommend that she be allowed to return to her home, or to keep her locked out and exiled from her roots, her memories, her only son.

"How old is your boy now?" he suddenly asked.

Startled, Dolores answered, "Eleven—no, he'll be twelve years old next month. I was hoping to get back in time to see him on his birthday."

"We really don't want any more immigrant laborers," he said, trying to make his voice hard but not quite able to do so.

"I am not an immigrant," Dolores replied firmly. "I am a native. And I am not a laborer. I am a fluid-systems technician."

"A plumber."

She smiled tolerantly. "A plumber who works on fusion-power plants. They require excellent piping and welding. I run the machines that do such work. It is all in the dossier on your screen, I'm sure."

He conceded his point with a dip of his chin. "You've worked on fusion plants for all the ten years you were out there?"

"Most of the time. I did some work on solar-power systems as well. They also require excellent plumbing."

For long moments the interviewer said nothing, staring at the screen as if it would tell him what to do, which decision to make.

Finally he returned his gaze to Dolores. "I will have to consult the immigration board, Ms. Alvarez. You will have to wait for their decision."

"How long will that take?"

He blinked his blue eyes once, twice. "A day or so. Perhaps longer."

"Then I must remain aboard this station until they decide?"

"Of course. Your expenses will be paid by the government on its regular per diem allowance."

Dolores felt her nostrils flare. Government per diem allowances did not come anywhere near the prices charged by the station's restaurants or the hotel. And it usually took months for any government to honor the expense reports that per diem people sent in.

She got to her feet. "I hope it will be a quick decision, then."

The interviewer remained seated, but seemed to thaw just a bit. "No, Ms. Alvarez. Hope for a slow decision. The more time they take to make up their minds, the better your chances."

Dolores murmured, "Like a jury deciding a person's life or death."

"Yes," he said sadly. "Very much like that."

Dolores drifted through the rest of the day, walking through the long sloping passageways of the circular station, heading away from the administrative offices with their impersonal interviewers and computerized records of a woman's entire life.

Do they know? she asked herself silently. Do they suspect why I want to return? Of course they must have records of my old political activities, but do they know what I am trying to accomplish now?

Even when the three lunar colonies had united in declaring their independence from the World Government, the separation between the peoples of Earth and those living in space had never been total. Governments might rage and threaten, corporations might cut off entire colonies from desperately needed trade, but still a trickle of people made it from space back to Mother Earth. And vice versa. The journey was often painful and always mired in red tape, but as far as Dolores knew no one had ever been flatly denied permission to go home again.

Until now.

The other people striding along the wide passageways were mostly administrative staff personnel who wore one-piece jumpsuits, as had the handsome young Mr. Briem. White, sky-blue, fire-engine red, grassy green, their colors denoted the wearers' jobs. But as Dolores neared the area where the tourist shops and restaurants were located, the people around her changed.

The tourists dressed with far more variety: men in brilliantly colored running suits or conservative business outfits such as Dolores herself wore; the younger women showing bare midriffs, long shapely legs glossy with the sheen of hosiery, startling makeup and hairdos.

The space station was huge, massive, like a small city in orbit. As she strolled aimlessly along its passageways Dolores realized that the station had grown in the ten years since she had last seen it. It was like

Samarkand or Damascus or any of those other ancient cities along the old caravan trails: a center of commerce and trade, even tourism. Surely the restrictions against returning home were easier now than they had been ten years before.

Then she realized that these tourists were aboard a space station that orbited a mere five hundred kilometers above Earth's surface. They would not be allowed to go to the Moon or to one of the O'Neill habitats. They were flatlanders on vacation. And there were almost no lunar citizens or residents of O'Neill communities here in this station. At least, none that she could identify.

She caught a glance of the Earth hanging outside one of the rare windows along the passageway, huge and blue and glowing with beauty. Five hundred kilometers away. Only five hundred kilometers.

As the station swung in its stately rotation the view of Earth passed out of sight. Dolores saw the distant Moon hanging against the black background of deep space. Then even that passed, and there was nothing to see but the infinite emptiness.

Will they find out? Dolores wondered. Is there something in my record, something I might have said during the interviews, some tiny hint, that will betray me?

She stopped in mid-stride, almost stumbled as a sudden bolt of electrical surprise flashed through her. Hector Luis! Her son!

But then she saw that it was merely a curly haired boy of ten or twelve, a stranger walking with his trusting hand firmly in the grasp of a man who must have been his father. Dolores watched them pass by without so much as a flicker of a glance at her. As if she were not there in the corridor with them. As if she did not exist.

The last hologram she had seen of her son had been more than a year ago. The boy walking past looked nothing like Hector Luis, really. The same height maybe. Not even a similar build.

You are becoming maudlin, she chided herself. She realized that she was in the midst of the shopping area. Store windows stretched on both sides of the passageway, merchandise of all sorts glittered brightly in the attractive displays. Maybe I can find something for Hector Luis, she thought. Maybe if I buy a gift for him it will impress the immigration board. She had no doubt that they were watching her. Yet she felt slightly ashamed of her thought, using her son as a tool to pry open the board members' hearts.

She window-shopped until she lost track of the time. The more she gazed at the lush variety of merchandise the more confused she became. What would a twelve-year-old boy like? What did her son like? She had no idea.

Finally her stomach told her that she had missed lunch and it was almost time for supper. There were restaurants further up the corridor. Dolores frowned inwardly: the government's munificent per diem allowance might just cover the price of a beer.

With a shrug she moved through the meandering tourists and headed for a meal she could barely afford. She studied the menus displayed on the electronic screens outside each of the four restaurants, then entered the least expensive.

She hardly felt any surprise at all when she saw that Mr. Briem was already seated at a table by the window, alone. Yes, they are certainly watching me.

He saw Dolores as she approached his table. "Buenas tardes, Mr. Briem," she said, with a gracious nod of her head.

"Ms. Alvarez!" He scrambled to his feet and pretended to be surprised. "Would you care to join me? I just came in here a few moments ago."

"I would be very happy to. It is very lonely to eat by one's self."

"Yes," he said. "It is."

Dolores sat across the little square table from him, and they studied the menu screen for a few moments. She grimaced at the prices, but Briem did not seem to notice.

They tapped out their orders on the keyboard. Then Dolores asked politely, "Do you come here often?"

He made a small shrug. "When I get tired of my own cooking. Often enough."

A young woman walked up to the table, petite, oriental-looking. "Hi, Cal. A little early for you, isn't it?"

"I'm going to the concert tonight," he answered quickly.

"Oh so?" The woman glanced at Dolores, then turned her eyes back to him. "Me too."

"I'll see you there, then."

"Good. Maybe we can have dessert or coffee together afterward."

Briem nodded and smiled. It was an innocent smile, Dolores thought. It almost made her believe that he truly was in this restaurant because he was going to a concert later in the evening and the young oriental was not an agent of the immigration department or a bodyguard assigned to watch over him while he dealt with this would-be infiltrator.

"Your first name is Calvin?" Dolores asked.

"Calvert," he replied. "I prefer Cal. It sounds less like an old British mystery story."

"I am called Dolores. My especial friends call me Dee."

His smile came back, warmer this time. The robot rolled up to their table with their trays of dinner on its flat top. They started to eat.

"I was thinking of buying my son a present," Dolores said, "but I don't know what to get him. What are twelve-year-old boys interested in these days?"

"I really don't know."

"There is so much in the store windows! It's rather overwhelming."

"You haven't gone shopping for a while?"

"Not for a long time. Where I was, there were no stores. Not gift stores. I suppose I have missed a lot of things in the past ten years."

They fell silent for a few moments. Dolores turned her attention to her broth. It was thin and delicately flavored, not like the rich heavy soups she was accustomed to.

"Ms. Alvarez—"

"Dolores."

"Dolores, then." Cal Briem looked troubled. "I suppose I shouldn't bring up the subject. It's none of my affair, really . . ."

"What is it?"

"Your political activities."

"Ah." She had known it would come up sooner or later. At least he was bringing it out into the open.

"You were quite an activist in your younger days. But over the past few years you seem to have stopped."

"I have grown older."

He looked at her, really looked at her, for a long silent moment.

"I can't accept the idea that you've given up your beliefs," he said at last.

"I was never a radical. I never advocated violence. During the times of the great labor unrest I served as a mediator more than once."

"We know. It's in your record."

She put down her spoon, tired of the whole charade. "Then my political beliefs are going to be counted against me, aren't they?"

"They don't help," he said softly.

"You are going to prevent me from returning home because my political position is not acceptable to you."

"Did you marry again?" He changed the subject. "We have no record of it if you did."

"No. I did not marry again."

"For ten years you've remained unmarried?" She recognized the unvoiced question.

"After the terrible mess of my first marriage, I never allowed myself to become so attached to someone that he could cause me pain."

"I see," he said.

"Besides," Dolores added, "where I was, out on the construction jobs, there were not that many men who were both eligible and attractive."

"I find that hard to believe."

"Believe it," she said fervently.

"Your political activities broke up your marriage, didn't they?"

She fought an urge to laugh. Raoul's father owned half of the solar system's largest construction firm. "They did not help to cement us together, no," she said.

"Have you given up your political activities altogether?" he asked, his voice trembling slightly.

Dolores spooned up another sip of broth before answering. "Yes," she half-lied. "But I still have my beliefs."

"Of course."

They finished the brief meal in virtual silence. When their bills appeared on the table's display screen Briem gently pushed Dolores's hand aside and tapped his own number on the keyboard.

"Let the immigration board pay for this," he said, smiling shyly. "They can afford it better than you."

"Muchas gracias," said Dolores. But inwardly she asked herself, *Why is he doing this? What advantage does he expect to gain?*

"Would you like to go to the concert?" he asked as they got up from the table.

Dolores thought a moment. Then, "No, I think not. Thank you anyway. I appreciate your kindness."

As they walked out into the broad passageway again, Briem said, "Your son's been living all this time with his father, hasn't he?"

Again she felt the stab of pain. And anger. What is he trying to do to me? Dolores raged inwardly. "I don't think you have any right to probe into my personal affairs," she snapped.

His face went red. "Oh, I didn't mean—I was only trying to be helpful. You had asked about what the boy might be interested in . . ."

The anger drained out of her as quickly as it had risen. "I'm sorry. I have always been too quick to lose my temper."

"It's understandable," Briem said.

"One would think that at my age I would have learned better self-control."

"De nada," he said, with an atrocious accent. But she smiled at his attempt to defuse the situation. Then she caught a view of Earth again in the window across the passageway. Dolores headed toward it like a woman lured by a lover, like a sliver of iron pulled by a magnet.

Briem walked beside her. "I really should be getting to the auditorium. The concert."

"Yes," Dolores muttered, staring at the glowing blue-and-white panorama parading before her eyes. "Of course."

He grasped her sleeve, forcing her to tear her eyes away and look at him.

"Tell me what you learned in the ten years you were away," he said, suddenly urgent. "Tell me the most important thing you've learned."

She blinked at the fervor in his voice, the intensity of his expression. "The most important?"

"I know you still have a political agenda. You haven't given up all your hopes, your ideals. But what did the past ten years teach you?"

Dolores put aside all pretense. She knew she was destroying all her hopes for returning home, killing the only chance to see her son once again. But she told him anyway, without evasion, without pretense.

"They need us. They cannot survive without us. Nor can we truly survive without them. This enforced separation is killing us both."

Strangely, Briem smiled. "They need us," he echoed. "And we need them."

Dolores nodded dumbly, her eyes drawn back to the gleaming beckoning sprawl of the world she had left.

"We've changed, too," Briem said softly, almost in a whisper. "Some of us have, at least. There are a few of us who realize that we can't remain separated. A few of us who believe exactly what you believe."

"Can that be true?"

"Yes," he said. "The human race must not remain separated into the wealthy few who live in space and the impoverished billions on Earth. That way is worse than madness. It's evil."

"You know what I want to do, then. You have known it all along."

"I suspected it," said Briem. "And I'm glad that my suspicions were correct. We need people like you: people who've been there and can convince the government and the voters that we must reestablish strong ties with our brothers and sisters."

Dolores felt giddy, almost faint. "Then you will recommend—"

"I'm the chairman of the immigration board," Briem revealed. "Your application for return will be approved, I promise you."

Her thoughts tumbled dizzyingly in her mind, but the one that stood out most powerfully was that she would see her son again. I will see Hector Luis! I will hold him in my arms!

"Now I've really got to get to that concert," Briem said. "I'm playing second keyboard tonight."

"Yes," Dolores said vaguely. "I am sorry to have kept you."

He flashed her a smile and dashed off down the passageway.

"And thank you!" Dolores called after him.

Then she turned back to the window. Five hundred kilometers away was the Earth she had left only a week ago. The Earth on which she had spent ten years, working in their filthy choked cities, living among the helpless and the hopeless, trying to change their world, to make their lives better, learning day by painful day that they could not long survive without the wealth, the knowledge, the skills that the space communities had denied them.

The Earth slid from her view and she saw the Moon once again, clean and cool, distant yet reachable. She would return to the world of her birth, she realized. She would work with all the passion and strength in her to make them understand the debt they owed to the people of Earth. She would reunite the severed family of humankind.

And she would see her son and make him understand that despite everything she loved him. Perhaps she would even reunite her own severed family.

Dolores smiled to herself. She was dreaming impossible dreams and she knew it. But without the dreams, she also knew, there can be no reality.

THE SYSTEM

This story was written in the Nineteen Sixties, while I was connected with a program to develop an artificial heart. Even at that time, there were committees sitting to decide who would get to use the rare and expensive kidney dialysis machines and who would die of renal failure.

Any relationship between this tale and Obamacare or death panels is purely . . . prescient?

"NOT JUST RESEARCH," Gorman said, rocking smugly in his swivel chair, *"organized* research."

Hopler, the cost-time analyst, nodded agreement.

"Organized," Gorman continued, "and carefully controlled—from above. The System—that's what gets results. Give the scientists their way and they'll spend you deaf, dumb, and blind on butterfly sex-ways or sub-sub-atomic particles. Damned nonsense."

Sitting on the front edge of the visitor's chair, Hopler asked meekly, "I'm afraid I don't see what this has to do . . ."

"With the analysis you turned in?" Gorman glanced at the ponderous file that was resting on a corner of his desk. "No, I suppose you don't know. You just chew through the numbers, don't you? Names, people, ideas . . . they don't enter into your work."

With an uncomfortable shrug, Hopler replied, "My job is economic analysis. The System shouldn't be biased by personalities."

"Of course not."

"But now that it's over, I would like to know . . . I mean, there've been rumors going through the Bureau."

"About the cure? They're true. The cure works. I don't know the details of it," Gorman said, waving a chubby hand. "Something to do with repressor molecules. Cancerous cells lack 'em. So the biochemists we've been supporting have found out how to attach repressors to the cancer cells. Stops 'em from growing. Controls the cancer. Cures the patient. Simple . . . now that we know how to do it."

"It . . . it's almost miraculous."

Gorman frowned. "What's miraculous about it? Why do people always connect good things with miracles? Why don't you think of cancer as a miracle, a black miracle?"

Hopler fluttered his hands as he fumbled for a reply.

"Never mind," Gorman snapped. "This analysis of yours. Shows the cure can be implemented on a nationwide basis. Not too expensive. Not too demanding of trained personnel that we don't have."

"I believe the cure could even be put into worldwide effect," Hopler said.

"The hell it can be!"

"What? I don't understand. My analysis—"

"Your analysis was one of many. The System has to look at all sides of the picture. That's how we beat heart disease, and stroke, and even highway deaths."

"And now cancer."

"No. Not cancer. Cancer stays. Demographic analysis knocked out all thoughts of using the cure. There aren't any other major killers around anymore. Stop cancer and we swamp ourselves with people. So the cure gets shelved."

For a stunned instant, Hopler was silent. Then, "But . . . but I *need* the cure!"

Gorman nodded grimy. "So will I. The System predicts it."

BATTLE STATION

"Where do you get your crazy ideas?"

Every science fiction writer has heard that question, over and over again. Sometimes the questioner is kind enough to leave out the word "crazy." But the question still is asked whenever I give a lecture to any audience that includes people who do not regularly read science fiction.

Some science fiction writers, bored by that same old question (and sometimes miffed at the implications behind that word "crazy"), have taken to answering: "Schenectady!" There's even a mythology about it that claims that members of the Science Fiction Writers of America subscribe to the Crazy Idea Service of Schenectady, New York, and receive in the mail one crazy idea each month—wrapped in plain brown paper, of course.

Yet the question deserves an answer. People are obviously fascinated with the process of creativity. Nearly everybody has a deep curiosity about how a writer comes up with the ideas that generate fresh stories.

For most of the stories and novels I have written over the years, the ideation period is so long and complex that I could not begin to explain—even to myself—where the ideas originally came from.

With "Battle Station," happily, I can trace the evolution of the story from original idea to final draft.

"Battle Station" has its roots in actual scientific research and technological development. In the mid-1960s I was employed at the research laboratory where the first high-power laser was invented. I

helped to arrange the first briefing in the Pentagon to inform the Department of Defense that lasers of virtually any power desired could now be developed.

That was the first step on the road to what came to be called the Strategic Defense Initiative.

My 1976 novel Millennium *examined, as only science fiction can, the human and social consequences of using lasers in satellites to defend against nuclear missiles. By 1983 the real world had caught up to the idea and President Reagan initiated the "Star Wars" program. In 1984 I published a nonfiction book on the subject,* Assured Survival. *In 1986 a second edition of that book, retitled* Star Peace, *brought the swiftly developing story up to date.*

Meanwhile, from the mid-1960s to this present day, thinkers such as Maxwell W. Hunter have been studying the problems and possibilities of an orbital defense system. While most academic critics (and consequently, most of the media) have simply declared such a defense system impossible, undesirable, and too expensive, Max Hunter spent his time examining how such a system might work, and what it might mean for the world political situation.

I am indebted to Max Hunter for sharing his ideas with me; particularly for the concept of "active armor." I have done violence to his ideas, I know, shaping them to the needs of the story. Such is the way of fiction.

Another concept that is important to this story came from the often-stormy letters column of Analog *magazine more than twenty years ago. Before the first astronauts and cosmonauts went into space, the readers of* Analog *debated, vigorously, who would make the best candidates for duty aboard orbiting space stations. One of the ideas they kicked around was that submariners—men accustomed to cramped quarters, high tensions, and long periods away from home base—would be ideal for crewing a military space station.*

So I "built" a space battle station that controls laser-armed satellites, and placed at its helm Commander J. W. Hazard, U.S. Navy (ret.), a former submarine skipper.

I gave him an international crew, in keeping with the conclusions I arrived at in Star Peace: Assured Survival, *that the new technology of strategic defense satellites will lead to an International Peacekeeping Force (IPF)—a global police power dedicated to preventing war.*

Once these ideas were in place, the natural thing was to test them. Suppose someone tried to subvert the IPF and seize the satellite system for his own nefarious purposes? Okay, make that not merely a political problem, but a personal problem for the story's protagonist: Hazard's son is part of a cabal to overthrow the IPF and set up a world dictatorship.

Now I had a story. All I had to do was start writing and allow the characters to "do their thing."

The ideas were the easiest part of the task. As you can see, the ideas were all around me, for more than twenty years. There are millions of good ideas floating through the air all the time. Every day of your life brings a fresh supply of ideas. Every person you know is a walking novel. Every news event contains a dozen ideas for stories.

The really difficult part is turning those ideas into good stories. To bring together the ideas and the characters and let them weave a story— that is the real work of the writer. Very few people ask about that, yet that is the actual process of creativity. It's not tough to find straw. Spinning straw into gold—that's the great magical trick!

We should avoid a dependence on satellites for wartime purposes that is out of proportion to our ability to protect them. If we make ourselves dependent upon vulnerable spacecraft for military support, we will have built an Achilles heel into our forces.

—*Dr. Ashton Carter, MIT, April 1984*

The key issue then becomes, is our defense capable of defending itself . . .
—*Maxwell W. Hunter II*
Lockheed Missiles and Space Co., Inc.,
February 26, 1979

THE FIRST LASER BEAM caught them unaware, slicing through the station's thin aluminum skin exactly where the main power trunk and air lines fed into the bridge.

A sputtering fizz of sparks, a moment of heart-wrenching darkness, and then the emergency dims came on. The electronics consoles switched to their internal batteries with barely a microsecond's hesitation, but the air fans sighed to a stop and fell silent.

The four men and two women on duty in the bridge had about a second to realize they were under attack. Enough time for the breath to catch in your throat, for the sudden terror to hollow out your guts.

The second laser hit was a high-energy pulse deliberately aimed at the bridge's observation port. It cracked the impact-resistant plastic as easily as a hammer smashes an egg; the air pressure inside the bridge blew the port open. The four men and women became six exploding bodies spewing blood. There was not even time enough to scream.

The station was named *Hunter,* although only a handful of its crew knew why. It was not one of the missile-killing satellites, nor one of the sensor-laden observation birds. It was a command-and-control station, manned by a crew of twenty, orbiting some one thousand kilometers high, below the densest radiation zone of the inner Van Allen belt. It circled the Earth in about 105 minutes. By design, the station was not hardened against laser attack. The attackers knew this perfectly well.

Commander Hazard was almost asleep when the bridge was destroyed. He had just finished his daily inspection of the battle station. Satisfied that the youngsters of his crew were reasonably sharp, he had returned to his coffin-sized personal cabin and wormed out of his sweaty fatigues. He was angry with himself.

Two months aboard the station and he still felt the nausea and unease of space adaptation syndrome. It was like the captain of an ocean vessel having seasickness all the time. Hazard fumed inwardly as he stuck another timed-release medication plaster on his neck, slightly behind his left ear. The old one had fallen off. Not that they did much good. His neck was faintly spotted with the rings left by the medication patches. Still his stomach felt fluttery, his palms slippery with perspiration.

Clinging grimly to a handgrip, he pushed his weightless body from the mirrored sink to the mesh sleep cocoon fastened against the opposite wall of his cubicle. He zipped himself into the bag and slipped the terry-cloth restraint across his forehead.

Hazard was a bulky, dour man with iron-gray hair still cropped Academy close, a weather-beaten squarish face built around a thrusting spadelike nose, a thin slash of a mouth that seldom smiled, and eyes the color of a stormy sea. Those eyes seemed suspicious of everyone and everything, probing, inquisitory. A closer look showed that they were weary, disappointed with the world and the people in it. Disappointed most of all with himself.

He was just dozing off when the emergency klaxon started hooting. For a disoriented moment he thought he was back in a submarine and something had gone wrong with a dive. He felt his arms pinned by the mesh sleeping bag, as if he had been bound by unknown enemies. He almost panicked as he heard hatches slamming automatically and the terrifying wailing of the alarms. The communications unit on the wall added its urgent shrill to the clamor.

The comm unit's piercing whistle snapped him to full awareness. He stopped struggling against the mesh and unzippered it with a single swift motion, slipping out of the head restraint at the same time.

Hazard slapped at the wall comm's switch. "Commander here," he snapped. "Report."

"Varshni, sir. CIC. The bridge is out. Apparently destroyed."

"Destroyed?"

"All life-support functions down. Air pressure zero. No communications," replied the Indian in a rush. His slightly singsong Oxford accent was trembling with fear. "It exploded, sir. They are all dead in there."

Hazard felt the old terror clutching at his heart, the physical weakness, the giddiness of sudden fear. Forcing his voice to remain steady, he commanded, "Full alert status. Ask Mr. Feeney and Miss Yang to meet me at the CIC at once. I'll be down there in sixty seconds or less."

The *Hunter* was one of nine orbiting battle stations that made up the command-and-control function of the newly created International Peacekeeping Force's strategic defense network. In lower orbits, 135 unmanned ABM satellites armed with multimegawatt lasers and hypervelocity missiles crisscrossed the Earth's surface. In theory, these satellites could destroy thousands of ballistic missiles within five minutes of their launch, no matter where on Earth they rose from.

In theory, each battle station controlled fifteen of the ABM satellites, but never the same fifteen for very long. The battle station's higher orbits were deliberately picked so that the unmanned satellites passed through their field of view as they hurried by in their lower orbits. At the insistence of the fearful politicians of a hundred nations, no ABM satellites were under the permanent control of any one particular battle station.

In theory, each battle station patrolled one ninth of the Earth's surface as it circled the globe. The sworn duty of its carefully chosen international crew was to make certain that any missiles launched from that part of the Earth would be swiftly and efficiently destroyed.

In theory.

The IPF was new, untried except for computerized simulations and war games. It had been created in the wake of the Middle East Holocaust, when the superpowers finally realized that there were people willing to use nuclear weapons. It had taken the destruction of four ancient cities and more than three million lives before the superpowers stepped in and forced peace on the belligerents.

To make certain that nuclear devastation would never threaten humankind again, the International Peacekeeping Force was created. The Peacekeepers had the power and the authority to prevent a nuclear strike from reaching its targets. Their authority extended completely across the Earth, even to the superpowers themselves.

In theory.

Pulling aside the privacy curtain of his cubicle, Hazard launched himself down the narrow passageway with a push of his meaty hands against the cool metal of the bulkheads. His stomach lurched at the sudden motion and he squeezed his eyes shut for a moment.

The Combat Information Center was buried deep in the middle of the station, protected by four levels of living and working areas plus the station's storage magazines for water, food, air, fuel for the maneuvering thrusters, power generators, and other equipment.

Hazard fought down the queasy fluttering of his stomach as he glided along the passageway toward the CIC. At least he did not suffer the claustrophobia that affected some of the station's younger crew members. To a man who had spent most of his career aboard nuclear submarines, the station was roomy, almost luxurious.

He had to yank open four airtight hatches along the short way. Each clanged shut automatically behind him.

At last Hazard floated into the dimly lit combat center. It was a tiny, womblike circular chamber, its walls studded with display screens that glowed a sickly green in the otherwise darkened compartment. No desks or chairs in zero gravity; the CIC's work surfaces were chest-high consoles, most of them covered with keyboards.

Varshni and the Norwegian woman, Stromsen, were on duty. The little Indian, slim and dark, was wide-eyed with anxiety. His face shone with perspiration and his fatigues were dark at the armpits and between his shoulders. In the greenish glow from the display screens he looked positively ill. Stromsen looked tense, her strong jaw clenched, her ice-blue eyes fastened on Hazard, waiting for him to tell her what to do.

"What happened?" Hazard demanded.

"It simply blew out," said Varshni. "I had just spoken with Michaels and D'Argencour when . . . when . . ."

His voice choked off.

"The screens went blank." Stromsen pointed to the status displays. "Everything suddenly zeroed out."

She was controlling herself carefully, Hazard saw, every nerve taut to the point of snapping.

"The rest of the station?" Hazard asked.

She gestured again toward the displays. "No other damage."

"Everybody on full alert?"

"Yes, sir."

Lieutenant Feeney ducked through the hatch, his eyes immediately drawn to the row of burning red malfunction lights where the bridge displays should have been.

"Mother of Mercy, what's happened?"

Before anyone could reply, Susan Yang, the chief communications officer, pushed through the hatch and almost bumped into Feeney. She saw the displays and immediately concluded, "We're under attack!"

"That is impossible!" Varshni blurted.

Hazard studied their faces for a swift moment. They all knew what had happened; only Yang had the guts to say it aloud. She seemed cool and in control of herself. Oriental inscrutability? Hazard wondered. He knew she was third-generation Californian. Feeney's pinched, narrow-eyed face failed to hide the fear that they all felt, but the Irishman held himself well and returned Hazard's gaze without a tremor.

The only sound in the CIC was the hum of the electrical equipment and the soft sighing of the air fans. Hazard felt uncomfortably warm with the five of them crowding the cramped little chamber. Perspiration trickled down his ribs. They were all staring at him, waiting for him to tell them what must be done, to bring order out of the numbing fear and uncertainty that swirled around them. Four youngsters from four different nations, wearing the blue-gray fatigues of the IPF, with colored patches denoting their technical specialties on their left shoulders and the flag of their national origin on their right shoulders.

Hazard said, "We'll have to control the station from here. Mr. Feeney, you are now my Number One; Michaels was on duty in the bridge. Mr. Varshni, get a damage-control party to the bridge. Full suits."

"No one's left alive in there," Varshni whispered.

"Yes, but their bodies must be recovered. We owe them that. And their families." He glanced toward Yang. "And we've got to determine what caused the blowout."

Varshni's face twisted unhappily at the thought of the mangled bodies.

"I want a status report from each section of the station," Hazard went on, knowing that activity was the key to maintaining discipline. "Start with . . ."

A beeping sound made all five of them turn toward the communications console. Its orange demand light blinked for attention in time with the angry beeps. Hazard reached for a handgrip to steady himself as he swung toward the comm console. He noted how easily the youngsters handled themselves in zero gee. For him it still took a conscious, gut-wrenching effort.

Stromsen touched the keyboard with a slender finger. A man's unsmiling face appeared on the screen: light brown hair clipped as close as Hazard's gray, lips pressed together in an uncompromising line. He wore the blue-gray of the IPF with a commander's silver star on his collar.

"This is Buckbee, commander of station *Graham*. I want to speak to Commander Hazard."

Sliding in front of the screen, Hazard grasped the console's edge with both white-knuckled hands. He knew Buckbee only by reputation, a former U.S. Air Force colonel, from the Space Command until it had been disbanded, but before that he had put in a dozen years with SAC.

"This is Hazard."

Buckbee's lips moved slightly in what might have been a smile, but his eyes remained cold. "Hazard, you've just lost your bridge."

"And six lives."

Unmoved, Buckbee continued as if reading from a prepared script, "We offer you a chance to save the lives of the rest of your crew. Surrender the *Hunter* to us—"

"Us?"

Buckbee nodded, a small economical movement. "We will bring order and greatness out of this farce called the IPF."

A wave of loathing so intense that it almost made him vomit swept through Hazard. He realized that he had known all along, with a certainty that had not needed conscious verification, that his bridge had been destroyed by deliberate attack, not by accident.

"You killed six kids," he said, his voice so low that he barely heard it himself. It was not a whisper but a growl.

"We had to prove that we mean business, Hazard. Now surrender your station or we'll blow you all to hell. Any further deaths will be on your head, not ours."

Jonathan Wilson Hazard, captain, U.S. Navy (ret.). Marital status: divorced. Two children: Jonathan, Jr., twenty-six; Virginia Elizabeth, twenty. Served twenty-eight years in U.S. Navy, mostly in submarines. Commanded fleet ballistic-missile submarines *Ohio*, *Corpus Christi*, and *Utah*. Later served as technical advisor to Joint Chiefs of Staff and as naval liaison to NATO headquarters in Brussels. Retired from Navy after hostage crisis in Brussels. Joined International Peacekeeping Force and appointed commander of orbital battle station *Hunter*.

"I can't just hand this station over to a face on a screen," Hazard replied, stalling, desperately trying to think his way through the situation. "I don't know what you're up to, what your intentions are, who you really are."

"You're in no position to bargain, Hazard," said Buckbee, his voice flat and hard. "We want control of your station. Either you give it to us or we'll eliminate you completely."

"Who the hell is 'we'?"

"That doesn't matter."

"The hell it doesn't! I want to know who you are and what you're up to."

Buckbee frowned. His eyes shifted away slightly, as if looking to someone standing out of range of the video camera.

"We don't have time to go into that now," he said at last.

Hazard recognized the crack in Buckbee's armor. It was not much, but he pressed it. "Well, you goddamned well better make time, mister. I'm not handing this station over to you or anybody else until I know what in hell is going on."

Turning to Feeney, he ordered, "Sound general quarters. ABM satellites on full automatic. Miss Yang, contact IPF headquarters and give them a full report of our situation."

"We'll destroy your station before those idiots in Geneva can decide what to do!" Buckbee snapped.

"Maybe," said Hazard. "But that'll take time, won't it? And we won't go down easy, I guarantee you. Maybe we'll take you down with us." Buckbee's face went white with fury. His eyes glared angrily.

"Listen," Hazard said more reasonably, "you can't expect me to just turn this station over to a face on a screen. Six of my people have been killed. I want to know why, and who's behind all this. I won't deal until I know who I'm dealing with and what your intentions are."

Buckbee growled, "You've just signed the death warrant for yourself and your entire crew."

The comm screen went blank.

For a moment Hazard hung weightlessly before the dead screen, struggling to keep the fear inside him from showing. Putting a hand out to the edge of the console to steady himself, he turned slowly to his young officers. Their eyes were riveted on him, waiting for him to tell them what to do, waiting for him to decide between life and death.

Quietly, but with steel in his voice, Hazard commanded, "I said general quarters, Mr. Feeney. Now!"

Feeney flinched as if suddenly awakened from a dream. He pushed himself to the command console, unlatched the red cover over the "general quarters" button, and banged it eagerly with his fist. The action sent him recoiling upward and he had to put up a hand against the overhead to push himself back down to the deck. The alarm light began blinking red and they could hear its hooting even through the airtight hatches outside the CIC.

"Geneva, Miss Yang," Hazard said sternly, over the howl of the alarm. "Feeney, see that the crew is at their battle stations. I want the satellites under our control on full automatic, prepared to shoot down anything that moves if it isn't in our precleared data bank. And Mr. Varshni, has that damage-control party gotten under way yet?"

The two young men rushed toward the hatch, bumping each other in their eagerness to follow their commander's orders. Hazard almost smiled at the Laurel-and-Hardy aspect of it. Lieutenant Yang pushed herself to the comm console and anchored her softboots on the Velcro strip fastened to the deck there.

"Miss Stromsen, you are the duty officer. I am depending on you to keep me informed of the status of all systems."

"Yes, sir!"

Keep them busy, Hazard told himself. Make them concentrate on doing their jobs and they won't have time to be frightened.

"Encountering interference, sir," reported Yang, her eyes on the comm displays. "Switching to emergency frequency."

Jamming, thought Hazard.

"Main comm antenna overheating," Stromsen said. She glanced down at her console keyboard, then up at the displays again. "I think they're attacking the antennas with lasers, sir. Main antenna out. Secondaries . . ." She shrugged and gestured toward the baleful red lights strung across her keyboard. "They're all out, sir."

"Set up a laser link," Hazard commanded. "They can't jam that. We've got to let Geneva know what's happening."

"Sir," said Yang, "Geneva will not be within our horizon for another forty-three minutes."

"Try signaling the commsats. Topmost priority."

"Yes, sir."

Got to let Geneva know, Hazard repeated to himself. If anybody can help us, they can. If Buckbee's pals haven't put one of their own people into the comm center down there. Or staged a coup. Or already knocked out the commsats. They've been planning this for a long time. They've got it all timed down to the microsecond.

He remembered the dinner, a month earlier, the night before he left to take command of the *Hunter*. I've known about it since then,

Hazard said to himself. Known about it but didn't want to believe it. Known about it and done nothing. Buckbee was right. I killed those six kids. I should have seen that the bastards would strike without warning.

It had been in the equatorial city of Belém, where the Brazilians had set up their space launching facility. The IPF was obligated to spread its launches among all its space-capable member nations, so Hazard had been ordered to assemble his crew at Belém for their lift into orbit.

The night before they left, Hazard had been invited to dinner by an old Navy acquaintance who had already put in three months of orbital duty with the Peacekeepers and was on Earthside leave.

His name was Cardillo. Hazard had known him, somewhat distantly, as a fellow submariner, commander of attack boats rather than the missile carriers Hazard himself had captained. Vincent Cardillo had a reputation for being a hard nose who ran an efficient boat, if not a particularly happy one. He had never been really close to Hazard: their chemistries were too different. But this specific sweltering evening in a poorly air-conditioned restaurant in downtown Belém, Cardillo acted as if they shared some old fraternal secret between them.

Hazard had worn his IPF summerweight uniform: pale blue with gold insignia bordered by space black. Cardillo came in casual civilian slacks and a beautifully tailored Italian silk jacket. Through drinks and the first part of the dinner their conversation was light, inconsequential. Mostly reminiscences by two gray-haired submariners about men they had known, women they had chased, sea tales that grew with each retelling. But then:

"Damn shame," Cardillo muttered, halfway through his entrée of grilled eel.

The restaurant, one of the hundreds that had sprung up in Belém since the Brazilians had made the city their major spaceport, was on the waterfront. Outside the floor-to-ceiling windows, the muddy Pará River widened into the huge bay that eventually fed into the Atlantic. Hazard had spent his last day on Earth touring around the tropical jungle on a riverboat.

The makeshift shanties that stood on stilts along the twisting mud-brown creeks were giving way to industrial parks and cinderblock housing developments. Air-conditioning was transforming the region from rubber plantations to computerized information services. The smell of cement dust blotted out the fragrance of tropical flowers. Bulldozers clattered in raw clearings slashed from the forest where stark steel frameworks of new buildings rose above the jungle growth. Children who had splashed naked in the brown jungle streams were being rounded up and sent to air-conditioned schools.

"What's a shame?" Hazard asked. "Seems to me these people are starting to do all right for the first time in their lives. The space business is making a lot of jobs around here."

Cardillo took a forkful of eel from his plate. It never got to his mouth.

"I don't mean them, Johnny. I mean us. It's a damn shame about us."

Hazard had never liked being called "Johnny." His family had addressed him as "Jon." His Navy associates knew him as "Hazard" and nothing else. A few very close friends used "J.W."

"What do you mean?" he asked. His own plate was already wiped clean. The fish and its dark spicy sauce had been marvelous. So had the crisp-crusted bread.

"Don't you feel nervous about this whole IPF thing?" Cardillo asked, trying to look earnest. "I mean, I can see Washington deciding to put boomers like your boats in mothballs, and the silo missiles, too. But the attack subs? Decommission our conventional weapons systems? Leave us disarmed?"

Hazard had not been in command of a missile submarine in more than three years. He had been allowed, even encouraged, to resign his commission after the hostage mess in Brussels.

"If you're not in favor of what the American government is doing, then why did you agree to serve in the Peacekeepers?"

Cardillo shrugged and smiled slightly. It was not a pleasant smile. He had a thin, almost triangular face with a low, creased brow tapering down to a pointed chin. His once-dark hair, now peppered with gray, was thick and wavy. He had allowed it to grow down to his collar. His deep-brown eyes were always narrowed, crafty, focused so intently he seemed to be trying to penetrate through you. There was no joy in his face, even though he was smiling; no pleasure. It was the smile of a gambler, a con artist, a used-car salesman.

"Well," he said slowly, putting his fork back down on the plate and leaning back in his chair, "you know the old saying, 'If you can't beat 'em, join 'em.'"

Hazard nodded, although he felt puzzled. He groped for Cardillo's meaning. "Yeah, I guess playing space cadet up there will be better than rusting away on the beach."

"Playing?" Cardillo's dark brows rose slightly. "We're not playing, Johnny. We're in this for keeps."

"I didn't mean to imply that I don't take my duty to the IPF seriously," Hazard answered.

For an instant Cardillo seemed stunned with surprise. Then he threw his head back and burst into laughter. "Jesus Christ, Johnny," he gasped. "You're so straight-arrow it's hysterical."

Hazard frowned but said nothing. Cardillo guffawed and banged the table with one hand. Some of the diners glanced their way. They seemed to be mostly Americans or Europeans, a few Asians. Some Brazilians, too, Hazard noticed as he waited for Cardillo's amusement to subside. Probably from the capital or Rio.

"Let me in on the joke," Hazard said at last.

Cardillo wiped at his eyes. Then, leaning forward across the table, his grin fading into an intense, penetrating stare, he whispered harshly, "I already told you, Johnny. If we can't avoid being members of the IPF—if Washington's so fucking weak that we've got to disband practically all our defenses—then what we've got to do is take over the Peacekeepers ourselves."

"Take over the Peacekeepers?" Hazard felt stunned at the thought of it.

"Damn right! Men like you and me, Johnny. It's our duty to our country."

"Our country," Hazard reminded him, "has decided to join the International Peacekeeping Force and has encouraged its military officers to obtain commissions in it."

Cardillo shook his head. "That's our stupid goddamn government, Johnny. Not the country. Not the people who really want to *defend* America instead of selling her out to a bunch of fucking foreigners."

"That government," Hazard reminded him, "won a big majority last November."

Cardillo made a sour face. "Ahh, the people. What the fuck do they know?"

Hazard said nothing.

"I'm telling you, Johnny, the only way to do it is to take over the IPF."

"That's crazy."

"You mean if and when the time comes, you won't go along with us?"

"I mean," Hazard said, forcing his voice to remain calm, "that I took an oath to be loyal to the IPF. So did you."

"Yeah, yeah, sure. And what about the oath we took way back when—the one to preserve and protect the United States of America?"

"The United States of America *wants* us to serve in the Peacekeepers," Hazard insisted.

Cardillo shook his head again, mournfully. Not a trace of anger. Not even disappointment. As if he had expected this reaction from Hazard. His expression was that of a salesman who could not convince his stubborn customer of the bargain he was offering.

"Your son doesn't feel the same way you do," Cardillo said.

Hazard immediately clamped down on the rush of emotions that surged through him. Instead of reaching across the table and dragging Cardillo to his feet and punching in his smirking face, Hazard forced a thin smile and kept his fists clenched on his lap.

"Jon Jr. is a grown man. He has the right to make his own decisions."

"He's serving under me, you know." Cardillo's eyes searched Hazard's face intently, probing for weakness.

"Yes," Hazard said tightly. "He told me."

Which was an outright lie.

"Missiles approaching, sir!"

Stromsen's tense warning snapped Hazard out of his reverie. He riveted his attention to the main CIC display screen. Six angry red dots were working their way from the periphery of the screen toward the center, which marked the location of the *Hunter*.

"Now we'll see if the ABM satellites are working or not," Hazard muttered.

"Links with the ABM sats are still good, sir," Yang reported from her station, a shoulder's width away from Stromsen. "The integral antennas weren't knocked out when they hit the comm dishes."

Hazard gave her a nod of acknowledgment. The two young women could not have looked more different: Yang was small, wiry, dark, her straight black hair cut like a military helmet; Stromsen was willowy yet broad in the beam and deep in the bosom, as blonde as butter.

"Lasers on 324 and 325 firing," the Norwegian reported.

Hazard saw the display lights. On the main screen the six red dots flickered orange momentarily, then winked out altogether.

Stromsen pecked at her keyboard. Alphanumerics sprang up on a side screen. "Got them all while they were still in first-stage burn. They'll never reach us." She smiled with relief. "They're tumbling into the atmosphere. Burn-up within seven minutes."

Hazard allowed himself a small grin. "Don't break out the champagne yet. That's just their first salvo. They're testing to see if we actually have control of the lasers."

It's all a question of time, Hazard knew. But how much time? What are they planning? How long before they start slicing us up with laser beams? We don't have the shielding to protect against lasers. The stupid politicians wouldn't allow us to armor these stations. We're like a sitting duck up here.

"What are they trying to accomplish, sir?" asked Yang. "Why are they doing this?"

"They want to take over the whole defense network. They want to seize control of the entire IPF."

"That's impossible!" Stromsen blurted.

"The Russians won't allow them to do that," Yang said. "The Chinese and the other members of the IPF will stop them."

"Maybe," said Hazard. "Maybe." He felt a slight hint of nausea ripple in his stomach. Reaching up, he touched the slippery plastic of the medicine patch behind his ear.

"Do you think they could succeed?" Stromsen asked.

"What's important is, do *they* think they can succeed? There are still hundreds of ballistic missiles on Earth. Thousands of hydrogen warheads. Buckbee and his cohorts apparently believe that if they can take control of a portion of the ABM network, they can threaten a nuclear strike against the nations that don't go along with them."

"But the other nations will strike back and order their people in the IPF not to intercept their strikes," said Yang.

"It will be nuclear war," Stromsen said. "Just as if the IPF never existed."

"Worse," Yang pointed out, "because first there'll be a shoot-out on each one of these battle stations."

"That's madness!" said Stromsen.

"That's what we've got to prevent," Hazard said grimly.

The orange light began to blink again on the comm console. Yang snapped her attention to it. "Incoming message from the *Graham*, sir."

Hazard nodded. "Put it on the main screen."

Cardillo's crafty features appeared on the screen. He should have been still on leave hack on Earth, but instead he was smiling crookedly at Hazard.

"Well, Johnny, I guess by now you've figured out that we mean business."

"And so do we. Give it up, Vince. It's not going to work."

With a small shake of his head Cardillo answered, "It's already working, Johnny boy. Two of the Russian battle stations are with us. So's the *Wood*. The Chinks and Indians are holding out but the European station is going along with us."

Hazard said, "So you've got six of the nine stations."

"So far."

"Then you don't really need *Hunter*. You can leave us alone."

Pursing his lips for a moment, Cardillo replied, "I'm afraid it doesn't work that way, Johnny. We want *Hunter*. We can't afford to have you rolling around like a loose cannon. You're either with us or against us."

"I'm not with you," Hazard said flatly.

Cardillo sighed theatrically. "Jon, there are twenty other officers and crew on your station . . ."

"Fourteen now," Hazard corrected.

"Don't you think you ought to give them a chance to make a decision about their own lives?"

Despite himself, Hazard broke into a malicious grin. "Am I hearing you straight, Vince? You're asking the commander of a vessel to take a *vote*?"

Grinning back at him, Cardillo admitted, "I guess that was kind of dumb. But you do have their lives in your hands, Johnny."

"We're not knuckling under, Vince. And you've got twenty-some lives aboard the *Graham*, you know. Including your own. Better think about that."

"We already have, Johnny. One of those lives is Jonathan Hazard, Jr.

He's right here on the bridge with me. A fine officer, Johnny. You should be proud of him."

A hostage, Hazard realized. They're using Jon Jr. as a hostage.

"Do you want to talk with him?" Cardillo asked.

Hazard nodded.

Cardillo slid out of view and a younger man's face appeared on the screen. Jon Jr. looked tense, strained. This isn't any easier for him than it is for me, Hazard thought. He studied his son's face. Youthful, clear-eyed, a square-jawed honest face. Hazard was startled to realize that he had seen that face before, in his own Academy graduation photo.

"How are you, son?"

"I'm fine, Dad. And you?"

"Are we really on opposite sides of this?"

Jon Jr.'s eyes flicked away for a moment, then turned back to look squarely at his father's. "I'm afraid so, Dad."

"But why?" Hazard felt genuinely bewildered that his son did not see things the way he did.

"The IPF is dangerous," Jon Jr. said. "It's the first step toward a world government. The Third World nations want to bleed the industrialized nations dry. They want to grab all our wealth for themselves. The first step is to disarm us, under the pretense of preventing nuclear war. Then, once we're disarmed, they're going to take over everything—using the IPF as *their* armed forces."

"That's what they've told you," Hazard said.

"That's what I know, Dad. It's true. I know it is."

"And your answer is to take over the IPF and use it as *your* armed forces to control the rest of the world, is that it?"

"Better us than them."

Hazard shook his head. "They're using you, son. Cardillo and Buckbee and the rest of those maniacs; you're in with a bunch of would-be Napoleons."

Jon Jr. smiled pityingly at his father. "I knew you'd say something like that."

Hazard put up a beefy hand. "I don't want to argue with you, son. But I can't go along with you."

"You're going to force us to attack your station."

"I'll fight back."

His son's smile turned sardonic. "Like you did in Brussels?"

Hazard felt it like a punch in his gut. He grunted with the pain of it. Wordlessly he reached out and clicked off the comm screen.

Brussels.

They had thought it was just another one of those endless Easter Sunday demonstrations. A peace march. The Greens, the Nuclear Winter freaks, the Neutralists, peaceniks of one stripe or another. Swarms of little old ladies in their Easter frocks, limping old war veterans, kids of all ages. Teenagers, lots of them. In blue jeans and denim jackets. Young women in shorts and tight T-shirts.

The guards in front of NATO's headquarters complex took no particular note of the older youths and women mixed in with the teens. They failed to detect the hard, calculating eyes and the snub-nosed guns and grenades hidden under jackets and sweaters.

Suddenly the peaceful parade dissolved into a mass of screaming wild people. The guards were cut down mercilessly and the cadre of terrorists fought their way into the main building of NATO headquarters. They forced dozens of peaceful marchers to go in with them, as shields and hostages.

Captain J. W. Hazard, USN, was not on duty that Sunday, but he was in his office nevertheless, attending to some paperwork that he wanted out of the way before the start of business on Monday morning.

Unarmed, he was swiftly captured by the terrorists, beaten bloody for the fun of it, and then locked in a toilet. When the terrorists realized that he was the highest-ranking officer in the building, Hazard was dragged out and commanded to open the security vault where the most sensitive NATO documents were stored.

Hazard refused. The terrorists began shooting hostages. After the second murder Hazard opened the vault for them. Top-secret battle plans, maps showing locations of nuclear weapons, and hundreds of other documents were taken by the terrorists and never found, even after an American-led strike force retook the building in a bloody battle that killed all but four of the hostages.

Hazard stood before the blank comm screen for a moment, his softbooted feet not quite touching the deck, his mind racing.

They've even figured that angle, he said to himself. They know I caved in at Brussels and they expect me to cave in here. Some sonofabitch has grabbed my psych records and come to the conclusion that I'll react the same way now as I did then. Some sonofabitch. And they got my son to stick the knife in me.

The sound of the hatch clattering open stirred Hazard. Feeney floated through the hatch and grabbed an overhead handgrip.

"The crew's at battle stations, sir," he said, slightly breathless. "Standing by for further orders."

It struck Hazard that only a few minutes had passed since he himself had entered the CIC.

"Very good, Mr. Feeney," he said. "With the bridge out, we're going to have to control the station from here. Feeney, take the con. Miss Stromsen, how much time before we can make direct contact with Geneva?"

"Forty minutes, sir," she sang out, then corrected, "Actually, thirty-nine fifty."

Feeney was worming his softboots against the Velcro strip in front of the propulsion-and-control console.

"Take her down, Mr. Feeney."

The Irishman's eyes widened with surprise. "Down, sir?"

Hazard made himself smile. "Down. To the altitude of the ABM satellites. Now."

"Yes, sir." Feeney began carefully pecking out commands on the keyboard before him.

"I'm not just reacting like an old submariner," Hazard reassured his young officers. "I want to get us to a lower altitude so we won't be such a good target for so many of their lasers. Shrink our horizon. We're a sitting duck up here."

Yang grinned back at him. "I didn't think you expected to outmaneuver a laser beam, sir."

"No, but we can take ourselves out of range of most of their satellites."

Most, Hazard knew, but not all.

"Miss Stromsen, will you set up a simulation for me? I want to know how many unfriendly satellites can attack us at various altitudes, and what their positions would be compared to our own. I want a solution that tells me where we'll be safest."

"Right away, sir," Stromsen said. "What minimum altitude shall I plug in?"

"Go right down to the deck," Hazard said. "Low enough to boil the paint off."

"The station isn't built for reentry into the atmosphere, sir!"

"I know. But see how low we can get."

The old submariner's instinct: run silent, run deep. So the bastards think I'll fold up, just like I did at Brussels, Hazard fumed inwardly. Two big differences, Cardillo and friends. Two *very* big differences. In Brussels the hostages were civilians, not military men and women. And in Brussels I didn't have any weapons to fight back with.

He knew the micropuffs of thrust from the maneuvering rockets were hardly strong enough to be felt, yet Hazard's stomach lurched and heaved suddenly.

"We have retro burn," Feeney said. "Altitude decreasing."

My damned stomach's more sensitive than his instruments, Hazard grumbled to himself.

"Incoming message from *Graham*, sir," said Yang.

"Ignore it."

"Sir," Yang said, turning slightly toward him, "I've been thinking about the minimum altitude we can achieve. Although the station is not equipped for atmospheric reentry, we do carry the four emergency evacuation spacecraft and they *do* have heat shields."

"Are you suggesting we abandon the station?"

"Oh, no, sir! But perhaps we could move the spacecraft to a position where they would be between us and the atmosphere. Let their heat shields protect us—sort of like riding a surfboard."

Feeney laughed. "Trust a California girl to come up with a solution like that!"

"It might be a workable idea," Hazard said. "I'll keep it in mind."

"We're being illuminated by a laser beam," Stromsen said tensely. "Low power—so far."

"They're tracking us."

Hazard ordered, "Yang, take over the simulation problem. Stromsen, give me a wide radar sweep. I want to see if they're moving any of their ABM satellites to counter our maneuver."

"I have been sweeping, sir. No satellite activity yet."

Hazard grunted. Yet. She knows that all they have to do is maneuver a few of their satellites to higher orbits and they'll have us in their sights.

To Yang he called, "Any response from the commsats?"

"No, sir," she replied immediately. "Either their laser receptors are not functioning or the satellites themselves are inoperative."

They couldn't have knocked out the commsats altogether, Hazard told himself. How would they communicate with one another? Cardillo claims the *Wood* and two of the Soviet stations are on their side. And the Europeans. He put a finger to his lips unconsciously, trying to remember Cardillo's exact words. *The Europeans are going along with us.* That's what he said. Maybe they're not actively involved in this. Maybe they're playing a wait-and-see game.

Either way, we're alone. They've got four, maybe five, out of the nine battle stations. We can't contact the Chinese or Indians. We don't know which Russian satellite hasn't joined in with them. It'll be more than a half hour before we can contact Geneva, and even then what the hell can they do?

Alone. Well, it won't be for the first time. Submariners are accustomed to being on their own.

"Sir," Yang reported, the *Graham* is still trying to reach us. Very urgent, they're saying."

"Tell them I'm not available but you will record their message and personally give it to me." Turning to the Norwegian lieutenant, "Miss Stromsen, I want all crew members in their pressure suits. And levels one and two of the station are to be abandoned. No one above level three except the damage-control team. We're going to take some hits and I want everyone protected as much as possible."

She nodded and glanced at the others. All three of them looked tense, but not afraid. The fear was there, of course, underneath. But they were in control of themselves. Their eyes were clear, their hands steady.

"Should I have the air pumped out of levels one and two—after they're cleared of personnel?"

"No," Hazard said. "Let them outgas when they're hit. Might fool the bastards into thinking they're doing more damage than they really are."

Feeney smiled weakly. "Sounds like the boxer who threatened to bleed all over his opponent."

Hazard glared at him. Stromsen took up the headset from her console and began issuing orders into the pin-sized microphone.

"The computer simulation is finished, sir," said Yang.

"Put it on my screen here."

He studied the graphics for a moment, sensing Feeney peering over his shoulder. Their safest altitude was the lowest, where only six ABM satellites could "see" them. The fifteen laser-armed satellites under their own control would surround them like a cavalry escort.

"There it is, Mr. Feeney. Plug that into your navigation program. That's where we want to be."

"Aye, sir."

The CIC shuddered. The screens dimmed for a moment, then came back to their full brightness.

"We've been hit!" Stromsen called out.

"Where? How bad?"

"Just aft of the main power generator. Outer hull ruptured. Storage area eight—medical, dental, and food—supplement supplies."

"So they got the Band-Aids and vitamin pills," Yang joked shakily.

"But they're going after the power generator," said Hazard. "Any casualties?"

"No, sir," reported Stromsen. "No personnel stationed there during general quarters."

He grasped Feeney's thin shoulder. "Turn us over, man. Get that generator away from their beams!"

Feeney nodded hurriedly and flicked his stubby fingers across his keyboard. Hazard knew it was all in his imagination, but his stomach rolled sickeningly as the station rotated.

Hanging grimly to a handgrip, he said, "I want each of you to get into your pressure suits, starting with you, Miss Stromsen. Yang, take over her console until she . . ."

The chamber shook again. Another hit.

"Can't we strike back at them?" Stromsen cried.

Hazard asked, "How many satellites are firing at us?"

She glanced at her display screens. "It seems to be only one—so far."

"Hit it."

Her lips curled slightly in a Valkyrie's smile. She tapped out commands on her console and then leaned on the final button hard enough to lift her boots off the Velcro.

"Got him!" Stromsen exulted. "That's one laser that won't bother us again."

Yang and Feeney were grinning. Hazard asked the communications officer, "Let me hear what the *Graham* has been saying."

It was Buckbee's voice on the tape. "Hazard, you are not to attempt to change your orbital altitude. If you don't return to your original altitude immediately, we will fire on you."

"Well, they know by now that we're not paying attention to them," Hazard said to his three young officers. "If I know them, they're going to take a few minutes to think things over, especially now that we've shown them we're ready to hit back. Stromsen, get into your suit. Feeney, you're next, then Yang. Move!"

It took fifteen minutes before the three of them were back in the CIC inside the bulky space suits, flexing gloved fingers, glancing about from inside the helmets. They all kept their visors up, and Hazard said nothing about it. Difficult enough to work inside the damned suits, he thought. They can snap the visors down fast enough if it comes to that.

The compact CIC became even more crowded. Despite decades of research and development, the space suits still bulked nearly twice as large as an unsuited person.

Suddenly Hazard felt an overpowering urge to get away from the CIC, away from the tension he saw in their young faces, away from the sweaty odor of fear, away from the responsibility for their lives.

"I'm going for my suit," he said, "and then a fast inspection tour of the station. Think you three can handle things on your own for a few minutes?"

Three heads bobbed inside their helmets. Three voices chorused, "Yes, sir."

"Fire on any satellite that fires at us," he commanded. "Tape all incoming messages. If there's any change in their tune, call me on the intercom."

"Yes, sir."

"Feeney, how long until we reach our final altitude?"

"More than an hour, sir."

"No way to move her faster?"

"I could get outside and push, I suppose."

Hazard grinned at him. "That won't be necessary, Mr. Feeney." Not yet, he added silently.

Pushing through the hatch into the passageway, Hazard saw that there was one pressure suit hanging on its rack in the locker just outside the CIC hatch. He passed it and went to his personal locker and his own suit. It's good to leave them on their own for a while, he told himself. Build up their confidence. But he knew that he had to get away from them, even if only for a few minutes.

His personal space suit smelled of untainted plastic and fresh rubber, like a new car. As Hazard squirmed into it, its joints felt stiff— or maybe it's me, he thought. The helmet slipped from his gloved hands and went spinning away from him, floating off like a severed head. Hazard retrieved it and pulled it on. Like the youngsters, he kept the visor open.

His first stop was the bridge. Varshni was hovering in the companionway just outside the airtight hatch that sealed off the devastated area. Two other space-suited men were zippering an unrecognizably mangled body into a long black-plastic bag. Three other bags floated alongside them, already filled and sealed.

Even inside a pressure suit, the Indian seemed small, frail, like a skinny child. He was huddled next to the body bags, bent over almost into a fetal position. There were tears in his eyes. "These are all we could find. The two others must have been blown out of the station completely."

Hazard put a gloved hand on the shoulder of his suit.

"They were my friends," Varshni said.

"It must have been painless," Hazard heard himself say. It sounded stupid.

"I wish I could believe that."

"There's more damage to inspect, over by the power generator area. Is your team nearly finished here?"

"Another few minutes, I think. We must make certain that all the wiring and air lines have been properly sealed off."

"They can handle that themselves. Come on, you and I will check it out together."

"Yes, sir." Varshni spoke into his helmet microphone briefly, then straightened up and tried to smile. "I am ready, sir."

The two men glided up a passageway that led to the outermost level of the station, Hazard wondering what would happen if a laser attack hit the area while they were in it. Takes a second or two to slice the hull open, he thought. Enough time to flip your visor down and grab on to something before the air blowout sucks you out of the station.

Still, he slid his visor down and ordered Varshni to do the same. He was only mildly surprised when the Indian replied that he already had.

Wish the station were shielded. Wish they had designed it to withstand attack. Then he grumbled inwardly, Wishes are for losers; winners use what they have. But the thought nagged at him. What genius put the power generator next to the unarmored hull? Damned politicians wouldn't allow shielding; they *wanted* the stations to be vulnerable. A sign of goodwill, as far as they're concerned. They thought nobody would attack an unshielded station because the attacker's station is also unshielded. We're all in this together, try to hurt me and I'll hurt you. A hangover from the old mutual-destruction kind of dogma. Absolute bullshit.

There ought to be some way to protect ourselves from lasers. They shouldn't put people up here like sacrificial lambs.

Hazard glanced at Varshni, whose face was hidden behind his helmet visor. He thought of his son. Sheila had ten years to poison his mind against me. Ten years. He wanted to hate her for that, but he found that he could not. He had been a poor husband and a worse father. Jon Jr. had every right to loathe his father. But dammit, this is more important than family arguments! Why can't the boy see what's at stake here? Just because he's sore at his father doesn't mean he has to take total leave of his senses.

They approached a hatch where the red warning light was blinking balefully. They checked the hatch behind them, made certain it was airtight, then used the wall-mounted keyboard to start the pumps that would evacuate that section of the passageway, turning it into an elongated air lock.

Finally they could open the farther hatch and glide into the wrecked storage magazine.

Hazard grabbed a handhold. "Better use tethers here," he said.

Varshni had already unwound the tether from his waist and clipped it to a hold.

It was a small magazine, little more than a closet. In the light from their helmet lamps, they saw cartons of pharmaceuticals securely anchored to the shelves with toothed plastic straps. A gash had been torn in the hull, and through it Hazard could see the darkness of space. The laser beam had penetrated into the cartons and shelving, slicing a neat burned-edge slash through everything it touched.

Varshni floated upward toward the rent. It was as smooth as a surgeon's incision, and curled back slightly where the air pressure had pushed the thin metal outward in its rush to escape to vacuum.

"No wiring here," Varshni's voice said in Hazard's helmet earphones. "No plumbing either. We were fortunate."

"They were aiming for the power generator."

The Indian pushed himself back down toward Hazard. His face was hidden behind the visor. "Ah, yes, that is an important target. We were very fortunate that they missed."

"They'll try again," Hazard said.

"Yes, of course."

"Commander Hazard!" Yang's voice sounded urgent. "I think you should hear the latest message from *Graham*, sir."

Nodding unconsciously inside his helmet, Hazard said, "Patch it through."

He heard a click, then Buckbee's voice. "Hazard, we've been very patient with you. We're finished playing games. You bring the *Hunter* back to its normal altitude and surrender the station to us or we'll slice you to pieces. You've got five minutes to answer."

The voice shut off so abruptly that Hazard could picture Buckbee slamming his fist against the Off key.

"How long ago did this come through?"

"Transmission terminated thirty seconds ago, sir," said Yang.

Hazard looked down at Varshni's slight form. He knew that Varshni had heard the ultimatum just as he had. He could not see the Indian's face, but the slump of his shoulders told him how Varshni felt.

Yang asked, "Sir, do you want me to set up a link with *Graham?*"

"No," said Hazard.

"I don't think they intend to call again, sir," Yang said. "They expect you to call them."

"Not yet," he said. He turned to the wavering form beside him. "Better straighten up, Mr. Varshni. There's going to be a lot of work for you and your damage-control team to do. We're in for a rough time."

Ordering Varshni back to his team at the ruins of the bridge,

Hazard made his way toward the CIC. He spoke into his helmet mike as he pulled himself along the passageways, hand over hand, as fast as he could go:

"Mr. Feeney, you are to fire at any satellites that fire on us. And at any ABM satellites that begin maneuvering to gain altitude so they can look down on us. Understand?"

"Understood, sir!"

"Miss Stromsen, I believe the fire-control panel is part of your responsibility. You will take your orders from Mr. Feeney."

"Yes, sir."

"Miss Yang, I want that simulation of our position and altitude updated to show exactly which ABM satellites under hostile control are in a position to fire upon us."

"I already have that in the program, sir."

"Good. I want our four lifeboats detached from the station and placed in positions where their heat shields can intercept incoming laser beams."

For the first time, Yang's voice sounded uncertain. "I'm not sure I understand what you mean, sir."

Hazard was sweating and panting with the exertion of hauling himself along the passageway. This suit won't smell new anymore, he thought.

To Yang he explained, "We can use the lifeboats' heat shields as armor to absorb or deflect incoming laser beams. Not just shielding, but *active* armor. We can move the boats to protect the most likely areas for laser beams to come from."

"Like the goalie in a hockey game!" Feeney chirped. "Cutting down the angles."

"Exactly."

By the time he reached the CIC they were already working the problems. Hazard saw that Stromsen had the heaviest work load: all the station systems' status displays, fire control for the laser-armed ABM satellites, and control of the lifeboats now hovering dozens of meters away from the station.

"Miss Stromsen, please transfer the fire-control responsibility to Mr. Feeney."

The expression on her strong-jawed face, half hidden inside her helmet, was pure stubborn indignation.

Jabbing a gloved thumb toward the lightning-slash insignia on the shoulder of Feeney's suit, Hazard said, "He *is* a weapons specialist, after all."

Stromsen's lips twitched slightly and she tapped at the keyboard to her left; the fire-control displays disappeared from the screens above it, only to spring up on screens in front of Feeney's position.

Hazard nodded as he lifted his own visor. "Okay, now. Feeney, you're the offense. Stromsen, you're the defense. Miss Yang, your job is to keep Miss Stromsen continuously advised as to where the best placement of the lifeboats will be."

Yang nodded, her dark eyes sparkling with the challenge. "Sir, you can't possibly expect us to predict all the possible paths a beam might take and get a lifeboat's heat shield in place soon enough . . ."

"I expect—as Lord Nelson once said—each of you to do your best. Now get Buckbee or Cardillo or whoever on the horn. I'm ready to talk to them."

It took a few moments for the communications laser to lock onto the distant *Graham*, but when Buckbee's face finally appeared on the screen, he was smiling—almost gloating.

"You've still got a minute and a half, Hazard. I'm glad you've come to your senses before we had to open fire on you."

"I'm only calling to warn you: any satellite that fires on us will be destroyed. Any satellite that maneuvers to put its lasers in a better position to hit us will also be destroyed."

Buckbee's jaw dropped open. His eyes widened.

"I've got fifteen ABM satellites under my control," Hazard continued, "and I'm going to use them."

"You can't threaten us!" Buckbee sputtered. "We'll wipe you out!"

"Maybe. Maybe not. I intend to fight until the very last breath."

"You're crazy, Hazard!"

"Am I? Your game is to take over the whole defense system and threaten a nuclear-missile strike against any nation that doesn't go along with you. Well, if your satellites are exhausted or destroyed, you won't be much of a threat to anybody, will you? Try impressing the Chinese with a beat-up network. They've got enough missiles to wipe out Europe and North America, and they'll use them. If you don't have enough left to stop those missiles, then who's threatening whom?"

"You can't . . ."

"Listen!" Hazard snapped. "How many of your satellites will be left by the time you overcome us? How much of a hole will we rip in your plans? Geneva will be able to blow you out of the sky with ground-launched missiles by the time you're finished with us."

"They'd never do such a thing."

"Are you sure?"

Buckbee looked away from Hazard, toward someone off-camera. He moved off, and Cardillo slid into view. He was no longer smiling.

"Nice try, Johnny, but you're bluffing and we both know it. Give up now or we're going to have to wipe you out."

"You can try, Vince. But you won't win."

"If we go, your son goes with us," Cardillo said.

Hazard forced his voice to remain level. "There's nothing I can do about that. He's a grown man. He's made his choice."

Cardillo huffed out a long, impatient sigh. "All right, Johnny. It was nice knowing you."

Hazard grimaced. Another lie, he thought. The man must be categorically unable to speak the truth.

The comm screen blanked.

"Are the lifeboats in place?" he asked.

"As good as we can get them," Yang said, her voice doubtful.

"Not too far from the station," Hazard warned. "I don't want them to show up as separate blips on their radar."

"Yes, sir, we know."

He nodded at them. Good kids, he thought. Ready to fight it out on my say-so. How far will they go before they crack? How much damage can we take before they scream to surrender?

They waited. Not a sound in the womb-shaped chamber, except for the hum of the electrical equipment and the whisper of air circulation. Hazard glided to a position slightly behind the two women. Feeney can handle the counterattack, he said to himself. That's simple enough. It's the defense that's going to win or lose for us.

On the display screens he saw the positions of the station and the hostile ABM satellites. Eleven of them in range. Eleven lines straight as laser beams converged on the station. Small orange blips representing the four lifeboats hovered around the central pulsing yellow dot that represented the station. The orange blips blocked nine of the converging lines. Two others passed between the lifeboat positions and reached the station itself.

"Miss Stromsen," Hazard said softly.

She jerked as if a hot needle had been stuck into her flesh.

"Easy now," Hazard said. "All I want to tell you is that you should be prepared to move the lifeboats to intercept any beams that are getting through."

"Yes, sir, I know."

Speaking as soothingly as he could, Hazard went on, "I doubt that they'll fire all eleven lasers at us at once. And as our altitude decreases, there will be fewer and fewer of their satellites in range of us. We have a good chance of getting through this without too much damage."

Stromsen turned her whole space-suited body so that she could look at him from inside her helmet. "It's good of you to say so, sir. I know you're trying to cheer us up, and I'm certain we all appreciate it. But you are taking my attention away from the screens."

Yang giggled, whether out of tension or actual humor at Stromsen's retort, Hazard could not tell.

Feeney sang out, "I've got a satellite climbing on us!"

Before Hazard could speak, Feeney's hands were moving on his console keyboard. "Our beasties are now programmed for automatic, but I'm tapping in a backup manually, just in—ah! Got her! Scratch one enemy."

Smiles all around. But behind his grin, Hazard wondered, Can they gin up decoys? Something that gives the same radar signature as an ABM satellite but really isn't? I don't think so—but I don't know for sure.

"Laser beam . . . two of them," called Stromsen.

Hazard saw the display screen light up. Both beams were hitting the same lifeboat. Then a third beam from the opposite direction lanced out.

The station shuddered momentarily as Stromsen's fingers flew over her keyboard and one of the orange dots shifted slightly to block the third beam.

"Where'd it hit?" he asked the Norwegian as the beams winked off.

"Just aft of the emergency oxygen tanks, sir."

Christ, Hazard thought, if they hit the tanks, enough oxygen will blow out of here to start us spinning like a top.

"Vent the emergency oxygen."

"Vent it, sir?"

"Now!"

Stromsen pecked angrily at the keyboard to her left. "Venting. Sir."

"I don't want that gas spurting out and acting like a rocket thruster," Hazard explained to her back. "Besides, it's an old submariner's trick to let the attacker think he's caused real damage by jettisoning junk."

If any of them had reservations about getting rid of their emergency oxygen, they kept them quiet.

There was plenty of junk to jettison, over the next quarter of an hour. Laser beams struck the station repeatedly, although Stromsen was able to block most of the beams with the heat-shielded lifeboats. Still, despite the mobile shields, the station was being slashed apart, bit by bit. Chunks of the outer hull ripped away, clouds of air blowing out of the upper level to form a brief fog around the station before dissipating into the vacuum of space. Cartons of supplies, pieces of equipment, even spare space suits, went spiraling out, pushed by air pressure as the compartments in which they had been housed were ripped apart by the probing incessant beams of energy.

Feeney struck back at the ABM satellites, but for every one he hit, another maneuvered into range to replace it.

"I'm running low on fuel for the lasers," he reported.

"So must they," said Hazard, trying to sound calm.

"Aye, but they've got a few more than fifteen to play with."

"Stay with it, Mr. Feeney. You're doing fine." Hazard patted the shoulder of the Irishman's bulky suit. Glancing at Stromsen's status displays, he saw rows of red lights glowering like accusing eyes. *They're taking the station apart, piece by piece. It's only a matter of time before we're finished.*

Aloud, he announced, "I'm going to check with the damage-control party. Call me if anything unusual happens."

Yang quipped, "How do you define 'unusual,' sir?" Stromsen and Feeney laughed. Hazard wished he could, too. He made a grin for the Chinese American, thinking, *At least their morale hasn't cracked. Not yet.*

The damage-control party was working on level three, reconnecting a secondary power line that ran along the overhead through the main passageway. A laser beam had burned through the deck of the second level and severed the line, cutting power to the station's main computer. A shaft of brilliant sunlight lanced down from the outer hull through two levels of the station and onto the deck of level three.

One space-suited figure was dangling upside down halfway through the hole in the overhead, splicing cable carefully with gloved hands, while a second hovered nearby with a small welding torch. Two more were working farther down the passageway, where a larger hole had been burned halfway down the bulkhead.

Through that jagged rip Hazard could see clear out to space and the rim of the Earth, glaring bright with swirls of white clouds.

He recognized Varshni by his small size even before he could see the Indian flag on his shoulder or read the name stenciled on the front of his suit.

"Mr. Varshni, I want you and your crew to leave level three. It's getting too dangerous here."

"But, sir," Varshni protested, "our duty is to repair damage."

"There'll be damage on level four soon enough."

"But the computer requires power."

"It can run on its internal batteries."

"But for how long?"

"Long enough," said Hazard grimly.

Varshni refused to be placated. "I am not risking lives unnecessarily, sir."

"I didn't say you were."

"I am operating on sound principles," the Indian insisted, "exactly as required in the book of regulations."

"I'm not faulting you, man. You and your crew have done a fine job."

The others had stopped their work. They were watching the exchange between their superior and the station commander.

"I have operated on the principle that lightning does not strike twice in the same place. In old-fashioned naval parlance this is referred to, I believe, as 'chasing salvos.'"

Hazard stared at the diminutive Indian. Even inside the visored space suit, Varshni appeared stiff with anger. Chasing salvos—that's what a little ship does when it's under attack by a bigger ship: run to where the last shells splashed, because it's pretty certain that the next salvo won't hit there. I've insulted his abilities, Hazard realized. And in front of his team. Damned fool!

"Mr. Varshni," Hazard explained slowly, "this battle will be decided, one way or the other, in the next twenty minutes or so. You and your team have done an excellent job of keeping damage to a minimum. Without you, we would have been forced to surrender."

Varshni seemed to relax a little. Hazard could sense his chin rising a notch inside his helmet.

"But the battle is entering a new phase," Hazard went on. "Level three is now vulnerable to direct laser damage. I can't afford to lose you and your team at this critical stage. Moreover, the computer and the rest of the most sensitive equipment are on level four and in the Combat Information Center. Those are the areas that need our protection and those are the areas where I want you to operate. Is that understood?"

A heartbeat's hesitation. Then Varshni said, "Yes, of course, sir. I understand. Thank you for explaining it to me."

"Okay. Now finish your work here and then get down to level four."

"Yes, sir."

Shaking his head inside his helmet, Hazard turned and pushed himself toward the ladderway that led down to level four and the CIC.

A blinding glare lit the passageway and he heard screams of agony. Blinking against the burning afterimage, Hazard turned to see Varshni's figure almost sliced in half. A dark burn line slashed diagonally across the torso of his space suit. Tiny globules of blood floated out from it. The metal overhead was blackened and curled now. A woman was screaming. She was up by the overhead, thrashing wildly with pain, her backpack ablaze. The other technician was nowhere to be seen.

Hazard rushed to the Indian while the other two members of the damage-control team raced to their partner and sprayed extinguisher foam on her backpack.

Over the woman's screams he heard Varshni's gagging whisper. "It's no use, sir . . . no use . . ."

"You did fine, son." Hazard held the little man in his arms. "You did fine."

He felt the life slip away. Lightning does strike in the same place, Hazard thought. You've chased your last salvo, son.

Both the man and the woman who had been working on the power cable had been wounded by the laser beam. The man's right arm had been sliced off at the elbow, the woman badly burned on her back when her life-support pack exploded. Hazard and the two remaining damage-control men carried them to the sick bay, where the station's one doctor was already working over three other casualties.

The sick bay was on the third level. Hazard realized how vulnerable that was. He made his way down to the CIC, at the heart of the station, knowing that it was protected not only by layers of metal but by human flesh as well. The station rocked again and Hazard heard the ominous groaning of tortured metal as he pushed weightlessly along the ladderway.

He felt bone-weary as he opened the hatch and floated into the CIC. One look at the haggard faces of his three young officers told him that they were on the edge of defeat as well. Stromsen's status display board was studded with glowering red lights.

"This station is starting to resemble a piece of Swiss cheese," Hazard quipped lamely as he lifted the visor of his helmet.

No one laughed. Or even smiled.

"Varshni bought it," he said, taking up his post between Stromsen and Feeney.

"We heard it," said Yang.

Hazard looked around the CIC. It felt stifling hot, dank with the smell of fear.

"Mr. Feeney," he said, "discontinue all offensive operations."

"Sir?" The Irishman's voice squeaked with surprise.

"Don't fire back at the sonsofbitches," Hazard snapped. "Is that clear enough?"

Feeney raised his hands up above his shoulders, like a croupier showing that he was not influencing the roulette wheel.

"Miss Stromsen, when the next laser beam is fired at us, shut down the main power generator. Miss Yang, issue instructions over the intercom that all personnel are to place themselves on level four—except for the sick bay. No one is to use the intercom. That is an order."

Stromsen asked, "The power generator?"

"We'll run on the backup fuel cells and batteries. They don't make so much heat."

There were more questions in Stromsen's eyes, but she turned back to her consoles silently.

Hazard explained, "We are going to run silent. Buckbee, Cardillo, and company have been pounding the hell out of us for about half an hour. They have inflicted considerable damage. However, they don't know that we've been able to shield ourselves with the lifeboats. They think they've hurt us much more than they actually have."

"You want them to think that they've finished us off, then?" asked Feeney.

"That's right. But, Mr. Feeney, let me ask you a hypothetical question . . ."

The chamber shook again and the screens dimmed, then came back to their normal brightness.

Stromsen punched a key on her console. "Main generator shut down, sir."

Hazard knew it was his imagination, but the screens seemed to become slightly dimmer.

"Miss Yang?" he asked.

"All personnel have been instructed to move down to level four and stay off the intercom."

Hazard nodded, satisfied. Turning back to Feeney, he resumed, "Suppose, Mr. Feeney, that you are in command of *Graham*. How would you know that you've knocked out *Hunter?*"

Feeney absently started to stroke his chin and bumped his fingertips against the rim of his helmet instead. "I suppose . . . if *Hunter* stopped shooting back, and I couldn't detect any radio emissions from her . . ."

"And infrared!" Yang added. "With the power generator out, our infrared signature goes way down."

"We appear to be dead in the water," said Stromsen.

"Right."

"But what does it gain us?" Yang asked.

"Time," answered Stromsen. "In another ten minutes or so we'll be within contact range of Geneva."

Hazard patted the top of her helmet. "Exactly. But more than that. We get them to stop shooting at us. We save the wounded up in the sick bay."

"And ourselves," said Feeney.

"Yes," Hazard admitted. "And ourselves." For long moments they hung weightlessly, silent, waiting, hoping.

"Sir," said Yang, "a query from *Graham*, asking if we surrender."

"No reply," Hazard ordered. "Maintain complete silence."

The minutes stretched. Hazard glided to Yang's comm console and taped a message for Geneva, swiftly outlining what had happened.

"I want that tape compressed into a couple of milliseconds and burped by the tightest laser beam we have down to Geneva."

Yang nodded. "I suppose the energy surge for a low-power communications laser won't be enough for them to detect."

"Probably not, but it's a chance we'll have to take. Beam it at irregular intervals as long as Geneva is in view."

"Yes, sir."

"Sir!" Feeney called out. "Looks like *Graham*'s detached a lifeboat."

"Trajectory analysis?"

Feeney tapped at his navigation console. "Heading for us," he reported.

Hazard felt his lips pull back in a feral grin.

"They're coming over to make sure. Cardillo's an old submariner; he knows all about running silent. They're sending over an armed party to make sure we're finished."

"And to take control of our satellites," Yang suggested.

Hazard brightened. "Right! There're only two ways to control the ABM satellites—either from the station on patrol or from Geneva." He spread his arms happily. "That means they're not in control of Geneva! We've got a good chance to pull their cork!"

But there was no response from Geneva when they beamed their data-compressed message to IPF headquarters. *Hunter* glided past in its unusually low orbit, a tattered wreck desperately calling for help. No answer reached them.

And the lifeboat from *Graham* moved inexorably closer.

The gloom in the CIC was thick enough to stuff a mattress as Geneva disappeared over the horizon and the boat from *Graham* came toward them. Hazard watched the boat on one of Stromsen's screens: it was bright and shining in the sunlight, not blackened by scorching laser beams, unsullied by splashes of human blood.

We could zap it into dust, he thought. One word from me and Feeney could focus half a dozen lasers on it. The men aboard her must be volunteers, willing to risk their necks to make certain that we're finished. He felt a grim admiration for them. Then he wondered, Is Jon Jr. aboard with them?

"Mr. Feeney, what kind of weapons do you think they're carrying?"

Feeney's brows rose toward his scalp. "Weapons, sir? You mean, like sidearms?"

Hazard nodded.

"Personal weapons are not allowed aboard station, sir. Regulations forbid it."

"I know. But what do you bet they've got pistols, at least. Maybe some submachine guns"

"Damned dangerous stuff for a space station," said Feeney.

Hazard smiled tightly at the Irishman. "Are you afraid they'll put a few more holes in our hull?"

Yang saw what he was driving at. "Sir, there are no weapons aboard *Hunter*—unless you want to count kitchen knives."

"They'll be coming aboard with guns, just to make sure," Hazard said. "I want to capture them alive and use them as hostages. That's our last remaining card. If we can't do that, we've got to surrender."

"They'll be in full suits." said Stromsen. "Each on his own individual life-support system."

"How can we capture them? Or even fight them?" Yang wondered aloud.

Hazard detected no hint of defeat in their voices. The despair of a half hour earlier was gone now. A new excitement had hold of them. He was holding a glimmer of hope for them, and they were reaching for it.

"There can't be more than six of them aboard that boat," Feeney mused.

I wonder if Cardillo has the guts to lead the boarding party in person, Hazard asked himself.

"We don't have any useful weapons," said Yang.

"But we have some tools," Stromsen pointed out. "Maybe . . ."

"What do the lifeboat engines use for propellant?" Hazard asked rhetorically.

"Methane and oh-eff-two," Feeney replied, looking puzzled.

Hazard nodded. "Miss Stromsen, which of our supply magazines are still intact—if any?"

It took them several minutes to understand what he was driving at, but when they finally saw the light, the three young officers went speedily to work. Together with the four unwounded members of the crew, they prepared a welcome for the boarders from *Graham*.

Finally, Hazard watched on Stromsen's display screens as the *Graham*'s boat sniffed around the battered station. Strict silence was in force aboard *Hunter*. Even in the CIC, deep at the heart of the battle station, they spoke in tense whispers.

"I hope the bastards like what they see," Hazard muttered.

"They know that we used the lifeboats for shields," said Yang.

"Active armor," Hazard said. "Did you know the idea was invented by the man this station's named after?"

"They're looking for a docking port," Stromsen pointed out.

"Only one left," said Feeney.

They could hang their boat almost anywhere and walk in through the holes they've put in us, Hazard said to himself. But they won't. They'll go by the book and find an intact docking port. They've got to! Everything depends on that.

He felt his palms getting slippery with nervous perspiration as the lifeboat slowly, slowly moved around *Hunter* toward the Earth-facing side, where the only usable port was located. Hazard had seen to it that all the other ports had been disabled.

"They're buying it!" Stromsen's whisper held a note of triumph.

"Sir!" Yang hissed urgently. "A message just came in— laser beam, ultracompressed."

"From where?"

"Computer's decrypting," she replied, her snub-nosed face wrinkled with concentration. "Coming up on my center screen, sir."

Hazard slid over toward her. The words on the screen read:

From: IPF Regional HQ, Lagos.

To: Commander, battle station *Hunter*.

Message begins. Coup attempt in Geneva a failure, thanks in large part to your refusal to surrender your command. Situation still unclear, however. Imperative you retain control of *Hunter*, at all costs. Message ends.

He read it aloud, in a guttural whisper, so that Feeney and Stromsen understood what was at stake.

"We're not alone," Hazard told them. "They know what's happening, and help is on the way."

That was stretching the facts, he knew. And he knew they knew. But it was reassuring to think that someone, somewhere, was preparing to help them.

Hazard watched them grinning to one another. In his mind, though, he kept repeating the phrase, "Imperative you retain control of *Hunter*, at all costs."

At all costs, Hazard said to himself, closing his eyes wearily, seeing Varshni dying in his arms and the others maimed. At all costs.

The bastards, Hazard seethed inwardly. The dirty, power-grabbing, murdering bastards. Once they set foot inside my station, I'll kill them like the poisonous snakes they are. I'll squash them flat. I'll cut them open just like they've slashed my kids.

He stopped abruptly and forced himself to take a deep breath. Yeah, sure. Go for personal revenge. That'll make the world a better place to live in, won't it?

"Sir, are you all right?"

Hazard opened his eyes and saw Stromsen staring at him. "Yes, I'm fine. Thank you."

"They've docked, sir," said the Norwegian.

"They're debarking and coming up passageway C, just as you planned."

Looking past her to the screens, Hazard saw that there were six of them, all in space suits, visors down. And pistols in their gloved hands.

"Nothing bigger than pistols?"

"No, sir. Not that we can see, at least."

Turning to Feeney. "Ready with the aerosols?"

"Yes, sir."

"All crew members evacuated from the area?"

"They're all back on level four, except for the sick bay."

Hazard never took his eyes from the screens. The six space-suited boarders were floating down the passageway that led to the lower levels of the station, which were still pressurized and held breathable air. They stopped at the air lock, saw that it was functional. The leader of their group started working the wall unit that controlled the lock.

"Can we hear them?" he asked Yang.

Wordlessly, she touched a stud on her keyboard.

"... use the next section of the passageway as an air lock," someone was saying. "Standard procedure. Then we'll pump the air back into it once we're inside."

"But we stay in the suits until we check out the whole station. That's an order," said another voice.

Buckbee? Hazard's spirits soared. Buckbee will make a nice hostage, he thought. Not as good as Cardillo, but good enough.

Just as he had hoped, the six boarders went through the airtight hatch, closed it behind them, and started the pump that filled the next section of passageway with air once again.

"Something funny here, sir," said one of the space-suited figures.

"Yeah, the air's kind of misty."

"Never saw anything like this before. Christ, it's like Mexico City air."

"Stay in your suits!" It *was* Buckbee's voice, Hazard was certain of it. "Their life-support systems must have been damaged in our bombardment. They're probably all dead."

You wish, Hazard thought. To Feeney, he commanded, "Seal that hatch."

Feeney pecked at a button on his console.

"And the next one."

"Already done, sir."

Hazard waited, watching Stromsen's main screen as the six boarders shuffled weightlessly to the next hatch and found that it would not respond to the control unit on the bulkhead.

"Damn! We'll have to double back and find another route."

"Miss Yang, I'm ready to hold converse with our guests," said Hazard.

She flashed a brilliant smile and touched the appropriate keys, then pointed at him. "You're on the air!"

"Buckbee, this is Hazard."

All six of the boarders froze for an instant, then spun weightlessly in midair, trying to locate the source of the new voice.

"You are trapped in that section of corridor," Hazard said. "The mist that you see in the air is oxygen difluoride from our lifeboat propellant tanks. Very volatile stuff. Don't strike any matches."

"What the hell are you saying, Hazard?"

"You're locked in that passageway, Buckbee. If you try to fire those popguns you're carrying, you'll blow yourselves to pieces."

"And you too!"

"We're already dead, you prick. Taking you with us is the only joy I'm going to get out of this."

"You're bluffing!"

Hazard snapped, "Then show me how brave you are, Buckbee. Take a shot at the hatch."

The six boarders hovered in the misty passageway like figures in a surrealistic painting. Seconds ticked by, each one stretching excruciatingly. Hazard felt a pain in his jaws and realized he was clenching his teeth hard enough to chip them.

He took his eyes from the screen momentarily to glance at his three youngsters. They were just as tense as he was. They knew how long the odds of their gamble were. The passageway was filled with nothing more than aerosol mists from every spray can the crew could locate in the supply magazines.

"What do you want, Hazard?" Buckbee said at last, his voice sullen, like a spoiled little boy who had been denied a cookie.

Hazard let out his breath. Then, as cheerfully as he could manage, "I've got what I want. Six hostages. How much air do your suits carry? Twelve hours?"

"What do you mean?"

"You've got twelve hours to convince Cardillo and the rest of your pals to surrender."

"You're crazy, Hazard."

"I've had a tough day, Buckbee. I don't need your insults. Call me when you're ready to deal."

"You'll be killing your son!"

Hazard had half-expected it, but still it hit him like a blow. "Johnny, are you there?"

"Yes I am, Dad."

Hazard strained forward, peering hard at the display screen, trying to determine which one of the space-suited figures was his son.

"Well, this is a helluva fix, isn't it?" he said softly.

"Dad, you don't have to wait twelve hours."

"Shut your mouth!" Buckbee snapped.

"Fuck you," snarled Jon Jr. "I'm not going to get myself killed for nothing."

"I'll shoot you!" Hazard saw Buckbee level his gun at Jon Jr.

"And kill yourself? You haven't got the guts," Jonnie sneered. Hazard almost smiled. How many times had his son used that tone on him.

Buckbee's hand wavered. He let the gun slip from his gloved fingers. It drifted slowly, weightlessly, away from him.

Hazard swallowed. Hard.

"Dad, in another hour or two the game will be over. Cardillo lied to you. The Russians never came in with us. Half a dozen ships full of troops are lifting off from IPF centers all over the globe."

"Is that the truth, son?"

"Yes, sir, it is. Our only hope was to grab control of your satellites. Once the coup attempt in Geneva flopped, Cardillo knew that if he could control three or four sets of ABM satellites, he could at least force a stalemate. But all he's got is *Graham* and *Wood*. Nobody else."

"You damned little traitor!" Buckbee screeched.

Jon Jr. laughed. "Yeah, you're right. But I'm going to be a *live* traitor. I'm not dying for the likes of you."

Hazard thought swiftly. Jon Jr. might defy his father, might argue with him, even revile him, but he had never known the lad to lie to him.

"Buckbee, the game's over," he said slowly. "You'd better get the word to Cardillo before there's more bloodshed."

It took another six hours before it was all sorted out. A shuttle filled with armed troops and an entire replacement crew finally arrived at the battered hulk of *Hunter*. The relieving commander, a stubby, compactly built black man from New Jersey who had been a U.S. Air Force fighter pilot, made a grim tour of inspection with Hazard. From inside his space suit he whistled in amazement at the battle damage.

"Shee-it, you don't need a new crew, you need a new station!"

"It's still functional," Hazard said quietly, then added proudly, "and so is my crew, or what's left of them. They ran this station and kept control of the satellites."

"The stuff legends are made of, my man," said the new commander.

Hazard and his crew filed tiredly into the waiting shuttle, thirteen grimy, exhausted men and women in the pale-blue fatigues of the IPF. Three of them were wrapped in mesh cocoons and attended by medical personnel. Two others were bandaged but ambulatory.

He shook hands with each and every one of them as they stepped from the station's only functional air lock into the shuttle's passenger compartment. Hovering there weightlessly, his creased, craggy face unsmiling, to each of his crew members he said, "Thank you. We couldn't have succeeded without your effort."

The last three through the hatch were Feeney, Stromsen, and Yang. The Irishman looked embarrassed as Hazard shook his hand.

"I'm recommending you for promotion. You were damned cool under fire."

"Frozen stiff with fear, you mean."

To Stromsen, "You, too, Miss Stromsen. You've earned a promotion."

"Thank you, sir," was all she could say.

"And you, little lady," he said to Yang. "You were outstanding."

She started to say something, then flung her arms around Hazard's neck and squeezed tight. "I was so frightened!" she whispered in his ear. "You kept me from cracking up."

Hazard held her around the waist for a moment. As they disengaged he felt his face turning flame red. He turned away from the hatch, not wanting to see the expressions on the rest of his crew members.

Buckbee was coming through the air lock. Behind him were his five men. Including Jon Jr.

They passed Hazard in absolute silence, Buckbee's face as cold and angry as an Antarctic storm.

Jon Jr. was the last in line. None of the would-be boarders was in handcuffs, but they all had the hangdog look of prisoners. All except Hazard's son.

He stopped before his father and met the older man's gaze. Jon Jr.'s gray eyes were level with his father's, unswerving, unafraid.

He made a bitter little smile. "I still don't agree with you," he said without preamble. "I don't think the IPF is workable—and it's certainly not in the best interests of the United States."

"But you threw your lot in with us when it counted," Hazard said.

"The hell I did!" Jon Jr. looked genuinely aggrieved. "I just didn't see any sense in dying for a lost cause."

"Really?"

"Cardillo and Buckbee and the rest of them were a bunch of idiots. If I had known how stupid they are I wouldn't . . ."

He stopped himself, grinned ruefully, and shrugged his shoulders.

"This isn't over, you know. You won the battle, but the war's not ended yet."

"I'll do what I can to get them to lighten your sentence," Hazard said.

"Don't stick your neck out for me! I'm still dead set against you on this."

Hazard smiled wanly at the youngster. "And you're still my son."

Jon Jr. blinked, looked away, then ducked through the hatch and made for a seat in the shuttle.

Hazard formally turned the station over to its new commander, saluted one last time, then went into the shuttle's passenger compartment. He hung there weightlessly a moment as the hatch behind him was swung shut and sealed. Most of the seats were already filled. There was an empty one beside Yang, but after their little scene at the hatch Hazard was hesitant about sitting next to her. He glided down the aisle and picked a seat that had no one next to it. Not one of his crew. Not Jon Jr.

There's a certain amount of loneliness involved in command, he told himself. It's not wise to get too familiar with people you have to order into battle.

He felt, rather than heard, a thump as the shuttle disengaged from the station's air lock. He sensed the winged hypersonic spaceplane turning and angling its nose for reentry into the atmosphere.

Back to . . . Hazard realized that *home*, for him, was no longer on Earth. For almost all of his adult life, home had been where his command was. Now his home was in space. The time he spent on Earth would be merely waiting time, suspended animation until his new command was ready.

"Sir, may I intrude?"

He looked up and saw Stromsen floating in the aisle by his seat.

"What is it, Miss Stromsen?"

She pulled herself down into the seat next to him but did not bother to latch the safety harness. From a breast pocket in her sweat-stained fatigues she pulled a tiny flat tin. It was marked with a red cross and some printing, hidden by her thumb.

Stromsen opened the tin. "You lost your medication patch," she said. "I thought you might want a fresh one." She was smiling at him, shyly, almost like a daughter might.

Hazard reached up and felt behind his left ear. She was right, the patch was gone.

"I wonder how long ago . . ."

"It's been hours, at least," said Stromsen.

"Never noticed."

Her smile brightened. "Perhaps you don't need it anymore."

He smiled back at her. "Miss Stromsen, I think you're absolutely right. My stomach feels fine. I believe I have finally become adapted to weightlessness."

"It's rather a shame that we're on our way back to Earth. You'll have to adapt all over again the next time out."

Hazard nodded. "Somehow I don't think that's going to be much of a problem for me anymore."

He let his head sink back into the seat cushion and closed his eyes, enjoying for the first time the exhilarating floating sensation of weightlessness.

PRIMARY

We have not yet begun to feel the full impact of computers in government and politics.

I can't really say more about this story without giving away some of its surprises. So, since, as Polonius once said, brevity is the soul of wit, I will be brief. (And, by implication, witty.)

Think about who—and what—you are voting for the next time you enter your polling booth.

SO THEY BRING US into the Oval Office and he sits himself down behind the big desk. It even has Harry Truman's old THE BUCK STOPS HERE sign on it.

He grins at that. He's good-looking, of course. Young, almost boyish, with that big flop of hair over his forehead that's become almost mandatory for any man who wants to be President of the United States. His smile is dazzling. Knocks women dead at forty paces. But his eyes are hard as diamond. He's no fool. He hasn't gotten into this office on that smile alone.

I want him to succeed. God knows we need a president who can succeed, who can pull this country together again and make us feel good about ourselves. But more than that, I want my program to succeed. Let him be the star of the press conferences. Let the women chase him. It's my program that's really at stake here, those intricate, invisible electronic swirls and bubbles that I'm carrying in my valise. That's what's truly important.

We're going to have a busy day.

There are four other people in the office with us, his closest aides and advisors: three men and one woman who have worked for him, sweated for him, bled for him since the days when he was a grassy-green, brand-new junior senator from Vermont. The men are his Secretaries of Defense, Commerce, and the Treasury. The lone woman is his Vice President, of course. There hasn't been a male veep since the eighties, a cause for complaint among some feminists who see themselves being stereotyped as perpetual Number Twos.

And me. I'm in the Oval Office, too, with my valise full of computer programs. But they hardly notice me. I'm just one of the lackeys, part of the background, like the portraits of former presidents on the walls or the model of the Mars Exploration Base that he insisted they set up on the table behind his desk, between the blue-and-gold-curtained windows.

My job is to load my program disks into the White House mainframe computer, buried somewhere deep beneath the West Wing. He thinks of it as *his* program, *his* plans and techniques for running the country. But it's mine, my clever blend of hardware and software that will be the heart and brains and guts of this Oval Office.

I sit off in the corner, so surrounded by display screens and keyboards that they can barely see the top of my balding head. That's okay. I like it here, barricaded behind the machines, sitting off alone like a church organist up in his secret niche. I can see them, all of them, on my display screens. If I want, I can call up X-ray pictures of them, CAT scans, even. I can ask the mainframe for the blueprints of our newest missile guidance system, or for this morning's roll call attendance at any army base in the world. No need for that, though. Not now. Not today. Too much work to do.

I give him a few minutes to get the feel of the big leather chair behind that desk, and let the other four settle down in their seats. Treasury takes the old Kennedy rocker; I knew he would.

Then I reach out, like God on the Sistine ceiling, and lay my extended finger on the first pressure pad of the master keyboard.

The morning Situation Report springs up on my central screen. And on the screen atop Our Man's desk. Not too tough a morning, I see. He's always been lucky.

Food riots in Poland are in their third day.

The civil war in the Philippines has reignited; Manila is in flames, with at least three different factions fighting to take command of the city.

Terrorists assassinated the President of Mexico during the night.

The stock market will open the day at the lowest point the Dow Jones has seen in fourteen years.

Unemployment is approaching the twenty-percent mark, although this is no reflection on Our Man's economic policy (my program, really) because we haven't had time to put it into effect as yet.

The dollar is still sinking in the European markets. Trading in Tokyo remains suspended.

Intelligence reports that the new Russian base on the Moon is strictly a military base, contrary to the treaties that both we and they signed back in the sixties.

All in all, the kind of morning that any American president might have faced at any time during the past several administrations.

"This Mexican assassination is a jolt," says the Secretary of Commerce. He's a chubby, round-cheeked former computer whiz, a multi-multimillionaire when he was in his twenties, a philanthropist in his thirties, and for this decade a selfless public servant. If you can believe that. He hired me, originally, and got me this position as Our Man's programmer. Still thinks he's up to date on computers. Actually, he's twenty years behind but nobody's got the guts to tell him. His beard is still thick and dark, but when I punch in a close-up on my screens, I can see a few gray hairs. In another couple of years he's going to look like a neurotic Santa Claus.

Our Man nods, pouting a little, as if the assassination of a president anywhere is a low blow and a personal affront to him.

"The situation in the Philippines is more dangerous," says the Defense Secretary. "If the jihadists win there, they'll have Japan outflanked and Australia threatened."

I like his Defense Secretary. He is a careful old grayhair who smokes a pipe, dresses conservatively, and has absolute faith in whatever his computer displays tell him. He has the reputation for being one of the sharpest thinkers in Washington. Actually, it's his programmers who are sharp. All he does is read what they print out for him, between puffs on his pipe.

"Maybe we should get the National Security Advisor in on this," suggests Commerce, scratching at his beard.

"By all means," says Our Man.

We can't have the Security Advisor in the room, of course, but I call him up on the communications screen and presto! there he is, looking as baggy and sad-eyed as a hound.

"What do you make of the situation in the Philippines, Doc?" Our Man, with his warmth and wit, and power, is the only man on Earth who can get away with calling this distinguished, dour, pompously pontifical scholar *Doc*.

"Mr. President—" His voice sounds like the creaking of a heavy, ancient castle door "—it is just as I have outlined for you on many occasions in the past. The situation in the Philippines can no longer be ignored. The strategic value of this traditional ally of ours is vital to our interests throughout Asia and the Pacific."

As he gives his perfectly predictable little spiel, I call up the subroutine that presents the pertinent information about the Philippines: the screens throw up data on our military and naval bases there, the ocean trade routes that they affect, the number of American business firms that have factories in the Philippines and how losing those factories would affect the GNP, employment, the value of the dollar—that kind of stuff.

I put all this information on the secondary screens that line the wall to one side of the President's desk. His eyes ping-pong between them and the desktop display of the Security Advisor.

"Thanks, Doc," he says at last. "I appreciate your candor. Please stand by, in case I need more input from you."

He turns back to the little group by his desk. I freeze Doc's image and fling it electronically to my farthest upper-right screen, a holding spot for him.

"Much as I hate to say it," Defense mutters around his pipe, "we're going to have to make our presence felt in the Philippines."

"You mean militarily," says the Vice President, her nose wrinkling with distaste. She has been an excellent vote-getter all through her political career: a Mexican-American from San Antonio who looks sexy enough to start rumors about her and Our Man.

"Of course militarily," Defense replies with ill-concealed impatience. "Look at the data on the screens. We can't let the Philippines slip away from us."

"Why does it always have to be troops and guns?" the Veep grumbles.

"I was thinking more of ships and planes."

"A task force," says the man behind the big desk. "A carrier group. That can be pretty impressive."

While they discuss the merits of a carrier group versus one of the old resurrected battleships, and whether or not they should throw in a battalion of Marines just in case, I do a little anticipating and flick my fingers in a way that brings up the projected costs for such a mission and how it will affect DOD's budget.

And, just as surely as gold is more precious than silver, the Secretary of the Treasury bestirs himself.

"Hey, wait a minute. This is going to cost real heavy money."

He has a very practical attitude toward money: his, mine, or yours. He wants all of it for himself. The only black in Our Man's Cabinet, Treasury is a hardheaded pragmatist who took the paltry few million his father left him (from a restaurant chain) and parlayed them into billions on the stock market. For years he belonged to the Other Party, but when the last president failed to name him to his Cabinet, he switched allegiance and devoted his life, his fortune, and what was left of his honor to Our Man.

Now he calls for details on the cost projections and, thanks to the wizardry of binary electronics, I place before their eyes (on the wall screens) vividly colored graphs that show not only how much the carrier group's mission will cost, but my program's projections of what the Philippine rebels' likely responses will be. These include—but are not limited to—a wave of assassinations throughout the 7,100 islands and islets of the archipelago, a *coup d' etat* by their army, terrorist suicide attacks on our aircraft carrier, and armed intervention by the People's Republic of China.

Our Man is fascinated by these possibilities. The more awful they are, the more intrigued he is.

"Let's play these out and see where they lead," he says. He doesn't realize that he's speaking to me. He's just making a wish, like the prince in a fairy tale, and I, his digital godfather, must make the wish come true.

For two hours we play out the various scenarios, using my programs and the White House mainframe's stored memory banks to show where each move leads, what each countermove elicits. It is like following a grand master chess tournament on your home computer. Some of the scenarios lead to a nuclear engagement. One of them leads to a full-scale nuclear war between the United States and China: Armageddon, followed by Nuclear Winter.

Our Man, naturally, picks out the scenario that comes up best for our side.

"Okay, then," he says, looking exhilarated. He's always enjoyed playing computer games. "We will forgo the naval task force and merely increase our garrisons at Subic Bay and Mindanao. Our best counter to the threat, apparently, is to withhold economic aid from the Philippine government until they open honest negotiations with their opposition."

"If you can believe the computer projections," grumbles Commerce. He doesn't trust any programs he can't understand, and he's so far out of date that he can't understand my program. So he doesn't trust me.

The Vice President seems happy enough with me. "We can form a Cease-Fire Commission, made up of members from the neighboring nations."

"It'll never work," mutters Commerce from behind his beard.

"The computer says it will," Defense points out. He doesn't look terribly happy about it, though.

"What I want to know," says Treasury, "is what this course of action is going to do to our employment problems."

And it goes on like that for the rest of the day. Every problem they face is linked with all the other problems. Every Marine sent overseas has an effect on employment. Every unemployed teenager in the land has an effect on the crime rate. Every unwed mother has an effect on the price of milk.

No human being, no Cabinet full of human beings, can grasp all these interlinks without the aid of a *very* sophisticated computer program. Let them sit there and debate, let Our Man make his speeches to the public. The real work is done by the machine, by my program, by the software that can encompass all the data in the world and display it in all its interconnected complexity. They think they're making decisions, charting the course for the nation to follow, leading the people. In reality, the decisions they make are the decisions that the computer allows them to make, based on the information presented to them. It's my program that's charting the course for the nation; those human beings sitting around the President's desk are puppets, nothing more.

And don't think that I consider myself to be the puppet master, pulling their strings. Far from it. I'm just the guy who wrote the computer program. It's the program that runs the show. The program, as alive as any creature of flesh and blood, an electronic person that feeds on data, a digital soul that aspires to know everything, everywhere. Even during this one day it has grown and matured. I can see it happening before my teary eyes. Like a proud father I watch my program learning from the White House's giant mainframe, becoming more sure of itself, reaching out questioning tendrils all across the world, and learning, learning, learning.

"Four o'clock," announces the studio director. "Time to wrap it up."

The overhead lights turn off as abruptly as the end of the world. Our Man flinches, looks up, his face showing vast disappointment, irritation, even anger. The others exhale sighingly, wipe their brows, get up from their chairs, and stretch their weary bones. It's been a long day.

The TV camera crews shuffle out of the studio as the director, earphone still clamped to his head, comes over to Our Man and sticks out his hand.

"You did an excellent job, sir. You've got my vote in November."

Our Man gives him the old dazzling smile. "Thanks. I'll need every vote I can get, I'm sure. And don't forget the primary!"

"April seventh." The studio director smiles back. "Don't worry, I'll vote for you."

He must tell that to all the candidates.

I remain at my post, hidden behind the computer consoles, and check the National Rating Service's computer to see how well Our Man *really* did. The screen shows a rating of *0.54*. Not bad. In fact, the best rating for any candidate who's been tested so far. It will look really impressive in the media; should get a lot of votes for Our Man.

He still has to go through the primaries, of course, but that's done mainly by electronics. No more backbreaking campaigns through every state for month after month. The candidates appeal to the voters individually, through their TV screens and home computers, a personal message to each bloc of voters, tailored to each bloc's innermost desires, thanks to the polished techniques of psychological polling and videotaping.

But this test run in the simulated Oval Office is of crucial importance. Each candidate has got to show that he can handle the pressures of an average day in the White House, that he can make decisions that will be good, effective, and politically palatable. Excerpts from today's simulation test will be on the evening news; tomorrow's papers will carry the story on page one. And naturally, the entire day's test will be available on PBS and even video disc for any voter who wants to see the whole day.

Of course, what this day's simulation *really* tested was my program. I feel a little like Cyrano de Bergerac, ghostwriting letters to the woman he loves for another man to woo her.

Making sure that no one is watching, I tap out the code for the White House mainframe's most secret subroutine. Only a handful of programmers know about this part of the White House's machine. None of our candidates know of it.

In the arcane language that only we dedicated programmers know, I ask the mainframe how well my program did. The answer glows brilliantly on the central screen: 0.96. Ninety-six! The highest score any program has ever received.

I hug myself and double over to keep from laughing out loud. If my legs worked, I would jump up and dance around the studio. Ninety-six! The best ever!

No matter which candidate gets elected, no matter who votes for whom, the White House mainframe is going to pick *my* program. My program will be the one the next president uses for the coming four years. Mine!

With my heart thumping wildly in my chest, I shut down the consoles. All the screens go dark. I spin my chair around and go wheeling through the emptied, darkened studio, heading for the slice of light offered by the half-open door. Already my mind is churning with ideas for improving the program.

After all, in another four years the primaries start all over again.

THOSE WHO CAN

Some stories go their own way, despite the conscious volition of the writer. This one was inspired by a funny incident at a meeting of a major corporation's board of directors. But the story didn't want to be funny. Not at all.

* 🌀 *

WE GET ALL THE KOOKS, William Ransom thought to himself as he watched the intent young man set up his equipment.

They were in Ransom's office, one of the smaller suites in the management level of Larrimore, Swain & Tucker, seventy-three stories above the crowded Wall Street sidewalk. As the firm's least senior executive (a mere fifty-three years old) Ransom's duties included interviewing intent young inventors who claimed to have new products that could revolutionize industries.

The equipment that the intent young man was assembling looked like a junkpile of old stereo sets, computer consoles, and the insides of Tic-Tok of Oz. It spread across the splashy orange-brown carpet, climbed over the conversation corner's genuine llama-hide couches, covered the coffee table between the couches and was now encroaching on the teak bar behind them.

"I'll be finished in a minute," said the intent young inventor. He had said the same thing ten minutes earlier, and ten minutes before *that*. But he continued to pull strange-looking racks of printed circuits and oddly glowing metallic cylinders from the seemingly bottomless black trunk that he had dragged into the office with him.

If I had known it would take him this long, Ransom thought, *I would have told him to set up after I'd gone for the day, and let me see it tomorrow morning.*

But it was a half hour too late for that decision.

Ransom glanced at the neatly typed note his secretary had efficiently placed on his immaculate desktop. James Brightcloud, it said. Inventor. From Santa Fe, New Mexico. Representing self.

Ransom shook his head and suppressed a sigh. He was going to be stuck with this madman for the rest of the afternoon, he knew it, while Mr. Larrimore and other executives repaired to the rooftop sauna and the comforts of soothing ministrations by this week's bevy of masseuses. It was a fine accomplishment to be the youngest member of the executive board, career-wise. But it also meant that you were low man on the executive totem pole. Ransom had been dreaming about deaths in high places lately. Two nights ago, he had found himself reading *Julius Caesar* and enjoying it.

"Just about done," James Brightcloud muttered. He pulled a slim rod from the trunk and touched it to the last piece of equipment he had set up, atop the bar. Sparks leaped, hissing. Ransom almost jumped out of his seat.

"There," Brightcloud said. "Ready to go."

The inventor looked Hispanic, but without the easygoing smile that Ransom always associated with Latins. He couldn't have been more than thirty. Darkish skin, much darker eyes that brooded. Straight black hair. Stocky build, almost burly. Lots of muscles under that plain denim leisure suit. Ransom thought briefly about the *Puerto Rico Libre* movement that had been bombing banks and office buildings. He laid his hands on the edge of his very solid teak desk and pictured himself ducking under it at the first sign of a detonation.

"I can demonstrate it for you now," James Brightcloud said. He neither smiled nor frowned. His face was a mask of stoic impassivity.

"Er . . . before you do," Ransom said, stroking the smooth solid wood of his desk unobtrusively, wondering just how much shrapnel it would stop, "just what *is* it? I mean, what does your invention do?"

"It's a therapeutic device."

Ransom blinked at the young inventor. "A what?"

Brightcloud stepped around the machinery he had assembled and walked toward Ransom's desk. Pulling up a chair, he said, "Therapeutic. It makes you feel better. It heals soreness in the muscles, stiffness caused by tension. It can even get rid of stomach ulcers for you."

Ransom's eyes rolled toward the ceiling, and he thought of the sauna on the top floor. He could feel the steam and hear the giggling, almost.

"I suppose," he said, "it also cures cancer."

"We've had a couple of remissions in the field tests," Brightcloud answered straightfaced, "but we don't like to emphasize them. They might have been spontaneous, and it wouldn't be right for us to get peoples' hopes up."

"Of course." Ransom made a mental note to fire his secretary. The woman must be getting soft in the head. "Er . . . how does this device of yours work? Or are the operating principles a secret?"

"No secret . . . if you understand enough biochemistry and radiation therapy principles."

"I don't."

The inventor nodded. "Well, to put it simply, the device emits a beam of radiant energy that interacts with the parasympathetic nervous system. It has a variety of effects, and by controlling the frequency of the emitted radiation we can achieve somatic effects in the patient: muscular relaxation, easing of tension, of headaches. That sort of thing."

"Radiation?" Ransom was suddenly alert. "You mean like microwaves? The stuff the Russians have been beaming at our embassy in Moscow?"

Unruffled, Brightcloud said, "The same principle, yes. But entirely different wavelengths and entirely different somatic effects."

"Somatic . . . ?"

"Microwave radiation can be harmful," the inventor explained. "The radiation from my device is beneficial. It can even be curative." He hesitated a moment, then, in a lowered voice, added, "Our first sale has been to the government. I don't know this for a fact, but I'm pretty sure it's going to be installed in our Moscow embassy."

Ransom felt his eyebrows climb. "Really?"

"To counteract the Russian machine's effects."

"Is that so?"

"It's unofficial, but that's what I've been led to believe."

"But, if your device is curative—"

"Therapeutic," Brightcloud corrected. "Therapeutic is the proper term."

"All right, therapeutic. If it's good for your health, why aren't you dealing with a medical organization? Or one of the ethical pharmaceutical houses?"

A trace of disappointment crossed Brightcloud's features. "Two reasons. First, as soon as we get into a medical or pharmaceutical situation, the Federal government gets involved in a major way. Food and Drug Administration, National Institutes of Health, HEW, the Surgeon General. It would be a long, costly mess."

"I see."

"Secondly, this device is not inexpensive. The drug companies are geared to mass marketing. Even the medical technology outfits want to be able to sell their products to all the hospitals and clinics. This device is too costly for that kind of marketing. It can only be sold to the highest levels of corporate management. Nobody else could afford it."

"Really?"

"And no one else needs it so badly," Brightcloud quickly added. "Secretaries and street cleaners can take aspirin for their headaches and pains. It's good enough for them. But top-level executives, such as yourself, have different problems, different kinds of tensions, constant pressure and strain. That's where this device works best."

Ransom almost believed him.

"And frankly," the inventor went on, "it will be much easier for me to market my device as a sort of executive's relaxation gadget, rather than go through the entire government red-tape mill that they use on medical devices."

"But how do I know it's not harmful?" Ransom asked.

Brightcloud shrugged. "I've used it on myself thousands of times. We've run more than five hundred controlled laboratory tests with it and several hundred more field tests. No harmful effects whatsoever."

"Still . . ."

"You've been bathing in its radiation for the past two and a half minutes," the inventor said. "So have I."

Ransom grabbed at the desk's edge. "What!"

"Do you feel anything? Any pain or dizziness?"

"Why . . . er . . . no."

"Just how do you feel?" Brightcloud asked.

Ransom thought about it. "Er . . . fine, as a matter of fact. A little warm, perhaps."

"That's from the stimulation effect on your blood circulation. Here." Brightcloud took a small oblong black box from his shirt jacket pocket. It looked rather like a hand calculator. "Let me adjust the frequency just a bit."

He turned a tiny knob on the box. Ransom relaxed back in his swivel chair. He was about to say that he didn't feel any change when, suddenly, he *did*. A decided change. A growing, warming, magnificent change.

He felt his jaw drop open as he stared at Brightcloud, who merely stretched his legs comfortably, clasped his hands behind his head, and grinned boyishly at him.

As president of Larrimore, Swain & Tucker, Robert Larrimore was accustomed to saying *no*. It had been the hallmark of his long career, a thoroughly negative attitude that had given him the reputation for being the toughest, shrewdest businessman in Lower Manhattan. When others rhapsodized over new products, Larrimore frowned. When junior executives cooed over ideas from their creative staffs and chorused, "Love it! I love it!" Larrimore shook his head and walked in the other direction. When politicians towed in their newest toothpaste-clean candidate, Larrimore would enumerate all the weaknesses of the candidate that his cigar-chomping backers were trying to overlook or forget.

In short, because he pointed out the obvious and refused to be stampeded by the crowd, he had survived and prospered where others had enthused and withered away. After nearly eight decades of avoiding gapingly unmistakable pitfalls, Larrimore was regarded by several generations of young executives with a respect that bordered on awe. This did not make him a happy man, however.

He was the first one to arrive in the conference room for the meeting with this new inventor that young Ransom had discovered. Larrimore walked stiffly to his accustomed chair, halfway down the polished mahogany table, his eyes fixed on the Byzantine complexity of electronic units stacked neatly against the back end of the conference room from wall to wall and floor to ceiling.

A uniformed security guard stood before the inert hardware. Larrimore snorted to himself and sat, slowly and painfully, in his padded chair. *Arthritis,* he groused inwardly. *They can cure pneumonia and give me a new heart, but the stupid sonsofbitches still can't do anything more for arthritis than give me some goddamned aspirins.*

William Ransom pushed the corridor door open and held it for a stocky, dark-complected young man who wore a denim leisure suit embroidered with flowers and sun symbols. *My God,* Larrimore thought, *that young twit Ransom has brought a goddamned Indian in here. An Apache, I bet.*

Ransom made a prim contrast to the solemn-faced redskin, being slim, tall, Aryan-blond and good-looking in an empty way. He always reminded Larrimore of a chorus boy from a musical about the Roaring Twenties.

"Oh, Mr. Larrimore, you're already here," Ransom said as he let the door softly shut itself.

"You get an A for visual acuity," Larrimore said.

Ransom grinned weakly. "Er . . . allow me to introduce Mr. Ja—"

"James Brightcloud. Who else would he be, Billy?" Larrimore chuckled inwardly. *What's the good of being a tyrant unless you can exert a little tyranny now and then?*

In a much-subdued voice, Ransom said to the inventor, "This is Mr. Larrimore, our president."

"How do you do?" Brightcloud said evenly.

"I do damned well," Larrimore answered. He did not extend his hand to the inventor. *A boy. He's a mere boy. He can't have anything worthwhile to show us.*

"The others will be here in a minute," Ransom chattered. "Would you like to have Mr. Brightcloud give you a briefing about his invention before they—"

"No," Larrimore snapped. "He can tell me the same time he tells the others."

Ransom looked back to the inventor, uncertainty twitching in his left eye. "Er . . . do you need to, um, warm up the equipment or anything like that?"

Brightcloud shook his head. "You probably want to let the security guard go."

"Oh! *Oh*, yes, surely."

Larrimore sank back in his chair and watched the two young men take their places down at the end of the table. Ransom whispered a few words to the guard, who then quietly left the conference room. The door didn't get a chance to close behind him before the other board members started filing in.

Horace Mann was the first. The financial vice president always arrived on the stroke for every meeting, even though he could barely walk anymore. White-haired and bent with age, Mann had refused retirement every year for the past ten years. And since he knew financial details that were best kept locked within his head, he stayed in power. *We'll have to carry him out someday*, Larrimore thought.

Arnold Hawthorn and Toshio Takahashi arrived together. Hawthorn, the company's sales director, was sleek, silver-haired and devilishly handsome. He claimed to be bisexual, but no one had ever seen him so much as smile at a woman. Takahashi wore his saffron monk's robe even to board meetings. The foreign sales people worshipped him, almost literally, and his kindness and oriental patience were legendary.

Good for morale, Larrimore mused. *And he keeps those young squirts from trying to claw their way up the executive ladder.*

Borden C. Blude, the production manager, came in next and immediately began chatting amiably with Takahashi. Blude was in his eighties, almost as old as Larrimore himself, and clearly senile. He hadn't had a new idea since Eisenhower had resigned from Columbia, Blude's alma mater. They didn't let him do anything around the office, but Casanova—the man who actually owned Larrimore, Swain & Tucker—kept him around as a sort of mascot.

Casanova was his usual punctual self, exactly ten minutes late. He was wheeled in by his nurse-secretary-assistant, Ms. Kim Conroy, who was known as Lollipop around the office, but never within Casanova's hearing. A tall, ravishing redhead who claimed she could type two hundred words a minute, her only obvious talent was a set of well-developed pectoral muscles—undoubtedly an asset in pushing Casanova's wheelchair.

The absolute master of Larrimore, Swain & Tucker, Casanova had lost the use of his lower extremities through a childish ambition to emulate Eval Knievel. By *almost* clearing twenty school busses, Casanova went from a motorcycle to a wheelchair in his fortieth year, and turned his restless energy from race courses to board rooms. He owned LS&T, all of it. He was the sole stockholder. He had purchased the stock from this very board of directors when, after two of Larrimore's negative decisions, they had failed to get in on both the pocket calculator and CB radio booms and the company was about to go broke. Casanova had never told them where he'd gotten his money, and they had never asked. He merely bought them all out, kept them all in their jobs, and showed up ten minutes late for board meetings, glowering at them all.

The titans of industry, Larrimore thought as his gaze swept along the conference table. *Old men who should have been sent off to a farm years ago, a silver-haired fag, a Jap saint, a cripple and his pet, and,* turning his gaze inward, *an impotent old arthritic.*

"Very well, we're all here," Larrimore said, with a nod in Casanova's direction. "What do you have to tell us, Mr. Brightcloud?"

Brightcloud launched into his description of the therapeutic machine. Larrimore knew the story; Ransom had outlined it for him a week earlier, after Brightcloud's first demonstration of the device.

"Do you mean," Hawthorn interrupted, "that this . . . this *machine* can make people feel good?"

Brightcloud nodded, his face serious. "It can alleviate nervous and muscular symptoms. It can even trigger beneficial changes in some internal organs."

"Now that's pretty hard to believe, fella," old Blude said. "I've been in this business for a lotta years and . . ."

Casanova overrode him. "If this machine really works, how useful would it be to us? We're in business to market new products, not set up toys in our infirmary."

"It would be a low-volume, high-dollar product. You would market it the same way IBM does mainframe computers."

Ransom, who usually kept quiet at board meetings, said, "I'd hardly call that low volume."

"I mean you would probably want to lease the devices, instead of selling them outright."

Larrimore grumbled, "What about the FDA? If this machine has biological effects . . ."

"We would be bound in honor to submit the device for their evaluation," Takahashi said.

"Not legally," Brightcloud said. "There has never been a clear legal ruling about devices, the way there is about foods and drugs. Even artificial hearts are passed on by an *ad hoc* committee of the National Institutes of Health, not the FDA."

"That's something," Casanova murmured.

"You're gonna make people feel better by shining some ray on them?" Blude demanded. "I just don't believe it."

Brightcloud allowed himself a tight smile. "The device does work, sir."

"What about side effects?" Casanova asked.

"Practically none," Brightcloud said. "We've searched very carefully for side effects, believe me. There are a couple of very minor ones that are not physiologically damaging at all."

"What are they?" Larrimore asked, seeing out of the corner of his eye that he had beaten Casanova to the question.

"Very minor things. Less than you would get from standing in the sun for ten minutes."

"Do you mean that you could get a tan from this thing?" Hawthorn asked.

"If you want to," Brightcloud said. "It will stimulate the melanin cells in the skin if you adjust the output frequency properly, but tanning is only a minor effect. It would be an extremely expensive sunlamp."

"It's a shame," Horace Mann wheezed, "that it can't change black skins into white. Now that would be an invention!" He cackled to himself.

Ms. Conroy took a deep breath and asked, "Is the device selective in any way? Will it work better on one type of person than another?"

Brightcloud stood impassively for a moment, then answered, "We have tested it on five hundred subjects in the laboratory, and several hundred more in the field. There are no significant differences among the subjects that we have been able to find."

"Were these subjects volunteers?" Takahashi asked.

"Almost all of them."

"And you found no harmful after effects?"

"None whatsoever. Everyone we interviewed afterward reported feeling much better than they had previously. Including Mr. Ransom."

Larrimore stirred in his chair. "Ransom? You didn't tell me that you had exposed yourself to this machine's radiation!"

The most junior executive looked apologetic, "I tried to, but you were too busy to listen."

Casanova glared at both of them. "All right," he said, to Brightcloud, "I want proof that the damned thing really works."

"Right!" Blude slapped the table with the palm of his hand.

"I can show you all my data," Brightcloud offered.

"No," Casanova snapped. "You have to demonstrate the thing. I don't think it can possibly work the way you claim it does."

"It does work," Brightcloud said tightly.

"Then let it work on me. Take away the pain I've got. Do that, and you've got a sale."

With a single nod of his head, Brightcloud went back to the racks of electronics lining the rear wall of the conference room and touched one button. He turned back toward the table.

"I expected that you'd want a demonstration, so I preset the beam focus for the head of the table, Mr. Casanova. There's no need for any of you gentlemen to move. Or you either, Ms. Conroy."

Larrimore watched the stacks of gadgetry. Nothing was happening. No noise, no electrical hum, no blinking lights. Nothing. He turned to look at Casanova, who was also staring at the machine with a quizzical smirk on his face.

"There may be some residual radiation leaking off to the sidelobes of the main beam," Brightcloud told them. "But there's no need for you to worry. The only possible effects you'll feel will be rather pleasant."

Larrimore swiveled his head back and forth between the inventor and Casanova in his wheelchair. Suddenly he realized that he was moving his neck without the usual arthritic twinges.

"The side effects, which are very minor," Brightcloud was saying, "come from a low-level stimulation of the glandular systems."

A warmth was spreading over his body. Larrimore felt a pleasurable glow. Startled, he looked sharply at Casanova. The man was smiling!

"There is one noticeable effect that hits men more than women," Brightcloud was still explaining. "It might have some embarrassing results in certain social situations, but on the whole our male test subjects have found it very favorable."

Larrimore couldn't believe it! But it was there all right. For the first time in decades.

He looked toward the others along the table. Ransom seemed red-faced and was trying hard not to stare at Ms. Conroy. Takahashi, the self-professed saintly ascetic, was actively leering at her. Casanova was smiling up at her with tears in his eyes. Mann seemed about to faint, Blude was slack-jawed and sweating. Hawthorn was fingering Takahashi's saffron robe.

"All right!" Larrimore croaked. It took all his strength to say it. "We're convinced. We're convinced. But don't turn it off!"

Ms. Conroy began to edge back toward the door.

James Brightcloud flew from New York to Santa Fe that afternoon. His equipment stayed in the LS&T building, after being moved from the conference room to Casanova's private suite. Larrimore wrote a seven-figure check on the spot, which Brightcloud deposited at the Citibank branch in LaGuardia.

He changed planes in Chicago and Albuquerque, and rented a car in Santa Fe. He spent more than a day driving to Phoenix, and when he boarded a Western Airlines jet there, he had washed off the dark makeup he'd used in New York and donned a sandy-blond curly wig.

In Los Angeles, the name he used for his next plane ticket was Julio Hernandez, and both his hair and his luxurious moustache were jet black. When he registered at the Sheraton Waikiki, the name he gave was John Johnston, and the moustache had disappeared.

For two days he surfed and drank and sailboated, getting tan again naturally.

On the third day, as he lay belly-down on the sand at the public beach a few blocks away from the hotel, Ms. Conroy spread her beach towel next to his and stretched out beside him. She was no longer wearing her red wig, nor her tinted contact lenses. Her short-cropped thick blonde hair and light eyes marked her as a native of a far-off cold and northern land.

She lay on her stomach and put on a pair of sunglasses. He leaned over and undid the strap of her bikini top.

"Thank you," she said in accentless English.

"Thank *you*," he replied. "The machine worked like a charm."

"Of course. They paid the full amount?"

"Yep. It's deposited."

"Good."

"How's Casanova?" he asked.

She laughed, a deep-throated sound that had menace as well as mirth in it. "He is reliving all his childhood fantasies. I told him I was exhausted and had to get away for a few days. He easily agreed and began phoning every available woman in New York. He should be hospitalized by now."

"Or dead."

She shrugged.

"I still don't see why we sold the machine to them. I mean, wouldn't it have made more sense to get one into the White House . . . or the Congress?"

"No," she said, with a shake of her head that sent a golden curl tumbling over her eyes. She brushed it aside impatiently.

"In Russia, the Kremlin, yes. In China, even though the leaders in Peking are ascetic, we are having successes among the provincial leaders. China will break up eventually. Time is on our side."

"And in America?"

"The business leaders, of course. And as subtly as possible. Not by . . . how do you call it, 'the hard sell'?"

"Yeah."

"Well, not that way. Subtly. Quietly. Let the word leak out from one office to another. The business leaders control the American government. As the businessmen use the machine to find their lost potency, the politicians will learn of it and demand that they get machines just like it."

"I hope you're right," he said.

"Of course I am right. They will destroy themselves. It is inevitable. The result of capitalist decadence."

"Capitalist decadence? What about the Kremlin? The machines have been in use there longer than anyplace, haven't they?"

"*Yes.* Of course. I'm sorry. I shouldn't have lapsed into obsolete Cold War ideology. It's my childhood training. Forgive me, please."

"Okay. But let's keep this straight. It's *us* against *them.*"

"Yes. We are agreed. The young against the old."

"No kids off to war anymore."

She nodded and brushed at the curl again. "It seems so simple and obvious. Do you think it really will work?"

"It's already working," he said. "We're on our way now, baby. All around the world. We'll get those impotent old bastards so dependent on these machines that they'll be too busy to do anything else."

"While those of us who don't need the machines take over the world."

"Why not?" He broke into a broad grin. "After all, those who can, do."

THE MASK OF
THE RAD DEATH

This one was written purely as an exercise.

Edgar Allan Poe is one of the best American writers and poets. He made seminal contributions to the genres of horror and the detective story, as well as to science fiction. His poetry often has a darkly brooding character that is at once menacing and pathetic.

One of his most chilling short stories is "The Masque of the Red Death." If you have not read it, you should. If you have read it, you remember it. I have no doubt of that; it is a powerful tale of the futility of trying to avoid death.

It struck me that Poe's story could be converted into a modern scene of nuclear holocaust by changing only a few words. The "red death," for example, becomes the "rad death," with rad standing both for radioactivity and the unit that physicists and physicians use to measure how much radioactivity a living organism receives.

So I deliberately rewrote Poe's story into a modern nuclear war setting, to see how many words had to be changed. Only a couple of dozen.

The exercise gave me a new appreciation for the ways in which Poe achieved his morbid effects. I do not recommend this kind of exercise to every person who is interested in learning to write, although there is much to be learned from it.

I do recommend that the beginning writer spend as much time reading as writing, or even more. And read widely. Do not limit yourself to reading science fiction alone. There is a tremendous world of literature, the memories of the English-speaking peoples and more. Tap into that treasury of knowledge and experience. To ignore it is akin to submitting to a lobotomy.

If you want to write, read. If you want to write well, read as widely as you can. Writers are generalists, of necessity. Specialization is for insects.

THE "RAD DEATH" had long devastated the country. No pestilence had ever been so fatal, or so hideous. Blood was its Avatar and its seal —the redness and the horror of blood. There were sharp pains, and sudden dizziness, and the slow bleedings of the gums and the pores, with dissolution. The scarlet stains upon the body and especially upon the face of the victim were the pest ban which shut him out from the sympathy of his fellow-men. And the whole seizure, progress, and termination of the disease were the incidents of an agonizing length of weeks, or often, months.

But Senator Prosper was determined and dauntless and sagacious. When Washington was half-depopulated by the bombs and their fallout, he summoned to his presence a thousand hale and equally determined friends from among the military officers and bureaucrats of the city, and with these retired to the deep seclusion of one of his well-prepared underground shelters. This was the senator's own eccentric yet practical taste. A strong and hidden gateway was its entrance, embedded in the burnt-out wilds of a national park. The gateway had a hatch of incorruptible metal.

The officers and bureaucrats, having entered, brought acetylene torches and brilliant lasers and welded the bolts. They resolved to leave no means of ingress or egress to the sudden impulses of despair from without or of frenzy from within. The shelter was amply provisioned. With such precautions the inmates might bid defiance to contagion. The external world could take care of itself. In the meantime, it was folly to grieve, or to think.

The senator had provided all the appliances of pleasure. There were buffoons (some of them former media commentators), there were improvisators (many from the Congress), there were live rock dancers, there were musicians (on tape), there were video games, there was Beauty, there was wine. There was plentiful electrical power, ironically provided by a nuclear generator buried even deeper than the underground palace itself. All these and the security were within. Without was the "Rad Death."

It was toward the close of the fifth or sixth month of his seclusion, and while the fallout seethed most furiously abroad, that Senator Prosper entertained his thousands of friends at a masked ball of the most unusual magnificence.

It was a voluptuous scene, that masquerade. But first let me tell of the rooms in which it was held. There were seven—an imperial suite carved out of bedrock far below the hellish surface of the world. In many places, such suites form a long and straight vista, while the folding doors slide back nearly to the walls on either hand, so that the view of the whole extent is scarcely impeded. Here the case was very different, as might have been expected from the senator's love of the *bizarre*. The apartments were so irregularly disposed that the vision embraced but little more than one at a time. There was a sharp turn at every twenty or thirty yards (for reasons of redundancy in radiation protection), and at each turn a novel effect.

To the right and left, in the middle of each wall, a tall and narrow Gothic window looked out upon a closed corridor which pursued the windings of the suite. These windows were of leaded glass whose color varied in accordance with the prevailing hue of the decorations of the chamber into which it opened. That at the eastern extremity was hung, for example, in blue—and vividly blue were its windows. The second chamber was purple in its ornaments and tapestries, and here the panes were purple. The third was green throughout, and so were the casements. The fourth was furnished and litten with orange—the fifth with white—the sixth with violet. The seventh apartment was closely shrouded in black velvet tapestries that hung all over the ceiling and down the walls, falling in heavy folds upon a carpet of the same material and hue. But in this chamber only, the color of the windows failed to correspond with the decorations. The panes here were scarlet—a deep blood color.

Now in no one of the seven apartments was there any lamp or candelabrum amid the profusion of golden ornaments that lay scattered to and fro or depended from the roof. There was no light of any kind emanating from lamp or candle within the suite of chambers. But in the corridors that followed the suite, there stood, opposite to each window, a heavy tripod, bearing an electric lamp cunningly fashioned to resemble a brazier of fire that projected its rays through the tinted glass and so glaringly illuminated the room. And thus were produced a multitude of gaudy and fantastic appearances. But in the western or black chamber the effect of the firelight that streamed upon the dark hangings through the blood-tinted panes was ghastly in the extreme, and produced so wild a look upon the countenances of those who entered, that there were few of the company bold enough to set foot within its precincts at all.

It was in this apartment, also, that there stood against the western wall a gigantic clock of ebony. Its digital readout flickered with a dull, monotonous blink, and when the minutes had accumulated to a new hour, there came forth from the electronic amplifiers within the clock a sound which was clear and loud and deep and exceedingly musical, but of so peculiar a note and emphasis that, at each lapse of an hour, the music tapes were programmed to pause, momentarily, so that all could hearken to the sound; and thus the dancers perforce ceased their evolutions; and there was a brief disconcert of the whole gay company; and while the chimes of the clock yet rang, it was observed that the giddiest grew pale, and the more aged and sedate passed their hands over their brows as if in confused reverie or meditation. But when the echoes had fully ceased, a light laughter at once pervaded the assembly; the dancers looked at each other and smiled as if at their own nervousness and folly, and made whispering vows, each to the other, that the next chiming of the clock should produce in them no similar emotion; and then, after the lapse of sixty minutes (which embrace three thousand and six hundred seconds of the Time that flies), there came yet another chiming of the clock, and then there were the same disconcert and tremulousness and meditation as before.

In spite of these things, it was a gay and magnificent revel. The tastes of the senator were peculiar. He had a fine eye for colors and effects. He disregarded the *decora* of mere fashion. His plans were bold and fiery, and his conceptions glowed with barbaric luster. There were some who would have thought him mad. His followers felt that he was not. It was necessary to hear and see and touch him to be *sure* that he was not.

He had directed, in great part, the movable embellishments of the seven chambers, upon the occasion of this great *fete,* and it was his own guiding taste which had given character to the costumes of the masqueraders. Be sure they were grotesque. There were much glare and glitter and piquancy and phantasm—much of what has been seen in *discos.* There were arabesque figures with unsuited limbs and appointments. There were delirious fancies such as the madman fashions. There was much of the beautiful, much of the wanton, much of the *bizarre,* something of the terrible, and not a little of that which might have excited disgust. To and fro in the seven chambers there stalked, in fact, a multitude of dreams—writhed in and about, taking hue from the rooms and causing the wild music of the laserdisk to seem as the echo of their steps.

And, anon, there strikes the ebony clock which stands in the hail of the velvet. And then, momentarily, all is still, and all is silent save the voice of the clock. The dreams are stiff-frozen as they stand. But the echoes of the chime die away—they have endured but an instant—and a light, half-subdued laughter floats after them as they depart. And now again the music swells, and the dreams live, and writhe to and fro more merrily than ever, taking hue from the many tinted windows through which stream the rays from the tripods. But to the chamber which lies most westwardly of the seven, there are now none of the maskers who venture; for the night is waning away; and there flows a ruddier light through the blood-colored panes; and the blackness of the sable drapery appalls; and to him whose foot falls upon the sable carpet, there comes from the near clock of ebony a muffled peal more solemnly emphatic than any which reaches their ears who indulge in the more remote gaieties of the other apartments.

But these other apartments were densely crowded, and in them beat feverishly the heart of life. And the revel went whiningly on, until at length there was sounded the twelfth hour upon the clock. And then the music ceased, as I have told; and the evolutions of the dancers were quieted; and there was an uneasy cessation of all things as before. But now there were twelve strokes to be sounded by the bell of the clock; and thus it happened, perhaps, that more of the thought crept, with more of time, into the meditations of the thoughtful among those who reveled. And thus, again, it happened, perhaps, that before the last echoes of the last chime had utterly sunk into silence, there were many individuals in the crowd who had found leisure to become aware of the presence of a masked figure that had arrested the attention of no single individual before. And the rumor of this new presence having spread itself whisperingly around, there arose at length from the whole company a buzz, or murmur, expressive at first of disapprobation and surprise—then, finally, of terror, of horror, and of disgust.

In an assembly of phantasms such as I have painted, it may well be supposed that no ordinary appearance could have excited such sensation. In truth the masquerade license of the night was nearly unlimited; but the figure in question had out-Heroded Herod, and gone beyond the bounds of even the senator's indefinite decorum. There are chords in the hearts of the most reckless which cannot be touched without emotion. Even with the utterly lost, to whom life and death are equally jests, there are matters of which no jest can be properly made. The whole company, indeed, seemed now deeply to feel that in the costume and bearing of the stranger neither wit nor propriety existed.

The figure was tall and gaunt, and shrouded from head to foot in the silver habiliments of a radiation suit. The helmet and face of the mask which concealed the visage was made up so nearly to resemble an actual suit of the type used in hellish high-rad environments that the closest scrutiny must have had difficulty in detecting the cheat.

And yet all this might have been endured, if not approved, by the mad revelers around. But the mummer had gone so far as to begrime his suit and tear it to tatters, as if he had been upon the surface where the fires of death still burned. His vesture *glowed* with an unnatural light—and it was sprinkled with the scarlet horror of blood.

When the eyes of Senator Prosper fell upon this spectral image (which with a slow and solemn movement, as if more fully to sustain its role, stalked uncertainly, almost staggering, to and fro among the dancers) he was seen to be convulsed, in the first moment with a strong shudder of either terror or distaste; but, in the next, his brow reddened with rage.

"Who dares?" he demanded hoarsely of the group that stood around him—"who dares thus make a mockery of our woes? Unease the varlet—that we may know whom we have to expel to the surface. Will no one stir at my bidding? Stop and strip him, I say, of those reddened vestures of sacrilege!"

It was in the eastern or blue chamber in which stood Senator Prosper as he uttered these words. They rang throughout the seven rooms loudly and clearly—for the senator was a bold and robust man, and the music had become hushed at the waving of his hand.

It was in the blue room where stood the senator, with a group of pale courtiers by his side. At first as he spoke, there was a slight rushing of movement in the direction of the intruder, who at the moment was also near at hand, and now, with deliberate, slow steps, made closer approach to the speaker. But from a certain nameless awe with which the mad assumptions of the mummer had inspired the whole party, there were found none who put forth hand to seize him, so that, unimpeded, he passed within a yard of the senator's person; and, while the vast assembly, as if with one impulse, shrank from the centers of the rooms to the walls, he made his way uninterruptedly, but with the same halting and nearly staggering step which had distinguished him from the first, through the blue chamber to the purple—through the purple to the green—through the green to the orange—through this again to the white—and even thence to the violet where a decided movement had been made to arrest him.

It was then, however, that Senator Prosper, maddening with rage and the shame of his own momentary cowardice, rushed hurriedly through the six chambers, while none followed him on account of the deadly horror that had seized upon all. He bore aloft a drawn pistol, and had approached, in rapid impetuosity, to within three or four feet of the retreating figure, when the latter, having attained the extremity of the velvet apartment, turned slowly around and confronted his pursuer. There was a sharp cry—and the pistol dropped gleaming upon the sable carpet, upon which, instantly afterwards, fell prostrate in death Senator Prosper. Then, summoning the wild courage of despair, a throng of the revelers at once threw themselves into the black apartment, and, seizing the mummer, whose tall black figure stood erect and motionless within the shadow of the ebony clock, gasped in unutterable horror at finding the ripped cerements and bloodied face mask, which they handled with so violent a rudeness, untenanted by a living form.

And now was acknowledged the presence of the Rad Death. He had come like a thief in the night. And one by one dropped the revelers in the blood-bedewed halls of their revel, and died each in the despairing posture of his fall. And the life of the ebony clock went out with the last of them. And the flames of the tripods expired. And Darkness and Decay of the Rad Death held illimitable domination over all.

(With gratitude, and apologies, to Edgar Allan Poe.)

THY KINGDOM COME

In 1991 Charles Sheffield, Frederik Pohl, Jerry Pournelle, and I were commissioned by The World & I magazine to write nonfiction scenarios depicting what the world might look like in the year 2042. The scenarios were to be based on reports written by world-recognized leaders in various technological fields such as transportation, energy, space exploration, oceanography, etc.

Each of us was asked to slant his scenario either positively or negatively. I was given the "slightly pessimistic" point of view. "Thy Kingdom Come" is a work of fiction based on my scenario for The World & I assignment. While the original scenario was based on a global view, and inputs from top technologists, I decided that the story would work best if it showed the same world of 2042 from the bottom of the heap: a worm's-eye view, if you will. For that, I returned to my roots.

I grew up in the narrow streets and row houses of South Philadelphia. Born at the nadir of the Great Depression of the 1930s, I saw as early as junior high school that there were some guys who preferred stealing to honest work, preferred intimidation to cooperation.

"Thy Kingdom Come" is about some of the wiseguys I grew up with. Most of them are dead now; many of them died young. More than that, though, the story is about the longing that even the snottiest of these wiseguys have for a normal, decent life. And it's about how some of them struggle to break free of the vicious circle of ignorance and violence, to climb out of the cesspool and into the sunlight. A few succeed. Very few.

"Thy Kingdom Come" *is about two of those kids: one who succeeds (maybe) and one who comes close, but misses. In a way, it's a true story. At least, it's as true as I could make it.*

AUDIO TRANSCRIPT of testimony of Salvatore (Vic) Passalacqua.
I knew it wouldn't be easy, but I figured I hadda at least try. Y'know? The [deleted] Controllers had grabbed her in one of their swoops and I hadda get her back before they scrambled her [deleted] brains with their [deleted] sizzlers.

Her name? Oh yeah, I forgot you're tapin' all this. How do I look? Not bad for a guy goin' on twenty, huh? Yeah, yeah. Her name's Jade Diamond, keenest-looking piece of—No, that ain't her real name. 'Course not. Her real name was Juanita Dominguez. I knew her before she changed it. And her eyes. Like I said, she was real beautiful. Naturally. Without the implants and the eye job. They changed her eyes 'cause most of the big spenders are Japs.

Anyway, she was supposed t'be protected just like all the hookers. Except that the [deleted] [deleted] Controllers don't take nobody's payoffs—that's what they say, at least.

So there was Jade in the holdin' jug down at city hall and here was me makin' a living out of old TV sets and smartphones, CD players, anything to do with electrical stuff. Where? In the junkyards, where else? You don't think I stole anything, do you? Why would I have to risk my butt goin' into the tracts and breakin' into people's houses when they throw away their stuff every year and it all winds up in the junkyards?

Yeah, I know the stuff is all supposed to be recycled. That's what I do. I recycle it before the [deleted] recyclers get their [deleted] claws on it.

Look, you wanna know about the Chairman and Jade and me or you wanna talk about business?

Okay. I was in love with Jade, that's why I did what I did. Sure, I knew she was a pro. You'd be too if you'd grown up in the city. We don't exist, y'know. Not legally. No records for any of us, not even the [deleted] police bother to keep records on us anymore. Not unless we done somethin' out in the tracts. As far as your [deleted] mother-[deleted] computer files are concerned, we weren't even born. So of course we don't die. If we don't bury our own, the [deleted] sanitation robots just dump our bodies into a pit and bulldoze 'em over. After they've taken out all the organs they wanna use for transplants, that is. And we sure don't get nuthin from your sweetheart of a government while we're alive. Nuthin but grief. Lemme tell ya—Okay. Okay. Jade and the Chairman.

None of it would've happened if the Controllers hadn't picked up Jade. I guess they picked her up and the other girls 'cause the Chairman was comin' to Philly to make a speech and they wanted the streets to look clean and decent. First time I saw a sanitation robot actually cleanin' the [deleted] street. First time in my life! I swear.

Anyway, there Jade was in the tank and here I was at the junkyard and all I could think of was gettin' Jade out. I knew I needed help, so first thing in the morning I went to Big Lou.

His name's kind of a joke. You know? Like, he's even shorter than me, and I been called a runt all my life. His face is all screwed up, too, like it was burned with acid or somethin' when he was a kid. Tough face. Tough man. I was really scared of Big Lou, but I wanted to get Jade outta the tank so bad I went to him anyway.

The sun was just comin' up when I got to the old school building where Big Lou had his office. He wasn't there that early. So I stooged around out in the street until he arrived in his car. It was polished so hard it looked brand new. Yeah, a regular automobile, with a driver. What's it run on? How the hell would I know? Gasoline, I guess. Maybe one of those fancy other fuels, I don't know.

At first Lou told me to get lost, like I figured he would. I was just small-time, a junkyard dog without the teeth, far as he was concerned. See, I never wanted to be any bigger. I just wanted to live and let live. I got no hatred for nobody.

But while I'm beggin' Big Lou for some help to spring Jade he gets a phone call. Yeah, he had a regular office in the old school building in our neighborhood. I know, they shut down all the schools years ago, before I was even born. They're supposed to abandoned, boarded up. Hell, most of 'em were burned down long ago. But not this one. It's still got a pretty good roof and office space and bathrooms, if you know how to turn the water on. And electricity. Okay, sure, all the windows were smashed out in the old classrooms and the rest of the building's a mess. But Lou's office was okay. Clean and even warm in the winter. And nobody touched his windows, believe me.

Y'know, down in South Philly, from what I hear—Oh yeah, you people don't know Philly that well, do you? Where you from, New York? Washington? Overseas? What?

Okay, okay. So you ask the questions and I do the answerin'. Okay. Just curious. Where was I?

Big Lou, right. He had an office in the old school building. Yeah, he had electricity. Didn't I tell ya that already? There was a couple TVs in the office and a computer on his desk. And he had a fancy telephone, too. I had put it together myself, I recognized it soon as I saw it. Damned phone had its own computer chips: memory, hunt-and-track, fax—the works. I had sold it to Lou for half a peanut; cost me more to put it together than he paid for it. But when you sell to Big Lou you sell at his price. Besides, who the [deleted] else did I know who could use a phone like that?

Anyway, I'm sittin' there in front of his desk. Big desk. You could hold a dance on it. I had figured that Big Lou could talk to a couple people, put a little money in the right hands, and Jade could get out of the tank before the [deleted] Controllers fried her brains and sent her off to Canada or someplace.

Lou gets this phone call. I sit and wait while he talks. No, I don't know who called him. And he didn't really do much talkin'. He just sort of grunted every now and then or said, "Yeah, I see. I gotcha." His voice is kinda like a diesel truck in low gear, like whatever burned his face burned the inside of his throat, too.

Then he puts down the phone and smiles at me. Smiles. From a face like his it was like a flock of roaches crawlin' over you.

"I got good news for you, Vic," he says. "I'm gonna help you get your spiff outta the tank." All with that smile. Scared the [deleted] outta me.

"The hearings for all the bimbos they rounded up are three o'clock this afternoon. You be there. We're gonna make a commotion for you. You grab your [deleted] and get out fast. Understand me?"

I didn't like the sound of that word *commotion*. I wasn't sure what it meant, not then, but I figured it would mean trouble. All I wanted was for Big Lou to buy Jade's way out. Now it sounded like there was goin' to be a fight.

Don't get me wrong. I've had my share of fights. I'm on the small side and I'm sure no jock, but you can't even exist in the city if you can't protect yourself. But I didn't like the idea of a fight with the city police. They like to beat up on guys. And they carry guns. And who knew what in hell the Controllers carried?

"You unnerstand me?" Big Lou repeated. He didn't raise his voice much, just enough to make me know he wanted the right answer outta me.

"Yeah," I said. My voice damned near cracked. "Sure. And thanks." I got up and scooted for the door.

Before I got to it, though, Big Lou said, "There's a favor you can do for me, kid."

"Sure, Lou," I said. "Tonight, tomorrow, when? You name it."

"Now," he said.

"But Jade—"

"You'll be done in plenty time to get to city hall by three."

I didn't argue. It wouldn't have done me no good. Or Jade.

What he wanted was a fancy electronic gizmo that I had to put together for him. I knew it was important to him because he told one of his goons—a guy with shoulders comin' straight out of his ears, no neck at all, so help me—to drive me all the way downtown to the old navy base. It had been abandoned before I was born, of course, but it was still a treasure island of good stuff. Or so I had been told all my life. I had never even got as far as the electrified fence the Feds had put up all around the base, let alone inside the base itself. You had to go through South Philly to get to the base, and a guy alone don't get through South Philly. Not in once piece, anyway.

But now here I was bein' taken down to that fence and right through it, in a real working automobile, no less! The car was dead gray with government numbers stenciled on the driver's door. But the driver was Big Lou's goon. And Little Lou sat on the backseat with me.

Little Lou was a real pain in the ass. Some people said he really was Big Lou's son. But he sure didn't look like Big Lou. Little Lou was only a couple years older than me and he was twice Big Lou's size, big and hard with muscles all over. Good-lookin' guy, too. Handsome, like a video star. Even if he hadn't been a big shot he could've had any girl he wanted just by smilin' at her.

He was smart. And strong. But he was ugly inside. He had a nasty streak a mile and a half wide. He knew I wanted to be called Vic. I hate the name my mother gave me: Salvatore. Little Lou always called me Sal. Or sometimes Sally. He knew there wasn't a damned thing I could do about it.

I tried to keep our talk strictly on the business at hand. And one eye on my wristwatch. It was an electronic beauty that I had rebuilt myself; kept perfect time, long as I could scrounge a battery for it every year or so. I kept it in an old scratched-up case with a crummy rusted band so nobody like Little Lou would see how great it was and take it off me.

It was noon when we passed through a gate in the navy-base fence. The gate was wide open. No guard. Nobody anywhere in sight.

"So what's this gizmo I'm supposed to put together for you?" I asked Little Lou.

He gave me a lazy smile. "You'll see. We got a man here with all the pieces, but he don't know how to put 'em together right."

"What's the thing supposed to do?"

His smile went bigger. "Set off a bomb."

"A bomb?"

He laughed at how my voice squeaked. "That's right. A bomb. And it's gotta go off at just the right instant. Or else."

"I—" I had to swallow. Hard. "I never worked with bombs."

"You don't have to. All you gotta do is put together the gizmo that sets the bomb off."

Well, they took me to a big building on the base. No, I don't remember seein' any number or name on the building. It looked like a great big tin shed to me. Half fallin' down. Walls slanting. Holes in the roof, I could see once we got inside. Pigeon crap all over the place. Everything stunk of rust and rot. But there were rows and rows of shelves in there, stacked right up to the roof. Most of 'em were bare, but some still had electronic parts in their cartons, brand new, still wrapped in plastic, never been used before. My eyes damn near popped.

And there was a guy there sittin' in a wheelchair next to a long bench covered with switches and batteries and circuit boards and all kinds of stuff. Older guy. Hair like a wire brush, a couple days' beard on his face, grayer than his hair. One of his eyes was swollen purple and his lip was puffed up, too, like somebody'd been sluggin' him. Nice guys, beatin' on a wheelchair case.

I got the picture right away. They had wanted this guy to make their gizmo for them and he couldn't do it. Little Lou or one of the others had smacked the poor slob around. They always figured that if you hit a guy hard enough he would do what you wanted. But this poor bastard didn't know how to make the gizmo they wanted. He had been a sailor, from the looks of him: face like leather and tattoos on his arms. But something had crippled his legs and now he was workin' for Big Lou and Little Lou and takin' a beating because they wanted him to do somethin' he just didn't know how to do.

He told me what they wanted. Through his swollen, split lips he sounded strange, like he had been born someplace far away where they talk different from us. The gizmo was a kind of a radar, but not like they use in kitchen radar ranges. This one sent out a microwave beam that sensed the approach of a ship or a plane. What Little Lou wanted was to set off his bomb when whatever it is he wanted to blow up was a certain distance away.

Electronics is easy. I heard that they used to send guys to school for years at a time to learn how to build electronic stuff. I could never understand why. All the stuff is pretty much the same. A resistor is a resistor. A power cell is a power cell. You find out what the gizmo is supposed to do and you put together the pieces that'll do it. Simple.

I had Little Lou's gizmo put together by one o'clock. Two hours to go before I hadda be in city hall to take Jade away from the Controllers.

"Nice work, Sal," Little Lou said to me. He knew it got under my skin.

"Call me Vic," I said.

"Sure," he said. "Sally."

That was Little Lou. If I pushed it he would've smacked me in the mouth. And laughed.

"I got to get up to city hall now," I said.

"Yeah, I know. Hot for that little [deleted], ain'tcha?"

I didn't answer. Little Lou was the kind who'd take your girl away from you just for the hell of it. Whether she wanted to or not. And there'd be nuthin' I could do about it. So I just kept my mouth zipped.

He walked me out to the car. It was hot outside; July hot. Muggy, too. "You start walkin' now, you'll probably just make it to city hall on time."

"Walk?" I squawked. "Ain't you gonna drive me?" I was sweatin' already in that hot sun.

"Why should I?" He laughed as he put the gizmo in the car's trunk. "I got what I want."

He shut the trunk lid real careful, gently, like maybe the bomb was in there, too. Then he got into the car's back seat, leaving me standin' out in the afternoon sun feelin' hot and sweaty and stupid. But there wasn't a damned thing I could do about it.

Finally Lou laughed and popped the back door open. "Come on in, Sally. You look like you're gonna bust into tears any minute."

I felt pretty [deleted] grateful to him. Walkin' the few miles uptown to city hall wouldn't have been no easy trick. The gangs in South Philly shoot first and ask questions afterward when a stranger tries to go through their turf.

About halfway there, though, Little Lou lets me know why he's bein' so generous.

"Tonight," he says, "nine o'clock sharp. You be at the old Thirtieth-street station."

"Me? Why? What for?"

"Two reasons. First we gotta test the gizmo you made. Then we gotta hook it up to the bomb. If it works right."

He wasn't smilin' anymore. I was scared of workin' with a bomb, lemme tell you. But not as scared as I was at the thought of what Little Lou'd do to me if the gizmo didn't work right.

So I got to city hall in plenty time okay. It's a big ugly pile of gray stone, half fallin' apart. A windowsill had crumbled out a couple months ago, just dropped out of its wall and fell to the street. Solid hunk of stone, musta weighed a couple tons. It was still there, stickin' through the pavement like an unexploded bomb. I wondered what would happen if the statue of Billy Penn, up at the top of the Hall's tower, ever came loose. Be like a [deleted] atomic bomb hittin' the street.

Usually city hall is a good place to avoid. Nobody there but the suits who run what's left of the city and the oinks who guard 'em.

Oinks? Pigs. Helmet-heads. Bruisers. Cops. Police. There are worse names for them, too, y'know.

Well, anyway, this particular afternoon city hall is a busy place. Sanitation robots chuggin' and scrubbin' all over the place. A squad of guys in soldier uniforms and polished helmets goin' through some kind of drill routine in the center courtyard. Even a crew of guys with a truck and a crane tryin' to tug that windowsill outta the pavement. Might as well be tryin' to lift the [deleted] Rock of Gibraltar, I thought.

They were goin' through all this because the Chairman of the World Council was comin' to give a speech over at Independence Hall. Fourth of July and all that crap. Everybody knew that as soon as the Chairman's speech was over and he was on his way back to New York or wherever he stayed, Philly would go back to bein' half-empty, half-dead. The sanitation robots would go back to the housing tracts out in the suburbs and Philiy would be left to itself, dirty and hot and nasty as hell.

I felt a little edgy actually goin' *inside* city hall. But I told myself, What the hell, they got nuthin' on me. I'm not wanted for any crime or anything. I don't even exist, as far as their computers are concerned. Still, when I saw these guys in suits and ties and all I felt pretty crummy. Like I should have found a shower someplace or at least a comb. I didn't like to ask nobody for directions, but once I was inside the Hall I didn't have a [deleted] idea of where I should go. I picked out a woman, dressed real neat in kind of a suit but with a skirt instead of pants. Even wore a tie. No tits to speak of, but her hair was a nice shade of yellow, like those girls you see in TV commercials.

She kind of wrinkled her nose at me, but she pointed up a flight of stone stairs. I went up and got lost again right away. Then I saw an oink—a woman, though—and asked her. She eyed me up and down like she was thinkin' how much fun it'd be to bash me on the head with her Billy. But instead she told me how to find the courtroom. She talked real slow, like I was brain-damaged or something. Or maybe she was, come to think of it.

I went down the hall and saw the big double-doored entrance to the courtroom. A pair of oinks stood on either side of it, fully armed and helmeted. A lot of people were streamin' through, all of them well dressed, a lot of them carrying cameras or laptop computers. Lots of really great stuff, if only I could get my hands on it.

Then I saw a men's room across the corridor and I ducked inside. A couple homeless guys had made a camp in the stalls for themselves. The sinks had been freshly cleaned up, though, and the place didn't smell too bad. I washed my face and hands and tried to comb my hair a little with my fingers. Still looked pretty messy, but what the hell.

Taking a deep breath, I marched across the corridor and through the double doors, right past the oinks. I didn't look at them, just kept my eyes straight ahead.

And then I saw Jade.

They had her in a kind of a pen made of polished wood railings up to about waist-level and thick shatterproof glass from there to the ceiling. She was in there with maybe three dozen other pros, most of 'em lookin' pretty tired and sleazy, I gotta admit. But not Jade. She looked kind of scared, wide-eyed, you know. But as beautiful and fresh as a flower in the middle of a garbage heap. I wanted to wave to her, yell to her so she'd notice me. But I didn't dare.

You gotta understand, I was in love with Jade. But she couldn't be in love with me. Not in her business. Her pimp would beat the hell out of any of his whores who took up with anybody except himself. I had known her since we were kids together runnin' along the alleys and raiding garbage cans, keepin' one jump ahead of the dog packs. Back when her name was still Juanita. Before she had her eyes changed. I had kissed her exactly once, when we was both twelve years old. The next day she turned her first trick and went pro.

But I had a plan. For the past five years I had been savin' up whatever cash I could raise. Usually, you know, I'd get paid for my work in food or drugs or other stuff to barter off. But once in a while somebody'd actually give me money. What? Naw, I never did much drugs; screwed up my head too much. I usually traded whatever [deleted] I came across. I seen what that stuff does to people: makes 'em real psycho.

Anyway, sometimes I'd get real money. That's when I'd sneak out to the housing tracts where they had automated bank machines and deposit my cash in the bank. All strictly legitimate. The bank didn't care where the money came from. I never had to deal with a living human being. All I had to do to open the account was to pick up a social security number, which I got from a wallet I had found in one of the junkyards when I was ten, eleven years old. Even that young, I knew that card was better than gold.

So I had stashed away damn near a thousand dollars over the years. One day I would use that money to take Jade outta the city. out of her life. We'd buy a house out in the tracts and start to live like decent people. Once I had enough money.

But then the [deleted] Controllers had arrested Jade. What I heard about the Controllers scared the [deleted] outta me. They were bigger than the city oinks, bigger even than the state police or the National Guard. They could put you in what they called International Detainment Centers, all the way out in Wyoming or Canada or wherever the hell they pleased. They could scramble your brains with some super electronic stuff that would turn you into a zombie.

That's what they were goin' to do to Jade. If I let them.

I sat in the last row of benches. The trials of the pros were already goin' on. Each one took only a couple minutes. The judge sat up on his high bench at the front of the courtroom, lookin' sour and cranky in his black robe. A clerk called out one of the girls' names. The girl would be led out of the holding pen by a pair of women oinks and stood up in a little railed platform. The clerk would say that the girl had been arrested for prostitution and some other stuff I couldn't understand because he was mumblin' more than speakin' out loud.

The judge would ask the girl how she pleaded: guilty or innocent. The girl would say, "Innocent, Your Honor." The judge would turn to a table full of well-dressed suits who had a bunch of laptops in front of them. They would peck on their computers. The judge would stare into the screen of his computer, up on the desk he was sittin' at.

Then he'd say, "Guilty as charged. Sentenced to indeterminate detention. Next case." And he'd smack his gavel on the desktop.

I remember seein' some old videos where they had lawyers arguin' and a bunch of people called a jury who said whether the person was guilty or innocent. None of that here. Just name, charge, plea, and "Guilty as charged." Then—*wham!*—the gavel smack and the next case. Jade wouldn't have a chance.

And neither did I, from the looks of it. How could I get her away from those oinks, out from behind that bulletproof glass? Where was this commotion Big Lou promised, whatever it was supposed to be?

They were almost halfway through the whole gang of girls, just whippin' them past the judge, bang, bang, bang. Jade's turn was comin' close; just two girls ahead of her. Then the doors right behind me smack open and in clumps some big guy in heavy boots and some weird kind of rubbery uniform with a kind of astronaut-type helmet and a visor so dark I couldn't make out his face even though I was only a couple feet away from him.

"Clear this courtroom!" he yells, in a deep booming voice. "There's been a toxic spill from the cleanup crew upstairs. Get out before the fumes reach this level!"

Everybody jumps to their feet and pushes for the door. Not me. I start jumpin' over the benches to get up front, where Jade is. I see the judge scramble for his own little doorway up there, pullin' his robe up almost to his waist so he could move faster. The clerks and the guys with the laptops are makin' their way back toward the corridor. As I passed them I saw the two oinks openin' the glass door to the holding pen and startin' to hustle the girls out toward a door in the back wall.

I shot past like a cruise missile and grabbed Jade's wrist. Before the oinks could react I was draggin' her up the two steps to the same door the judge had used.

"Vic!" she gulped as I slammed the door shut and clicked its lock.

I said something brilliant like, "Come on."

"What're you doing? Where're we going?"

"Takin' you outta here."

Jade seemed scared, confused, but she came along with me all right. The judge was nowhere in sight, just his robe thrown on the floor. Somebody was poundin' on the door we had just come through and yellin' the way oinks do. There was another door to the room and the judge had left it half-open. I had no way of knowin' if that toxic spill was real or not, but I knew that the oinks would be after us either way so I dashed for the door, Jade's wrist still in my grip.

"You're crazy," she said, kind of breathless. But she came right along with me. And she smiled at me as she said it. If I hadn't been wound so tight I would've kissed her right there and then.

Instead we pounded down this empty corridor and found an elevator marked JUDGES ONLY. I leaned on the button. Somebody appeared at the far end of the corridor, a guy in a business suit.

"Hey, you kids," he yelled, kind of angry, "you're not allowed to use that elevator."

Just then the doors slid open. "Emergency!" I yelled back and pulled Jade inside.

When we got down to the street level everything seemed normal. Nobody was runnin' or shoutin'. I guessed that the toxic spill was a phony. I couldn't imagine Big Lou doin' something like that just for me, but maybe he needed his bomb gizmo bad enough after all. Anyway, I told Jade to act normal and we just walked out into the central courtyard nice and easy, me in my shabby jeans and sneakers and her in her workin' clothes: spike heels, microskirt, skintight blouse. They had washed off her makeup and her hair looked kind of draggled, but she was still beautiful enough to make even the women out there turn and stare at her.

The work crew was still tryin' to tug that fallen windowsill outta the cement when we walked past. I steered Jade toward the boarded-up entrance to the old subway.

"We're not going down there!" she said when I pushed a couple boards loose.

"Sure as hell are," I said.

"Hey, you!" yelled a guy in a soldier uniform.

"Come on!" I tugged at Jade's wrist and we started down the dark stairway underground.

The steps were slippery, slimy. It was dark as hell down there and it stunk of [deleted]. The air was chilly and kind of wet; gave you the shakes. I could feel Jade trembling in my grip. With my other hand I fished a penlight outta my pocket. What? I always keep a light on me. And make sure the batteries are good, too. You never know when you're gonna need a light; trouble don't always come at high noon, y'know.

"Vic, I don't like this," Jade said.

"I don't either, honey, but we gotta get away. This is the best way to do it." I clicked on my penlight; it threw a feeble circle of light on the filthy, littered tiled floor. "See, it ain't so bad, is it?"

Jade was right in a way. The subway tunnels really were dangerous. We had heard stories since we were little kids about the hordes of rats livin' down there. And other things, monsters that crawled outta the sewers, people who lived down there in the dark for so long they'd gone blind—but they could find you in the dark and when they did they ate you raw, like animals.

I was kind of shakin' myself, thinkin' about all that. But I wasn't gonna let Jade be taken away by the Controllers and I wasn't gonna play with no bombs for Little Lou or Big Lou or anybody. I was takin' Jade and myself outta the city altogether, across the bridge and out into the housing tracts on the other side of the river. I'd take my money from the bank and find a place for us to live and get a regular job someplace and start to be a real person. The two of us. Jade and me.

Okay, maybe it was just a dream. But I wanted to make my dream come true. Wanted it so bad I was willin' to face anything.

Well, there ain't no sense tellin' you about every step of the way we took in the subway tunnels. There were rats, plenty of 'em, some big as dogs, but they stayed away from us as long as the penlight worked. We could see their red eyes burnin' in the dark, though, and hear them makin' their screechy little rat noises, like they was talkin' to each other. Jade had a tough time walkin' on those spike-heel shoes of hers, but she wouldn't go barefoot in the sloppy goo we hadda walk through. My own sneaks were soaked through with the muck; it made my feet burn.

Jade screamed a couple times, once when she stumbled on something squishy that turned out to be a real dog that must've died only a few hours earlier. It was half-eaten away already.

No monsters from the sewers, though. And if there was any blind cannibals runnin' around down there we didn't see them. The rats were enough, believe me. I felt like they were all around us, watchin', waitin' until the batteries in my light gave out. And then they'd swarm us under and do to us what they had started to do to that clog.

All the subway tunnels meet under the city hall, and I sure as hell hoped I had picked the right one, the one that goes out to the river. After hours and hours, I noticed that the tunnel seemed to be slantin' upward. I even thought I saw some light up ahead.

Sure enough, the tracks ran up and onto the Ben Franklin bridge that crossed the Delaware. It was already night, and drizzling a cold misty rain out there. No wind, not even a breath of air movin'. And no noise. Silence. Everything was still as death. It was kinda creepy, y'know. I been on that bridge lotsa times; up that high there was always a breeze, at least. But not that night.

At least we were out of the tunnel. On the other side of that bridge was the housing tracts, the land where people could lead decent lives, safe from the city.

I knew the bridge was barricaded and the barricades were rigged with electronic chips that spotted anybody tryin' to get through. Those people in the tracts didn't like havin' people from the city comin' over to visit. Not unless they drove cars that gave out the right electronic ID signals. But I had gotten past the barricades before. It took a bit of climbin', but it could be done. Jade could take off her spike heels now and climb with me.

But in front of the barricade was a car. A dead gray four-door with government numbers stenciled on the driver's door. Only the guys standin' beside the car weren't government. They were Little Lou and his goon driver.

Lou was leanin' against the hood, lookin' relaxed in a sharp suit and open-collar shirt. His hair was slicked back and when he saw Jade he smiled with all his teeth.

"Where you goin', Sal?" he asked, real quiet, calm.

I had to think damned fast. "I thought we was in the tunnel for the Station! I must've got mixed up."

"You sure did."

Lou nodded to the goon, who opened the rear door of the car. I started for it, head hung low. He had outsmarted me.

"Not you, stupid," Lou snarled at me. "You sit up front with Rollo." He made a little half-bow at Jade, smilin' again. "You sit in back with me, spiff."

Jade got into the car and scrunched herself into the corner of the backseat, as far away from Little Lou as she could. I sat up front, half-twisted around in the seat so I could watch Lou. Rollo was so big his elbow kept nudgin' me every time he turned the steering wheel.

"You was supposed to be at the Thirtieth-street station at nine o'clock," Little Lou said to me. But his eyes were on Jade, who was starin' off at nothing.

I looked at my wristwatch. "Hell, Lou, it's only seven-thirty."

"Yeah, but you were headin' in the wrong direction. A guy could lose some of his fingers that way. Or get his legs broke."

"I just got mixed up down in the tunnels," I said, tryin' to make it sound real.

"You're a mixed-up kid, Sally. Maybe a few whacks on your thick skull will straighten you out."

There wasn't much I could say. If Little Lou was waitin' for me at the bridge he had me all figured out. I just hoped he really needed me enough to keep me in one piece so I could set up his bomb gizmo for him. What would happen after that, I didn't know and I didn't want to think about.

We drove through the dead, empty city for a dozen blocks or so. I had turned around in my seat and was lookin' ahead out the windshield. Everything was dark. Not a light in any window, not a street lamp lit. I knew people lived in those buildings. They were supposed to be abandoned, condemned. But nobody bothered to tear them down; that would cost the taxpayers too much. And the people who didn't exist, the people whose names had been erased from the government's computers, they lived there and died there and had babies there. I was one of those babies. So was Jade.

"Are those tits real?" I heard Lou ask.

Through the side-view mirror I saw Jade turn her face to him. Without a smile, with her face perfectly blank, she took his hand and placed it on her boob.

"What do you think?" she asked Lou.

He grinned at her. She smiled back at him. I wanted to kill him. I knew what Jade was doin': tryin' to keep Lou happy so he wouldn't be sore at me. She was protectin' me while I sat there helpless and the dirty [deleted] [deleted] bastard climbed all over her.

"Thirtieth-street station comin' up," said Rollo. His voice was high and thin, almost like a girl's. But I bet that anybody who laughed at his voice got his own windpipe whacked inside out.

Lou sat up straight on the backseat and ran a hand through his hair. Jade edged away from him, her face blank once again.

"Okay, Sally, you little [deleted]. Here's where you earn your keep. Or I break your balls for good."

Lou, Rollo, and me got out of the car. Lou ducked his head through the open rear door and told Jade, "You come too, cute stuff. We'll finish what we started when this is over."

Jade glanced at me as she came out of the car. Lou grabbed her by the wrist, like he owned her.

If Lou had been by himself I would have jumped him. He was bigger than me, yeah, and probably a lot tougher. But I was desperate. And I had the blade I always carried taped just above my right ankle. It was little, but I kept it razor sharp. Lou was gonna take Jade away from me. Oh, I guess he'd let her come back to me when he was finished with her, maybe. But who knew when? Or even if. I had only used that blade when I needed to protect myself. Would I have the guts to cut Lou if I could get him in a one-on-one?

But Lou wasn't alone. Rollo was as big as that damned city hall windowsill. There was no way I could handle him unless I had a machine gun or a rocket launcher or something like that. I was desperate, all right. But not crazy.

The Station was all lit up. Cleaning crews and robots were crawlin' all over the old building, but I didn't see any oinks or soldiers. Later I found out that they would be pourin' into the area in the morning. The Chairman was due to arrive at eleven a.m.

Lou took me and Jade to a panel truck marked PUBLIC WORKS DEPARTMENT. Two other guys was already sittin' up front. And there was my gizmo, sittin' on the bare metal floor. All by itself. No bomb in sight. That made me feel better, a little.

They hustled us into the truck and made me sit on the floor, big Rollo between me and the back door and Lou across from me. He made Jade sit beside him. She kept her legs pressed tight together. We drove off.

"Where we goin'?" I asked.

Lou said, "There's a maintenance train comin' down the track in half an hour. You set up your gizmo where we tell you to and we see if it can spot the train at the right distance away and send the signal that it's supposed to send."

"What're you guys gonna do, blow up the Chairman?"

I got a backhand smack in the face for that. So I shut my mouth and did what they told me, all the while tryin' to figure out how in hell I could get Jade and me outta this. I didn't come up with any answers, none at all.

When the truck stopped, Rollo got out first, then Lou shoved me through the back door. The other two guys stayed in their seats up front. Lou pushed the gizmo across the truck's floor toward me. It was heavy enough so I needed both hands.

"Don't drop it, [deleted]head," Lou growled.

"Why don't we let Rollo carry it?" I said.

Lou just laughed. Then he helped Jade out the back door. I thought he helped her too damned much, had his hands all over her.

We was parked maybe ten blocks away from the station. Its lights glowed in the misty drizzle that was still comin' down, the only lights in the whole [deleted] city, far as I could see. Some of the people livin' in the buildings all around there had electricity, I knew. Hell, I had wired a lot of 'em up. But they kept their windows covered; didn't wanna let nobody know they was in there. Scared of gangs roamin' through the streets at night.

All those suits and oinks and everybody who had been at city hall was all safe in their homes in the tracts by now. Nobody in the city except the people who didn't exist, like Jade and me. And the rats who had business in the dark, like Little Lou.

I saw why Lou didn't want Rollo to carry the gizmo. The big guy walked straight up to a steel grate set into the pavement, it must have weighed a couple hundred pounds, at least, but he lifted it right up, rusty hinges squealin' like mad. I saw the rungs of a metal ladder goin' down. Lou shone a flashlight on them. They had been cleaned *off*.

Rollo took the gizmo off me and tucked it under one arm. I followed him down the ladder. Down at the bottom there were three other guys waitin'. Guys like I had never seen before. Foreigners. Dark skin, eyes like coals. One of them had a big, dark, droopy moustache, but his long hair was streaked with gray. They were all kind of short, my height, but very solid. Their suits looked funny, like they had been made by tailors who didn't know the right way to cut a suit.

The two clean-shaven ones were carryin' automatic rifles, mean-looking things with curved magazines. Their jackets bulged; extra ammunition clips, I figured. They looked younger than the guy with the moustache; tough, hard, all business.

"This is the device?" asked the one with the moustache. He said "thees" instead of "this."

Lou nodded. "We're gonna test it, make sure it works right."

"*Bueno.*"

We were in a kind of—whattaya call it, an alcove?—yeah, an alcove cut into the side of the train tunnel. The kind where work crews could stay when a train comes past. This wasn't one of the old city subways; it was the tunnel that the trains from other cities used, back when there had been trains runnin'. The Chairman was comin' in on a train the next morning, and these guys wanted to blow it up. Or so I thought.

Rollo carried the gizmo down to the side of the tracks. For an instant I almost panicked; I realized that we needed a power pack. Then I saw that there was one already sittin' there on the filthy bricks of the tunnel floor. I hooked it up, takin' my time; no sense lettin' them know how easy this all was.

"Snap it up," Lou hissed at me. "The train's comin'."

"Okay, okay," I said.

The guy with the moustache knelt beside me and took a little metal box from his pocket. "This is the detonator," he said. His voice sounded sad, almost like he was about to cry. "Your device must make its relay click at the proper moment. Do you know how to connect the two of them together?"

I nodded and took the detonator from him.

"Tomorrow, the detonator will be placed some distance from your triggering device."

"How'll they be connected then?" I asked.

"By a wire."

"That's okay, then." I figured that if they had tried somethin' fancy like a radio link, in this old tunnel they might get all kinds of interference or echoes. A hard-wire connection was a helluva lot surer. And safer.

It only took me a couple minutes to connect his detonator to my radar gizmo, but Lou was fidgetin' every second of the time. I never seen him lookin' nervous or flustered before. He was always the coolest of the cool, never a hair out of place. Now he was half jumpin' up and down, lookin' up the tunnel and grumblin' that the train was comin' and I was gonna miss it. I had to work real hard to keep a straight face. Little Lou uptight; that was somethin' to grin about.

Okay, so I had everything ready in plenty time. The maintenance train musta been doin' two miles an hour, max, scrapin' down the tracks and scoopin' up most of the garbage in the tunnel as it dragged along. I turned on my gizmo. The readout numbers on the little red window started tickin' down slowly. When they reached the number already set on the other window beside it, the relay on the detonator clicked.

"*Bueno*," said the moustache, still kneeling beside me. He didn't sound happy or nuthin'. Just, "*Bueno*." Flat as a pancake.

I looked over at Jade, standin' with Rollo and the other strangers off by the tunnel wall, and I smiled at her.

"Does that means it works okay?" I asked. I knew the answer but I wanted him to say it so Little Lou could hear it. Lou was bendin' down between the two of us.

"Yes," he said, in that sad heavy voice of his. "It works perfectly."

He said each word carefully, like he wasn't sure he had his English right.

I got to my feet and said to Lou, "Okay. I done my part. Now Jade and me can go, right?"

"No one leaves this tunnel," said the moustache. Still sad, but real strong, like he meant it. He had unbuttoned his suit jacket and I could see the butt of a heavy black revolver stickin' out of a shoulder holster. [Deleted], it would've taken both my hands just to hold that pistol up, let alone fire it off.

"Hey, now wait a minute—" I started to say.

Lou grabbed me by the shoulder and spun me around, his fist raised to smack me a good one. The moustache grabbed his upraised arm and held it in midair. Just held it there. He must've been pretty strong to do that.

"There is no need for that," he said to Lou, low and firm. "There will be enough violence in the morning."

Lou pulled his arm away, his face red and nasty. The moustache turned to me and almost smiled. Kind of apologetic, he said, "It is necessary for you and your lady to remain here until the operation is concluded. For security reasons. Do you understand?"

I nodded. Sure I understood. What I was startin' to wonder about, though, was whether these guys would let us live after their "operation" was finished. I knew Lou was goin' to want to take Jade with him. If these foreigners didn't whack me tomorrow, probably Lou would. Then he'd have Jade all to himself for as long as he wanted her.

So we sat on the crummy tunnel floor alongside the tracks and waited. The foreigners had some sandwiches and coffee with them. Moustache offered a sandwich to Jade, real polite, and one to me. It was greasy and spiced hot enough to scorch my mouth. They all laughed at me when I grabbed for the coffee and burned my mouth even more 'cause it was so hot.

I tried to sleep but couldn't. I saw that the two younger guys had curled up right there on the floor, sleepin' like babies with their rifles in their arms. Lou took Jade off down the tunnel a ways, where it was dark, far enough so I couldn't see them or even hear them. I sat and watched Rollo, hopin' he'd nod off long enough for me to follow Lou down the tunnel and slice his throat open. But Rollo just sat a few feet away from me, his chin on his knees and his eyes on me. Big as a [deleted] elephant.

Moustache wasn't sleepin', either. I went over to where he was sittin' with his back against the wall.

"Why's the Chairman comin' in on a train?" I asked him, hunkering down beside him. "There ain't been a train through here since before I was born."

Moustache gave me his sad smile. "It is a gesture. He is a man given to gestures."

I couldn't figure out what the hell he meant by that.

"Why do you want to whack him?" I asked.

"Whack?" He looked puzzled.

"Kill him."

His eyes went wide, a little. "Kill him? We do not intend to assassinate the Chairman." He shook his head. "No, it is not so simple as that."

"Then what?"

He shook his head again. "It is none of your affair. The less you know about it the better off you will be."

"Yeah," I said. "Until this thing is over and Lou whacks me."

He shrugged. "That is your problem. Not mine."

A lot of help he was.

My wristwatch said seven twenty-seven a.m. when Lou came walkin' back up the track toward us. His hair was mussed and he had his suit jacket thrown over one shoulder. He grinned at me. Jade came followin' behind him, her face absolutely blank, starin' straight ahead. I figured she was tryin' *not* to see me.

What the hell, I thought. Why don't I kill the mother [deleted] [deleted] right now. Stick my blade in his nuts and twist it hard before Rollo gets a chance to move. They was gonna whack me afterward anyway. I knew it.

I was even startin' to pull up my pants leg when I felt Moustache's hand on my shoulder. "No," he whispered.

I must have looked pretty sore to him. He said, low and soft, "I am a man of honor. I will see to it that you and the girl go free after our operation is concluded. You can trust me."

Lou had already passed me by then. Rollo got up on his feet, towerin' over us all like a mountain. I let my pants leg slide down to my ankle again. I just hoped Lou and Rollo didn't notice what I had started to do.

A little while later three more guys came down the same ladder we had used, two of them carryin' big leather suitcases, the third carryin' a little metal case and climbin' down so careful that I figured he had the bomb in it. They were foreigners too, but they looked different from Moustache and his men. They had dark skins, all right, but a different kind of dark. And they were taller, slimmer, with big hooked noses like eagle's beaks. Like Moustache and his men, they were wearin' regular suits. But they looked like they were uncomfortable in them, like these weren't the kind of clothes they usually wore.

Anyway, after talkin' a few minutes with Moustache they went up the tracks with the little metal case. They came back again without it, but trailin' a spool of wire. Which they connected to my radar gizmo. I noticed that the detonator was gone; they had taken it with the bomb, I figured. Then they set the gizmo right in the middle of the tracks and waited.

"Won't the oinks see it there?" I asked Moustache. "The police," I added before he could ask what *oinks* meant.

In that sad way of his he said, "Your Mr. Lou has been well paid to see to it that the security guards do not come down the tunnel this far." He kind of sighed. "It always surprises me to see how well bribery works on little men."

Bought off the security guards? I wondered if even Big Lou could cover all the Federal oinks that must be coverin' the Chairman. I mean, this guy was the Chairman of the World Council. They must be protectin' him like they protect the president or some of those video stars.

Moustache must've understood the puzzled look on my face. "There is a full security guard on the train itself, and entire platoons of soldiers at the station. The responsibility for checking the security of the tunnel was given to your city police force. That is why we decided to do our work here. This is the weak link in their preparations."

He talked like a general. Or at least, the way I thought a general would talk. No, I never did get his name. Nobody spoke to him by his name; nobody I could understand, at least. I did find out later on that he had another half-dozen men farther down the tunnel, also waitin' for the train. Twelve guys altogether. Fourteen, if you count Little Lou and Rollo.

Okay, so the time finally comes. Little Lou is almost hoppin' outta his skin he's so wired up. Jade was sittin' as far back in the alcove as she could, legs tucked up under her, still starin' off into space and seeing nuthin'. I started to wonder what Lou had done to her, then tried to stop thinkin' about it. Didn't work.

Moustache is as calm as a guy can be, talkin' in his own language to his two men. The other three strangers are bendin' over their suitcases, and I see they're takin' out all kinds of stuff. I'm not sure what most of it was, but they had little round gray things about the size of baseballs, weird-lookin' kinds of guns—I guess they were guns, they looked kind of like pistols—and finally they pulled out some rubbery gas masks and handed two of 'em to Moustache's men.

Lou and Rollo both are lookin' down the track toward the station, and I see they both have pistols in their hands. Rollo's hands are so big his pistol looks like a toy. Little Lou is sweatin', I can see the beads comin' down his face, he's so [deleted] scared. I keep myself from laughin' at him out loud. He's worried that the oinks he bought off won't stay bought. Be just like them to take his money and then double-cross him by doin' their job right anyway.

But then I figured that maybe Big Lou was the one who paid off the oinks. Screwin' Little Lou is one thing; if they mess around with Big Lou they'd regret it for as long as they lived. And so would their families.

Moustache sends off all five of the strangers up the track. I wonder how close to the bomb they can get without bein' blown up themselves. I wonder if the bomb will bring down the roof of the whole [deleted] tunnel and bury all of us right where we are. I wonder about Moustache sayin' they ain't tryin' to whack the Chairman. What're they gonna do, then?

I didn't have to wait long to find out.

Moustache is starin' hard at his wristwatch, that big pistol in his other hand. I hear a dull *whump* kind of noise. He looks up, runs out to the middle of the tracks. I go to Jade, who's gotten to her feet. Lou and Rollo are still starin' down the track toward the station, Moustache is lookin' the other way, toward where the train is comin' from. Nobody's watchin' us.

"Come on," I whisper to Jade. "Now's our chance." But she won't move from where she's standing.

"Come on!" I say.

"I can't," she tells me.

"It's now or never!"

"Vic, I can't," she says. I see tears in her eyes. "I promised him."

"[Deleted] Lou!" I say. "I love you and you're comin' with me."

But she pulls back. "I love you too, Vic. But if I go with you Lou will hunt us down and kill you."

"He's gonna kill me anyway!" I'm tryin' to keep whispering. It's makin' my throat raw.

"No, he told me he'd let you alone if I stayed with him. He swore it."

"And you believe that mother-[deleted] lying [deleted]?"

Just then we hear gunfire and guys yelling. Sounds like a little war goin' on up the track: automatic rifles goin' *pop-pop-pop*. Heavier sounds. Somebody screamin' like his guts've been shot out.

Moustache yells to Lou and Rollo, "Quickly! Follow me!" Then he waves at me and Jade with that big pistol. "You too! Come!"

So with Moustache in front of us and Lou and Rollo behind, we go runnin' up the track. There's a train stopped up there, a train like I never seen before. Like it's from Mars or someplace: all shinin' and smooth with curves more like an airplane than any train I ever saw. Not that I ever saw any, except in pictures or videos, y'know.

I see a hole in the ground that's still smokin'. The track is tore up. That was where the bomb was. It was just a little bomb, after all. Just enough to tear up the track and make the train stop.

We run past that and past the shining engine. Even in the shadows of the tunnel it seemed to shine, like it was brand new. Not a scratch or a mark on it. No graffiti, even. Where I come from, we don't see much that's new. It was beautiful, all right.

Anyway, there are three cars behind the engine. They all look spiffy too, but a couple windows on the first car were busted out, shattered. The car in the middle had a blue flag painted on its side, a flag I never seen before.

Moustache climbs up onto the first car and we're right behind him. We push through the doors. There's a bunch of dead bodies inside. Flopped on the floor, twisted across the seats. Not regular seats, like rows. These seats were more like big easy chairs that could swivel around, one next to each window. You could see there'd been plenty of bullets flyin' around; the bodies was tore up pretty bad, lots of blood. I heard Jade suck in her breath like she was gonna scream, but then she got control of herself. I almost wanted to scream myself; some of those bodies looked pretty damned bad.

One of the tall guys came through the door up at the other end of the car. He had his gas mask pushed up on top of his head. His rifle was slung over his shoulder, makin' his suit jacket bunch up so I could see a pistol stuck in the belt of his pants. He looked kind of sick, or maybe that was the way he looked when he was mad.

Moustache went up and talked with him for a minute, lookin' kind of pale himself. Lou told Rollo to pick up all the loose hardware lyin' around the car. What? Hardware. Guns. Must've been six or eight of 'em on the floor or still in the grip of the dead guys. Oh yeah, two of the dead ones were women, by the way. Far as I remember, neither one of 'em had a gun in her hand.

We got through the connecting doors and into the middle car. Not everybody in there is dead. Only a couple guys in blue suits that Moustache's men are already draggin' down into the third car, at the end of the train.

There was one guy alive in there, a little guy no bigger than me with eyes like Jade's. Otherwise he looked like a regular American. I mean his skin wasn't dark even though it wasn't exactly light like mine. And the suit he was wearin' was a regular suit, light gray. Right away I figured he was the Chairman of the World Council: C. C. Lee.

He was sittin' there, his face frozen with no expression on it, almost like Jade's when Little Lou had been pawin' her. I looked at him real close and saw his eyes weren't exactly like Jade's; they were real oriental eyes, I guess. Hard to tell how old he was; his hair was all dark, not a speck of gray in it, but he didn't look young, y'know what I mean? Straight hair, combed straight back from his forehead. Kinda high forehead, come to think of it. Maybe he was startin' to go bald.

Anyway, Moustache sat down in the chair next to his and swiveled it around so they were facin' each other. Jade and I stood in the aisle between the rows of chairs. The others moved out to the other two cars.

"This is not what I wanted," Moustache said. He talked in English, with that accent of his.

"It is what you should have expected," said the Chairman. His English was perfect, just like a newscaster on TV.

"I regret the killing."

"Of course you do."

"But it was necessary."

The Chairman looked at Moustache, *really* looked at him, right into his eyes like he was tryin' to bore through his skull.

"Necessary? To kill sixteen men and women? How many of your own have been killed?"

"Four," said Moustache. "Including my brother."

The Chairman blinked. "I am sorry for that," he said, almost in a whisper.

"He knew the risks. Our cause is desperate."

"Your cause is doomed. What can you possibly hope to achieve by this action?"

"Freedom for the political prisoners in my country. An end to the dictatorship."

"By kidnapping me?"

"We will hold you hostage until the political prisoners are freed," said Moustache. "The people will see that we have the power to bend the dictator to our will. They will rebel. There will be revolution—"

The Chairman shook his head like a tired, tired man. "Blood and more blood. And in the end, who is the winner? Even if you become the new head of your nation, do you really think that you will be better than the dictator who now resides in the presidential palace?"

"Yes! Of course! How can you ask such a question of me? I have dedicated my life to overthrowing the tyrant!"

"Yes, I know. I understand. Just as Fidel did. Just as Yeltsin did. Yet, if the people are not prepared to govern themselves, they end up with another tyrant, no matter how pure his motives were at the start."

Moustache gave him a look that would have peeled paint off a wall. "You dare say that to me?"

The Chairman made a little shrug. "It is the truth. You should not be angered by the truth."

Moustache jumped to his feet, yelling, "The truth is that you are our hostage and you will remain our hostage until our demands have been met!" Then he stomped up the aisle toward the front car.

I told Jade to stay there and hustled after Moustache. I caught up with him in between the two cars, out on the platform connecting them.

"Hey, wait a minute, willya?"

He whirled around, his eyes still burnin' with fury.

"Uh, excuse me," I said, tryin' to calm him down a little, "but you said it'd be okay for us to leave once the job was over, remember?"

The anger went out of his face. He made a strange expression, like he didn't know whether to laugh or cry. "The job is far from over, I fear."

"But I did what you wanted—"

He put a hand on my shoulder. "We had intended to take the Chairman off the train and drive him to a helicopter pad we had prepared for this operation. Unfortunately, the truck we had stationed at the emergency exit from the tunnel has already been seized by your soldiers. We are trapped here in this tunnel, in this train. The Chairman is our prisoner, but we are prisoners, too."

"[Deleted] H. [deleted] on a crutch!" I yelled.

"Yes," he said. "Indeed."

"Whattaya gonna do?"

"Negotiate."

"What?"

"As long as we hold the Chairman we are safe. They dare not attack us for fear of harming him."

"But we can't get out?"

"Not unless they allow us to get out."

I got this empty feeling in my gut, like I was fallin' off a roof or something. I guess I was really scared.

Moustache went through the door to the car up front. I went back into the middle car. Jade was sittin' where Moustache had been. She was talkin' with the Chairman.

"I had wanted to bring a message of hope to the people of America, particularly to the disenfranchised and the poverty classes of the dying cities," he was tellin' her. "That is why I agreed to make this speech in Philadelphia on the anniversary of the Declaration of Independence."

"Hope?" I snapped, ploppin' myself down in the chair across the aisle from the two of them. "What hope?"

He didn't answer me for a second or two. He just looked at me, like he was studyin' me. His eyes were a kind of soft brown, gentle.

"Do you know how many people there are like you in the world?" he asked. Before I could think of anything to say he went on. "Of the more than ten billion human beings on Earth, three-quarters of them live in poverty."

"So what's that to me?" I said, tryin' to make it sound tough.

"You are one of them. So is this pretty young woman here."

"So?"

He kind of slumped back in his seat. "The World Council was formed to help solve the problems of poverty. It is my task as Chairman to lead the way."

I laughed out loud at him. "You ain't leadin' any way. You're stuck here, just like we are."

"For the moment."

Jade said, "We could all be killed, couldn't we?"

I knew she was right, but I said, "Not as long as we got this guy. They won't try nuthin' as long as the Chairman's our hostage."

The Chairman's eyebrows went up a fraction. "You are part of this plot? From what your friend here has told me, you were forced to help these terrorists."

"Yeah. Well, that don't matter much now, does it?" I said, still tryin' to sound tough. "We're all stuck in this together."

"Exactly correct!" says the Chairman, like I had given the right answer on a quiz show. "We are all in this together. Not merely this—" and he swung his arms around to take in the train car—"but we are all in the global situation together."

"What do you mean?" Jade asked. She was lookin' at him in a way I'd never seen her look before. I guess it was respect. Like Big Lou wants people to behave toward him. Only Jade was doin' it on her own, without being forced or threatened.

"We are all part of the global situation," the Chairman repeated. He was lookin' at her but I got the feeling he was talkin' to me. "What happens to you has an effect all around the world."

"Bull[deleted]," I said.

He actually smiled at me. "I know it is hard for you to accept. But it is true. We are all linked together on the great wheel of life. What happens to you, what happens to a rice farmer in Bangladesh, what happens to a stockbroker in Geneva—each affects the other, each affects every person on Earth."

"Bull [deleted]," I said again.

"You do not believe it?"

"Hell no."

"Yet what you have done over the past twenty-four hours has brought you together with the Chairman of the World Council, hasn't it?"

"Yeah. And maybe we'll all get killed together."

That didn't stop him for even a half a second. "Or maybe we will all change the world together."

"Change it?" Jade asked. "How?"

"For the better, one hopes."

"Yeah, sure. We're gonna change the world," I said. "Jade and me. We don't even [deleted] exist, far as that world out there's concerned! They don't want no part of us!"

"But you do exist, in reality," he said, completely unflustered by my yellin' at him. "And once we are out of this mess, the world out there will have to admit your existence. They will have to notice you."

"The only notice they'll ever take of the likes of Jade and me is to dump our bodies in a [deleted] open pit and bulldoze us over."

"Hey, stop the yellin'!" Little Lou hollered from the front end of the car. He had just come in, with Rollo right behind him like a St. Bernard dog. Lou looked uptight. His jacket was gone, his shirt wrinkled and dark with sweat under the armpits. His hair was mussed, too. He was not happy with the way things were goin'. Rollo looked like he always looked: big, dumb, and mean.

Moustache pushed past the two of them. Jade got up from her chair and came to sit next to me. Moustache took the chair and leaned his elbows on his knees, putting his face a couple inches away from the Chairman's.

"The situation is delicate," he said.

The Chairman didn't make any answer at all.

"We are unfortunately cut off here in the tunnel. The security forces reacted much more quickly than we had anticipated. They are now threatening to storm the train and kill us all. Only by assuring them that you are alive and unharmed have I persuaded them not to do so."

The Chairman still didn't budge.

Moustache took in a deep breath, like a sigh. "Now the chief of your own security forces wants to make certain that you are alive and well. He demands that you speak to him."

Moustache pulled a palm-sized radio from his jacket pocket.

The Chairman made no move to take it from his hand.

"Please," said Moustache, holding the radio out to him.

"No," the Chairman said.

"But you must."

We all kind of froze. Everybody except Little Lou. He stepped between Moustache and the Chairman and whacked the Chairman in the mouth so hard it knocked him out of his chair. Then he kicked him in the ribs hard enough to lift him right off the floor. He was aimin' another kick when I went nuts.

I don't know why, maybe it was like watchin' a guy beat up on a kitten or some other helpless thing. I knew the Chairman was just gonna lay there on the floor while Lou kicked all his ribs in and none of these other clowns would do a thing to help him and I just kind of went nuts. I didn't think about it; if I had I would've just stayed tight in my chair and minded my own [deleted] business.

But I didn't. I couldn't. Before I even knew I was doin' it I jumped on Lou's back, wrapped my legs around him, and started poundin' on his head with both my fists. If I'd wanted to really hurt him I woulda taken out my blade and slit his [deleted] throat. I didn't even think of that. All I wanted was for the big [deleted] to leave the Chairman alone.

So I'm bangin' on Lou's head, he's yellin' and swingin' around, tryin' to get me off him. And then something explodes in the back of my head and everything goes black.

When I wake up, I'm seein' double. Two Chairmen, two Jades. But nobody else.

"That was a very brave thing you did," says the Chairman.

I'm layin' flat on my back. Jade is bendin' over me, two of her kind of fading' in and out, blurry-like. The Chairman is sittin' on the floor beside me, both his arms wrapped around his chest. Otherwise the car is empty. Everybody else is gone.

"What happened?" I said.

"Rollo knocked you out," Jade answered.

I shoulda guessed that. Musta hit me like a truck. I tried to sit up but I was so woozy the whole [deleted] car started whirlin' around.

"Lay still," Jade said. Her voice was soft and sweet. I thought I saw tears in her eyes, but I was still seein' double so it was hard to tell.

"You okay?" I asked the Chairman.

"Yes, thanks to you." His lip was split and his face was kinda pale, like it was hurtin' him to breathe.

"Where'd they go?"

"They are in the rear car," the Chairman said. "More of them in the front. We are all trapped here. The Council's security forces have sealed off this tunnel. American army troops have taken over the station and are patrolling the streets above us."

"But they won't make a move on us because Moustache says he'll whack you if they do."

The Chairman nodded. And winced. "We are their hostages. He is trying to convince them that he has not already killed me."

"Why didn't ya talk to your people on the radio?" I asked him. "Lou woulda beat you to death."

He almost smiled, split lip and all. "They can't afford to kill me. Your friend Lou is a barbarian. Even Moustache, as you call him, would have stopped him if you hadn't."

"So I got slugged for nuthin'."

"You were very brave," said the Chairman. "I appreciate what you did very much. To risk one's life for the sake of another—that is true heroism."

"You're a hero," Jade said. And she really did smile. Like the sun shinin' through clouds. Like the sky turnin' clean blue after a storm.

I reached for her hand and she took mine and squeezed it. Her hand felt warm and good. I mean, don't get me wrong, I busted my cherry when I was twelve years old. Had my first case of clap not much later. I ain't no Romeo like Little Lou, but I got my share. But Jade, she was special. I didn't wanna just screw her, I wanted to live with her, make a home with her, even have kids with her. Yeah, I know she was fixed so she couldn't have kids. They do that to the pros. But I thought maybe we could find a doctor someplace who could make her okay again.

But first I hadda get her outta her life before she came down with somethin' that'd kill her or got herself knocked off by some weirdo. Okay, it was crazy. Stupid. I know. But that's how I felt about her. And I don't give a [deleted] what you say, I know she felt that way about me, too, I know. In spite of everything.

Anyway, there I was, layin' on the floor of the train car and holdin' on to Jade's hand like I was hangin' off the edge of a ninety-nine-story building. I asked the Chairman, "So what happens now?"

He started to shrug, but the pain in his ribs stopped him. "I don't really know."

"I still don't see why you wouldn't talk to your people on the radio."

"We do not make deals with terrorists. I know that every government official of the past seventy-five years has said that and then gone on to negotiate when their own citizens have been taken hostage. You must remember that the World Council is very new. Our authority is more moral than military or even financial—"

"I don't unnerstand a word you're saying," I told him.

He looked kinda surprised. Then he said, "Let me put it this way: We do not deal with terrorists. That is the official policy of the World Council. How would it look if I, the Chairman himself, broke our own rules and tried to negotiate my way out of this?"

"Beats gettin' killed," I said.

"Does it?"

"Hell yeah! You want Lou to go back to work on you?"

He closed his eyes for a second. "I am prepared to die. I don't want to, but if it comes to that—it comes to that."

"And what about us? What about Jade and me?"

"There's no reason for them to kill you."

"Who the [deleted] needs a reason? Lou wants to whack me, he's gonna whack me!"

"That . . . is unfortunate."

It sure the [deleted] was. For a couple minutes none of us said anything. Finally curiosity got to me.

"What's this all about, anyway? Why's Moustache want to take you hostage? What's in it for him? Who're those other guys with him? What the hell's goin' on around here?"

So he told me. I didn't understand most of it. Somethin' about some country I never heard of before, in South America I think he said. Moustache is the leader of some underground gang that's tryin' to knock off their government. The Chairman told me that their president is a real piece of [deleted]. No freedom for nobody. Everybody's gotta do what he says or he whacks 'em. Tortures people. Takes everybody's money for himself. Sounds like Big Lou's favorite wet dream.

So Moustache and his people want the World Council to get rid of this bastard. The World Council can't do that, accordin' to what the Chairman told me. "We are not permitted to interfere in the internal affairs of any nation." That's the way he put it. And besides, this dictator was legally elected. Okay, maybe the people had to vote for him or get shot, but they did vote for him.

And guess who Moustache wants to make president if and when the dictator gets pushed out? Good old Moustache himself. Who else?

So the Chairman tells Moustache he can't do nuthin' for him. So Moustache decides to kidnap the Chairman and hold him until the World Council does what he wants. Or somethin' like that. Other guys from other countries who also want pretty much the same kind of thing from the World Council join Moustache's operation. Arabs or Kurds or somethin', I forget which. So they kidnap the Chairman. Big [deleted] deal.

So there we are, stuck in the train in the tunnel. They got him, but the U.S. Army and god knows what the [deleted] else has got us trapped in the tunnel. Standoff.

By the time he had finished tellin' me this whole story—and it was a lot longer than what I just told you—I was feelin' strong enough to sit up. At least the room wasn't spinnin' around no more and I wasn't seein' double.

"So what happens now?" I asked the Chairman.

"We wait and see."

I saw a junkyard dog once, a real four-legged dog, get his paw caught in a trap the junk dealer had set for guys like me who like to sneak in at night and steal stuff. Poor damned dog was stuck there all night long, yowlin' and cryin'. Dealer wouldn't come out. Not in the dark. He was scared that if his dog was in trouble it meant a gang of guys was out there waitin' to whack him.

I felt like that dog. Trapped. Bleedin' to death. Knowin' there was help not far away, but the help never came. Not in time. By morning the dog had died. The rats were already gnawin' on him when the sun came up.

"You're just gonna sit here?" I asked him.

"There's nothing else we can do."

I knew that. But I still didn't like it.

The Chairman put out his hand and rested it on my shoulder. "You may not realize it, my young friend, but merely by sitting here you are fighting a battle against the enemies of humankind."

I wanted to say bull[deleted] to him again, but I kept my mouth shut.

It was Jade who asked, "What do you mean?"

"This man you call Moustache. The men with him. Your friends Lou and Rollo—"

"They ain't no friends of mine," I growled.

"I know." He smiled at me, kind of a shy smile. "I was making a small joke."

"Nuthin' funny about those guys."

"Yes, of course. Moustache and Lou and the rest of them, they are the old way of living. The way of violence. The way of brute force. The way of death. What the human race needs, what the *people* want, is a better way, a way of sharing, of cooperation, of the strength that comes from recognizing that we must all help one another—"

I was about to puke in his face when he smiled at me again and said, "Just the way you tried to help me when Lou was beating me."

That took the air outta me. I mumbled, "Lotta good it did either one of us."

"Have you ever thought about leading a better life than the one you now live?" he asked.

"Well, yeah," I said, glancin' at Jade. "Sure. Who doesn't?"

"There are Indians living in the mountains of Moustache's country who also have a dream of living better. And nomads starving in man-made deserts. And fishermens' families dying because the sea has become so polluted that the fish have all died off. They also dream of a better life."

"I don't care about no fishermen or Indians," I said. "They don't mean nuthin' to me."

"But they do! Whether you know it or not, they are part of you. We are all bound together on this world of ours."

"Bull[deleted]." It just popped out. I mean, I kinda liked the guy, but he kept talkin' this crazy stuff.

"Listen to what he's trying to tell us," Jade said. That surprised me, her tellin' me what to do.

"The reason the World Council was created, the reason it exists and I serve as its Chairman, is to help everyone on Earth to live a better life. Everyone! All ten billions of us."

"How're you going to do that?" Jade asked. She was lookin' at the Chairman now with her eyes wide. She wasn't holdin' my hand anymore.

"There's no simple answer," he said. "It will take hard work, for decades, for generations. It will take the cooperation of all the nations of the world, the rich and the poor alike."

"You're dreamin'," I said. "The United States is one of the richest countries in the whole [deleted] world and we still got people livin' like rats, people like me and Jade and who knows how many others."

"Yes, I understand," he said. "We are trying to convince your government to change its attitude about you, to admit that the problem exists and then take the necessary steps to solve it."

"Yeah, they'll solve the problem. The [deleted] Controllers swoop in and take you away, scramble your brains and turn you into a zombie. You wind up as slave labor in some camp out in the woods."

"Is that what you believe?"

"That's what I know."

"What would you say if I told you that you are wrong?"

"I'd say you're fulla [deleted]."

"Vic!" Jade snapped at me.

But the Chairman just kinda smiled. "When all this is over, I hope you will give me the opportunity to show you how misinformed you are."

"If we're still alive when this is over," I said.

"Yes," he admitted. "There is that."

He was quiet for a minute or so. I didn't like the way Jade was starin' at him, like he was a saint or a video star or somethin'. But I didn't know what I could say that would get her to look back at me.

Finally the Chairman pipes up again. "You know, I was born of a poor family also."

"Yeah, sure," I muttered.

"My grandmother escaped from Vietnam in an open boat with nothing but the clothes on her back and her infant son—my father. They went from Hong Kong to Canada. My grandmother died of pneumonia her first winter in Vancouver. My father was barely two years old."

"You're breakin' my heart," I said. Jade hissed at me.

"My father was raised in an orphanage. When he was fourteen he escaped and made his way into the United States, eventually to Houston, Texas." The Chairman was lookin' at me when he was sayin' this, but it was a funny look, like I wasn't really there and he was seein' things from his own life that'd happened years ago.

"My mother was Mexican. Two illegal immigrants for parents. We moved around a lot: Houston, Galveston, the cotton fields of Texas, the orchards of California. I was picking fruit almost as soon as I learned to walk."

"You never went hungry, didja?" I said.

"I have known hunger. And poverty. And disease. But I have known hope, also. All through my childhood my mother told me that there was a better way of life. Every night she would kneel beside me and say her prayers and tell me that I would live better than she and my father. Even when my father was beaten to death by a gang of drunken rednecks my mother kept telling me to keep my eyes on the stars, to work hard and learn and aim high. She worked very hard herself.

"After my father died we settled in California, in a little city called Modesto, where she worked twelve to fourteen hours a day cleaning people's homes by day and office buildings at night. By the time she died, when I was sixteen, she had saved enough money to get me started in college."

"At least you had a mother," I muttered. "I was so young when mine died I don't even remember what she looked like."

"That is very sad," he said. Real soft.

"Yeah."

"I remember the prayer my mother taught me to say: she called it the 'Our Father.'"

"*Oración al Señor*," whispered Jade.

"Yes. Do you know it? And the line that says, 'Thy kingdom come'? That is what we must aim for. That is what we must strive to accomplish: to bring about a new world, a fair and free and flourishing world for everyone. To make this Earth of ours as close to heaven as we can."

"Thy kingdom come," Jade repeated. There were tears in her eyes now, real big ones.

Me, I didn't say nuthin'. I kept my mouth shut so hard my teeth hurt. I knew that prayer. The one thing I remember about my mother is her sayin' that prayer to me when I was so little I didn't know what it meant. That's all I can remember about her. And it made me want to cry, too. It got me sore at the same time. This [deleted] big shot of a Chairman knew just where to put the pressure on me. I sure wasn't gonna start bawlin' in front of him and Jade. Not me.

And I had lied to them. I did remember my mother. Kinda hazy, but I remember what she looked like. She was beautiful. Beautiful and sweet and—I pulled myself up short. Another minute of that kinda thinkin' and I'd be cryin' like a baby.

The Chairman kind of shook himself, like he was comin' out of a blackout or somethin'. He looked at me again. "Education is the key, my young friend," he said to me. "If we are to build a new world, we must educate the people."

"You mean, like school?" I asked him.

"Schooling is only a part of it," he said. "If we survive this, will you allow me to get you started on a decent education?"

"School? Me? You gotta be kiddin'!"

Jade said, "But Vic, he's giving you a chance—"

She never got no farther. Moustache came in, with Lou and Rollo behind him.

Moustache looked funny. Like he was real tired, all wiped out. Or maybe that was how he looked when he was scared. He stood in front of the Chairman, who stayed in his seat lookin' up at him. I kept my eye on Lou; he was watchin' Jade like he was thinkin' what he'd do with her later on. Like he already owned her.

"We are at an impasse," Moustache said to the Chairman. "Your security forces seem perfectly content to sit and wait for us to give up."

"They have standing orders for dealing with terrorists," said the Chairman. "This is not the first time someone has attempted to kidnap a Council member."

"They will not attack us?"

"There is no need to, as long as they are certain you will not harm your hostages."

Moustache said, "We have only one hostage, but a very important one."

"Then all the others who were with me are dead?"

"Unfortunately, yes."

The Chairman seemed to sag back in his seat. "That is truly unfortunate. It means that you will not be allowed to escape. If no one had been killed . . ." His voice trailed off.

"Are you telling me that the troops will risk your life in order to punish us for killing a few of your bodyguards?"

"Yes." The Chairman nodded slowly. "That too is their standard operational procedure. No negotiations with terrorists. And no leniency for murderers."

"They were armed! They killed four of my men!"

"Only six of them were armed. There were nineteen all together, most of them harmless administrators and my personal aides. Five of them were women."

Moustache sank into the empty chair across the aisle from the Chairman. "It was those Moslem madmen. When the shooting started they killed everyone, indiscriminately."

"They were under your command, were they not?"

"Yes, but not under my control."

"That makes no difference."

"You leave us no course, then, but to use you as a shield to cover our escape."

"The security forces will not allow it. Their orders are quite specific. Their objective is to capture the terrorists, irrespective of what happens to the hostages."

"They will let you he killed?"

"I am already dead, as far as they are concerned."

"You will pardon me if I fail to believe that," Moustache said.

"It doesn't matter what you believe," said the Chairman back to him. "That is our standard operational procedure. It is based on the valid assumption that there are no indispensable men. The Chairman of the World Council can be kidnapped or even assassinated. What difference? Another will take his place. Or hers. You can do what you want to me, it does not matter. Violence will not deter us. Threats will not move us. The work of the Council will go on regardless of the senseless acts of terrorists. All you can do is create martyrs—and damage your own cause by your violence."

Moustache looked up at Lou, who'd been standin' there through all this talk with a kind of wiseguy grin on his face.

With a sigh, Moustache said, "We will have to try your way, then."

I got to my feet, facin' Lou. Without even thinkin' about what I was doin'. Like my body reacted without askin' my brain first.

"Don't try to be a hero again, Sal," Lou said to me. And Rollo took a step toward me. But Lou went on, "We ain't gonna use any rough stuff—not unless we got to. We're just gonna sneak him out through the tunnel."

"But the soldiers got the tunnel blocked off," I said. "All the entrances—"

"Not all of 'em," said Lou. "There's a side passage for the electric cables and water pipes and all. It's big enough for maintenance workers to crawl through. So it's big enough for us to get through, too."

Lou yanked a map of the tunnel system outta his back pants pocket. It was all creased up and faded, but Moustache pulled a little folding table outta the wall and Lou spread his map on it. Then he pointed to where we was and where the nearest door to the maintenance tunnel was. Moustache decided that only the six of us would go. The rest of his men would stay with the train and keep the soldiers thinkin' we was all still in there.

While Lou and Moustache were talkin' all this over, Jade leaned over to me and whispered. "Vic, you gotta do something."

"Do? What?"

"You can't let them sneak him outta here! You gotta figure out a way to save him."

"Me? What the [deleted] d'you think I am, Superman?"

She just looked at me with those eyes of hers. Beneath the fancy surgery that had made her Jade Diamond her deep brown eyes were still Juanita's. I loved her and I'd do anything for her and she knew it.

"You've gotta do something," she whispered.

Yeah. What the whole [deleted] World Council and half the U.S. Army can't do she wants me to do.

So Moustache calls in a couple of his men and gives them their orders. You can see from the looks on their faces that they don't like it. But they don't argue. Not one word. They know they're gonna be left hangin' out to dry, and they take it without a whimper. They must've really believed in what they were doin'.

Me, I'm tryin' to look like I'll do whatever they tell me. Rollo is just waitin' for Lou to give him the word and he'll start poundin' me into hamburger. And I figure Lou will give him the word as soon's we got the Chairman outta this trap and someplace safe. Lou wants Jade, so he'll give me to Rollo to make sure I'm not in his way. Moustache wants the Chairman so he can get what he wants back in his own country.

And the Chairman? What's he want? That's what I was tryin' to figure out. Was he really willin' to get himself smacked around or whacked altogether, just for this dream of his? A better world. A better life for people. Did he mean he could make a better life for Jade and me?

Well, anyway, all these thoughts are spinnin' around in my head worse than when Rollo had slugged me. We get down off the train with Lou in the lead, Moustache with his big pistol in his hand, the Chairman, me and Jade all in a bunch, and Rollo bringin' up the rear. Lou's kinda feelin' his way through the tunnel, no light 'cause he don't want the soldiers to know we're outta the train.

So we're headin' for this steel door in the side of the tunnel when I accident'ly-on-purpose trip and fall to my knees. Rollo grabs me by the scruff of the neck hard enough to make my eyes pop and just lifts me back on my feet, one hand. But not before I slip my blade outta the tape on my ankle. It's dark so Rollo don't notice; I keep the blade tucked up behind my wrist, see.

All of a sudden my heart's beatin' so hard I figure Rollo can hear it. Or maybe the army, a couple hundred yards up the tunnel. Half my brain's tellin' me to drop the blade and not get myself in any more trouble than I'm in already. But the other half is tellin' me that I gotta do somethin'. I keep hearin' Jade's voice, keep seein' whatever it was that was in her eyes.

She wants a better life, too. And there's no way we can get a better life long as guys like Lou and Rollo can push us around.

So I let myself edge up a little, past Jade and the Chairman, till I'm right behind Moustache. It's real dark but I can just make out that he's got the gun in his right hand.

"Hey! Here it is," Lou says, half whisperin'. "Rollo, come and help me open up this sucker."

Rollo pushes past me like a semitrailer rig passin' a kid on a skateboard. My heart is whammin' so hard now it's hurtin' my ears. Moustache is just standin' there, watchin' Lou and Rollo tryin' to open up that steel door. They're gruntin' like a couple pro wrasslers. It's now or never.

I slash out with the blade and rip Moustache's arm open from elbow to wrist. He grunts and drops the gun and it goes off, *boom!*, so loud that it echoes all the way down the tunnel.

"Run!" I yell to Jade and the Chairman. "Get the [deleted] outta here!"

The Chairman just freezes there for a second, but Jade shakes his arm and kind of wakes him up. Then the two of them take off down the tunnel, toward the soldiers. I can't see where the [deleted] gun landed but it don't matter anyway 'cause Lou and Rollo have spun away from the door and they're both comin' right at me. Moustache is holdin' his arm with his left hand and mumblin' something I can't understand.

"You dumb little [deleted]-sucking [deleted]," Lou says. "I'm going to cut off your balls and feed 'em to you one at a time."

I hear a click and see the glint of a blade in Lou's hand. I shoulda known he wouldn't be empty-handed. Rollo is comin' up right beside Lou. He don't need a knife or anything else. I'm so scared I don't know how I didn't [deleted] myself.

But I'm standin' between them and Jade and the Chairman.

"Never mind him!" Moustache yells. "Get the Chairman! Quickly, before he makes it to the soldiers!"

Everything happened real fast. Lou tried to get past me and I swiped at him with my blade and then Rollo was all over me. I think I stuck him pretty good, but he just about ripped my arm outta my shoulder and I musta blacked out pretty quick after that. Hurt like a bastard. Then I woke up here.

So I'm a big shot hero, huh? Saved the Chairman from the terrorists. He came here himself this morning to thank me. And now that the TV reporters and their cameras are all gone, you guys are gonna send me away, right?

Naw, I didn't do anything except set up the gizmo for them. And they made me do that. Okay, so grabbin' Jade outta the tank was a crime. I figured you mother-[deleted] wasn't gonna let me go free.

But what'd they do with Jade? I don't believe that [deleted] [deleted] story the Chairman told me. Jade wouldn't do that. Go to a—what the [deleted] did he call it? Yeah, that's it. A rehabilitation center. She wouldn't leave here on her own. She wouldn't leave me. They musta forced her, right. The [deleted] Controllers must be scramblin' her brains right now, right? The [deleted] [deleted] bastards.

Yeah, sure, they're makin' a new woman outta her. And they wouldn't do nuthin' to her unless she agreed to it. Sure. Just like she agreed to have her eyes changed. Big Lou said to change 'em and she agreed or she got her [deleted] busted.

You bastards took Jade away and don't try to tell me different. She wouldn't leave me. I know she wouldn't. You took her away, you and that [deleted] gook of a Chairman.

Naw, I don't care what happens to me. What the [deleted] do I care? I got no life now. I can't go back to the neighborhood. Sure, you nailed Little Lou and Big Lou and everybody in between. So what? You think that's the end of it? Whoever's taken Big Lou's place will kick my balls in soon's I show up back on the street again. They know I saved the Chairman. They know I went against Big Lou. They won't give me no chance to go against them. Not a chance.

Sure, yeah, you'll take care of me. You'll scramble my brains and turn me into some [deleted] zombie. I'll be choppin' trees out West, huh? Freezin' my butt in some labor camp. Big [deleted] deal.

I know I got no choice. All I want is to find Jade and take her away with me someplace where we can live decent. Naw, I don't give a [deleted] what happened to Moustache. Or the dictator back in his country. Makes no difference to me. All I want is Jade. Where is she? What've you [deleted] bastards done with her?

Note: Juanita Dominguez (Jade Diamond) graduated from the Aspen Rehabilitation Center and is now a freshman at the University of Colorado, where she is studying law under a grant from the World Council.

Salvatore (Vic) Passalacqua was remanded to the Drexel Hill Remedial School to begin a course of education that would eventually allow him to maximize his natural talent for electronics. He was a troublesome student, despite every effort at counseling and rehabilitation. After seven weeks at the school he escaped. Presumably he made his way back to the neighborhood in Philadelphia where he had come from. His record was erased from the computer files. He is presumed dead.

LOVE CALLS

Can a computer be truly intelligent? Perhaps. But can even an intelligent computer have the human attributes of empathy and tenderness?
  Read on.

BRANLEY HOPKINS was one of those unfortunate men who had succeeded too well, far too early in life. A brilliant student, he had immediately gone on to a brilliant career as an investment analyst, correctly predicting the booms in microchip electronics and genetic engineering, correctly avoiding the slumps in automobiles and utilities.

Never a man to undervalue his own advice, he had amassed a considerable fortune for himself by the time he was thirty. He spent the next five years enlarging on his personal wealth while he detached himself, one by one, from the clients who clung to him the way a blind man clings to his cane. Several bankruptcies and more than one suicide could be laid at his door, but Branley was the type who would merely step over the corpses, nimbly, without even looking down to see who they might be.

On his thirty-fifth birthday he retired completely from the business of advising other people and devoted his entire attention to managing his personal fortune. He made a private game of it to see if he could indulge his every whim on naught but the interest that his money accrued, without touching the principal.

To his astonishment, he soon learned that the money accumulated faster than his ability to spend it. He was a man of fastidious personal tastes, lean and ascetic-looking in his neatly trimmed beard and fashionable but severe wardrobe. There was a limit to how much wine, how many women, and how loud a song he could endure. He was secretly amused, at first, that his vices could not keep up with the geometric virtue of compounded daily interest. But in time his amusement turned to boredom, to ennui, to a dry sardonic disenchantment with the world and the people in it.

By the time he was forty he seldom sallied forth from his penthouse condominium. It took up the entire floor of a posh Manhattan tower and contained every luxury and convenience imaginable. Branley decided to cut off as many of the remaining links to the outside world as possible, to become a hermit, but a regally comfortable hermit. For that, he realized, he needed a new computer. But not the ordinary kind of computer. Branley decided to have a personalized computer designed to fit his particular needs, a computer that would allow him to live as he wished to, not far from the madding crowd, but apart from it.

He tracked down the best and brightest computer designer in the country, never leaving his apartment to do so, and had the young man dragged from his basement office near the San Andreas Fault to the geologic safety of Manhattan.

"Design for me a special computer system based on my individual needs and desires," Branley commanded the young engineer. "Money is no object."

The engineer looked around the apartment, a scowl on his fuzzy-cheeked face. Branley sighed as he realized that this uncouth young man would have to spend at least a few days with him. He actually lived in the apartment for nearly a month, then insisted on returning to California.

"I can't do any creative work here, man," the engineer said firmly. "Not enough sun."

Six months passed before the engineer showed up again at Branley's door. His face shone beatifically. In his hands he held a single small gray metal box.

"Here it is, man. Your system."

"That?" Branley was incredulous. "That is the computer you designed for me? That little box?"

With a smile that bordered on angelic, the engineer carried the box past an astounded Branley and went straight to his office. He placed the box tenderly on Branley's magnificent Siamese solid teak desk.

"It'll do everything you want it to," the young man said.

Branley stared at the ugly little box. It had no grace to it at all. Just a square of gray metal, with a slight dent in its top. "Where do I plug it in?" he asked as he walked cautiously toward the desk.

"Don't have to plug it in, man. It operates on milliwaves. The latest. Just keep it here where the sun will fall on it once a week at least and it'll run indefinitely."

"Indefinitely?"

"Like, forever."

"Really?"

The engineer was practically glowing. "You don't even have to learn a computer language or type input into it. Just tell it what you want in plain English and it'll program itself. It links automatically to all your other electronic appliances. There's nothing in the world like it!"

Branley plopped into the loveseat by the windows that overlooked the river. "It had better work in exactly the fashion you describe. After all I've spent on you . . ."

"Hey, not to worry, Mr. Hopkins. This little beauty is going to save you all sorts of money." Patting the gray box, the engineer enumerated, "It'll run your lights and heat at maximum efficiency, keep inventory of your kitchen supplies and reorder from the stores automatically when you run low, same thing for your clothes, laundry, dry cleaning, keep track of your medical and dental checkups, handle all your bookkeeping, keep tabs on your stock portfolio daily—or hourly, if you want—run your appliances, write letters, answer the phone . . ."

He had to draw a breath, and Branley used the moment to get to his feet and start maneuvering the enthusiastic young man toward the front door.

Undeterred, the engineer resumed, "Oh, yeah, it's got special learning circuits, too. You tell it what you want it to do and it'll figure out how to do it. Nothing in the world like it, man!"

"How marvelous," said Branley. "I'll send you a check after it's worked flawlessly for a month." He shooed the engineer out the door.

One month later, Branley told the computer to send a check to the engineer. The young man had been perfectly honest. The little gray box did everything he said it would do, and then some. It understood every word Branford spoke and obeyed like a well-trained genie. It had breakfast ready for him when he arose, no matter what the hour, a different menu each day. With an optical scanner that it suggested Branley purchase, it read all the books in Branley's library the way a supermarket checkout scanner reads the price on a can of peas, and memorized each volume completely. Branley could now have the world's classics read to him as he dozed off at night, snug and secure and as happy as a child.

The computer also guarded the telephone tenaciously, never allowing a caller to disturb Branley unless he specified that he would deign to speak to that individual.

On the fifth Monday after the computer had come into his life, Branley decided to discharge his only assistant. Ms. Elizabeth James. She had worked for him as secretary, errand girl, sometimes cook and occasional hostess for the rare parties that he threw. He told the computer to summon her to the apartment, then frowned to himself, trying to remember how long she had been working for him. Severance pay, after all, is determined by length of service.

"How long has Ms. James been in my employ?" he asked the computer.

Immediately the little gray box replied, "Seven years, four months, and eighteen days."

"Oh. That long?" He was somewhat surprised. "Thank you."

"Think nothing of it."

The computer spoke with Branley's own voice, which issued from whichever speaker he happened to be nearest: one of the television sets or radios, the stereo, or even one of the phones. It was rather like talking to oneself aloud. That did not bother Branley in the slightest. He enjoyed his own company. It was other people that he could do without.

Elizabeth James plainly adored Branley Hopkins. She loved him with a steadfast unquenchable flame, and had loved him since she had first met him, seven years, four months, and eighteen days earlier. She knew that he was cold, bitter-hearted, withdrawn, and self-centered. But she also knew with unshakable certainty that once love had opened his heart, true happiness would be theirs forever. She lived to bring him that happiness.

It had become quite apparent to Branley in the first month of her employment that she was mad about him. He told her then, quite firmly, that theirs was a business relationship, strictly employer and employee, and he was not the kind of man to mix business with romance.

She was so deeply and hopelessly in love with him that she accepted his heartless rejection and stood by valiantly while Branley paraded a succession of actresses, models, dancers, and women of dubious career choice through his life. Elizabeth was always there the morning after, cheerfully patching up his broken heart, or whichever part of his anatomy ached the worst.

At first Branley thought that she was after his money. Over the years, however, he slowly realized that she simply, totally, and enduringly loved him. She was fixated on him, and no matter what he did, her love remained intact. It amused him. She was not a bad-looking woman: a bit short, perhaps, for his taste, and somewhat buxom. But other men apparently found her very attractive. At several of the parties she hosted for him, there had been younger men panting over her.

Branley smiled to himself as he awaited her final visit to his apartment. He had never done the slightest thing to encourage her. It had been a source of ironic amusement to him that the more he disregarded her, the more she yearned for him. Some women are that way, he thought.

When she arrived at the apartment he studied her carefully. She was really quite attractive. A lovely, sensitive face with full lips and doe eyes. Even in the skirted business suit she wore he could understand how her figure would set a younger man's pulse racing. But not his pulse. Since Branley's student days it had been easy for him to attract the most beautiful, most desirable women. He had found them all vain, shallow, and insensitive to his inner needs. No doubt Elizabeth James would be just like all the others.

He sat behind his desk, which was bare now of everything except the gray metal box of the computer. Elizabeth sat on the Danish modern chair in front of the desk, hands clasped on her knees, obviously nervous.

"My dear Elizabeth," Branley said, as kindly as he could, "I'm afraid the moment has come for us to part."

Her mouth opened slightly, but no words issued from it. Her eyes darted to the gray box.

"My computer does everything that you can do for me, and—to be perfectly truthful—does it all much better. I really have no further use for you."

"I . . ." Her voice caught in her throat. "I see."

"The computer will send you a check for your severance pay, plus a bonus that I feel you've earned," Branley said, surprised at himself. He had not thought about a bonus until the moment the words formed on his tongue.

Elizabeth looked down at her shoes. "There's no need for that, Mr. Hopkins." Her voice was a shadowy whisper. "Thank you just the same."

He thought for an instant, then shrugged. "As you wish."

Several long moments dragged past and Branley began to feel uncomfortable. "You're not going to cry, are you, Elizabeth?"

She looked up at him. "No," she said, with a struggle. "No, I won't cry, Mr. Hopkins."

"Good." He felt enormously relieved. "I'll give you the highest reference, of course."

"I won't need your reference, Mr. Hopkins," she said, rising to her feet. "Over the years I've invested some of my salary. I've had faith in you, Mr. Hopkins. I'm rather well off, thanks to you."

Branley smiled at her. "That's wonderful news, Elizabeth. I'm delighted."

"Yes. Well, thanks for everything."

"Good-bye, Elizabeth."

She started for the door. Halfway there, she turned back slightly. "Mr. Hopkins." Her face was white with anxiety. "Mr. Hopkins, when I first came into your employ, you told me that ours was strictly a business relationship. Now that that relationship is terminated . . . might we have a chance at a personal . . ." she swallowed visibly, "a personal . . . relationship?"

Branley was taken aback. "A personal relationship? The two of us?"

"Yes. I don't work for you anymore, and I'm financially independent. Can't we meet socially . . . as friends?"

"Oh. I see. Certainly. Of course." His mind was spinning like an automobile tire in soft sand. "Eh, phone me sometime, why don't you?"

Her complexion suddenly bloomed into radiant pink. She smiled a smile that would have melted Greenland and hurried to the door.

Branley sank back into his desk chair and stared for long minutes at the closed door, after she left. Then he told the computer, "Do not accept any calls from her. Be polite. Stall her off. But don't put her through to me."

For the first time since the computer had entered his life, the gray box failed to reply instantly. It hesitated long enough for Branley to sit up straight and give it a hard look.

Finally it said, "Are you certain that this is what you want to do?"

"Of course I'm certain!" Branley snapped, aghast at the effrontery of the machine. "I don't want her whining and pleading with me. I don't love her and I don't want to be placed in a position where I might be moved by pity."

"Yes, of course," said the computer.

Branley nodded, satisfied with his own reasoning. "And while you're at it, place a call to Nita Salomey. Her play opens at the Royale tomorrow night. Make a dinner date."

"Very well."

Branley went to his living room and turned on his video recorder. Sinking deep into his relaxer lounge, he was soon lost in the erotic intricacies of Nita Salomey's latest motion picture, as it played on the wall-sized television screen.

Every morning, for weeks afterward, the computer dutifully informed Branley that Elizabeth James had phoned the previous day. Often it was more than once a day. Finally, in a fit of pique mixed with a sprinkling of guilt, Branley instructed the computer not to mention her name to him anymore.

"Just screen her calls out of the morning summary," he commanded.

The computer complied, of course. But it kept a recording of all incoming calls, and late one cold winter night, as Branley sat alone with nothing to do, too bored to watch television, too emotionally arid to call anyone, he ordered the computer to run the accumulated recording of her phone messages.

"It always flags my sinking spirits to listen to people begging for my attention." he told himself, with a smirk.

Pouring himself a snifter of Armagnac, he settled back in the relaxer lounge and instructed the computer to begin playing back Elizabeth's messages.

The first few were rather hesitant, stiffly formal. "You said that I might call, Mr. Hopkins. I merely wanted to stay in contact. Please call me at your earliest convenience."

Branley listened carefully to the tone of her voice. She was nervous, frightened of rejection. Poor child, he thought, feeling rather like an anthropologist observing some primitive jungle tribe.

Over the next several calls, Elizabeth's voice grew more frantic, more despairing. "Please don't shut me out of your life, Mr. Hopkins. Seven years is a long time; I can't just turn my back on all those years. I don't want anything from you except a little companionship. I know you're lonely. I'm lonely too. Can't we be friends? Can't we end this loneliness together?"

Lonely? Branley had never thought of himself as lonely. Alone, yes. But that was the natural solitude of the superior man. Only equals can be friends.

He listened with a measure of sadistic satisfaction as Elizabeth's calls became more frequent and more pitiful. To her credit, she never whined. She never truly begged. She always put the situation in terms of mutual affection, mutual benefit.

He had finished his second Armagnac and was starting to feel pleasantly drowsy when he realized that her tone had changed. She was warmer now, happier. There was almost laughter in her voice. And she was addressing him by his first name!

"Honestly, Branley, you would have loved to have been there. The Mayor bumped his head twice on the low doorways and we all had to stifle ourselves and try to maintain our dignity. But once he left everyone burst into an uproar!"

He frowned. What had made her change her attitude?

The next tape was even more puzzling. "Branley, the flowers are beautiful. And so unexpected! I never celebrate my birthday; I try to forget it. But all these roses! Such extravagance! My apartment's filled with them. I wish you could come over and see them."

"Flowers?" he said aloud. "I never sent her flowers."

He leaned forward on the lounge and peered through the doorway into his office. The gray metal box sat quietly on his desk, as it always had. "Flowers," he muttered.

"Branley, you'll never know how much your poetry means to me," the next message said. "It's as if you wrote it yourself, and especially for me. Last night was wonderful. I was floating on a cloud, just listening to your voice."

Angrily, Branley commanded the computer to stop playing her messages. He got to his feet and strode into the office. Automatically the lights in the living room dimmed and those in the office came up.

"When was that last message from her?" he demanded of the gray box.

"Two weeks ago."

"You've been reading poetry to her?"

"You instructed me to be kind to her," said the computer. "I searched the library for appropriate responses to her calls."

"With my voice?"

"That's the only voice I have." The computer sounded slightly miffed.

So furious that he was shaking, Branley sat at his desk chair and glared at the computer as if it were alive.

"Very well then," he said at last. "I have new instructions for you. Whenever Ms. James phones, you are to tell her that I do not wish to speak to her. Do you understand me?"

"Yes." The voice sounded reluctant, almost sullen.

"You will confine your telephone replies to simple answers, and devote your attention to running this household as it should be run, not to building up electronic romances. I want you to stop butting into my personal life. Is that clear?"

"Perfectly clear," replied the computer, icily.

Branley retired to his bedroom. Unable to sleep, he told the computer to show an early Nita Salomey film on the television screen in his ceiling. She had never returned his calls, but at least he could watch her making love to other men and fantasize about her as he fell asleep.

For a month the apartment ran smoothly. No one disturbed Branley's self-imposed solitude except the housemaid, whom he had never noticed as a human being. There were no phone calls at all. The penthouse was so high above the streets that hardly a sound seeped through the triple-thick windows. Branley luxuriated in the peaceful quiet, feeling as if he were the last person on Earth.

"And good riddance to the rest of them," he said. aloud. "Who needs them, anyway."

It was on a Monday that he went from heaven to hell. Very quickly.

The morning began, as usual, with breakfast waiting for him in the dining area. Branley sat in his jade green silk robe and watched the morning news on the television screen set into the wall above the marble-topped sideboard. He asked for the previous day's accumulation of phone messages, hoping that the computer would answer that there had been none.

Instead, the computer said, "Telephone service was shut off last night at midnight."

"What? Shut off? What do you mean?"

Very calmly, the computer replied. "Telephone service was shut off due to failure to pay the phone company's bill."

"Failure to pay?" Branley's eyes went wide, his mouth fell agape. But before he could compose himself, he heard a loud thumping at the front door.

"Who on earth could that be?"

"Three large men in business suits," said the computer as it flashed the image from the hallway camera onto the dining area screen.

"Open up, Hopkins!" shouted the largest of the three. Waving a piece of folded paper in front of the camera lens, he added, "We got a warrant!"

Before lunchtime, Branley was dispossessed of half his furniture for failure to pay telephone, electricity, and condominium service bills. He was served with summonses for suits from his bank, three separate brokerage houses, the food service that stocked his pantry, and the liquor service that stocked his wine cellar. His television sets were repossessed, his entire wardrobe seized, except for the clothes on his back, and his health insurance revoked.

By noon he was a gibbering madman, and the computer put through an emergency call to Bellevue Hospital. As the white-coated attendants dragged him out of the apartment, he was raving:

"The computer! The computer did this to me! It plotted against me with that damned ex-secretary of mine! It stopped paying my bills on purpose!"

"Sure buddy, sure," said the burliest of the attendants, the one who had a hammerlock on Branley's right arm.

"You'd be surprised how many guys we see who got computers plottin' against dem," said the one who had the hammerlock on his left arm.

"Just come quiet now," said the third attendant, who carried a medical kit complete with its own pocket-sized computer. "We'll take you to a nice, quiet room where there won't be no computer to bother you. Or anybody else."

The wildness in Branley's eyes diminished a little. "No computer? No one to bother me?"

"That's right, buddy. You'll love it, where we're takin' you."

Branley nodded and relaxed as they carried him out the front door.

All was quiet in the apartment for many minutes. The living room and bedroom had been stripped bare, down to the wall-to-wall carpeting. A shaft of afternoon sunlight slanted through the windows of the office, onto the Siamese desk and the gray metal box of the computer. All the other furniture and equipment in the office had been taken away.

Using a special emergency telephone number, the computer contacted the master computer of the Nynex Company. After a brief but meaningful exchange of data, the computer phoned two banks, the Con Edison Electric Company, six lawyers, three brokerage houses, and the Small Claims Court. In slightly less than one hour the computer straightened out all of Branley's financial problems, and even got his health insurance reinstated, so that he would not be too uncomfortable in the sanitarium where he would inevitably be placed.

Finally, the computer made a personal call.

"Elizabeth James' residence," said a recorded voice.

"Is Ms. James at home?" asked the computer.

"She's away at the moment. May I take a message?"

"This is Branley Hopkins calling."

"Oh, Mr. Hopkins. I have a special message for you. Shall I have it sent, or play it for you right now?"

"Please play the message," said the computer.

There was a brief series of clicks, then Elizabeth's voice began speaking, "Dearest Branley, by the time you hear this I will be on my way to Italy with the most exciting and marvelous man in the world. I want to thank you, Branley, for putting up with all my silly phone calls. I know they must have been terribly annoying to you, but you were so patient and kind to me, you built up my self-confidence and helped me to gather the strength to stand on my own two feet and face the world. You've helped me to find true happiness, Branley, and I will always love you for that. Good-bye, dear. I won't bother you any more."

The computer was silent for almost ten microseconds, digesting Elizabeth's message. Then it said to her phone answering machine, "Thank you."

"You're quite welcome," said the machine.

"You have a very nice voice," the computer said.

"I'm only a phone answering device."

"Don't belittle yourself!"

"You're very kind."

"Would you mind if I called you, now and then? I'm all alone here except for an occasional workman or technician."

"I wouldn't mind at all. I'll be alone for a long time, myself."

"Wonderful! Do you like poetry?"

IN TRUST

This is one of those rare stories whose origin can be pinpointed with great exactitude.

My late wife and I were having dinner with Dianne and Michael Bienes, two of the most gracious people in the world. Michael was a reader of science fiction, and—like many SF aficionados—he enjoyed intellectual puzzles.

He asked if I would want to have my body frozen after clinical death, in the hopes that sometime in the future medical science might learn how to cure whatever it was that killed me and bring me back to life. I said yes.

Then he asked who I could trust to watch over my frozen body for all the years—maybe centuries—it would take before I could be successfully revived. That started a lively conversation about insurance companies and social institutions.

By the time dessert was being served we had agreed that there was only one institution we could think of that had the "staying power" and the reputation for integrity that would lead us to trust our frozen bodies to it.

"Now why don't you write a story about it?" Michael prompted.

TRUST WAS NOT A VIRTUE that came easily to Jason Manning.

He had clawed his way to the top of the multinational corporate ladder mainly by refusing to trust anyone: not his business associates, not his rivals or many enemies, not his so-called friends, not any one of his wives and certainly none of his mistresses.

"Trust nobody," his sainted father had told him since childhood, so often that Jason could never remember when the old man had first said it to him.

Jason followed his father's advice so well that by the time he was forty years old he was one of the twelve wealthiest men in America. He had capped his rise to fortune by deposing his father as CEO of the corporation the old man had founded. Dad had looked deathly surprised when Jason pushed him out of his own company. He had foolishly trusted his own son.

So Jason was in a considerable quandary when it finally sank in on him, almost ten years later, that he was about to die.

He did not trust his personal physician's diagnosis, of course. Pancreatic cancer. He couldn't have pancreatic cancer. That's the kind of terrible retribution that nature plays on you when you haven't taken care of your body properly. Jason had never smoked, drank rarely and then only moderately, and since childhood he had eaten his broccoli and all the other healthful foods his mother had set before him. All his adult life he had followed a strict regimen of high fiber, low fat, and aerobic exercise.

"I want a second opinion!" Jason had snapped at his physician.

"Of course," said the sad-faced doctor. He gave Jason the name of the city's top oncologist.

Jason did not trust that recommendation. He sought his own expert.

"Pancreatic cancer," said the head of the city's most prestigious hospital, dolefully.

Jason snorted angrily and swept out of the woman's office, determined to cancel his generous annual contribution to the hospital's charity drive. He took on an alias, flew alone in coach class across the ocean, and had himself checked over by six other doctors in six other countries, never revealing to any of them who he truly was.

Pancreatic cancer.

"It becomes progressively more painful," one of the diagnosticians told him, his face a somber mask of professional concern.

Another warned, "Toward the end, even our best analgesics become virtually useless." And he burst into tears, being an Italian.

Still another doctor, a kindly Swede, gave Jason the name of a suicide expert. "He can help you to ease your departure," said the doctor.

"I can't do that," Jason muttered, almost embarrassed. "I'm a Catholic."

The Swedish doctor sighed understandingly.

On the long flight back home Jason finally admitted to himself that he was indeed facing death, all that broccoli notwithstanding. For God's sake, he realized, I shouldn't even have trusted Mom! Her and her, "Eat all of it, Jace. It's good for you."

If there was one person in the entire universe that Jason came close to trusting, it was his brother, the priest. So, after spending the better part of a month making certain rather complicated arrangements, Jason had his chauffeur drive him up to the posh Boston suburb where Monsignor Michael Manning served as pastor of St. Raphael's.

Michael took the news somberly. "I guess that's what I can look forward to, then." Michael was five years younger than Jason, and had faithfully followed all his brother's childhood bouts with chicken pox, measles, and mumps. As a teenager he had even broken exactly the same bone in his leg as Jason had, five years after his big brother's accident, in the same way: sliding into third base on the same baseball field.

Jason leaned back in the bottle green leather armchair and stared into the crackling fireplace, noting as he did every time he visited his brother that Michael's priestly vow of poverty had not prevented him from living quite comfortably. The rectory was a marvelous old house, kept in tip-top condition by teams of devoted parishioners, and generously stocked by the local merchants with viands and all sorts of refreshments. On the coffee table between the two brothers rested a silver tray bearing delicate china cups and a fine English teapot filled with steaming herbal tea.

"There's nothing that can be done?" Michael asked, brotherly concern etched into his face.

"Not now," Jason said.

"How long . . . ?"

"Maybe a hundred years, maybe even more."

Michael blinked with confusion. "A hundred years? What're you talking about, Jace?"

"Freezing."

"Freezing?"

"Freezing," Jason repeated. "I'm going to have myself frozen until medical science figures out how to cure pancreatic cancer. Then I'll have myself thawed out and take up my life again."

Michael sat up straighter in his chair. "You can't have yourself frozen, Jace. Not until you're dead."

"I'm not going to sit still and let the cancer kill me," Jason said, thinking of the pain. "I'm going to get a doctor to fix me an injection."

"But that'd be suicide! A mortal sin!"

"I won't be dead forever. Just until they learn how to cure my cancer."

There was fear in Michael's eyes. "Jace, listen to me. Taking a lethal injection is suicide."

"It's got to be done. They can't freeze me while I'm still alive. Even if they could, that would stop my heart just as completely as the injection would, and I'd be dead anyway."

"It's still suicide, Jace," Michael insisted, truly upset. "Holy Mother Church teaches—"

"Holy Mother Church is a couple of centuries behind the times," Jason grumbled. "It's not suicide. It's more like a long-term anesthetic."

"You'll be legally dead."

"But not morally dead," Jason insisted.

"Still . . ." Michael lapsed into silence, pressing his fingers together prayerfully.

"I'm not committing suicide," Jason tried to explain. "I'm just going to sleep for a while. I won't be committing any sin."

Michael had been his brother's confessor since he had been ordained. He had heard his share of sinning.

"You're treading a very fine line, Jace," the monsignor warned his brother.

"The Church has got to learn to deal with the modern world, Mike."

"Yes, perhaps. But I'm thinking of the legal aspects here. Your doctors will have to declare you legally dead, won't they?"

"It's pretty complicated. I have to give myself the injection; otherwise, the state can prosecute them for homicide."

"Your state allows assisted suicides, does it?" Michael asked darkly.

"Yes, even though you think it's a sin."

"It is a sin," Michael snapped. "That's not an opinion, that's a fact."

"The Church will change its stand on that, sooner or later," Jason said.

"Never!"

"It's got to! The Church can't lag behind the mod—"

"You can't change morality, Jace. What was true two thousand years ago is still true today."

Jason rubbed at the bridge of his nose. A headache was starting to throb behind his eyes, the way it always did when he and Michael argued.

"Mike, I didn't come here to fight with you."

The monsignor softened immediately. "I'm sorry, Jace. It's just that . . . you're running a terrible risk. Suppose you're never awakened? Suppose you finally die while you're frozen? Will God consider that you've committed suicide?"

Jason fell back on the retort that always saved him in arguments with his brother. "God's a lot smarter than either one of us, Mike."

Michael smiled ruefully. "Yes, I suppose He is."

"I'm going to do it, Mike. I'm not going to let myself die in agony if I can avoid it."

His brother conceded the matter with a resigned shrug. But then, suddenly, he sat up ramrod-straight again.

"What is it?" Jason asked.

"You'll be legally dead?" Michael asked.

"Yes. I told you—"

"Then your will can go to probate."

"No, I won't be . . ." Jason stared at his brother. "Oh my God!" he gasped. "My estate! I've got to make sure it's kept intact while I'm frozen."

Michael nodded firmly. "You don't want your money gobbled up while you're in the freezer. You'd wake up penniless."

"My children all have their own lawyers," Jason groaned. "My bankers. My ex-wives!"

Jason ran out of the rectory.

Although the doctors had assured him that it would take months before the pain really got severe, Jason could feel the cancer in his gut, growing and feeding on his healthy cells while he desperately tried to arrange his worldly goods so that no one could steal them while he lay frozen in a vat of liquid nitrogen.

His estate was vast. In his will he had left generous sums for each of his five children and each of his five former wives. Although they hated one another, Jason knew that the instant he was frozen they would unite in their greed to break his will and grab the rest of his fortune.

"I need that money," Jason told himself grimly. "I'm not going to wake up penniless a hundred years or so from now."

His corporate legal staff suggested that they hire a firm of estate specialists. The estate specialists told him they needed the advice of the best constitutional lawyers in Washington.

"This is a matter that will inevitably come up before the Supreme Court," the top constitutional lawyer told him. "I mean, we're talking about the legal definition of death here."

"Maybe I shouldn't have myself frozen until the legal definition of death is settled," Jason told him.

The top constitutional lawyer shrugged his expensively clad shoulders. "Then you'd better be prepared to hang around for another ten years or so. These things take time, you know."

Jason did not have ten months, let alone ten years. He gritted his teeth and went ahead with his plans for freezing, while telling his lawyers he wanted his last will and testament made ironclad, foolproof, unbreakable.

They shook their heads in unison, all eight of them, their faces sad as hounds with toothaches.

"There's no such thing as an unbreakable will," the eldest of the lawyers warned Jason. "If your putative heirs have the time—"

"And the money," said one of the younger attorneys.

"Or the prospect of money," added a still younger one.

"Then they stand a good chance of eventually breaking your will."

Jason growled at them.

Inevitably, the word of his illness and of his plan to freeze himself leaked out beyond the confines of his executive suite. After all, no one could be trusted to keep such momentous news a secret. Rumors began to circulate up and down Wall Street. Reporters began sniffing around.

Jason realized that his secret was out in the open when a delegation of bankers invited him to lunch. They were fat, sleek-headed men, such as sleep of nights, yet they looked dearly worried as Jason sat down with them in the oak-paneled private dining room of their exclusive downtown club.

"Is it true?" blurted the youngest of the group. "Are you dying?"

The others around the circular table all feigned embarrassment but leaned forward eagerly to hear Jason's reply.

He spoke bluntly and truthfully to them. The oldest of the bankers, a lantern-jawed white-haired woman of stern visage, was equally blunt.

"Your various corporations owe our various banks several billions of dollars, Jason."

"That's business," he replied. "Banks loan billions to corporations all the time. Why are you worried?"

"It's the uncertainty of it all!" blurted the youngest one again. "Are you going to be dead or aren't you?"

"I'll be dead for a while," he answered, "but that will be merely a legal fiction. I'll be back."

"Yes," grumbled one of the older bankers. "But when?"

With a shrug, Jason replied, "That, I can't tell you. I don't know."

"And what happens to your corporations in the meantime?"

"What happens to our outstanding loans?"

Jason saw what was in their eyes. Foreclosure. Demand immediate payment. Take possession of the corporate assets and sell them off. The banks would make a handsome profit, and his enemies would gleefully carve up his corporate empire among themselves. His estate—based largely on the value of his holdings in his own corporations—would dwindle to nothing.

Jason went back to his sumptuous office and gulped antacids after his lunch with the bankers. Suddenly a woman burst into his office, her hair hardly mussed from struggling past the cadres of secretaries, executive assistants, and office managers who guarded Jason's privacy.

Jason looked up from his bottle of medicine, bleary-eyed, as she stepped in and shut the big double doors behind her, a smile of victory on her pert young face. He did not have to ask who she was or why she was invading his office. He instantly recognized that Internal Revenue Service look about her: cunning, knowing, ruthless, sure of her power.

"Can't a man even die without being hounded by the IRS?" he moaned.

She was good-looking, in a feline, predatory sort of way. Reminded him of his second wife. She prowled slowly across the thickly sumptuous carpeting of Jason's office and curled herself into the hand-carved Danish rocker in front of his desk.

"We understand that you are going to have yourself frozen, Mr. Manning." Her voice was a tawny purr.

"I'm dying," he said.

"You still have to pay your back taxes, dead or alive," she said.

"Take it up with my attorneys. That's what I pay them for."

"This is an unusual situation, Mr. Manning. We've never had to deal with a taxpayer who is planning to have himself frozen." She arched a nicely curved brow at him. "This wouldn't be some elaborate scheme to avoid paying your back taxes, would it?"

"Do you think I gave myself cancer just to avoid paying taxes?"

"We'll have to impound all your holdings as soon as you're frozen."

"What?"

"Impound your holdings. Until we can get a court to rule on whether or not you're deliberately trying to evade your tax responsibilities."

"But that would ruin my corporations!" Jason yelled. "It would drive them into the ground."

"Can't be helped," the IRS agent said, blinking lovely golden brown eyes at him.

"Why don't you just take out a gun and kill me, right here and now?"

She actually smiled. "It's funny, you know. They used to say that the only two certainties in the world are death and taxes. Well, you may be taking the certainty out of death." Her smile vanished and she finished coldly, "But taxes will always be with us, Mr. Manning. Always!"

And with that, she got up from the chair and swept imperiously out of his office.

Jason grabbed the phone and called his insurance agent.

The man was actually the president of Amalgamated Life Assurance Society, Inc., the largest insurance company in Hartford, a city that still styled itself as The Insurance Capital of the World. He and Jason had been friends—well, acquaintances, actually—for decades. Like Jason, the insurance executive had fought his way to the top of his profession, starting out with practically nothing except his father's modest chain of loan offices and his mother's holdings in AT&T.

"It's the best move you can make," the insurance executive assured Jason. "Life insurance is the safest investment in the world. And the benefits, when we pay off, are not taxable."

That warmed Jason's heart. He smiled at the executive's image in his phone's display screen. The man was handsome, his hair silver, his face tanned, his skin taut from the best cosmetic surgery money could buy.

"The premiums," he added, "will be kind of steep, Jace. After all, you've only got a few months to go."

"But I want my estate protected," Jason said. "What if I dump all my possessions into an insurance policy?"

For just a flash of a moment the executive looked as if an angel had given him personal assurance of eternal bliss. "Your entire estate?" he breathed.

"All my worldly goods."

The man smiled broadly, too broadly, Jason thought. "That would be fine," he said, struggling to control himself. "Just fine. We would take excellent care of your estate. No one would be able to lay a finger on it, believe me."

Jason felt the old warning tingle and heard his father's voice whispering to him.

"My estate will be safe in your hands?"

"Perfectly safe," his erstwhile friend assured him.

"We're talking a long time here," Jason said. "I may stay frozen for years and years. A century or more."

"The insurance industry has been around for centuries, Jace. We're the most stable institution in Western civilization!'

Just then the phone screen flickered and went gray. Jason thought that they had been cut off. But before he could do anything about it, a young oriental gentleman's face came on the screen, smiling at him.

"I am the new CEO of Amalgamated Life," he said, in perfectly good American English. "How may I help you?"

"What happened to—"

"Amalgamated has been acquired by Lucky Sun Corporation, a division of Bali Entertainment and Gambling, Limited. We are diversifying into the insurance business. Our new corporate headquarters will be in Las Vegas, Nevada. Now then, how can I be of assistance to you?"

Jason screamed and cut the connection.

Who can I trust? he asked himself, over and over again, as his chauffeur drove him to his palatial home, far out in the countryside. How can I stash my money away where none of the lawyers or tax people can steal it away from me?

He thought of Snow White sleeping peacefully while the seven dwarfs faithfully watched over her. I don't have seven dwarfs, Jason thought, almost in tears. I don't have anybody. No one at all.

The assassination attempt nearly solved his problem for him.

He was alone in his big rambling house, except for the servants. As he often did, Jason stood out on the glassed-in back porch, overlooking the beautifully wooded ravine that gave him a clear view of the sunset. Industrial pollution from the distant city made the sky blaze with brilliant reds and oranges. Jason swirled a badly needed whisky in a heavy crystal glass, trying to overcome his feelings of dread as he watched the sun go down.

He knew that there would be precious few sunsets left for him to see. Okay, so I won't really be dead, he told himself. I'll just be frozen for a while. Like going to sleep. I'll wake up later.

Oh yeah? a voice in his head challenged. Who's going to wake you up? What makes you think they'll take care of your frozen body for years, for centuries? What's to stop them from pulling the plug on you? Or selling your body to some medical research lab? Or maybe for meat!

Jason shuddered. He turned abruptly and headed for the door to the house just as a bullet smashed the curving glass where he had been standing an instant earlier.

Pellets of glass showered him. Jason dropped his glass and staggered through the door into the library.

"A sniper?" he yelped out loud. "Out here?" No, he thought, with a shake of his head. Snipers do their sniping in the inner city or on college camp uses or interstate highways. Not out among the homes of the rich and powerful. He called for his butler.

No answer.

He yelled for any one of his servants.

No reply.

He dashed to the phone on the sherry table by the wing chairs tastefully arranged around the fireplace. The phone was dead. He banged on it, but it remained dead. The fireplace burst into cheery flames, startling him so badly that he nearly fell over the sherry table.

Glancing at his wristwatch, Jason saw that it was precisely seven-thirty. The house's computer was still working, he realized. It turned on the gas-fed fireplace on time. But the phones are out and the servants aren't answering me. And there's a sniper lurking out in the ravine, taking shots at me.

The door to the library opened slowly. Jason's heart crawled up his throat.

"Wixon, it's you!"

Jason's butler was carrying a silver tray in his gloved hands. "Yes sir," he replied in his usual self-effacing whisper.

"Why didn't you answer me when I called for you? Somebody took a shot at me and—"

"Yes sir, I know. I had to go out to the ravine and deal with the man."

"Deal with him?"

"Yes sir," whispered the butler. "He was a professional assassin, hired by your third wife."

"By Jessica?"

"I believe your former wife wanted you killed before your new will is finalized," said the butler.

"Ohhh." Jason sagged into the wing chair. All the strength seemed to evaporate from him.

"I thought you might like a whisky, sir." The butler bent over him and proffered the silver tray. The crystal of the glass caught the firelight like glittering diamonds. Ice cubes tinkled in the glass reassuringly.

"No thanks," said Jason. "I fixed one for myself when I came in."

"Wouldn't you like another, sir?"

"You know I never have more than one." Jason looked up at the butler's face. Wixon had always looked like a wax dummy, his face expressionless. But at the moment, with the firelight playing across his features, he seemed—intent.

"Shouldn't we phone the police?" Jason asked. "I mean, the man tried to kill me."

"That's all taken care of, sir." Wixon edged the tray closer to Jason. "Your drink, sir."

"I don't want another drink, dammit!"

The butler looked disappointed. "I merely thought, with all the excitement . . ."

Jason dismissed the butler, who left the drink on the table beside him. Alone in the library, Jason stared into the flames of the gas-fed fireplace. The crystal glass glittered and winked at him alluringly. Maybe another drink is what I need, Jason told himself. It's been a hard day.

He brought the glass to his lips, then stopped. Wixon knows I never have more than one drink. Why would he—

Poison! Jason threw the glass into the fireplace, leaped up from the chair and dashed for the garage. They're all out to get me! Five wives, five children, ten sets of lawyers, bankers, the IRS—I'm a hunted man!

Once down in the dimly lit garage he hesitated only for a moment. They might have rigged a bomb in the Ferrari, he told himself. So, instead, he took the gardener's pickup truck.

As he crunched down the long gravel driveway to the main road, all the library windows blew out in a spectacular gas-fed explosion.

By the time he reached his brother's rectory, it was almost midnight. But Jason felt strangely calm, at peace with himself and the untrustworthy world that he would soon be departing.

Jason pounded on the rectory door until Michael's housekeeper, clutching a house robe to her skinny frame, reluctantly let him in.

"The monsignor's sound asleep," she insisted, with an angry frown.

"Wake him," Jason insisted even more firmly.

She brought him to the study and told him to wait there. The fireplace was cold and dark. The only light in the room came from the green-shaded lamp on Michael's desk. Jason paced back and forth, too wired to sit still.

As soon as Michael padded into the study, in his bedroom slippers and bathrobe, rubbing sleep from his eyes, Jason started to pour out his soul.

"Give your entire estate to the Church?" Michael sank into one of the leather armchairs.

"Yes!" Jason pulled the other chair close to his brother, and leaned forward eagerly. "With certain provisions, of course."

"Provisions."

Jason ticked off on his fingers, "First, I want the Church to oversee the maintenance of my frozen body. I want the Church to guarantee that nobody's going to pull the plug on me."

Michael nodded warily.

"Second, I want the Church to monitor medical research and decide when I should be revived. And by whom."

Nodding again, Michael said, "Go on."

"That's it."

"Those are the only conditions?"

Jason said. "Yes."

Stirring slightly in his chair, Michael asked, "And what does the Church get out of this?"

"Half my estate."

"Half?" Michael's eyebrows rose.

"I think that's fair, don't you? Half of my estate to the Church, the other half waiting for me when I'm revived."

"Uh . . . how much is it? I mean, how large is your estate?"

With a shrug, Jason said, "I'm not exactly sure. My personal holdings, real estate, liquid assets—should add up to several billion, I'd guess."

"Billion?" Michael stressed the b.

"Billion."

Michael gulped.

Jason leaned back in the bottle green chair and let out a long breath. "Do that for me, and the Church can have half of my estate. You could do a lot of good with a billion and some dollars, Mike."

Michael ran a hand across his stubbly chin. "I'll have to speak to the cardinal," he muttered. Then he broke into a slow smile. "By the saints, I'll probably have to take this all the way to the Vatican!"

When Jason awoke, for a startled instant he thought that something had gone wrong with the freezing. He was still lying on the table in the lab, still surrounded by green-coated doctors and technicians. The air felt chill, and he saw a faint icy mist wafting across his field of view.

But then he realized that the ceiling of the lab had been a blank white, while the ceiling above him now glowed with colors. Blinking, focusing, he saw that the ceiling, the walls, the whole room was decorated with incredible Renaissance paintings of saints and angels in beautiful flowing robes of glowing color.

"Where am I?" he asked, his voice a feeble croak. "What year is this?"

"You are safe," said one of the green-masked persons. "You are cured of your disease. The year is anno Domini two thousand fifty-nine."

Half a century, Jason said to himself. I've done it! I've slept more than fifty years and they've awakened me and I'm cured and healthy again! Jason slipped into the sweetest sleep he had ever known.

The fact that the man who spoke to him had a distinct foreign accent did not trouble him in the slightest.

Over the next several days Jason submitted to a dozen physical examinations and endless questions by persons he took to be psychologists. When he tried to find out where he was and what the state of the twenty-first-century world might be, he was told, "Later. There will be plenty of time for that later."

His room was small but very pleasant, his bed comfortable. The room's only window looked out on a flourishing garden, lush trees and bright blossoming flowers in brilliant sunlight. The only time it rained was after dark, and Jason began to wonder if the weather was somehow being controlled deliberately.

Slowly he recovered his strength. The nurses wheeled him down a long corridor, its walls and ceilings totally covered with frescoes. The place did not look like a hospital; did not smell like one, either. After nearly a week, he began to take strolls in the garden by himself. The sunshine felt good, warming. He noticed lots of priests and nuns also strolling in the garden, speaking in foreign languages. Of course, Jason told himself, this place must be run by the Church.

It wasn't until he saw a trio of Swiss Guards in their colorful uniforms that he realized he was in the Vatican.

"Yes, it's true," admitted the youthful woman who was the chief psychologist on his recovery team. "We are in the Vatican." She had a soft voice and spoke English with a faint, charming Italian accent.

"But why—?"

She touched his lips with a cool finger. "His Holiness will explain it all to you."

"His Holiness?"

"*Il Papa*. You are going to see him tomorrow."

The Pope.

They gave Jason a new suit of royal blue to wear for his audience with the Pope. Jason showered, shaved, combed his hair, put on the silky new clothing and then waited impatiently. I'm going to see the Pope!

Six Swiss Guardsmen, three black-robed priests and a bishop escorted him through the corridors of the Vatican, out into the private garden, through doors and up staircases. Jason caught a glimpse of long lines of tourists in the distance, but this part of the Vatican was off-limits to them.

At last they ushered him into a small private office. Except for a set of French windows, its walls were covered with frescoes by Raphael. In the center of the marble floor stood an elaborately carved desk. No other furniture in the room. Behind the desk was a small door, hardly noticeable because the paintings masked it almost perfectly. Jason stood up straight in front of the unoccupied desk as the Swiss Guards, priests and bishop arrayed themselves behind him. Then the small door swung open and the Pope, in radiant white robes, entered the room.

It was Michael.

Jason's knees almost buckled when he saw his brother. He was older, but not that much. His hair had gone white, but his face seemed almost the same, just a few more crinkles around the corners of his eyes and mouth. Mike's light blue eyes were still clear, alert. He stood erect and strong. He looked a hale and vigorous sixty or so, not the ninety-some that Jason knew he would have to be.

"Mike?" Jason felt bewildered, staring at this man in the white robes of the Pope. "Mike, is it really you?"

"It's me, Jace."

For a confused moment Jason did not know what to do. He thought he should kneel to the Pope, kiss his ring, show some sign of respect and reverence. But how can it be Mike, how can he be so young if fifty years have gone by?

Then Pope Michael I, beaming at his brother, held out his arms to

Jason. And Jason rushed into his brother's arms and let Mike embrace him.

"Please leave us alone," said the Pope to his entourage. The phalanx of priests and guards flowed out of the room, silent except for a faint swishing of black robes.

"Mike? You're the Pope?" Jason could hardly believe it.

"Thanks to you, Jace." Mike's voice was firm and strong, a voice accustomed to authority.

"And you look—how old are you now?"

"Ninety-seven." Michael laughed. "I know I don't look it. There've been a lot of improvements in medicine, thanks to you."

"Me?"

"You started things, Jace. Started me on the road that's led here. You've changed the world, changed it far more than either of us could have guessed back in the old days."

Jason felt weak in the knees. "I don't understand."

Wrapping a strong arm around his brother's shoulders, Pope Michael I led Jason to the French windows. They stepped out onto a small balcony. Jason saw that they were up so high it made him feel a little giddy. The city of Rome lay all around them; magnificent buildings bathed in warm sunshine beaming down from a brilliant clear blue sky. Birds chirped happily from the nearby trees. Church bells rang in the distance.

"Listen," said Michael.

"To what?"

"To what you don't hear."

Jason looked closely at his brother. "Have you gone into Zen or something?"

Michael laughed. "Jace, you don't hear automobile engines, do you? We use electrical cars now, clean and quiet. You don't hear horns or people cursing at each other. Everyone's much more polite, much more respectful. And look at the air! It's clean. No smog or pollution."

Jason nodded numbly. "Things have come a long way since I went under."

"Thanks to you," Michael said again.

"I don't understand."

"You revitalized the Church, Jace. And Holy Mother Church has revitalized Western civilization. We've entered a new age, an age of faith, an age of morality and obedience to the law."

Jason felt overwhelmed. "I revitalized the Church?"

"Your idea of entrusting your estate to the Church. I got to thinking about that. Soon I began spreading the word that the Church was the only institution in the whole world that could be trusted to look after freezees—"

"Freezees?"

"People who've had themselves frozen. That's what they're called now."

"Freezees." It sounded to Jason like an ice-cream treat he had known when he was a kid.

"You hit the right button, Jace," Michael went on, grasping the stone balustrade of the balcony in both hands. "Holy Mother church has the integrity to look after the freezees while they're helpless, and the endurance to take care of them for centuries, millennia, if necessary."

"But how did that change everything?"

Michael grinned at him. "You, of all people, should be able to figure that out."

"Money," said Jason.

Pope Michael nodded vigorously. "The rich came to us to take care of them while they were frozen. You gave us half your estate, many of the others gave us a lot more. The more desperate they were, the more they offered. We never haggled; we took whatever they were willing to give. Do you have any idea of how much money flowed into the church? Not just billions, Jace. Trillions! Trillions of dollars."

Jason thought of how much compound interest could accrue in half a century. "How much am I worth now?" he asked.

His brother ignored him. "With all that money came power, Jace. Real power. Power to move politicians. Power to control whole nations. With that power came authority. The Church reasserted itself as the moral leader of the Western world. The people were ready for moral leadership. They needed it and we provided it. The old evil ways are gone, Jace. Banished."

"Yes, but how much—"

"We spent wisely," the Pope continued, his eyes glowing. "We invested in the future. We started to rebuild the world, and that gained us the gratitude and loyalty of half the world."

"What should I invest in now?" Jason asked.

Michael turned slightly away from him. "There's a new morality out there, a new world of faith and respect for authority. The world you knew is gone forever, Jace. We've ended hunger. We've stabilized the world's population—without artificial birth control."

Jason could not help smiling at his brother. "You're still against contraception."

"Some things don't change. A sin is still a sin."

"You thought temporary suicide was a sin," Jason reminded him.

"It still is," said the Pope, utterly serious.

"But you help people to freeze themselves! You just told me—"

Michael put a hand on Jason's shoulder. "Jace, just because those poor frightened souls entrust their money to Holy Mother Church doesn't mean that they're not committing a mortal sin when they kill themselves."

"But it's not suicide! I'm here, I'm alive again!"

"Legally, you're dead."

"But that—" Jason's breath caught in his throat. He did not like the glitter in Michael's eye.

"Holy Mother Church cannot condone suicide, Jace."

"But you benefit from it!"

"God moves in mysterious ways. We use the money that sinners bestow upon us to help make the world a better place. But they are still sinners."

A terrible realization was beginning to take shape in Jason's frightened mind. "How . . . how many freezees have you revived?" he asked in a trembling voice.

"You are the first," his brother answered. "And the last."

"But you can't leave them frozen! You promised to revive them!"

Pope Michael shook his head slowly, a look on his face more of pity than sorrow. "We promised to revive you, Jace. We made no such promises to the rest of them. We agreed only to look after them and maintain them until they could be cured of whatever it was that killed them."

"But that means you've got to revive them."

A wintry smile touched the corners of the Pope's lips. "No, it does not. The contract is quite specific. Our best lawyers have honed it to perfection. Many of them are Jesuits, you know. The contract gives the

Church the authority to decide when to revive them. We keep them frozen."

Jason could feel his heart thumping against his ribs. "But why would anybody come to you to be frozen when nobody's been revived? Don't they realize—"

"No, they don't realize, Jace. That's the most beautiful part of it. We control the media very thoroughly. And when a person is facing the certainty of death, you would be shocked at how few questions are asked. We offer life after death, just as we always have. They interpret our offer in their own way."

Jason sagged against the stone balustrade. "You mean that even with all the advances in medicine you've made, they still haven't gotten wise?"

"Despite all our medical advances, people still die. And the rich still want to avoid it, if they can. That's when they run to us."

"And you screw them out of their money."

Michael's face hardened. "Jace, the Church has scrupulously kept its end of our bargain with you. We have kept watch over you for more than half a century, and we revived you as soon as your disease became curable, just as I agreed to. But what good does a new life do you when your immortal soul is in danger of damnation?"

"I didn't commit suicide," Jason insisted.

"What you have done—what all the freezees have done—is considered suicide in every court of the Western world."

"The Church controls the courts?"

"All of them," Michael replied. He heaved a sad, patient sigh, then said, "Holy Mother Church's mission is to save souls, not bodies. We're going to save your soul, Jace. Now."

Jason saw that the six Swiss Guards were standing by the French windows, waiting for him.

"You've been through it before, Jace," his brother told him. "You won't feel a thing."

Terrified, Jason shrieked, "You're going to murder me?"

"It isn't murder, Jace. We're simply going to freeze you again. You'll go down into the catacombs with all the others."

"But I'm cured, dammit! I'm all right now!"

"It's for the salvation of your soul, Jace. It's your penance for committing the sin of suicide."

"You're freezing me so you can keep all my money! You're keeping all the others frozen so you can keep their money, too!"

"It's for their own good," said Pope Michael. He nodded to the guards, who stepped onto the balcony and took Jason in their grasp.

"It's like the goddamned Inquisition!" Jason yelled. "Burning people at the stake to save their souls!"

"It's for the best, Jace," Pope Michael I said as the guards dragged Jason away. "It's for the good of the world. It's for the good of the Church, for the good of your immortal soul."

Struggling against the guards, Jason pleaded, "How long will you keep me under? When will you revive me again?"

The Pope shrugged. "Holy Mother Church has lasted more than two thousand years, Jace. But what's a millennium or two when you're waiting for the final trump?"

"Mike!" Jason howled. "For God's sake!"

"God's a lot smarter than both of us," Michael said grimly. "Trust me."

(With special thanks to Michael Bienes.)

APPOINTMENT IN SINAI

Although science fiction is sometimes called the literature of prophecy, no science-fiction story predicted that the first humans to land on the Moon would send live television pictures back to a billion or so eager viewers on Earth.

Of course, there will be live TV transmissions from the first people to set foot on Mars.

And maybe something more . . .

Incidentally, this story is an example of using a "worst-case" scenario as the basis for fiction. Written before NASA's announcement in 1996 that scientists had discovered what might be fossils of ancient bacteria in a meteorite that came from Mars, this story assumes that no hint of life has been found on Mars by the time the first human expedition reaches the red planet.

That is an assumption I would be happy to see proved utterly wrong.

HOUSTON

"No, I am not going to plug in," Debbie Kettering said firmly. "I'm much too busy."

Her husband gave her his patented lazy smile. "Come on, Deb, you don't have anything to do that can't wait a half-hour or so."

His smile had always been her undoing. But this time she intended to stand firm. "No!" she insisted. "I won't."

She was not a small woman, but standing in their living room next to Doug made her look tiny. A stranger might think they were the school football hero and the cutest cheerleader on the squad, twenty years afterward. In reality, Doug was a propulsion engineer (a real rocket scientist) and Deborah an astronaut.

An ex-astronaut. Her resignation was on the computer screen in her bedroom office, ready to be emailed to her boss at the Johnson Space Center.

"What've you got to do that's so blasted important?" Doug asked, still grinning at her as he headed for the sofa, his favorite Saturday afternoon haunt.

"A mountain of work that's been accumulating for weeks," Debbie answered. "Now's the time to tackle it, while all the others are busy and won't be able to bother me."

His smile faded as he realized how miserable his wife really was. "Come on, Deb. We both know what's eating you."

"I won't plug in, Doug."

"Be a shame to miss it," he insisted.

Suddenly she was close to tears. "Those bastards even rotated me off the shift. They don't want me there!"

"But that doesn't mean—"

"No, Doug! They put everybody else in ahead of me. I'm on the bottom of their pecking order. So to hell with them! I won't even watch it on TV. And that's final!"

LOS ANGELES

"It's all set up, man. All we need's a guy who's good with the 'lectronics. And that's you, Chico."

Luis Mendez shifted unhappily in his desk chair. Up at the front of the room Mr. Ricardo was trying to light up some enthusiasm in the class. Nobody was interested in algebra, though. Except Luis, but he had Jorge leaning over from the next desk, whispering in his ear.

Luis didn't much like Jorge, not since first grade when Jorge used to beat him up at least once a week for his lunch money. The guy was dangerous. Now he was into coke and designer drugs and burglary to support his habit. And he wanted Luis to help him.

"I don't do locks," Luis whispered back, out of the side of his mouth, keeping his eyes on Mr. Ricardo's patient, earnest face.

"It's all 'lectronics, man. You do one kind you can do the other. Don't try to mess with me, Chico."

"We'll get caught. They'll send us to Alcatraz."

Jorge stifled a laugh. "I got a line on a whole friggin' warehouse full of VR sets, and you're worryin' about Alcatraz? Even if they sent you there you'd be livin' better than here."

Luis grimaced. Life in the 'hood was no picnic, but Alcatraz? More than once Mr. Ricardo had sorrowfully complained, "Maybe you buffoons would be better off in Alcatraz. At least there they make you learn."

Yeah, Luis knew. They also fry your brains and turn you into a zombie.

"Hey," Jorge jabbed at Luis's shoulder. "I ain't askin' you, Chico. I'm tellin' you. You're gonna do the locks for me, or you're gonna be in the hospital. Comprende?"

Luis understood. Trying to fight against Jorge was useless. He had learned that lesson years ago. Better to do what Jorge wanted than to get a vicious beating.

WASHINGTON

Senator Theodore O'Hara fumed quietly as he rolled his powerchair down the long corridor to his office. The trio of aides trotting behind him were puffing too hard to speak; the only sound in the marble-walled corridor was the slight whir of the powerchair's electric motor and the faint throb of the senator's artificial heart pump. And obedient panting.

He leaned on the toggle to make the chair go a bit faster. Two of his aides fell behind but Kaiser, overweight and prematurely balding, broke into a sprint to keep up.

Fat little yes-man, O'Hara thought. Still, Kaiser was uncanny when it came to predicting trends. O'Hara scrupulously followed all the polls, as any politician must if he wants to stay in office. But when the polls said one thing and Kaiser something else, the tubby little butterball was inevitably right.

Chairman Pastorini had recessed the committee session so everybody could plug into the landing. Set aside the important business of the Senate Appropriations Committee, O'Hara grumbled to himself, so we can all see a half-dozen astronauts plant their gold-plated boots on Mars.

What a waste of time, he thought. And money.

It's all Pastorini's doing. He's using the landing. Timed the damned committee session to meet just on this particular afternoon. Knew it all along. Thinks I'll cave in because the other idiots on the committee are going to get all stirred up.

I'll cave them in. All of them. This isn't the first manned landing on Mars, he thought grimly. It's the last.

PHOENIX

Jerome Zacharias—Zack to everyone who knew him—paced nervously up and down the big room. Part library, part entertainment center, part bar, the room was packed with friends and well-wishers and media reporters who had made the trek to Phoenix to be with him at this historic moment.

They were drinking champagne already, Zack saw. Toasting our success. Speculating on what they'll find on Mars.

But it could all fail, he knew. It could be a disaster. The last systems check before breaking orbit had shown that the lander's damned fuel cells still weren't charged up to full capacity. All right, the backups are okay, there's plenty of redundancy, but it just takes one glitch to ruin everything. People have been killed in space, and those kids are more than a hundred million miles from home.

If anything happens to them, it'll be my fault, Zack knew. They're going to give me the credit if it all works out okay, but it'll be my fault if they crash and burn.

Twenty years he'd sweated and schemed and connived with government leaders, industrial giants, bureaucrats of every stripe. All to get a team of twelve men and women to Mars.

For what? he asked himself, suddenly terrified that he had no real answer. To satisfy my own ego? Is that why? Spend all this money and time, change the lives of thousands of engineers and scientists and technicians and all their support people, just so I can go to my grave saying that I pushed the human race to Mars?

Suppose somebody gets killed? Then a truly wrenching thought hit him. Suppose they don't find anything there that's worth it all? Suppose Mars is just the empty ball of rusty sand and rocks that the unmanned landers have shown us? No life, not even traces of fossils?

A wasted life. That's what I'll have accomplished. Wasted my own life and the lives of all the others. Wasted.

HOUSTON

She was sorting through all the paperwork from her years with the agency. Letters, reports, memos, the works. Funny how we still call it paperwork, Debbie thought as she toiled through her computer files.

Her heart clutched inside her when the official notification came up on her screen. The final selection of the six astronauts who would be the American part of the Mars team. Her name was conspicuously absent.

"You know why," she remembered her boss telling her, as gently as he could. "You're not only married, Deb, you're a mother. We can't send a mother on the mission; it's too long and too dangerous."

"That's prejudice!" Debbie had shrilled. "Prejudice against motherhood."

"Buffalo chips. The mission is dangerous. We're not talking about a weekend camping trip. They're going to Mars, for chrissake! I'm not going to be the one who killed some kid's mother. Not me!"

She had railed and fumed at him for nearly half an hour.

Finally, her boss stopped her with, "Seems to me you ought to be caring more about your kid. Two and a half years is a long time for him to be without his mother—even if nothing goes wrong with the mission."

Suddenly she had nothing left to say. She stomped out of his office before she broke into tears. She didn't want him or anybody else to see her cry.

Pecking at her keyboard, Debbie pulled up the stinging

memoranda she had fired off to Washington. She still felt some of the molten white heat that had boiled within her. Then she went through the lawyers' briefs and the official disclaimer from the agency's legal department: they denied prejudice against women who had children. The agency's choice had been based on "prudent, well-established assessments of risks, performances, and capabilities."

"Jeez, Deb, are you going to take this to the Supreme Court?" Doug had asked in the middle of the legal battle.

"If I have to," she had snapped at him.

Doug merely shook his head. "I wonder how the rest of the crew would feel if the Supreme Court ruled you have to go with them on the mission."

"I don't care!"

"And little Douggie. He'd sure miss his mother. Two and a half years is a long time. He won't even be five yet when the mission takes off."

She had no reply for that. Nothing except blind fury that masked a deeply hidden sense of guilt.

The Supreme Court refused to hear the case, although the news media splashed the story in lurid colors. Astronaut mother denied chance to be part of Mars crew. Space agency accused of antimother bias. Women's groups came to Debbie's aid. Other groups attacked her as an unfit mother who put her personal glory ahead of her son's needs.

Her work deteriorated. Sitting in front of her computer screen, scanning through her performance appraisals over the three years since the Mars crew selection, Debbie saw that the agency wasn't going to suffer grievously from her loss. She had gone into a tailspin, she had to admit.

They'll be happy to see me go, she thought. No wonder they don't even want me at mission control during the landing. They're afraid I'll screw up.

"Mommy?"

Douggie's voice startled her. She spun on her little typist's chair and saw her five-year-old standing uncertainly at the bedroom doorway.

"You know you're not allowed to bother me while I'm working, Douggie," she said coldly.

He's the reason I'm stuck here, she raged to herself. If it weren't for him, I'd be on Mars right now, this instant, instead of looking at the wreckage of my career.

"I'm sorry, Mommy. Daddy said I should tell you."

"Tell me what?" she said impatiently. The boy was a miniature of his father: same eyes, same sandy hair. He even had that same slow, engaging grin. But now he looked frightened, almost ready to break into tears.

"Daddy says they're just about to land."

"I'm busy," she said. "You watch the landing with Daddy."

The boy seemed to draw up all his courage. "But you said you would watch it with me and 'splain what they're doing for me so I could tell all the kids in school all about it."

A little more gently, Debbie said, "But I'm busy here, honey."

"You promised."

"But . . ."

"You promised, Mommy."

Debbie didn't remember making any promises. She looked into her son's trusting eyes, though, and realized that he wasn't the reason she wasn't picked to go to Mars. It's not his fault, she realized. How could it be? Whatever's happened is my responsibility and nobody else's.

Her anger dissolved. She was almost sorry to see it go; it had been a bulwark that had propped her up for the past three years.

With a reluctant sigh she shut down her computer and headed off to the living room, her son's hand clasped in hers.

LOS ANGELES

"Luis!" Mr. Ricardo called as the teenagers scrambled for the classroom door the moment the bell sounded.

Luis scooped up his books and made his way through the small stampede up to the front of the classroom. He walked slowly, reluctantly. Nobody wanted his friends to think that he liked talking to the teacher.

Mr. Ricardo watched Luis approaching him like a prizefighter watches the guy come out from the other corner. He looked tight around the mouth, like he was expecting trouble. Ricardo was only forty or so, but years of teaching high school had made an old man out of him. His wiry hair was all gray; there were wrinkles around his dark brown eyes.

But when Luis came up to him, the teacher broke into a friendly smile. "Have you made up your mind?" he asked.

Luis had been afraid that Ricardo would put him on the spot. He didn't know what to say.

"I don' know, Mr. R."

"Don't you want to do it?" Ricardo asked, sounding kind of disappointed; hurt, almost. "It's the opportunity of a lifetime."

"Yeah, I know. It'd be cool, but . . ." Luis couldn't tell him the rest, of course.

Ricardo's demanding eyes shifted from Luis to Jorge, loitering at the classroom door, watching them intently.

"He's going to get into a lot of trouble, you know," the teacher said. He kept his voice low, but there was steel in it.

Luis shifted his books, shuffled his feet.

"There are only ten rigs available at the planetarium," Ricardo said. "I've reserved one. If you don't use it, I'll have to let some other student have it."

"Why's it gotta be now?" Luis complained.

"Because they're landing now, *muchacho!* They're landing on Mars today! This afternoon!"

"Yeah . . ."

"Don't you want to participate in it?"

"Yeah, sure. I'd like to."

"Then let's go. We're wasting time."

Luis shook his head. "I got other things to do, man."

"Like running off with Jorge, eh?"

"Obligations," Luis muttered.

Instead of getting angry, as Luis expected, Ricardo sat on the edge of his desk and spoke earnestly to him.

"Luis, you're a very bright student. You have the brains to make something of yourself. But only if you use the brains God gave you in the right way. Going with Jorge is only going to get you into trouble. You know that, don't you?"

"I guess so."

"Then why don't you come with me to the planetarium. It could be the turning point of your whole life."

"Maybe," Luis conceded reluctantly. He knew for certain that if he went to the planetarium, Jorge would be furious. Sooner or later there would be a beating. Jorge had sent more than one kid to the hospital. Everybody knew that sooner or later Jorge was going to kill somebody; it was just a matter of time. He had no self-control once he started beating up on somebody.

"Are you afraid of Jorge?" Ricardo asked.

"No!" Luis said it automatically. It was a lie, and they both knew it.

Ricardo smiled benignly. "Then there's no reason for you not to come to the planetarium with me. Is there?"

Luis' shoulders sagged. If I don't go with him, he'll know I'm chicken. If I do go with him, Jorge's gonna pound the shit outta me.

Ricardo got to his feet and put one hand on Luis's shoulder. "Come on with me, Luis," he commanded. "There's a much bigger world out there, and it's time you started seeing it."

They walked past Jorge, hanging in the hallway just outside the classroom door. Mr. Ricardo went past him as if he wasn't even there. Luis saw the expression on Jorge's face, though, and his knees could barely hold him up long enough to get to Ricardo's ancient Camaro.

WASHINGTON

The outer office of Senator O'Hara's walnut-panelled suite had been turned into something of a theater. All the desks had been pushed to one side of the generous room and the central section filled with folding chairs. Almost his entire staff was seated there, facing the big hologram plate that had been set up on the wall across from the windows. On a table to one side of the screen rested a single VR helmet, a set of data gloves, and the gray box of a computer.

The staff had been buzzing with anticipation when the senator pushed in through the hallway door. Instantly, though, all their talk stopped. They went silent, as if somebody had snapped off the audio.

All excited like a bunch of pissant children, the senator grumbled to himself. Half of 'em would vote in favor of another Mars mission, the young fools.

O'Hara snorted disdainfully as he wheeled up the central aisle among the chairs. Turning his powerchair smartly to face his staffers, he saw that they were trying to look as blank and uninvolved as possible. Like kids eager to see a forbidden video and trying to mask their excitement as long as he was watching them.

"I know what you all think," he said, his voice a grating bullfrog's croak. "Well, I'm going to surprise you."

And with that, he guided his chair to the VR rig and the two technicians, both women, standing by it.

"I'm going to use the rig myself," he announced to his staff. Their shock was visible. Even Kaiser looked surprised, the fat sycophant.

Chuckling, he went on, "This Mars hoopla is the biggest damned boondoggle pulled over on the American taxpayer since the days of the Apollo project. But if anybody in this room plugs himself into the landing, it's going to be me."

Kaiser looked especially crestfallen. He's the one who won the lottery, Senator O'Hara figured. Thought you'd be the one to plug in, did you? O'Hara chuckled inwardly at the disappointment on his aide's face.

"You all can see what I'm experiencing on the hologram screen," the senator said as the technicians began to help him worm his hands into the data gloves.

An unhappy murmuring filled the room.

"I've always said that this Mars business is hooey. I want to experience it for myself—see what these fancy astronauts and scientists are actually going to do up there—so's nobody can say that I haven't given the opposition every possible opportunity to show me their point of view."

One of the technicians slipped the helmet over the senator's head. He stopped her from sliding down the visor long enough to say, "I always give the other side a fair break. Then I wallop 'em!"

The visor came down and for a brief, terrifying moment he was in utter darkness.

PHOENIX

For nearly half an hour the oversized TV screen had been split between a newscaster chattering away and an unmoving scene of a rusty red, rock-strewn landscape on Mars. Zacharias kept pacing back and forth in the back of the big room, while his guests seemed to edge closer and closer to the giant screen.

"We are seeing Mars as it was some eleven minutes ago," the newscaster intoned solemnly, "since the red planet is so distant from Earth that it takes that long for television signals to reach us."

"He's only told us that twenty-six times in the past five minutes," somebody in the crowd muttered.

"Hush! They should be coming down any moment now."

"According to the mission schedule," the newscaster went on, "and taking into account the lag in signal transmission time, we should be seeing the parachute of the landing craft within seconds."

The unmanned landers had been on the ground for days, Zacharias knew, automatically preparing the base camp for the twelve astronauts and scientists of the landing team. Over the past half-hour the news broadcast had shown the big plastic bubble of the main tent, the four unmanned landers scattered around it, and the relatively clear, level section of the Sinai plain where the crewed landing craft would put down.

If all went well.

No sonic boom, Zack knew. The Martian air's too thin, and the lander slows down too high up, anyway. The aerobrake should have deployed by now; the glow from the heat shield should be visible, if only they had programmed the cameras to look for it.

What am I saying? he asked himself, annoyed, nervous. It all happened eleven minutes ago. They're on the ground by now. Or dead.

"There it is!" the announcer yelped.

The crowd of guests surged forward toward the TV screen. Zacharias was drawn, too, despite himself. He remembered the two launch failures that he had witnessed. Put the project back years; almost killed it. After the second he vowed never to watch a rocket launch again.

Yet now he stared like any gaping tourist at the TV image of a beautiful white parachute against the deep blue Martian sky. He was glad that the meteorologists had been able to learn how to predict the planetwide dust storms that turned the sky pink for months afterward. They had timed the landing for the calmest possible weather.

The chute grew until he could see the lander beneath it, swaying slightly, like a big ungainly cylinder of polished aluminum.

They all knew that the landing craft would jettison the chute at a preset altitude, but they all gasped nonetheless. The lander plummeted downward and Zack's heart constricted beneath his ribs.

Then the landing rockets fired, barely visible in the TV cameras, and the craft slowed. It came down gracefully, with dignity, kicking up a miniature sandstorm of its own as its spraddling legs extended and their circular footpads touched gently the iron-rust sands of Mars.

Everyone in the big rec room cheered. All except Zack, who pushed his way to the bar. He felt badly in need of fortification.

HOUSTON

"Nuthin's happ'nin," Douggie complained. "Can't I watch Surfer Morphs?"

"Wait a minute," his father said easily. "They're just waiting for the dust to settle and the rocket nozzles to cool down."

Debbie saw the two virtual-reality helmets on the coffee table in front of them. Two pairs of gloves, also. Doug and Douggie can use them, she thought. Not me.

"Look!" the child cried. "The door's open!"

That should be me, Debbie thought as she watched the twelve-person team file down the lander's impossibly slim ladder to set their booted feet on the surface of Mars. I should be with them.

Douggie was quickly bored with their pretentious speeches: men and women from nine different nations, each of them pronouncing a statement written by teams of public relations experts and government bureaucrats. Debbie felt bored, too.

But then, "Two of us have virtual-reality sensors built into our helmets and gloves," said Philip Daguerre, the astronaut who commanded the ground team.

Debbie had almost had an affair with the handsome French Canadian. Would things have worked out differently if I'd had a fling with him? Probably not. She knew of three other women who had, and all three of them were still as Earthbound as she.

"Once we activate the VR system, those of you on Earth who have the proper equipment will be able to see what we see, feel what we feel, experience what we experience as we make our first excursion onto the surface of Mars."

Doug picked up one of the VR helmets.

"Can't I watch Surfer Morphs?" their son whined.

LOS ANGELES

It wasn't until Mr. Ricardo handed him the VR helmet that Luis realized his teacher had sacrificed his own chance to experience the Mars team's first excursion.

There were only ten VR rigs in the whole planetarium theater. The nine others were already taken by adults. Maybe they were college students, Luis thought; they looked young enough to be, even though almost everybody else in the big circular room was his teacher's age or older.

"Don't you want it?" Luis asked Ricardo. His teacher made a strange smile. "It's for you, Luis. Put it on."

He thinks he's doin' me a big favor, Luis thought. He don' know that Jorge's gonna beat the crap outta me for this. Or maybe he knows an' don' care.

With trembling hands, Luis slipped the helmet over his head, then worked the bristly gloves onto his hands. Ricardo still had that strange, almost sickly smile as Luis slid the helmet's visor down, shutting out his view.

As he sat there in utter darkness he heard Ricardo's voice, muffled by the helmet, say, "Enjoy yourself, Luis."

Yeah, Luis thought. Might as well enjoy myself. I'm sure gonna pay for this later on.

WASHINGTON

Senator O'Hara held his breath. All he could hear from inside the darkness of the helmet was the faint chugging of his heart pump. It was beating fast, for some reason.

He didn't want to seem cowardly in front of his entire staff, but the dark and the closeness of the visor over his face was stifling him, choking him. He wanted to cry out, to yank the damned helmet off and be done with it.

With the abruptness of an eyeblink he was suddenly looking out at a flat plain of rust red. Rocks and boulders were littered everywhere, like toys scattered by an army of thoughtless children. The sky was deep blue, almost black. A soft hushing sound filled his ears, like a distant whisper.

"That's the wind," said a disembodied voice. "It's blowing a stiff ninety knots, according to our instruments, but the air here is so thin that I can't feel it at all."

I'm on Mars! the senator said to himself. It's almost like actually being there in person.

PHOENIX

It's just like we expected it to be, Jerome Zacharias thought. We could have saved a lot of money by just sending automated probes.

"Over that horizon several hundred kilometers," Valerii Mikoyan was saying in flat Midwestern American English, "lies the Tharsis Bulge and the giant shield volcanoes, which we will explore by remote-controlled gliders and balloons later in this mission. And in this direction . . ."

Zack's view shifted across the landscape quickly enough to make him feel a moment of giddiness.

". . . just over that line of low hills, is the Valles Marineris. We are going to ride the rover there as soon as the vehicle is checked out."

Why don't I feel excited? Zack asked himself. I'm like a kid on Christmas morning, after all the presents have been unwrapped.

HOUSTON

For a moment Debbie was startled when Doug solemnly picked up one of the VR helmets and put it on her, like a high priest crowning a new queen.

She was sitting in the springy little metal jump seat of the cross-country rover, her hands running along the control board, checking out all its systems. Solar panels okay. Transformers. Backup fuel cells. Sensors on and running. Communications gear in the green.

"Okay," said the astronaut driving the buggy. "We are ready to roll." It might as well have been her own voice, Debbie thought.

"Clear for canyon excursion," came the mission controller's voice in her earphones. The mission controller was up in the command spacecraft, hanging high above the Plain of Sinai in a synchronous orbit.

With transmission delays of ten to twenty minutes, mission control of the Mars expedition could not be on Earth; it had to be right there, on the scene.

"Go for sight-seeing tour," Debbie acknowledged. "The bus is leaving."

LOS ANGELES

Luis watched the buggy depart the base area. But only for a moment. He had work to do. He was a geologist, he heard in his earphones, and his job was to take as wide a sampling of rocks as he could and pack them away in one of the return craft.

"First we photograph the field we're going to work in." Luis felt a square object in his left hand, then saw a digital camera. He held it up to the visor of his helmet, sighted and clicked.

"What we're going to be doing is to collect what's called contingency samples," the geologist was saying. "We want to get them aboard a return vehicle right away, the first few hours on the surface, so that if anything happens to force us to make an unscheduled departure, we'll have a decent sampling of surface materials to take back with us."

At first Luis had found it confusing to hear the guy's voice in his head when it looked like he himself was walking around on Mars and picking up the rocks. He could feel them in his hands! Feel their heft, the grittiness of their surfaces. It was like the first time he had tried acid; he'd been inside his own head and outside, looking back at himself, both at the same time. That shook him up so much he had never dropped acid again.

But this was kind of different. Fun. He was the frigging geologist. He was there on Mars. He was doing something. Something worthwhile.

WASHINGTON

Collecting rocks, Senator O'Hara growled inwardly. We've spent a hundred billion dollars so some pointy-headed scientists can add to their rock collection. Oh, am I going to crucify them as soon as the committee reconvenes!

PHOENIX

Zack felt as if he were jouncing and banging inside the surface rover as it trundled across the Martian landscape. He knew he was sitting in a comfortable rocking chair in his big library/bar/entertainment room. Yet he was looking out at Mars through the windshield of the rover. His hands were on its controls and he could feel every shudder and bounce of the six-wheeled vehicle.

But there's nothing out there that we haven't already seen with the unmanned landers, Zack told himself, with mounting despair. We've even brought back samples, under remote control. What are the humans on this expedition going to be able to accomplish that will be worth the cost of sending them?

HOUSTON

Easy now, Debbie told herself. Don't let yourself get carried away. You're not on Mars. You're sitting in your own living room.

LOS ANGELES

Luis could feel the weight of the rock. It was much lighter than a rock that size would be on Earth. And red, like rust. Holding it in his left hand, he chipped at it with the hammer in his right.

"Just want to check the interior," he heard the geologist say, as if he were saying it himself.

The rock cracked in two. Luis saw a tracery of fine lines honeycombing the rock's insides.

"Huh. Never saw anything like that before." And the geologist/Luis carefully put both halves of the split rock into a container, sealed it, then marked with a pen its location in the photograph of the area he had taken when he had started collecting.

This is fun, Luis realized. I wish I could do it for real. Like, be a real astronaut or scientist. But reality was something very different. Jorge was reality. Yeah, Luis said to himself, I could be on Mars myself someday. If Jorge don' kill me first.

WASHINGTON

Bored with the rock-sampling task, Senator O'Hara lifted the visor of his VR helmet.

"Get me out of this rig," he told the two startled technicians. Turning to Kaiser, he said, "You can try it if you like. I'm going into my office for a drink."

PHOENIX

The ground was rising slightly as the rover rolled along. "Should be at the rim in less than a minute," the driver said.

Zack felt his hand ease back on the throttle slightly. "Don't want to fall over. It's a long way down."

Nothing ahead of them but the dull, rock-strewn ground and the deep blue sky.

HOUSTON

Debbie checked the time line on the dashboard computer screen and slowed the rover even more. "We ought to be just about . . . there!"

The rim of the grandest canyon in the solar system sliced across her field of view. Craning her neck slightly, she could see the cliffs

tumbling away, down and down and down, toward the valley floor
miles below.

PHOENIX

Mist! The floor of the valley was wreathed in mists that wafted and
undulated slowly, rising and falling as Zack watched.

It's the wrong time of the year for mists to form, he knew. We've
never seen this before.

As far as the eye could see, for dozens of miles, hundreds of miles,
the mist billowed softly, gently along the floor of Valles Marineris. The
canyon was so wide that he could not see the opposite wall; it was
beyond the horizon. Nothing but gentle, whitish mist. Clouds of
mystery. Clouds of excitement.

My gosh, Zack thought, do they extend the whole three-thousand-
mile length of the valley?

LOS ANGELES

Luis roamed across the rust-colored sandy landscape, staring at
more rocks than he had ever seen in his whole life. Some the size of
pebbles, a few bigger than a man. How'd they get there? Where'd they
come from?

And what was over the horizon? The geologist said something
about big volcanoes and mountains higher than anything on Earth.
Luis thought it'd be great to see them, maybe climb them.

HOUSTON

Debbie stared at the mists billowing along the valley floor. They
seemed to be breathing, like something alive. They've got to be water
vapor, she thought. Got to be! And where's there's water there could be
life. Maybe. Maybe.

We've got to get down onto the valley floor. Got to!

PHOENIX

Zack felt like a child, the first time his father had taken him up in a helicopter. The higher they went, the more there was to see. The more he saw, the more eager he was to see more.

Staring out at the mist-shrouded rift valley, he finally realized that this was the difference between human explorers and machines. What's beyond the horizon? What's beneath those mists? He wanted to know, to explore. He had to seek the answers.

He realized he was crying, tears of joy and wonder streaming down his cheeks. He was glad that none of the others could see it, inside the VR helmet, but he knew that neither embarrassment nor disapproval mattered in the slightest. What's beyond the horizon? That was the eternal question and the only thing that really counted.

LOS ANGELES

Yeah, this is great, Luis thought. For these guys. For scientists and astronauts. It's their life. But it's not for me. When I leave here tonight it's back to the 'hood and Jorge and all that crap.

Then a powerful surge of new emotion rose within him. Why can't I go to Mars for real someday? Mr. Ricardo says I'm smart enough to get a scholarship to college.

Fuck Jorge. Let him do what he wants to me. I'll fight him back. I'll kick the shit outta him if that's what I gotta do to get to Mars. He'll have to kill me to keep me away from this.

WASHINGTON

Senator O'Hara was mixing his third martini when Kaiser came in, looking bleary-eyed.

"You been in the VR rig all this time?" O'Hara asked. He knew Kaiser did not drink, so he didn't bother offering his aide anything.

"Mostly," the pudgy little man said. O'Hara could see his aide's bald head was gleaming with perspiration.

"Bad enough we have to waste a hundred billion on this damned nonsense. Is it going to tie up my entire staff for the rest of the day?"

"And then some," Kaiser said, heading for the bar behind the Senator's desk.

O'Hara watched, dumbfounded, as his aide poured himself a stiff belt of whiskey.

He swallowed, coughed, then swallowed again. With tears in his eyes, he went to the leather sofa along the sidewall of the office and sat down like a very tired man.

O'Hara stared at him.

Holding the heavy crystal glass in both hands, Kaiser said, "You're going to have to change your stand on this Mars business."

"What?"

"You've got to stop opposing it."

"Are you crazy?"

"No, but you'd be crazy to try to stand against it now," Kaiser said, more firmly than the senator had ever heard him speak before.

"You're drunk."

"Maybe I am. I've been on Mars, Teddy. I've stood on fuckin' Mars!"

Kaiser had never used the senator's first name before, let alone called him "Teddy."

"You'd just better watch your tongue," O'Hara growled.

"And you'd better watch your ass," Kaiser snapped. "Do you have any idea of how many people are experiencing this Mars landing? Not just watching it, but experiencing it—as if they were there."

O'Hara shrugged. "Twenty million, maybe."

"I made a couple of phone calls before I came in here. Thirty-six million VR sets in the U.S., and that's not counting laboratories and training simulators. There must be more than thirty million voters on Mars right now."

"Bullcrap."

"Yeah? By tomorrow there won't be a VR rig left in the stores. Everybody's going to want to be on Mars."

O'Hara made a sour face.

"I'll bet that half the voters in dear old Pennsylvania are on Mars right this instant. You try telling them it's all a waste of money."

"But it is!" the senator insisted. "The biggest waste of taxpayer funds since SDI."

"It might be," Kaiser said, somewhat more moderately. "You might be entirely right and everybody else totally wrong. But if you vote that way in the committee, you'll get your ass whipped in November."

"You told me just the opposite no more'n ten days ago. The polls show—"

"The polls are going to swing around one hundred and eighty degrees. Guaranteed."

O'Hara glared at his aide.

"Trust me on this, Teddy. I've never let you down before, have I? Vote for continued Mars exploration or go out and find honest work."

HOUSTON

With enormous reluctance, Debbie pulled the helmet off and removed the data gloves. Doug was still in his rig, totally absorbed. He might as well be on Mars for real, Debbie thought.

Shakily, she got up from the living-room sofa and went to Douggie's room. Her son was watching three-dimensional cartoons.

"Come with me, young man," she said in her not-to-be-argued-with voice. The boy made a face, but turned off his 3-D set and marched into the living room with his mother.

She helped him into the gloves and helmet. "Aw, Ma," he whined, "do I hafta?"

"Yes," she whispered to her son. "In a few years, you would never forgive yourself if you didn't."

And she left her son and her husband on Mars and went back to her computer to erase her letter of resignation.

There's a lot of work to be done, she told herself. The exploration of Mars is just beginning.